BROKEN CHORD

BROKEN CHORD

A Music Row Mystery

ALICE A. JACKSON

WordCrafts

Published by WordCrafts Press
Cody, Wyoming 82414
www.wordcrafts.net

Prologue

She opened the door hesitantly, her heart pounding in her chest. She wasn't sure what she feared seeing in this room she had entered so often. It appeared the same—untouched, no crime tape to bar entry. Still, a pall of tragedy permeated the room. She felt her throat tighten.

It was a relatively sterile room, mostly devoid of any hint of the mercurial personality of its last occupant. The walls were painted a pale beige. The furnishings as austere as the walls: a wood desk lacking any ornamentation. Behind it, against the wall, a small credenza with a laptop computer and neatly stacked file folders. No framed photographs or colorful vases interrupted the blandness of the room. On the middle shelf of the credenza, a wooden mantle clock held lonely prominence, noisily ticking off the seconds and chiming on the hour.

The four chairs in a semi-circle in front of the desk were functional, but not matching. She reached down and touched the beige cloth cushion of a chair she had been sitting in only last Friday. The tears she had been choking back stung her eyes as she looked slowly around the room. Her eyes sought any reminder of her friend and saw none. The room, like the person who had inhabited it during working hours, was an enigma.

But then her friend had always been…

Chapter 1

Four Years Earlier

Sarah Ann turned the car sharply off the busy thoroughfare onto a side street as the green street sign flashed by her view. Jeb Stuart Boulevard. *Why the hell were streets always named after men in the South? Were there no Southern women after whom to name a street?* She pondered that thought as she whipped the car around the corner onto Nathan Bedford Forrest Avenue. No equally famous woman's name came to mind.

Two blocks later the tires squealed turning onto Robert E. Lee Street.

Damn! Didn't Mrs. Robert E. Lee ever do something to merit having a street named for her? Probably not! Southern women seem content to live in the shadow of their husbands. Look at the three women with whom Sarah Ann spent this evening celebrating her birthday. They certainly did—that is, live in the shadow of their husbands, especially the one now on her third husband.

But not her. John Bennett Boswell transferred his shielding shadow two years ago to a new, much younger wife.

Sarah Ann felt the tickle of a tear on her cheek. *I'm having a mid-life crisis,* she thought with rising despair. "I'm having more than a mid-life crisis," she cried aloud, her words slightly slurred. "Hell, I'm having a full-blown crisis of mids; mid-life, mid-menopause, and mid-career."

The trickle of tears became a gusher. Sarah Ann made no effort to quell the flow as she tore around the corner onto Shiloh Place and sped down the tree-lined boulevard, tears blurring a sign declaring the speed limit as twenty miles per hour when children were present. It was a sign she had advocated to the Franklin Board of Aldermen when her own children were young. An imposing Southern colonial home loomed ahead. She bounced into its driveway and slammed on the brakes as the car sailed under the broad portico supported by wide-girthed pillars.

Sarah Ann fished a crumpled tissue from the cluttered bottom of her leather purse and dabbed at her wet cheeks. "You're now fifty, girl! Get used to it," she admonished herself out loud. Her words provoked a new flow of tears.

She sat for several minutes sobbing loudly. Another tissue was drawn from the reaches of her purse to be quickly soaked by tears and nose blows.

I'm just drunk enough to have a crying jag, she reasoned silently, triggering a fresh heave of sobs. As the tears began to ebb, she leaned back against the smooth leather of the Lincoln sedan's seat and contemplated going into the house. She dreaded that most. The house would be empty except for her two Persians, Sammie Sue and Sadie Lou.

Why was it, anything or anyone Southern, had to have two names? she whined to herself. She was still Sarah Ann to her family and friends and had been since she was born. Why couldn't she just be plain and simple Sarah?

Plain and simple seemed misplaced adjectives where her life was concerned. Plain never described her. She had been beautiful since birth, blessed with her mother's porcelain complexion and her father's flashing green eyes and auburn hair. No one she knew had ever characterized her as simple. Complex, quirky, generous, funny, gregarious, bitchy, open-minded (on some things), savvy, intelligent. Never simple.

Maybe that was why her life was now so empty. Even a thimble full of simplicity might have encouraged more fulfillment. And she would not be slamming shut the car door at this moment to walk into a house to spend the rest of the night with two haughty, disdainful cats. She could expect no empathy from either of the snotty little bitches—not for being drunk and certainly not for the misery of turning fifty.

"You try blowing out that many candles," she hissed at the two pair of indifferent blue eyes looking at her from the down coverlet on the four-poster bed. The thought of the lavishly decorated cake, alight with fifty candles, set in front of her by the obsequious majordomo, prompted a wan smile which turned to a soft chuckle when she recalled the quartet of waiters singing "Happy Birthday" slightly off-key.

"They'd been drummed out of St. Theresa's choir for sure," she told the impervious little faces still staring at her. "Sister Imelda would never have put up with such off-key singing," she declared, wagging a limp finger at the two cats. "Never, never, never..." her voice trailed off and a fresh splash of tears tumbled down her cheeks as she recalled her high school choir teacher.

I'm talking like a crazy person to two cats who don't understand a word I've said, she thought absently, and crossed unsteadily to the curved mahogany dressing table. She leaned toward the ornately carved gilded mirror, wincing at her reflection, the swollen eyes reddened by too many gin and tonics and now tears.

"You look like shit," she slurred at the reflection, sitting down heavily on the cushioned bench. She lowered her swirling head to rest on the hard surface of the table as her chest heaved in sobs.

She had been unhappy with her reflection for weeks now. Maybe that was why Bobby Ray Kendal tried to be so soothing after firing her today. "Budget cuts by the foundation board," he had explained in a waxy voice that slowed and curled lazily over every vowel. It was the Kendal Foundation for godsakes! He ran it. The board had little say in anything. Did he really think she was so naive not to know the decision to fire her was his alone?

He understood this was a bad time. She had not been feeling well lately, had not been herself. He was sorry. What could he do to help? It was an offer he had made several times in recent weeks, in his typical syrupy way, when she had appeared at work late—more than two hours late on one occasion.

She feebly blamed her tardiness on new medication she was taking.

She then spurned his concern, assuring him with impatient vehemence it was misplaced.

She learned long ago, growing up across the street from the Kendal family, never to take Bobby Ray at his word or accept any offer of help. She knew what to expect when she accepted the job as vice-president in charge of community outreach.

Sincerity was never a hallmark of Bobby Ray's character, a character deficient in many other ways but overlooked by Franklin society, she thought bitterly, because he was a Kendal.

His great-great-grandfather fought at Chickamauga and Franklin. He survived to lose again at Nashville before riding his horse back to Franklin to spend the rest of his days hoarding Yankee gold he acquired before and during the Civil War—loot cleverly hidden from the bluecoat occupiers and carpetbaggers who descended on Tennessee following the end of conflict.

"Bobby Ray, you are a disingenuous fool and a bastard to boot," she hissed. "I was more the fool to have gone to work for you and your damned foundation."

The sting of embarrassment, mixed with the shame she felt at the foundation offices just hours ago, now returned. That shame was imprinted on her face as she lifted her head to stare into the mirror, feeling a deep emptiness as she studied the pained reflection.

Unmarried, unemployed, generally ignored by her son and daughter. Even her only grandchild wasn't being entrusted to her care as often. Signs of failure were evident all around her, and she had only herself to blame. She turned away from the haunted face in the mirror and half stumbled her way over to the bed.

"You generally make the bed you have to lie in," her staunch, strict and erect Grandmother Shepherd had reminded her often during her formative years. That admonishment terrified her now. The thought of sleeping in the bed she had made of her life was unfathomable. John had left. The settled security she wrapped herself in during her 26-year marriage had vanished with him. Even the children's affection and camaraderie had become more restrained, transferred in part to John's new wife.

She reached for a plastic bottle and rolled it absently with her thumb. The third time she called, Jim Rhodes finally agreed to prescribe something to help her sleep. Insomnia—it just goes with hot flashes, weight gain and irritability he had told her. Just part of the change of life territory he cooed in his most soothing and doctorly tone. The underlying message: just deal with it.

However, he failed to mention vaginal dryness, sagging boobs, thinning hair, except, of course, for the hair popping out on her upper lip, along with an occasional chin whisker that seemed to appear overnight.

Well, she was tired of dealing with it. Mostly, she was just tired. Men didn't have to deal with menopause, or hot flashes, or any of the rest of going through the change. Men hitting the high side of middle age, she thought bitterly, might find less hair on their legs and the need for Viagra, but it usually meant chasing around after younger women. If God were a woman, the menopause shoe would surely be on the other gender's foot.

And why was it that doctors always sounded so busy when you called? Maybe if they didn't have every weekend and Wednesday afternoon off, they would have more time for patients like her.

She glanced down at the plastic bottle. Just under the large prescription number was the description of the pills inside and beneath that, a red warning label not to drink or drive when taking this medication.

"Thank you for your comforting words," she spoke to the red label, before tossing the bottle savagely across the room. As it cracked against the far wall the two cats bolted off the bed and raced out of the room.

"Take a flying leap, you little whooshes," she jeered at the white tails disappearing into the hallway while fluffy hairs floated in the wake of their hasty retreat. Sarah Ann walked around the bed and bent to retrieve the pill bottle. It felt light in her hand compared with the tight heaviness gripping her stomach. Tears spilled out as she clutched a bed post. Her mind was a tangle of dismaying emotions snatching at her sanity.

Face it Sarah Ann Boswell, she thought, *if you swallowed every one of these damn pills, would anybody care?* Her children would probably be relieved. Embarrassed, of course, because their mother chose suicide as her means of dying instead of suffering a more socially acceptable bout with cancer, or better still, a rapid exit via a heart attack. Political correctness was not her forte. Hadn't Bobby Ray said as much today?

Sarah Ann looked down at the small container in her hand. The shame she felt was like a physical pain ripping at her insides. She shook the bottle and heard the pills knocking around. With these pills the pain could end.

She had not told her friends about being fired. Or about seeing John coming down the wide steps of the antebellum courthouse as she drove past on her way home following her firing. Or about being overwhelmed at that moment by how much she missed him. He was little changed, still strikingly handsome in a middle-aged, lawyerly way, his thick salt and pepper hair, mussed by a teasing afternoon breeze. His face was still lean and firm, accentuated by high cheek bones which underscored his deep-set blue eyes. She knew from the refection in the mirror their two years apart had not been as kind to her.

She held tightly to the bedpost as a new wave of sobs racked her body.

Hell, wasn't passing the age limit for an AARP membership a big enough damper on any celebration? Not really, she admitted to herself. It was fear of laying bare her shame before her four friends who sat around the circular table at Bell's this evening. If she had confided in them, they would have chewed on her problems with their Chateaubriand before issuing a glutton's portion of sympathy. They would have told her to consider the source of her misery and then would have labeled Bobby Ray Kendal a prick, threatened to kick him in the balls (not that he probably had much down there to aim at), and hoisted their flutes of champagne in a toast to finding a new life.

Well, she was tired of searching for that "new life." It had eluded her since John left.

Sarah Ann opened the plastic bottle and the yellow pills spilled into the palm of her left hand. Twenty in all. Enough.

Ignoring the thoughts that threatened to stall her movement, she stepped into the bathroom. Avoiding looking into the mirror, she opened a bottle of Perrier on the vanity. Filling a paper cup, she slung part of the cache of small pills into her mouth. They descended into her stomach with surprising ease.

I've done it. Now let's finish the job. The remaining pills slid down her throat with more gulps of Perrier. No clash of conscious battled over what she had just done. No sense of remorse. Only an overpowering feeling of exhaustion. She staggered over to the bed. Tears still dampened the silk coverlet as consciousness slipped away.

Chapter 2

The Prayer Group huddled around a table in the far corner of the visitor's lounge just outside the Intensive Care Unit. The praying, which began with clasped hands and whispered appeals to the Almighty, ceased abruptly when Della Sue Simpson dropped the hands holding hers and whispered in a low, petulant voice, "Why the heck would Sarah Ann try to commit suicide?"

Della Sue had given up cursing for Lent—again.

She was answered with silent shaking heads, raised eyebrows, and shrugs.

"I can't imagine what prompted her to do this," Jeanne Marie Osborne finally responded. "She seemed happy enough at dinner." She looked quickly away from the three faces staring at her as unwelcome tears stung the corners of her deep set brown eyes—eyes crowned by long, thick lashes that never seemed to need bolstering by mascara or rounding by an eyelash curler.

"Well, she obviously *wasn't* happy," concluded Angela Lane, the only member of the Prayer Group without a middle name. The omission was her mother's passive-aggressive penalty for Angela's challenging birth. As her mother so often complained, Angela had exited the birth canal feet first *which took an intolerable toll on mother's pain threshold*. And if that weren't enough, Angela had the audacity to weigh over eight pounds, despite her mother's strict rationing of food necessary to remain below the twenty-pound weight gain limit imposed by her physician. *After all, babies were nothing but little leeches lurking in the dark safety of the womb*, her mother frequently reminded her, *sucking away a woman's figure and firmness*. Her mother's advice:

don't conceive—adopt. *And if you must give birth*, she had cautioned, *have boys. They had the courtesy to pop out the way nature intended*—at least in the case of Angela's two older brothers.

Despite having to endure her mother's lifelong blame for being a breech delivery that widened her mother's hips and permanently thickened her waistline, Angela considered having a singular name an achievement second only to being born in the first place. She did feel fleeting guilt when she looked at her father's aging face and knew her birth was the reason he was banished from his wife's bed and forced to sleep in the monastic solitude of a second bedroom.

"I think Sarah Ann may be keeping secrets from us," Angela theorized.

"Obviously," Jeanne Marie replied tartly, as she lit a cigarette with a trembling hand. It was her first cigarette since dutifully parting with cigarettes on Ash Wednesday. This was an extraordinary situation. The Lord would just have to understand reneging on her annual pledge.

But the Lord seemed bent on her keeping the pledge in the form of Willie Dell Winstead. "May I remind you, Jeanne Marie, this is a non-smoking hospital. Go douse it in the toilet," Willie Dell ordered, "before a nurse spots you and sends a security officer charging our way."

Jeanne Marie threw him a peevish look but obediently headed toward the women's restroom just outside the waiting room. After two long draws on the filtered Camel, she reluctantly flipped it into a toilet bowl.

A hurt look clouded Angela's eyes as it always did when Jeanne Marie was being bitchy. This was not the time—certainly not the place. Their friend was in a room not far from them, near death, for reasons none of them could fathom. But Angela stifled any verbal retort to Jeanne Marie. Instead, she asked Willie Dell, "You're close with Sarah Ann. Why would she do such a thing?"

Willie Dell just shook his head in response to Angela's question and continued staring out the window at the parking lot below. He was too despondent to answer out loud, fearful any spoken words might betray the tightness in his throat. In all their years of monthly

Prayer Group meetings, he had never shed tears in the group's presence, and wasn't about to start now.

Still, the *why* of Sarah Ann's decision to end her life was as much a mystery to him as it was to the three women with whom he was sharing this end of the waiting room? It had been front and center on his mind since Della Sue's frantic call rocketed him out of a rare sound sleep. By the time he was dressed, Della Sue was honking impatiently in his driveway.

"Sarah Ann seemed so cheerful at her birthday party," insisted Della Sue, as she sped toward the hospital. "Joyful, merry…whatever upbeat word came to mind, it applied," she had added.

But then, Sarah Ann always appeared that way thought Willie Dell. She seldom complained—at least not to the Prayer Group, of which he was the lone male member.

They had been a Prayer Group for as long as any of them could remember. They began their supplications in third grade at St. Theresa's Elementary when most of their prayers were petitions for the Almighty to wreak mayhem on this nun or that nun, depending on what disciplinary travail had been suffered during the school day.

Sarah Ann's prayer requests at their monthly meetings were mostly benign; prayers for her children to be happy, an occasional plea for patience or one of the other virtues. Never like the requests made by the other three women.

A divorce. That was the repeated request by Della Sue. Also, a great time in bed with a lover who could insure just such an experience. To Willie Dell's thinking, neither request would ever be answered. Encroaching middle age had taken a toll on Della Sue's once slim figure, although the face remained youthfully beautiful with sensuous lips and luminous blue eyes that betrayed any secrets she might try to keep.

More money. That was eternally Angela. Now in her third marriage, she had managed to remain childless and seemed never content with a bank account that had grown with each exchange of "I do's."

Jeanne Marie most recently suggested a Caribbean cruise for her future if the Man upstairs was paying attention. It was a request quickly espoused by the other women and even Willie Dell, after his fellow Prayer Group members insisted they would not step foot on a sleek white cruise ship without him.

And always there were the oft-requested standards; lose weight; quit smoking; make menopause short lived and hot flash free; and last—but certainly not least—know when to get a facelift.

Willie Dell's requests generally involved his business. List more properties. Sell more quickly the properties already listed. Make more money…not that he needed it. Grandfather Sidmore's trust fund insured he would be financially secure for the rest of his life. In moments of candid self-assessment, he admitted money equaled satisfaction for him and gave him an elevated status in the community. Petitioning aloud for more money put him in league with Angela, whom he secretly considered materialistic and greedy. His head bowed slightly as he now made another silent request. *Please God, don't let my dear friend die.*

The tightness in his throat suddenly felt like a noose threatening to choke off his very breath as sadness engulfed him. He felt powerless to quell tears that began trailing slowly down his plump cheeks.

He had known Sarah Ann since a late summer morning when they were both six. She had scurried up the huge oak tree towering between their adjacent properties to trespass into a domain he held private and sacred, a tree house he guarded tenaciously against all invaders. His lone defenses—his fists—proved futile against the onslaught of an opponent who had honed her pugilistic skills in frequent fights with several cousins. He was left biting a bloody lip and rubbing a tender eye which developed into a multi-colored shiner by lunch time.

Deciding pragmatically that she needed companionship in her newly conquered play environment, Sarah Ann had welcomed Willie Dell back after lunch. It was in the shaded coolness of the flimsily constructed tree house that their friendship was sealed by a pact to keep all other intruders out.

His divorced mother had chosen the quaint, antebellum community of Franklin to escape from the world she had known as the wife of a wealthy and promiscuous banker and community leader in Memphis. Banished is the word Willie Dell would later use to describe the move from Memphis to Franklin.

He still lived with his mother in the same house on Shiloh Avenue. He had left only for the one year he was married to Beverly. Like a tornado Beverly Eddings had whirled through his life, threatening to plunder his financial security and despoiling his fragile self-esteem. His mother's home became a sanctuary. It was the only place he felt truly safe, the same sense of security he felt with Sarah Ann in the creaky confines of the old tree house, the remnants of which still clung precariously to the supporting branch now stretching even further into the reaches of her yard next door.

"You okay, buddyroo?"

He felt the gentle hand of Jeanne Marie on his shoulder. He reached up and patted it. "I'm fine. Thanks for asking."

"I'm making a coffee run. Can I get you something?"

"Not right now, thanks," he said, holding up a Styrofoam cup still half full.

Minutes later Jeanne Marie was back with three steaming cups of vending machine coffee, which, while bitter, were welcomed by the other women.

"Any word yet?" Jeanne Marie asked as she pressed cups into outstretched hands.

Della Sue shook her bottled blond head dolefully, her large eyes becoming blue pools.

"I'll go check at the desk," Willie Dell offered. He walked out of the lounge and down the short hallway to a circular desk. Two nurses sat silently watching monitors above their heads. He could hear the rhythmic bleeps of the monitors as he approached the counter.

"Can I help you?" asked the nurse nearest him, her lively dark eyes in sharp contrast to the weariness apparent on her round ebony face.

"Yes. I'm checking on Sarah Ann Boswell."

"Are you a family member?"

"No, ma'am, a close friend."

"Well, we can only provide information about a patient to family members. I'm sorry." She turned back to resume scanning the screens above her.

Willie Dell rankled at the dismissive tone. "Could I speak to the head nurse?"

The ebony face turned back to him, this time the large eyes flashed irritation. "Hold on. Let me page her."

Willie Dell glanced at the gold face of the Rolex on his wrist, his impatience apparent. The beeping of the monitors sounded in his head like alarm bells. The sudden fear he felt was further stoked by the antiseptic odors—hospital odors—that seemed to surround his senses. Looking up he saw the elevator door on the far side of the nurse's station open and felt a rush of relief. Stepping out were John Bennett Boswell, Jr. and his younger sister, Anna Leigh.

Willie Dell hailed Sarah Ann's children with a wave. "I'm waiting to get an update, Johnny," said Willie Dell, as he gripped the younger man's hand.

"Glad you're here, Willie Dell," Johnny said quietly. "Mom would like that… having you here." Looking at Sarah Ann's son, Willie Dell was struck, as always, by how close a son could favor a father in every way, from his good looks to his chosen profession—law.

Willie Dell turned to Sarah Ann's daughter, as beautiful as he remembered Sarah Ann being at that age. "How you holdin' up, Anna Leigh?" She had spent most of the morning at the hospital, along with her brother, before both were coaxed to leave and spend some time with their spouses and children.

She answered with sobs that shook her slender shoulders. Willie Dell pulled her to him. The concern he had for Sarah Ann now transferred to her child. He had known Anna Leigh and her brother since they were born. He had watched them blossom into adults and loved them as much as he loved their mother. Anna Leigh drew back and looked up at him. "Uncle Willie, we just can't understand why Mama would do this," she cried, as tears streamed down her cheeks.

Willie Dell cupped Anna Leigh's face in his plump hands. "Sometimes, we just don't know why people do what they do, baby girl. She'll survive. And we'll find out what's troubling her and then we'll make it right." He smiled wanly and kissed her forehead.

The floor supervisor approached, a look of consternation clouding her face. Willie Dell had always been one to head off trouble when he saw it coming. And trouble was what he was looking at as the supervisor stopped in front of him.

"Thank you for coming to see us," he began, in an attempt to part the clouds on the face peering warily into his. "These are Mrs. Boswell's children and I'm a longtime family friend. We're concerned about her condition. Can you enlighten us about any improvement?" Willie Dell underscored his words with just the right level of hopeful tone. The clouds receded. "Mrs. Boswell is holding her own," the supervisor responded. "Dr. Rhodes should be here shortly, and I'll make sure he gives you an update."

"Can I join her children at the bedside for a few moments?"

"Yes, of course," said the supervisor, who turned toward the nurse's station. "This family friend has requested to see Mrs. Boswell. He can go in."

When the supervisor turned to nod affirmation, the clouds had returned to her well-scrubbed, prematurely lined face. She turned and walked briskly toward double doors, punched the large, round button to open them and disappeared like a swirling vapor as they closed.

Willie Dell was not prepared for what he *now* saw. New tears stung his eyes. The face on the pillow was ghostly pale. A large tube was crammed into Sarah Ann's mouth while smaller oxygen tubes covered the openings of her nostrils. An IV bag hung above her dripping a clear liquid into her right arm. Her breathing came in regulated spurts, measured by the whooshing sound of the ventilator.

He wanted to turn and flee from this place where death stalked his dear friend. But his feet held firm.

A hand gently clasped his. "You've always been there for Mama, Uncle Willie. I know she knows you're here, even if she is in a coma." Tears glistened in Anna Leigh's green eyes. Willie Dell lifted her chin as he pulled a fresh linen hanky from his pocket and gently wiped away the tears. Looking into her face was like seeing a reflection of Sarah Ann. "There, there, baby girl," he said soothingly, pulling her into his arms.

Although she was an adult, Willie Dell still addressed Sarah Ann's daughter with the same words of endearment he had first used when he held her over the marble baptismal font at St. Theresa's Church and promised to protect her spiritual growth as her Godparent. He could not vouch, now or ever, to her practice of the Catholic faith, but he never forgot her birthday, or Johnny's, or the anniversary of their baptisms. Each child could count on receiving a sizable check.

It was Anna Leigh who had discovered her mother. She had arrived early at the country club for a tennis match she and her mother had booked two days before. When there was no response to repeated cell phone calls, Anna Leigh drove like a shot to her mother's home just before eight and found Sarah Ann lying prone, fully dressed on the big bed, barely alive.

"Why, why would she do this, Uncle Willie?" Anna Leigh's voice was muffled as he held her tightly against his chest.

"I don't have a clue, baby girl. Not a clue."

But he did know. Only last night that prick, Bobby Ray Kendal, had telephoned asking if he knew of someone who could step into the job just "vacated" by Sarah Ann. Kendal professed he was disappointed at losing her. Willie Dell knew that was a lie. He fully suspected Kendal had fired her. It doesn't pay for a community outreach person to overshadow, or worse, to be better at mingling with the community than the director of the foundation, especially a family foundation. From the time he was waist high, when every other boy in the neighborhood could stretch their arms and touch the top of their mother's head, Kendal had an ego that grew at twice the rate of the rest of him. *Big ego, small dick*, Willie Dell rationalized disdainfully of his childhood neighbor.

"When she wakes up, we'll have a good talk with your mama and find out what's troubling her." Willie Dell patted Anna Leigh's arm. "Whatever is wrong, we'll just have to make it right, baby girl," repeating his earlier promise.

They stood silently around the bed, staring at Sarah Ann's colorless face for some time before Jim Rhodes walked quietly in, a stethoscope draped around his neck.

"Hey, Willie Dell," the physician said, as he lightly squeezed Willie Dell's shoulder and nodded to his patient's children.

"I'd be less than honest if I told you this has not been touch-and-go. I think your mama will make it. But just by the skin of her teeth and maybe by the grace of God." He looked back down at Sarah Ann. "She's tough. No question there. Always has been. That's why this is so damn puzzling."

The physician shook his partially bald head sadly. This was a woman he had known since high school; whose children he delivered; a woman he considered as much friend as patient. "When she pulls out of this, we'll get to the bottom of why it happened." Rhodes pursed his thin lips and sighed deeply. "I'll look back in on your mama later tonight. Call me if you need anything."

None of those around the bed moved for some time after the doctor left as quietly as he had come. Willie Dell spoke first. "After you've had time with your mama I want you both to go back home to your families. I'll stay with her tonight." He rubbed his index finger back and forth across his upper lip. "I'll call you if there's any change." Willie Dell raised his head and looked at Sarah Ann's children. "She's gonna make it, you know." He nodded his head affirmatively as much to convince himself as Sarah Ann's children. "She's my best friend. I won't let her go."

"You sure about this...about staying tonight, Willie Dell?"

"Yeah, Johnny. Y'all go on home. Get a good night's sleep. She'll need you just as much in the morning."

"Thanks, Uncle Willie." Anna Leigh reached up and kissed his cheek. Johnny patted him lightly on the back before Willie Dell strode out of the room. When her children left sometime later, Willie Dell stepped back into the room and leaned over Sarah Ann to whisper, "Well missy, it's just you and us now. I'll get the others. It's time for some real powerful prayers, the likes of which you've never seen by this Prayer Group you founded."

When the hand holding and praying and the in-and-out visiting was finished, it was Willie Dell who remained at the bedside, cradling his friend's hand in his through the remainder of the long night, willing her not to leave him. He talked to her off and on, in a low voice, assuring Sarah Ann of the many reasons she needed to stay.

"Anyway," he said in a voice hoarse with fatigue, "how can I abide the Prayer Group without you."

Chapter 3

One Year Later

Sarah Ann watched with pensive fascination as two petulant mockingbirds scurried across the grassy median that separated the neighboring property from the concrete driveway leading to the rear parking lot. Their querulous chirping bit the air.

Had it really been a year since her chance meeting with Jill Edgerton in the hospital? The days, the weeks, the months, had raced by since she accepted the offer to join Edgerton Group. From the moment she had said "yes" her life seemed to launch forward at warp speed.

It was the eyes, those penetrating blue eyes reflecting from underneath dense blond eyebrows, recalling their first meeting. She had awakened to see Jill at the end of her hospital bed. "Hi. I'm Jill Edgerton. I'm in the next bed."

Sarah Ann had tried to respond but only a raspy whisper emanated from her throat which felt as if it had been roughly sandpapered. "Where am I…?"

"Don't try to talk. You probably had a tube down your throat." Jill had walked around and stood looking down at her curiously. "You're in the Williamson Medical Center. They wheeled you in here last night. Same as me. Seems there's a shortage of private rooms. I parted with my gall bladder." A shadow had clouded the congenial face. "I heard the nurses say you almost parted period."

It was then Sarah Ann remembered why she was there. The sudden realization stung, constricting her throat, evoking pain from every fiber of her body. She had turned away from the piercing blue eyes overwhelmed by shame. Failure had prompted her to swallow the pills. And she had even failed at that—the attempt to escape her failures.

"When you're ready you'll find me long on listening and short on advice." Sarah Ann recalled Jill's warm hand patting her feet reassuringly and urging her to rest.

Sarah Ann had slept. When she woke she had found herself looking into those same blue eyes now twinkling with sly mirth.

"I hate to be the one to tell you this. You need nasal surgery. You snore! Sometimes really loud."

A smile wafted across Sarah Ann's face as she recalled her indignation at hearing Jill's description of her sleeping habits. Then bursting out with laughter. "I'll put that on my list," Sarah Ann had shot back, "right behind a face lift, tummy tuck, maybe a little liposuction. Oh yeah! And that surgery they do to tighten your bladder, so when I laugh this hard I won't pee in my pants like I'm about to do right now."

"With a list that long," Jill had responded, sitting down on the side of Sarah Ann's bed, "You'll need a man with deep pockets." Jill had obviously noted the absence of a wedding ring.

It had felt so exhilarating to laugh. In those short moments the laughter seemed to lift constraints that had been weighing so long on her spirit, trumping the gloom of depression which had imprisoned her psychic since John dealt her a body blow when he walked out of her life.

Sarah Ann chortled silently remembering that moment. "So, what do you do when you're not exorcizing depression?" she had asked Jill.

Jill had looked askance and then giggled. "I've been accused of a lot of things. Never of being an exorcist! I leave exorcising to priests. Actually, I'm in the country music business." She then described her Nashville talent management firm in her usual understated way. "Moved here from Boston and set up shop in a house on Music Row. Office downstairs. My apartment upstairs."

A mischievous glint sparked in Sarah Ann's eyes. "So, I have a carpetbagger for a roommate," she proclaimed with a mocking exclamation in her voice. "And I suppose the next thing you'll tell me is you're a Democrat."

"Carpetbagger," Jill replied mockingly. "I guess I'll just have to add that to exorcist. And as for my political preference," she added, "I do prefer blue to red. Blue matches my Irish Catholic eyes, so forgive me, sister, for I have apparently sinned," she had responded with sardonic bemusement, her eyes lifted toward the ceiling.

"To err is only human," Sarah Ann declared still laughing and added, "As a faithful member of a prayer group I firmly believe forgiving is divine. For your penance, five Our Fathers and ten Hail Marys."

Jill had glided around the room and talked, describing her talent management firm as "I make a little. They make a lot. And we generally have a compatible relationship."

"Have you managed anybody famous," Sarah Ann had inquired.

Jill rattled off several names, none of whom Sarah Ann recognized.

"Really!" Sarah Ann tried to mask not recognizing any of the names and instantly knew she had failed, admitting sheepishly, "I have to confess, I'm not much of a country music fan."

"That's un-American," Jill had retorted with a flush of feigned indignation, "if you live so close to Nashville. Are you saying you're one of those suburban snobs who've never been to the Grand Ole Opry?"

"Guilty, I'm afraid."

"Then you didn't see Scooter Harrison." There had been a hint of regret in Jill's voice. "No problem. He was a one album wonder," she observed, sighing deeply. "I learned one thing from Scooter. Always let a man in a double-breasted suit, with an overstuffed briefcase and a hard-assed attitude, draw up an iron clad contract."

"It sounds like you could use the services of my former husband."

The sarcasm in Sarah Ann's voice had not been lost on Jill. "Then I guess that nice man who came and sat with you last night is not your ex. He introduced himself. Willie something-or-other. Three women joined him for a while." A sudden look of melancholy flashed across Jill's beautiful face. "You seem to have lots of caring friends."

Jill said Willie Dell had stayed the night, holding her hand even when his head slumped on the bed. He had slipped out while Jill was in the bathroom. Then Sarah Ann had told Jill about the

Prayer Group. "That explains a lot," Jill concluded. "He and those women held hands and prayed over you like a Greek god and his Vestal Virgins."

That image had prompted an immediate giggle from Sarah Ann. "Actually, Vestal Virgins looked after a Roman goddess," she corrected smugly.

Jill had taken no offense at the correction and continued to gently probe her with questions. In the year that had passed since their first meeting in the hospital, Sarah Ann had come to recognize Jill's innate curiosity about people as a feature of her personality which was at times a perceptive asset, and other times marked her as just plain nosy.

Sarah Ann remembered the weariness that seemed to rush over her like a flooding creek overflowing its banks. Jill observed her weariness and had walked around to the side of the bed and patted her shoulder. "When we both fly this astringent smelling coop, we'll have to meet for lunch one day—maybe on Music Row—and let you sink your Southern fried teeth into a little cowboy cooking while I educate you on the joys and travails of the music business."

And that was how it had happened—not over the "cowboy" food Jill described, but steaming clam lasagna at an Italian restaurant. Sarah Ann looked around her office and remembered that first day she had sat down at this desk after the job offer.

Jill had proved a patient and thorough mentor. Sarah Ann had rewarded Jill's confidence by being a quick study of a business that had a glamorous veneer, and at times, an unforgiving and ruthless underbelly. The synergy she and Jill developed in those early weeks had cemented their friendship and resulted in Sarah Ann becoming a partner.

What was it she had read recently…something Nicole Kidman had said…oh, yes! *Life has got all those twists and turns. You've got to hold on tight and off you go.*

"You're so right, girl," Sarah Ann whispered. The telephone intercom interrupted Sarah Ann's reverie.

"Miz Sarah, Abe Winters on line two."

"Thanks, Viola." Sarah Ann scowled at the blinking light on the telephone panel. *What does Abe want now?* she thought crossly, before realizing she was reacting like the birds which had captivated her attention just moments ago. She forced a smile on her face as she pressed the lit button.

"Abe, how are you?"

"Couldn't be better. Yourself?"

"Super. What can I do for you?" she asked, trying to get Abe right to the point of his call.

"Jill in today?"

"She is, if she's not out to lunch." Sarah Ann was trying to discourage what she suspected was coming.

"I've got a kid I think you and Jill should meet. Comes from Texas. Great voice. A terrific picker too. I caught him at the Blue Bird last night," Winters rushed on, referring to a Nashville watering hole nearly as revered as the Grand Ole Opry itself. "Can I bring him over?"

"Now!"

"I promise he won't disappoint."

Sarah Ann had heard that before from Abe Winters—too many times. She wanted to tell him she was too busy, her schedule too crowded, maybe another day, all of it a fabrication. Abe Winters was a pest, but a pest who had connected Edgerton Group with two of its current top talents, even if she and Jill had been forced to cull those two from among several other hopefuls he had finagled through their front door.

Abe Winters was a veteran of the country music business who had been hanging around Music Row for the better part of forty years, with little to show for those years except the expectation of a couple of free drinks served by sympathetic bartenders at the Blue Bird. She and Jill paid him generous finder's fees for the two talents who were now earning their keep on the county fair circuit. *We need to cut off his allowance,* she thought acerbically.

"Hang on, Abe, let me see if Jill's in," said Sarah Ann, making little attempt to hide her irritation. Before she could put him on hold, he hollered from the other end of the line. "She is. I already checked with Viola. That's why I got you."

Sarah Ann had a sudden urge to do a vocal lobotomy on the receptionist, but then remembered how wily Abe could be, even with a person who guarded Edgerton Group's drawbridge as doggedly as Viola.

"Okay, Abe. You win. How about bringing your boy by around three?"

"We'll be there. This is one appointment you'll kiss my ring for making."

Kiss my ass, was the silent reply hanging on her lips as the line clicked dead. Abe seldom said goodbye.

Abe Winters looked his usual rumpled, need-to-send-the-suit-to-the-cleaners self, as he deposited his short skinny frame into a chair in Jill's office.

The man who sat down directly across from Jill and Sarah Ann presented a very opposite appearance. Tall, with the build of an athlete, he had a face that appeared a cross between Marty Stuart and Vince Gill. Blue eyes focused unblinking on each woman as he shook their hands and bathed each with a slightly crooked smile that animated from his mouth to his large eyes. Those eyes held an expression of sincerity and confidence.

If this guy has anything, he has presence, Sarah Ann observed silently.

Jill was reaching the same silent conclusion. She slumped further down in the tall desk chair. From under her lowered eyes she fixed a perspicacious stare on the young man sitting across from her. "Tell us about yourself…Mr., ah, Parson was it?"

"Yes, ma'am. Jared Parson. I'm from Jacksonville, Texas. Born and raised there. Came by my music from my mama. She was the organist at the Sixth Avenue Baptist Church. Me being an only child, well…I got everything she could give me. And that included learnin' piano and guitar. The singin' just kinda followed."

There was fluidity in his voice, his words flowing like a small stream lazily winding its way through a mountain meadow. *If he sang as well as he talked, this could be a hot prospect,* Jill concluded.

Sarah Ann was making the same observation. It was part of the synergy which had developed between the two women since Sarah Ann yielded to Jill's persistent prodding and joined Edgerton Group. They seemed to view people and their talent through the same lens.

Whether it was acceptance or rejection, the two women seemed always on the same page before even having to consult. The synergy buttressed a business relationship which had begun so tentatively.

Jared Parson talked on about graduating from the University of Texas, writing songs in between classes and packing his suitcase and guitar and heading for Nashville immediately after securing a degree in business administration. It was his fallback position, he explained, if his burning ambition to be an entertainer failed to ignite. The small talk continued for some time, ending with Parson listing the titles of songs he had written—songs he planned for a first album.

Jill found his last statement leaping over optimism to cockiness. "You're a remarkable young man, Mr. Parson." Jill's bland tone masked any hint of a compliment.

"Not really, ma'am. I just wanna sing." Parson's face flushed with sincerity.

"Which song would you like us to hear?"

"Yes, ma'am." Parson opened the soft leather briefcase sitting unobtrusively by the side of his chair and pulled out a CD, handing it across to Jill.

"I wrote the song on there, ma'am. It's called *Parting Texas*." A faint smile drifted across his handsome face. "Kinda my goodbye song before leaving Texas in the rear view."

"Well, Mr. Parson, Sarah Ann and I will certainly listen to your song. Let our receptionist know how to get in touch with you. I'll walk you and Abe out." Sarah Ann knew Jill was taking the fall this time, knowing Abe would linger at the door pitching his prospect even further, hoping to pry some commitment from Jill.

When Abe left ten minutes later, Jill stopped at Sarah Ann's office. "Got a moment?"

"Of course, silly. Got the CD?"

Jill handed it to her and slipped into the chair across from Sarah Ann. What they heard coming from the shelf stereo during the next three minutes precipitated a current of excitement in each woman.

Sarah Ann clapped her hands. "He's good! Really good!"

"Hold tight," Jill responded, trying to mute her own excitement. "Let's hear it again at Arliss's, then make up our minds." She looked thoughtful as she started toward the door. "I've been screwed too often in this business to rush to this quick a judgment. Let Arliss hear him. He has a great ear."

Jill paused at the door. "By the way, did Parson mention he has a wife and young daughter or did I miss it?"

"No, why?" Sarah Ann answered curiously.

"Abe told me. Trying to soften me up, I guess. Make me feel sorry for the guy." She went out but popped her head back around the doorway. "Strange that a guy would talk so much about his mother and not a word about his wife and kid."

Really strange, Sarah Ann mused silently.

Chapter 4

Arliss Hemming was one of Nashville's top producers, a man who honed his skills with the likes of Carl Smith, Johnny Cash, Eddie Rabbit, and a host of other top talent, and now sat quietly at the pinnacle of his craft. Clad in his usual white shirt, open at the neck, and faded blue jeans, Arliss Hemming did not look the part of a multi-millionaire music producer. Nowhere in his demeanor was reflected the power he held with record companies. The music industry awards that lined a shelf on the far side of his small, but neat office paid tribute to his success. They weren't invisible: just not the first thing you saw when you entered Arliss Hemming's world.

Jill was first through the open door of his office promptly at the time she had promised in her call earlier. Hemming had known Jill almost from the day she set up shop on Music Row. Never had he known her to be late. The sight of her sailing through the door, a smile accompanying her casual "Hey, Arliss" greeting, did the usual job on his emotions. He felt the familiar gnawing in his stomach and the predictable ripple of nervousness. Jill had the impact of a first date on him each time they came in contact. Accepting his reaction to the sight of her was something, which for him, was now routine. He gripped the handles of his chair to steady himself as he rose to greet her. Also routine, a hug and a soft peck on the cheek. There were times when he would have given anything for that particular routine to linger. It never did.

In those introspective moments he occasionally allowed himself, Hemming admitted he had been in love with Jill Edgerton almost from the first day they met. It was the day she brought her first client to meet him, her lovely face alight with enthusiasm. She stumbled through a rapid presentation of her client's talents and accomplishments, which were doubtful and unimpressive, in that order. Still, he had listened to her with patient amusement and even agreed to give the client a second look. The client never made it much past that point and soon packed up his guitar and hurried back to obscurity while Hemming exiled his attraction to Jill to a similar place.

Hemming had a wife, two grown kids, one grandchild, and a reputation for being one of the good guys in an industry which seemed to spawn dubious relationships.

In the decade since their first meeting, Hemming observed, with a certain proprietary pride, the morphing of the eager young promoter into a shrewd business woman with a practiced eye for good talent. The only thing still eluding her was snagging the big one—a talent who would become an industry legend. He never doubted it would eventually happen, especially since adding Sarah Ann Boswell as a partner.

Like just about everyone else along Music Row, Hemming questioned the choice of Sarah Ann. *No industry experience. No real business background. Just a year or so as a small foundation fundraiser. How did that qualify anyone for spotting country music talent and nurturing that talent to a lucrative career?* However, the more he came to know Sarah Ann, the more convinced he became that the former socialite was a sound choice.

Like Jill, Sarah Ann shunned the tight, 'good ole boy', make you or break you circuit, which still dominated the country music scene. Arliss Henning did not count himself a member of that lofty circuit. Nor did he consider himself an influence in the industry. He had been content to do things his way since graduating from the University of Tennessee with a degree in business administration. That degree emphasized the pragmatic side of his nature. His independence marked him as a maverick. His financial success gave him entrée into almost any door along Music Row.

During his years in the music business he had observed many changes. Maybe the biggest was that the 'good ole boys' now walking into their Music Row offices were wearing Gucci instead of leather cowboy boots and speaking with brusque dialects easier on the ears in New York or Los Angeles than in Nashville.

Hemming slipped the CD into a player feeding into a state-of-the-art sound system. It generated output to top grade speakers strategically placed around the circular mixing room where he sat with the two women. The mixing studio overlooked a larger studio, its blackened, sound-engineered space capacious enough to accommodate a full orchestra. Hemming designed the studio he now looked over. It was his dream—a million-dollar dream—the envy of most producers in Nashville and even some of the record companies.

"Ready, ladies?"

Hemming pressed the start button and leaned back in his chair, folded his hands comfortably behind his head and swung his booted feet onto the edge of the console, closed his eyes and keened his ears to the voice, the words, the sounds emanating from the speakers.

When the CD was finished he reached over with deliberate slowness to retrieve it, mentally measuring his own appraisal of what he had just heard and how to impart that to the two women sitting expectantly on either side of him. Hemming turned and handed the CD to Jill.

"Sign him."

As she slid behind the wheel of her powder blue Mercedes convertible, Jill erupted in giggles. She thumped the leather steering wheel with her right hand. "We got us a winner, Miss Sarah Ann Boswell! We got us a winner," she exclaimed between giggles. "I just know it."

Sarah Ann could hardly contain her own excitement, but found herself laughing more at the uncharacteristic reaction of Jill, who was usually more staid when evaluating new talent.

"So! When do we tell him?"

~

Jill pulled the car under the aluminum awning covered parking spot reserved for her behind the office. It was one of her few perks, prompted by an inordinate pride she always felt behind the wheel of the Mercedes. *That was the way it was and the way it would stay,* she thought, letting her eyes roam over the sleek convertible for a countless time. Jill made no move to exit the car. "Let's go celebrate at that new restaurant on West End."

Sarah Ann's smile evaporated. "I can't. Not tonight. I have Prayer Group."

"Cancel. Tell them you're working late."

Sarah Ann looked at the excitement radiating on Jill's face. It was the first time she had seen her partner so ebullient about a new talent. She hated to be the damper on that exuberance. "I have to go. I'm hosting. Sorry, Jill."

"You prefer the Vestal Virgins, plus one, to heavenly lasagna and red wine fit for the Last Supper?" Glibness was the shield behind which Jill always withdrew in the face of anything, in this case, disappointment. It registered for only a moment before being evicted by a bright smile.

"So why don't you come to Prayer Group with me?" Sarah Ann had extended that same invitation several times, an invitation always met with a polite rejection.

"No problem, partner. Enjoy the vee-vees," said Jill, employing the nickname with which she had baptized the female members of the Prayer Group some months before.

"Okay! I'll see you in the morning. What time do we make the big call?"

"Soon as you get here."

"Then I'll beat you in," parried Sarah Ann.

Chapter 5

"I will not go on a cruise surrounded by a bunch of fat, retired old couples," Della Sue insisted petulantly. "Carnival would be so much more fun."

"I agree," chimed in Angela. "Besides, Carnival has verandas cheaper than Holland America.

Jeanne Marie glared at Della Sue. "Face it. You're just hoping to get laid by some young stud. Who knows," she said with a sly smile, "you may find the cabin boys more to your liking on Holland America." She noted with secret relish the embarrassment registering on Della Sue's face. So, it might just be true. Della Sue may have been laid by that cabin steward last year. Angela had said as much. Jeanne Marie felt an instant pang of guilt, then the familiar pull in her chest that came with any hint of stress. She needed a cigarette. "Excuse me. I'll let y'all figure this out while I go outside and feed my habit." Because of her 'habit', Jeanne Marie had been banned from smoking inside during Prayer Group meetings. She gave Willie Dell a thump on the knee with her index finger as she passed and glided down the long front hall to the kitchen.

"Need a smoke," Jeanne Marie waved at Sarah Ann, as she pushed open the screen door leading to the back porch.

"Hurry! Food is about to be served." Sarah Ann pulled on a second insulated glove before picking up a platter heaped with barbecued ribs and headed for the dining room. "Come on in here, y'all. Everything's 'bout ready," Sarah Ann shouted across to the parlor.

Angela and Della Sue were still trying to coerce Willie Dell to their side of the cruise line choice as they trailed into the dining room, the oval mahogany table shimmering in the light cast by the crystal chandelier.

"Grab a seat. I set out some extra napkins." Sarah Ann pointed to the short stack of ivory linen napkins by the rib platter. "I'll go get Jeanne Marie."

"I'm here. Two puffs will hold me for a while, but only if you serve that great wine you had last time."

"Your wish is my command," replied Sarah Ann, as she turned the silver corkscrew in a merlot that had found favor with the entire group.

Jeanne Marie sat down beside Willie Dell, across from the Carnival conspirators, at whom she stuck out her tongue. "Willie Dell will go on whatever ship Sarah Ann chooses, won't you, darlin'?" she cooed, patting his arm. "And that settles that," she added dismissively.

"Settles what?" Sarah Ann asked as she took her seat at the table.

Jeanne Marie smirked at Della Sue. "Seems Della Sue feels the field of seduction prospects will be more ample on a Carnival ship, as opposed to being left with having to sort through cabin stewards on staid ole Holland America."

"Oh, for godsakes!" exclaimed Sarah Ann with feigned exasperation. "Then let's go on Norwegian or Celebrity. The lay of your dreams could be anywhere."

"Sarah Ann, the truce-maker has spoken. Let us pray." Willie Dell grasped Sarah Ann's hand and the hand of Jeanne Marie and the five heads gathered around the table were lowered. "Dear Lord, we thank you for this meal. We thank you for the friends about to enjoy this meal. And most of all, we thank you for not allowing any more bickering about anything the rest of the meeting."

"Amen," intoned Jeanne Marie emphatically, feeling smugly that she had vanquished Carnival from the choice of cruise ships the Prayer Group would book for their annual vacation.

"Speak for yourself, Wille Dell," Della Sue pounced. "I reserve the right to fuss and argue as much as I please. It would be totally out of character for me not to, don't you agree Sarah Ann?" she asked with an exaggerated drawl.

"With that I do agree. However, arguing gives one indigestion. I read that on WebMD just the other day. So, for the moment, let's use our mouths mostly for eating. Start those ribs around, Willie Dell," suggested Sarah Ann, pointing to the rib platter.

Laughter rippled among the five friends as they heaped their plates with ribs, cole slaw, scalloped potatoes, and cheese grits.

Angela looked ruefully at her plate as she picked up a rib slathered with the delicately spiced barbecue sauce concocted from ingredients Sarah Ann kept a close secret. She glanced at her friend. "You are evil, Sarah Ann Boswell. A pox on your culinary skills," Angela declared as her teeth chiseled the tender meat off the edge of a rib. "You know these ribs are *sooo* good. They slide right past my own ribs and just leap onto my butt, never to be dislocated. But they are *sooo* worth it," she added, a tiny smear of reddish brown sauce oozing out of each side of her mouth.

"Here, here." Willie Dell raised his glass of merlot. "Here's to endless ribs. And big butts be damned."

The 'butts-be-damned' sentiment appeared to win the evening. Sarah Ann had only an empty rib platter to take to the kitchen a half-hour later. The dessert was pecan pie, topped with a dollop of fresh whipped cream. As a dessert plate was placed in front of each guest, it was greeted with a moan. Despite the chorus of hypocritical moans, the dessert plates Sarah Ann and Angela removed minutes later were as empty as the rib platter.

"Heavenly, as always, my dear," Della Sue gushed, as Sarah Ann refilled glasses with the merlot. "When I'm winging my way toward those pearly gates, I'm taking you along to bribe that old goat, Saint Peter, with some of your delectable Southern cuisine. You will be my culinary insurance policy for eternal life."

"I hope that's not all it takes. What if Saint Peter's on Nutrisystem?" countered Sarah Ann.

"Then I'll be eternally damned, I guess," drawled Della Sue. "But you know I prefer warmer climates anyway."

"That seems a good opening for prayer requests," inserted Willie Dell. "Since your name starts with the first letter of the alphabet, you first, Angela."

"My first request is that Charlie will have the balls to get a new job.

He has an interview early next week. Then maybe, just maybe, we can wave goodbye to those related-by-blood sons-of-bitches he calls daddy and brother." Angela rarely concealed her disdain for her husband's kin, often referring to them in terms far more execrable and obscene.

"Who with, Angela?" Jeanne Marie inquired.

"An insurance company that needs an accounting geek like Charlie to design software for their overseas clients. Not only will he make more money than what that impecunious ogre who passes for his father pays him, but he would be traveling for long periods, therefore, out of my hair."

"Oh God, where can I sign Beau up?" asked Della Sue excitedly. "I'd happily settle for a pay cut to get Beau off to China. Maybe Bora Bora or Pago Pago: some place where natives could make a meal of him."

"Della Sue, you couldn't do without Beaufort Oliver Simpson for ten seconds," drawled Willie Dell. "What would become of your dependency syndrome?"

"Oh, hush, Willie Dell. You know I couldn't part with my Beau, any more than I could my pet Black Mamba." Amid the chuckles, she added. "And while I have the floor, let me say I am willing to compromise on Celebrity instead of Carnival *if* it will smooth Jeanne Marie's prudish feathers. Also, I want God to keep all my friends at this table safe. And their families, too." After a pregnant pause she glanced around at her friends from lowered eyelids, "And yes, that includes Beau."

"I'm not sure how much sincerity God will be reading into that last request, but I'll put it down on the list." Willie Dell wrote with exaggerated flourish on the legal pad, "even Beau."

For the next few minutes the other women added this request or that request to the prayer list which Willie Dell dutifully recorded in his neat cursive. Only Sarah Ann remained silent. He looked over at his reticent friend. "So, what do you wish the Almighty to provide you with this month?"

"Well." Sarah Ann hesitated. *Should she share her hopes for Jared Parson with her friends? Why not? Prayers couldn't hurt.* "We are about to sign a new talent that has the looks of a young Vince Gill, hips like Elvis, and a voice to challenge Blake Shelton. My prayer is that we sign him. And that he is as successful as all three put together."

"When can I meet him," exclaimed Della Sue. "Or maybe you could bring him along on the cruise. Then I could really turn Holland America into a party ship."

"Be serious, Della Sue?" Sarah Ann scolded good-naturedly. "This could put Jill's agency on the map if he's as good as we think he is."

"By the way, it's your agency too. Or had you forgotten about the word 'partner' on that contract you signed?

"No, I haven't forgotten. But thanks, Della Sue, for reminding me of my wall of worry."

"Sarah Ann, I'm serious, darlin'. I'm speaking purely medicinally when I say I hanker for a good lookin' man." She looked around at her friends with a mischievous gleam in her eyes. "Willie Dell needs a hair restorative. I need restoration somewhere a little lower."

"You are wicked," declared Angela, between laughs.

"Well, it's time to pray fellow group members. Take a hand," ordered Willie Dell, as he neatly tore off the list of prayer requests and placed it in the center of the table amidst the five friends. Each reached for a hand on either side. With heads bowed, the silent prayers were offered. It was a prayer ritual the five friends had practiced since the first meeting of the Prayer Group in third grade. Only the written requests had changed, which no longer included asking the Almighty to heap havoc on unsuspecting nuns. Such prayer requests were now mostly reserved for husbands, ex-husbands or the occasional former lover.

As Sarah Ann lowered her head she became a supplicant on a mission—*on behalf of Jill and me, make Jared Parson the big find Jill has been searching for. Give her the success she has so long been seeking. Me too!* Then she suddenly realized as Jill's partner she would benefit equally. She and Jill could end up far wealthier women if Jared Parson lived up to the expectations placed on him by Arliss Hemming. *Thank you, God, for all your tender mercies. Most of all help make this success for Jill happen.*

Sarah Ann raised her head first. "Now, who's for more pecan pie?"

The chorus of affirmations was unanimous.

Chapter 6

Jill was already at her desk when Sarah Ann arrived at the office a half-hour early the next morning.

"Good morning, early bird," said Sarah Ann, as she poked her head into Jill's office.

"I've already got the signing contract. I filled in the name and added a couple of stipulations. Copies are almost finished printing." There was a flush of excitement on Jill's face. She rubbed her small, delicate hands together. "He's the one, Sarah Ann. I just know it. Good looking—drop dead handsome, actually—with a voice to rival the best in this business. He's the whole package, Sarah Ann. And he's *ours*." She turned to the tall, cherry credenza behind her and scooped several pages from the printer tray. "Just as soon as he puts his 'John Henry' on this document, of course."

"Of course," parroted Sarah Ann. "And the moment he does, and steps out the door, let's close up shop and head to Leiper's Fork where I will buy you the biggest burger and the tallest plate of onion rings Puckett's has to offer. Then we can celebrate with a full-on cholesterol high."

"And wine, maybe?"

Sarah Ann laughed. "That could be a challenge. We may have to smuggle a bottle in." She turned to walk to her own office and chirped over her shoulder, "You can take the girl to the sticks, but you can't remove those snooty New England habits."

"Spoken like a true Southern belle," Jill retorted.

Within an hour after Jared Parson answered Jill's call, he was sitting across from the two women, his blue eyes dancing with expectation. His hands were one moment tightly fisted, the next nervously gripping his knees, just above the 'factory made' frays in his well-worn jeans.

Jill had given Jared no hint of what they would be discussing. She called it a follow-up meeting. From the comfort of the soft leather couch sitting against a side wall, Sarah Ann observed the young man closely. He seemed tentative, almost vulnerable at this moment. Was he expecting rejection? It was the outcome for most who sat in the same chair as he did now. She wanted to smile encouragement; to hint at what he was about to hear; to ease the tension on his handsome features. Her own features remained impassive.

Jill did the honors. She stood and walked around and sat on the edge of her desk. In a business-like tone that camouflaged the excitement churning within her, Jill said, "Jared, we liked what we heard yesterday. We think you have potential." The fists gripping his knees tightened until the knuckles turned white. "We would like to sign you to a management contract. It would be a standard agreement with the typical probationary period to see if you can get a foothold in this business, something I might add, and I'm sure you well know, is tough at best…impossible for most who bring their dreams to Nashville." Jill waited for Jared's reaction.

It came in the form of a long sigh, as if he had been holding his breath for a prolonged period and released it with a whoosh. "Yes, ma'am. I think that would be terrific."

As Jill stood to walk back around the side of her desk, Jared leaped out of his chair and in one long stride had her in his grasp, wrapping her in a bear hug, and swinging her around and around, as her backless heels clattered to the floor. She felt the strength of his arms as his hold crushed her to his chest. She was nearly breathless when he finally placed her back on her bare feet.

"Thank you, ma'am," Jared said jubilantly. A flushed smile replaced the startled look on Jill's face. "Sorry, ma'am. Sometimes I get a little carried away when I get excited. But I can promise you this. You've just made the best decision you'll ever make."

"It's all right, Jared. I just wasn't expecting such a robust reaction," Jill added, fishing for one of her shoes under the desk.

Only then did Jared acknowledge Sarah Ann. "Thank you too, ma'am." She flinched slightly as he bounded toward her. "Not to worry, ma'am. I'll keep it to hand shaking this time."

Jill smoothed the front of her Ann Taylor silk blouse that matched the color of her eyes and sought sanctuary in the chair behind her desk. "Let's move on, Jared. Now we get to this thing that binds us together in joy, and sorrow—this contract." She pushed the several-page document across the desk. "Have a seat and give this a quick scan. Then I suggest you have an attorney look it over before you sign, because it wraps you up with Edgerton Group like salsa inside an omelet."

"Thank you for the advice, ma'am. No need for an attorney. Let me give this a good look-see." He studied the contract in silence for several minutes, rereading parts of it, but asked no questions. When he looked up, Jill reminded him it was a standard management contract that most talent managers could download from their computers, and she added, he could insert special requests that both she and Sarah Ann would initial, along with his. He had none.

"Then you agree, Arliss Hemming will produce your new album?"

"Yes, ma'am. If you hadn't suggested him, I would be initialing one of those special requests you mentioned just now."

Jill leaned forward in her chair, her hands steepled under her chin. "Interesting, Jared? Why would you have insisted on Arliss?"

Jared's face tightened with intensity. "Because he's the best in this town. I already checked him out. And if I'm gonna make it as big as I plan, I need to work with only the best."

"Is that why you chose us, Mr. Parson?" The question came from Sarah Ann, who had watched an intensity take almost a fanatic hold on Jared's frame, clinching his fists in another tight ball, paralyzing the animation that energized him moments before. When he finally turned to her, his face was bathed in a wide grin. "Yes, ma'am, with a little help from Abe. And please, ma'am, call me Jared."

"I'm curious, Mr.… Jared. What is it about Edgerton Group that makes you feel we can help you accomplish your goals?"

"It's quite simple, ma'am. Women work a lot harder than any men I know, with one exception, myself. Having two women gives my career the kinda workforce it needs to succeed." His face was once again swathed in a boyish grin.

"Since I've just been enlisted in your *workforce*, Jared, please call me Sarah Ann, or if you prefer, Sarah will do."

The same gripping intensity flashed across Jared's face before he relaxed back into his engaging grin. "I'll call you Sarah Ann, 'cause that appears to be what everyone calls you. But what you will be called in the future is millionaire, 'cause that's what I intend all of us to be just as soon as I can get into that studio with Arliss Hemming."

Jill said, "Before you can do that, Jared, you need to sign both copies of this in the places marked by the colored tabs." She handed him a pen.

After Jared left Jill's office, stopping to give another bear hug to a startled Viola before heading out the front door, Jill darted around her desk toward Sarah Ann. The two women danced arm-in-arm around the small office whooping for joy. "He's the big catch I've been angling for since I set up shop. I just know it." Jill held Sarah Ann at arm's length. "You made it happen, you know. You've been a good luck charm since your first day here."

Sarah Ann was pleased and self-conscious at the same time. "Don't sell yourself short, girl. You built this agency. I'm just one of your stepping stones."

"And now it's time to close up shop for the day and head out to Puckett's," proclaimed Jill. "If I remember correctly, I was promised the best tasting dose of high cholesterol a body can have. Let's go. My arteries are all a twitter."

Chapter 7

Arliss Hemmings slipped the CD into the plastic case and swiveled around to hand it to Jill standing behind him, culminating more than two months of work—work that began mid-day most days and often went well past mid-night. "You look bushed, lady," he said, noting the dark circles of weariness under her eyes.

"I am," she agreed. "It's the producer's fault, you know. He's that guy who makes me work all night—the same guy who's had his days and nights mixed up since he left the womb."

"That would be me." He smiled. She was right. He was a night person by choice and long habit, but their nights together were over. Jared had spent the afternoons and early evenings laying down tracks. Hemming did the mixing at night, with Jill in the chair next to his giving final approval. Sarah Ann had kept the office running. The pace was grueling, and it showed on both their faces.

"Have you lined up any listeners?" Hemming inquired.

"Sure have. Sarah Ann has an appointment for us with Len Shiring over at NCA Records first thing tomorrow." She glanced at the clock above the control panel. "Actually, make that today. Then, we're meeting Grasso from Emporium at Maggiano's for lunch."

"You won't be going to Maggiano's. Len's no fool," observed Hemming, tapping the CD Jill was holding. "This guy is another Alan Jackson—throw in Brad Paisley—all wrapped into one, and Len will know that after the first couple o' minutes."

"You really think he's that good, Arliss?"

"Yeah! I do. I predict a couple of cuts will be chart toppers." He looked toward the door as Jared came into the studio rubbing his eyes. "Hey, sleepy head, catch!" Hemmings tossed a cased CD at the startled Jared who had been getting a bag of chips from a vending machine in the hall. "Something to play while you talk your wife into having sex."

Jared grinned and tossed the CD in the air. "I've never had to sing for sex yet." His grin morphed into a smirk as he flopped into a chair next to Jill. An awkward silence fell between the three people positioned in a triangle near the console.

"Arliss thinks the CD is great," said Jill, breaking the uncomfortable silence. "He thinks Len Shiring at NCA will bite before anyone else has a chance to."

"Yes, ma'am. I hope you're right." Jared glanced over at Hemming. "If he does, I owe it to you, Arliss. Thanks for your patience with me. I know we had our moments, but you make me sound the best I can." Jared stuck out his hand.

"Good luck." Hemming's hand was enclosed in Jared's iron grip. "God gave you that voice, Jared. There wasn't a whole lot I did to improve on His handiwork."

Jill leaned over and kissed Hemming on the cheek. "Goodnight… make that morning. And thanks. I'll call you after we see Shiring." Jill stood and tucked her arm in Jared's, who waved at Hemming as the pair swept out of the studio, the younger man's arm now draped proprietarily over Jill's shoulder.

An almost triumphant exit, Hemmings thought, watching the pair disappear as the studio door shut tightly behind them. He leaned back in the chair and linked his arms behind his head. He wanted to feel Jill's exuberance, to share even a little of the elation he knew she was feeling after hearing the CD all the way through. As much as he wanted to, he could not summon even one ounce of her euphoria. Why? The kid seemed all smiles and sincerity on the outside. *Yes, sir this…yes, sir that.* But something prickled at the edges of Hemming's senses. He wasn't sure what.

"Shit!" he said out loud, trying to verbally banish the melancholy. He felt suddenly old and weary. Maybe it was too many successive nights in the studio. Maybe it was just jealousy because it wasn't his arm around Jill's shoulder walking down the hall.

He leaned back again and drifted into introspection. Jared Parson was going to be big in the country music business. In Hemming's opinion that was a given. He recalled Jill telling him about Jared's declaring he would make her and Sarah Ann millionaires the day he signed the management contract. That would likely happen, he conceded, without any envy. As the producer, he would get a fair share himself. So why wasn't he feeling a sense of success—a sense of accomplishment at what had just been completed? It was Parson. There was something troubling about the kid. Hemming had felt it the first time he met him. *But what?* He knew it was irrational to hold something against someone and not know what. Still, he did. And it was a feeling he could not shake.

I'm full of shit, he thought morosely, as he got up to leave. *I just told Jill he'd be bigger than Alan and Brad. Stow it,* he admonished himself. He flipped the switch that powered the long console and the computers that ran it, and then turned down the dimmer switch for the studio lights. Time to go home. Dejectedly, he pulled open the studio door. *Maybe I should try singing. Maybe that would get me some sex. What the hell? Nothing else had worked in months*. He felt a familiar pang of frustration and slammed the studio door shut.

~

Shortly after ten the next that same morning Len Shiring was listening to the last of the fifteen cuts on the CD Jill had handed him. When it finished, he reached over and turned off the CD player and methodically placed the disc back in its plastic case. His expression remained opaque as he handed it to Jill. "Think you got a winner here?" he asked, his eyes moving languidly from one female face to the other.

"The question is, do you?" was Sarah Ann's rejoinder.

She's a sharp one, he thought, looking at a face that even in middle age was still devoid of the usual encroachments of age. *For a grand-mother, Sarah Ann was still a helluva good looking woman*, he observed silently. *And a shrewd one. Even more so than the woman seated next to her*. He leaned back in his oversized leather chair. "Okay. I like it. I like it a lot," Shiring announced, a faint smile tugging at the edges of his mouth. Watching the two women, he could not decide whether their faces expressed relief or triumph. Maybe both.

"When do we sign?" Jill wasted no time in getting to the point of their being there.

"Whoooa, Jill. You know I've got to run this past Jim and a few others," referring to Jim Watkins, who handled marketing for the record label. "Give me a day or two and I'll get back to you."

"Jill and I are having lunch with Grasso at noon," Sarah Ann said. "Then we head over to his office. That gives you maybe an hour to make up your mind. We sign with whoever makes the first offer." Sarah Ann watched to see if her words dented the veil of inscrutability that had descended over Shiring's features. No change.

"You seem mighty sure Grasso's going to bite if I don't," he said finally.

Jill responded, "That boy is a feast and Grasso has never passed up a plate of food like this in his entire time in Nashville." Her tone was measured, her eyes fixed squarely on Shiring. This was a high stakes parry that could win them a contract or could invite a polite, but firm dismissal.

Shiring sat forward in his chair, his eyes trained on Jill's face. "Cancel your lunch with Grasso. We've got some talking and signing to do." Shiring turned to Sarah Ann whose face was dissected by a wide grin. "By the way, where is this Wunderkind? I better meet him before I start peddling his music."

"He's waiting in your lobby. I'll go get him." Sarah Ann almost bounded out the door.

Shiring liked what he saw. Good looking kid. Trim, muscular, thick hair and a cockiness that would give him balls on stage. Charisma oozed out of the guy. And he had a gift from God in his throat, as well as a Willie Nelson penchant for penning a good song. The whole package.

Shiring leaned back in his big chair with the confident air of a man who had been in charge a long time and held the future in his hands of eager young guys like the one in front of him now. "So, why'd you pick Nashville? You could peddle your voice in LA or New York."

"My mom and I used to listen to the Grand Ole Opry on TV. Every Saturday night. I've never wanted to be anywhere else but Nashville."

Shiring had heard that before. This time he believed it. "Once we sign a contract, me and everyone else in this place are going to work your butt off. And so are those two," he said, pointing at Jill and Sarah Ann. "Are you ready for that?"

"Yes, sir. I've been ready since the day I left Texas."

"Good. Come by tomorrow about this time and we'll have the contracts drawn up for you and your managers to sign." Shiring eyed Jared sagaciously. "And I'll have a $10,000 advance drawn up to help get you ready for the launch. Suit you?"

"Yes, sir. That will sure help."

Chapter 8

The next few weeks were a whirlwind of preparations for the launch of Jared Parson and his debut album. Other performers managed by the agency were handed off to a newly-hired administrative assistant, Natalie Holt. She was a bright young woman whom Sarah Ann had employed on the spot, seeing a high measure of energy and maturity in the newly graduated Belmont University music business major.

Shirings's promotion director, Jim Watkins, had been on the telephone pitching the album to Walmart, Target and Tower Records among others, and setting up distribution through the on-line firms emerging as major marketers of music, selling both albums and music downloads.

While Watkins worked the distribution sources, Jill and Sarah Ann were spinning in their own whirlwind—setting up a showcase in the posh ballroom of the Hermitage Hotel near the state capitol, issuing more than a thousand invitations and shooting out press releases to the entertainment editors of major magazines, newspapers and television outlets across the country. This would be the biggest launch of a performer by Edgerton Group ever. Covering all the bases with such a small staff made sleeping at the office look almost attractive to Sarah Ann on many workdays that ran well past the normal quitting time.

Jared was the model of cooperation. He spent several hours with a tailor selected by Jill who catered to the country music set. His jeans no longer read Wrangler on the rear pocket. They now sported tailor-made holes in the knees outlined by a threaded fringe that gave them a realistic worn look.

"A shortage of patches," Sarah Ann observed sardonically, when she walked past the small conference room just past the lobby at Edgerton Group. Jared was standing on a short stool in the designer jeans that were being altered for yet another photo shoot, this time for digitally autographed pictures to distribute with press releases. It's the 'in' look," Jill tossed back from inside her office across the hall. "Ever looked at Alan Jackson's knees?"

"Can't say I have. But I might just like to sometime," Sarah Ann replied as she sat down behind her desk. Jill called out, "You go, girl. Start with the knees and move directly up. You might find Mr. Jackson quite interesting."

"Speaking from experience, are we?"

"I wish," Jill laughed. "He was lassoed early-on and still carries the same brand."

Jared stood quietly on the tailor stand amused at the banter between the two women. The earnest looking tailor was not talking. His lips were pressed tight, clutching large straight pins which he inserted expertly to mark seams that would make the customized jeans skin tight. The slightly built tailor, with the last name of Woo, reviled chalk, and persisted in using pins which had long ago lost favor with others in his trade. As Mr. Woo pinned a long tuck up the inside of the left leg, he noted with male envy the bulge in the crotch area of the young man standing stark still in front of him. One of the cotton-filled wads he customized for several of his other famous clients to create just the right bulge would not be needed. Nature had provided well for Jared, who was now looking down at him.

"We about through, Mr. Woo? I could sure use a Pepsi."

Mr. Woo shook his head furiously, unable to speak because of pins still clinched between his lips.

"I'll get you one, Jared," Jill offered. "Be right back."

By the time she returned, the tailor's lips were devoid of the pins. He waved her impatiently out of the room before helping Jared carefully remove the jeans. When they were safely across his arm, Mr. Woo bobbed his small head and beamed at Jared. "I return these perfect tomorrow."

"Thank you, Mr. Woo," said Jill, as he passed by her. She opened the can of Pepsi and held it out to Jared who had just finished pulling on another pair of jeans. "About what time, Mr. Woo?"

"Morning, Madam. Everything ready then."

"That's perfect. Just bring them by the Hermitage. That's where we'll be."

That's cutting it close thought Sarah Ann, *since the showcase was in two days.* Her telephone buzzed. "Are you in?" inquired Viola. "It's County Scene returning your call."

"I'm in." The voice of the woman at the other end of the line was calling to book an interview with Jared and his wife before the big launch. "Sounds great, Lou. Hold on. Jared's here. Let me just double-check with him." She put the connection on hold and bolted for the conference room.

"Jared," she announced excitedly, "Country Scene wants to interview you and your wife before the showcase tomorrow. They can do it tomorrow around two. They also want to shoot some photos of you and LouAnn before the interview. Can LouAnn be there a little early?"

"I'm not sure…," he sounded hesitant. "LouAnn slipped picking up Willow and fell against a door a couple o' days ago. Got herself a bad shiner." And quickly added, "Luckily, she didn't drop Willow," referring to the couple's four-year-old daughter.

"I'm sorry. You hadn't mentioned the accident." Sarah Ann frowned deeply. This was a huge opportunity. A story in Country Scene. Maybe even a cover. It was an opportunity that didn't come often for someone just breaking into the business. An opportunity Sarah Ann had pushed hard for. She knew Shiring would hit the ceiling if Jared refused the interview. "Not to worry," Sarah Ann said briskly, "we can have the make-up artist there early. She will work wonders on your wife. And we can position LouAnn so the black eye won't show."

Anger streaked like a bullet across Jared's face. He glanced toward Jill who stood just inside the door. She nodded her head slightly. The anger that stormed across his face only a moment before was replaced with a bland expression. "I thought LouAnn didn't have to be involved with any of this. She's really shy."

"Just a minute, Jared." Sarah Ann went back to her office and pushed the hold button. "Lou, can I get right back to you on the time? Jared is thrilled at the opportunity," she explained quickly. "We just need to clear the time. You know how hectic it is when you're hosting a showcase with this many people coming." Another few seconds of silence and then she responded. "Back to you in ten. No later. I promise," and hung up the receiver.

Sarah Ann walked back to where Jared was slipping a belt through the loops in his jeans. "LouAnn won't have to do much talking. I'll be there to steer the interview and make sure they don't make her feel awkward." Sarah Ann reached out and touched Jared's arm reassuringly. "This is a big start for you. And for her. She might as well get used to the attention. The bigger you get; the more attention will be focused on her. It's just part of this business."

"Dolly Parton's husband doesn't get interviewed," Jared stubbornly insisted. "He's like a ghost, and it never held Dolly back."

Sarah Ann had no rejoinder for that analogy. It was true. Carl Dean was a phantom, and Parton seemed content for him to remain that way. Jared's was a different situation. He was just breaking into the business, and she knew that if his wife was not seen, it might encourage rumors about the stability of his marriage and spark speculation about affairs. The country music business had its ugly side. It was the gossip she and Jill must protect their young client from so he would achieve the 'God and Family' image demanded by the fans that would be purchasing his music.

Jared turned and glared at Jill. Sensing the awkwardness, Sarah Ann suggested, "Why don't I talk to LouAnn. Anyway, she's scheduled for a final fitting for her dress later this afternoon. Maybe I can help calm any butterflies she has about meeting with the reporter." Jared stood silently glaring at Jill who looked away only when her cell phone belted out *Rocky Top* and she stepped back across to her office to take the call. Jared looked steely when he turned to Sarah Ann but finally nodded assent.

"Good." Sarah Ann patted his arm and walked back to her desk to call the writer at Country Scene. Placing the receiver back on the phone she reflected on what she had just observed between Jared and Jill. She was both bewildered and disturbed. Sarah Ann couldn't recall exactly when Jill's cell phone rang. Had she heard all of the conversation between herself and Jared? Maybe not. Sarah Ann tried to quell the unsettling feeling enveloping her. The phone ringing was a welcome intrusion. She made a mental note to discuss it with Jill later as she lifted the receiver.

When they did discuss it early that afternoon in Jill's office, she was terse to the point of testy, a side of her business partner that Sarah Ann had not seen before. Jill questioned her decision to involve Jared's wife in the pre-showcase interview. "She could say inadvertent things. "Things," Jill repeated, "that could derail Jared before he even gets on track." Then added, "LouAnn's a hick compared to him."

Sarah Ann was shocked by Jill's assessment. They had met LouAnn together. She *was* shy. But it was an appealing shyness. And she certainly was *not* a "hick." Soft spoken, winsome and intelligent were terms Sarah Ann had applied to LouAnn Parson after she and Jill had met her for the first time at a Music Row restaurant shortly after Jared signed with their agency. And LouAnn was a looker. No mistaking that. She had somewhat unruly long blond hair, crystal blue eyes framed by thick lashes; with an innocent air about her that Sarah Ann found enchanting. Combining the right make-up with flattering clothes, LouAnn could easily go from very pretty to beautiful.

Both she and Jill had agreed on that assessment of LouAnn. *What had changed?* Sarah Ann wondered. "When The Tennessean called two weeks ago about interviewing Jared and LouAnn, you didn't raise any objections. Why now?" she asked Jill pointedly. The newspaper interview was set for the following week.

"Because I've been thinking about her and she could be a drag on Jared's career." Jill flung the words at Sarah Ann like a discus, anger distorting her lovely features. Jill played at straightening a small stack of framed records of clients who had landed on the record charts once, but never again. She had removed them to make space on the walls of her office in anticipation of the gold and platinum records she expected Jared to garner. With her back to Sarah Ann, Jill blurted out, "She really is a hick compared to him. No poise. No sophistication. I can't imagine why someone like Jared would marry anyone like that."

Again, Sarah Ann felt the shock of Jill's words. But she remained silent. *What could Jill have been thinking that so turned her against a young woman she had met only once* that she was aware of. In the nearly two years they had worked together Sarah Ann had seen the quirky side of Jill, even the edgy, angry side. Jill's temper could erupt over the most unlikely things. She would spew like a volcano. Then moments later apologize for her outburst. Sarah Ann had never witnessed this new side of Jill—judgmental and demeaning.

After a prolonged silence, Sarah Ann spoke. "They were high school sweethearts. That will add a romantic element to the story, don't you think?" she suggested, trying to temper Jill's objections.

Jill just shrugged her shoulders and Sarah Ann returned to her office stunned and even more bewildered. She shook her head as if to rid her mind of the puzzling response by Jill and looked back down at her laptop. She needed to finish the biographical sketch of Jared she promised to have ready for the Country Scene interviewer. She was still bent over her laptop an hour later when a soft knock interrupted her. It was LouAnn Parson. There was a hint of discomfort in the awkward smile that furrowed her deep dimples. "Miss Edgerton told me to see you."

"Oh, of course, LouAnn," said Sarah Ann, as she rose from her chair. "Come in and have a seat," she said graciously, pointing LouAnn to a chair by her desk. "You're here for the final fitting on you dress, right?"

"Yes, ma'am."

"Mr. Woo was here this morning for Jared's final fitting. He should be back around four to make sure your new dress is perfect." Glancing at the clock which showed 3:45, Sarah Ann asked if she could get LouAnn a cup of coffee or a soft drink.

"No, ma'am, but thanks."

"Did Jared come with you?" Sarah Ann asked.

"Yes, ma'am. He's in Miss Edgerton's office. He closed the door. Said they had something important to talk about."

"I'm sure they do, LouAnn. It's a busy time. Lots of last minute loose ends to tie up." Sarah Ann could not imagine what was so important that it had to be discussed behind a closed door and without her being invited to sit in. Unless it was about tomorrow's interview.

LouAnn saw the shadow of concern on Sarah Ann's face. "I can wait out front if I'm in the way here."

"You're not in the way at all, LouAnn." Sarah Ann pulled a chair from the corner of her office to sit closer to LouAnn. It was only then she noticed the deep blue and red swelling beneath LouAnn's left eye. The younger woman turned her head away in embarrassment.

"I've got a pretty good shiner, haven't I, Mrs. Boswell." LouAnn turned back toward Sarah Ann with a look that reminded her of a repentant puppy dog.

"I'm sorry you were injured," said Sarah Ann, trying to cover her own discomfort after seeing the bruise under the eye that extended partway down the cheek. "Jared said you fell against a doorway. I'm so sorry. Does it hurt very much?"

"No, ma'am. It just looks awful bad. Jared doesn't think I should do that interview you talked to him about, so I guess I'll have to decline, if you don't mind."

Sarah Ann's mouth opened, but the protest died silently. There was something painfully vulnerable in the face she was looking at. This was not the time to push an unwanted interview. "Of course not. We want you to feel comfortable. I'll let the magazine know. They'll understand."

Sarah Ann knew the reporter assigned to the interview would not understand and would throw a fit and probably threaten to back out. Country Scene was the biggest game in town where country music magazines were concerned. Landing an interview for Jared had been a coup on her part. And the reporter had specifically agreed to do the interview only if they had access to LouAnn as well. Well, she would just have to smooth it over. No amount of make-up, applied by the best make-up artist they could hire, would cover an eye and cheek as deeply bruised as that which Sarah Ann was now looking at with alarm. A chilling thought nagged at the edges of her mind; a thought she brushed aside as unthinkable.

~

"LouAnn won't be able to be here tonight," Jared told his two managers as he pulled on a new pair of ornately trimmed cowboy boots.

"The kid's kinda sick. She didn't want to leave her with the babysitter."

Jared Parson stood before Sarah Ann and Jill, his thumbs hooked in the pockets of the tailored jeans that had arrived with Mr. Woo only minutes before as Jared strolled into the hotel room at the Hermitage. The little man's round face was bathed in an obsequious smile as he stood back and perused his skillful work. The jeans fit as the little Chinese tailor had promised and the bill he handed Sarah Ann and Jill was larger than he had led them to expect. Unsmiling, Jill wrote the tailor a check while keeping her temper in check.

The reporter from Country Scene was clearly vexed that LouAnn would not be available for the interview. *Let her stew* thought Sarah Ann. She was on deadline and did not have time to cancel the story on Jared. Another bullet dodged on a day when she and Jill had begun to feel like the losing side at the OK Corral.

When Sarah Ann opened a package of menus this morning, with Jared's biography on the back, she discovered an error the printer had failed to correct. The reprinted menus were delivered only an hour ago.

The lighting crew positioned stand lights in several areas around the specially built stage that would prevent some guests from viewing the full stage. Following a verbal battle with the staging crew chief—won in a nearly chin-to-chin exchange between Jill and the lighting engineer—stand lights were either repositioned or eliminated. To make matters worse, the cell phones of both women were ringing frequently, jarring their nerves already on edge.

Then there was Len Shiring. As Sarah Ann predicted, he hit the ceiling when she told him LouAnn would not be available for the interview. Sarah Ann was not prepared for the string of profanity, followed by insistent demands for LouAnn to be interviewed, that ran a gamut from threatening to insulting. Shiring had telephoned at least a dozen times; so often Sarah Ann finally pushed him off to her assistant, Natalie, who then threatened to quit every time her cell phone rang. Shiring had not been informed yet that LouAnn would be a no-show at the showcase itself.

Sarah Ann sat down at one of the empty tables in the large room, sipped from the bottle of water she had been carrying around most of the afternoon like a third appendage and decided it was time to exhale. What else could go wrong?

It the next instant Jill's face was close to Sarah Ann's. The alarm was apparent on her flushed features as she whispered in Sarah Ann's ear, "Shiring's up in Jared's room, and he's getting Jared upset. Can you come and help me get rid of that meddling sonofabitch?"

The two women heard Shiring shouting "pompous ass" as they approached the door of Jared's hotel room. When they entered he was spewing more loud vitriol laced with profanity from the center of the room where he stood, his round face blotchy red with anger. Jared towered over the smaller man, silent but seething, his fists clenched tightly at his sides. A photographer appeared to be trying to make himself invisible in a far corner of the hotel room.

Sarah Ann squeezed Jill's arm to constrain any reaction and walked over to link her arm familiarly in Shiring's, and in her most soothing and patrician voice asked, "What's the problem, Len?"

Shiring let out a deep sigh before finally looking over at Sarah Ann. "This kid wants to sing a Willie Nelson classic to end the show. I keep telling him this is a showcase for his songs. Not a time to rehash someone else's music. He's just being an upstart jerk about everything." He pounded his chest with his right hand. "And I'm shelling out nearly thirty grand for this launch."

"Are you Jared? Are you being an upstart jerk?" Sarah Ann looked pointedly at Jared who stood with his balled fists jammed in his new tight-fitting jeans, his head lowered.

There was a period of strained silence before Jared finally looked up and replied, "Yes, ma'am, I guess I am," he conceded. He rammed his fists even deeper into the pockets. "But it's what I want to do, and Jill agrees. It's my showcase," he added defensively. "I'm not going to blow anything." He looked directly at Shiring. "This is a chance I've worked hard for. When it's over, I'll be on my way and that means you and your record label will get back all of its investment and a whole helluva lot more."

There was a smug tone in the last words not lost on Shiring. But the steam seemed to have evaporated in the record label executive. He unlatched himself from Sarah Ann and stormed out of the room, closing the door with an, *Awww shit*, echoing at his heels. The silence in the hotel room was prolonged following Shiring's exit. Finally, Jill walked over to Jared and pulled him into a hug. "As long as you kick ass out there tonight, Len isn't going to care what you sing."

Jill was right. Shiring was glowing with compliments as he embraced Jared Parson following his performance. "A rising new star of NCA Records," he declared. "Going to be big. The biggest, maybe!" The record company head gave Jared a hi-five and pumped several hands thrust at him by well-wishers. The kid had presence and energy on stage the like of which he hadn't seen in a while. Peering out from the crowd around Jared, Shiring spotted Sarah Ann standing near the edge of the stage observing the effusive scene around Jared. He walked over and gave her a rough peck on the cheek.

"Think you made a good choice, Len?"

"Not me, girl. You and Jill. You saw him first," he added graciously as he put his arm around her shoulders and pulled her close.

"Is he going to be big, Len?"

"Yeah! Could be as big as Garth." He patted her arm. "Hell, kid, with his looks and talent, he could be the biggest yet." Shiring looked over at Sarah Ann and grinned mischievously. "And he's gonna fatten your bank account. You and Jill both. Get ready to hire a big-time tax guy. "

"Then I'm happy for Jill. This is *her* dream, you know."

He gave her shoulder a squeeze and whispered, "She deserves it, kid," before starting back toward the throng surrounding Jared. Even though Shiring wore elevated shoes, Sarah Ann could see the bald spot at the back of the stubby man's crown which he had tried to disguise with a dark color spray. When he had taken only a few steps, Shiring stopped and turned back toward Sarah Ann and threw her a kiss. Then his smile faded into a look of sober reflection. "You're right about this, you know. Jared Parson will be Jill's dream weaver." He turned and in moments had melted into the crowd around his new star.

Chapter 9

$\mathbf{I}$t was a face he had last seen sitting in a battered Ford Taurus, scowling and silent. Now here was the bastard smiling up at him from the glossy front of the magazine. This time it was his turn to scowl as he picked up the magazine and debated paying nearly two bucks to buy it.

Hell with it, he hissed silently, roughly stuffing the magazine back in the rack at the convenience store. His money was better spent on a beer. He slapped down a twenty-dollar bill for the carton of cigarettes the clerk handed him. He walked across the street to the bar with a blinking neon sign that lit only half of the name of Bob's Bar and Grill. No matter. The bar had changed hands twice since the man whose name was on the sign had owned the bar.

He scooted his thin hips onto a wooden stool and signaled the woman behind the bar. He had become a regular. She knew what to put in front of him. He watched her fill the tall glass at an angle to minimize the foam. Her watery blue eyes were deeply shadowed in a narrow face with sunken cheeks prematurely grooved by deep lines. *That's what too much drinking will do to you*, he thought, as she set the beer in front of him and sullenly took his money.

They never spoke. Nothing left to say. He sipped the cool brew and wondered absently what the magazine would say about this woman with the pinched, sunken cheeks of an alcoholic working in a dimly lit bar and living in a ramshackle trailer. Would her boy be grinning then when the magazine found out about his mother? His lips curled in a malicious smile. How much would the boy be ready to pay to keep the magazine from finding out?

A plan formed in his head as he slowly sipped the beer. When he finished he pushed the empty glass aside and left the bar without glancing at the woman who might just become the centerpiece of a plan to prime the pump to fill up his chronically depleted checking account.

~

"Is he really the next Garth Brooks like they say in this magazine?"

Della Sue Simpson waved a copy of *Country Scene* at Sarah Ann with Jared on the cover, his handsome face creased by a sanguine smile. "Even on slick paper, his blue eyes look absolutely electric with sex appeal. If he's what they say he is in this article, I want an introduction." Della Sue hesitated for the effect of her words to sink in. "Then afterward, an autograph."

The Prayer Group members hooted with laughter. They were sitting in Sarah Ann's high-ceilinged parlor sipping port after a sumptuous dinner of Caesar salad, chateaubriand, steamed vegetables, and a delicate chocolate mousse prepared by Sarah Ann's new housekeeper, an ebony-skinned immigrant from Trinidad and Tobago named Monet. She spoke little English, cursed colorfully in at least three languages that Sarah Ann could discern, used words Sarah Ann was certain she did not want to know the meaning of, and lavished her abundant affection on the two cats. Both felines now totally ignored their mistress. It was a propitious situation Sarah Ann welcomed in terms of both cuisine and cats.

"Della Sue. Do you ever have anything but sex on your mind?" Willie Dell asked blandly.

Della Sue glanced across the round, gilded coffee table at her smiling nemesis waiting smugly for her answer. "Unlike you, Willie Dell, who is never horny, and appears shackled to the lifestyle of a castrated monk, I have a more seasoned approach to life. Be horny. Grab life by the horns, or whatever," she hesitated a moment to let his imagination upload her meaning before adding, "*Whenever* and *wherever* you can." Della Sue tipped her port glass toward Willie Dell.

"Touché," he responded.

Try as she may, Della Sue seemed never able to get under Willie

Dell's skin. Despite his frequent pointed barbs at her expense, theirs was a congenial give-and-take. She felt almost the same closeness to him that was shared between him and Sarah Ann. Besides her husband (most of the time, anyway), Willie Dell seemed the only man on whom Della Sue had no sexual designs.

Monet appeared (named after the French impressionist, she had told Sarah Ann during their interview, explaining her name with evident pride) to clear away dessert plates and refill port glasses. As the housekeeper approached, Angela raised her large gray eyes to Monet and raised her crystal port glass to be replenished. "That was an extraordinary meal, Monet. Just a tad more, if you please."

"Tank ya, Mes," Monet replied in her heavily accented English, frowning at the request. Port glasses were never to be more than half filled. That maintained the flavor of the Portuguese wine at its sweet peak. She grudgingly added an extra portion to Angela's glass, and then glanced quickly at Sarah Ann. Monet had been cautioned to avoid giving liquor to Angela unless it was requested. Angela's drinking was an ongoing concern for her fellow Prayer Group members. Sarah Ann's eyes held no admonishment.

"Careful there, Monet. That's clearly favoritism. If I can't smoke with the outside door open, Angela can't have more port than the rest of us." Jeanne Marie meant her words as a gentle reminder. Monet only glared silently as she bent over Jeanne Marie's empty glass, adding only the normal half portion before turning for the kitchen without another word.

"My, my! She's a bit touchy," observed Jeanne Marie tartly, after Monet disappeared into the kitchen.

Sarah Ann smiled across the table at her friend, trying to hide her own irritation and said mildly. "She's an excellent cook and an even better housekeeper. She's just a little sensitive to a perceived criticism."

"Well, I certainly didn't mean to offend her," Jeanne Marie huffed.

"Time for prayer requests," suggested Willie Dell, jumping in to neutralize Jeanne Marie's natural bitchiness.

For the next half-hour the prayer requests were offered and discussed. Sips of the elegant port added warmth to the words that flowed between the friends. The monthly meeting of the Prayer

Group was an evening set aside from any intrusion, save death or natural disaster. It had been that way from the beginning.

Following graduation from high school, the choice of a college was done by secret ballot. Della Sue's vote was cast for the University of Tennessee. A party school she scribbled on the note in describing her nomination. Angela's choice was Fordham University. It was as far from her mother as she could get and still attend a Catholic school. But a majority of three votes were cast for Vanderbilt University: sedate, secular, and close. Despite its geographic closeness, Angela finally relented and enrolled.

Vanderbilt dormitories were segregated by gender. Male visitors were restricted to the common rooms on the first floor of the women's dorm. Sneaking Willie Dell into one of the girl's rooms for the monthly meeting was a continuing challenge. Then slipping him out past the permanently scowling dorm mother was an even greater challenge. The friends questioned if she ever slept at night. Probably not, surmised Della Sue, who was most frequently tasked with secreting Willie Dell out the rear door of the dorm.

It was the day before the end of the winter semester of their junior year when disaster struck in the form of the dorm mother's voice ringing out in the dark hallway. "And just where do you think you are going, Miss Inman? And with whom?" The last three words sounded close to a snarl.

There was little that intimidated Della Sue Inman, but the sound of that stern voice had her quaking. Knowing she faced a severe reprimand, even expulsion, Della Sue quickly called in the cavalry. They charged at the determined dorm mother, stabbing at her unflinching demeanor with some of the most inventive excuses the dorm matriarch had ever heard for violating the strict prohibition of allowing a man into a woman's dorm room. She listened, at times even amused, without allowing her amusement to show.

In her many years as dorm mother of Latching Hall, Isabel Stuben could not recall such gifted liars. But she remained buttressed by her principles. The rules were the rules and it was her responsibility to enforce them. The five friends returned to their respective dorm rooms doomed.

It was Willie Dell's long-absent father who became their white knight. He was a Vanderbilt graduate. By virtue of the wealth he had accumulated and his propensity for sharing some of that wealth with his alma mater, he held a seat on the Vanderbilt Board of Regents. In his case, money talked. Miss Stuben remained dorm mother. The discipline ruling handed to his son and his son's four female friends did not.

The five friends made it through to graduation day together, Sarah Ann and Willie Dell clasping business degrees, Angela and Della Sue liberal arts degrees, and Jeanne Marie clutching a degree in journalism, with a minor in art history which she would turn into a successful gallery business for a time.

Two of the friends, Sarah Ann and Angela, sported engagement rings to balance the large gold class rings they wore on right hands. Surrounded by parents and siblings, graduation day for the Prayer Group had been a day of self-congratulatory elation. They had made it. Together.

And together they remained this night, in the soft light of the large parlor, sipping the last of the elegant port, reading their prayer requests, offering advice where needed, encouragement where it could help, and silently thanking the Lord for the friendship embraced so long ago.

Perhaps it was the meandering warmth of the final sip of port or just the convivial rapport between her four friends that sent a wave of contentment washing over Sarah Ann for the first time in weeks. This evening with her friends temporarily dissolved the doubts and disquiet that had crowded her mind since the showcase. Content to listen to the back and forth banter she let her mind drift back to the office.

Two weeks after the release of Jared's album, the title song raced to the top of the country music charts. The album itself was not far behind. It was a dizzying success neither she nor Jill had prepared for: calls for interviews; demands for appearances by Jared; and a schedule of concerts Len Shiring tossed at them that would keep one or the other of them or both on the road for the next six months. There was even a concert proposal from a European promoter. That presented the two partners with more than one set of problems. Signing contracts with a foreign entity was something Edgerton Group had never had to do. Sarah Ann and Jill agreed they needed an attorney with international law experience in case they decided to launch Jared across the pond.

"Know anyone like that?" Jill had asked.

"I know one. John Bennett Boswell." Sarah Ann had watched with wry humor as Jill reacted to her answer.

"Your ex-husband!" Jill exclaimed, looking totally flabbergasted.

"He's got a Yale degree to back up those credentials."

So, Jill had called John and to Sarah Ann's surprise, he had agreed to draw up all contracts, foreign and domestic, for Edgerton Group. After dealing with the efficiency John Bennett Boswell brought to the legal side of their business, both women agreed the Boswell firm should be retained for all agency business. Sarah Ann wasn't sure it was what you might call coming full circle, but it was a hell of a U-turn.

Then there was their office to run. It was exploding with new clients, several of them highly talented, especially one, Stella Wayne, a blue-eyed beauty from Oklahoma with a voice that ranged from angelic to seductive. Shiring was almost salivating after meeting her and predicted a lucrative future in which he would play a big part.

An agency's success spread fast around the relatively small geographic area called Music Row. Among those flocking to join Edgerton Group were several established artists, using out-clauses to bolt from long associations to try their luck with the new managers. With some canny negotiating skills and a little luck, Edgerton Group could have a corral full of top talent like Jared Parson and a front lobby lined with framed gold and platinum records.

During their meeting yesterday at a Green Hills restaurant, Jill settled one nagging issue by announcing she would accompany Jared on the road. He would need a manager at his side and she knew the road. Sarah Ann could stay in Nashville and put her business degree to good use, running the day-to-day operations, negotiating contracts and overseeing the hiring of new publicists and road managers for the contracted artists. It was her strength, Jill noted.

Sarah Ann was better at the business end. Plus, she could deal with their new law firm. Jill had not warmed to John Bennett Boswell's polite, but aloof Southern demeanor.

And after all, Sarah Ann had never been on the road. While she skillfully spooned a delicate angel hair pasta topped with the restaurant's signature meatball sauce, Jill described the rigors of riding in a tour bus from one concert location to another, packing and unpacking in hotel rooms or worse, bunking on a bus rolling down a highway all night. "And try to find time to wash your underwear."

Jill laughed, wiping away a squeeze of sauce from the sides of her mouth. "Not a life for a Southern belle. And you won't have to miss your Prayer Group." There was just a trace of sarcasm in those last words.

Sarah Ann had agreed, seeing little downside to the arrangement. There was no question Jill had the experience to handle Jared on the road. Office details, contracts, publicity agreements and the like bored her. Those were the reasons she brought Sarah Ann into Edgerton Group in the first place and quickly made her a full partner. Sarah Ann could not argue with Jill's logic, but doubt about the arrangement still troubled her. Why? Did she fear handling the office by herself? Not really. Jill would only be a cell phone call away if there were questions. Still, the nagging doubt.

Go with the flow Jill was always saying. *Get swept up in it. Let it take you where it will. That's the excitement of this business,* she reminded Sarah Ann often.

"Don't be such a worry wort," Jill had laughingly admonished as she slipped her American Express card into the discreet leather folder left by the waiter. "But, then that's why you're here, isn't it? To worry, so I don't have to," Jill had concluded.

"Hey, girl. Where are you?" Willie Dell's voice intruded softly into Sarah Ann's reverie.

"I'm still here, little brother. Just letting business encroach for a moment." She banished the worry lines by touching her fingers to his forehead and ruddy cheeks. "I think enough prayer requesting for the night. Let's open a bottle of merlot and business-be-damned."

"That's the spirit, girl. We'll deal with the hangovers tomorrow." Then he glanced over at Angela and wished Sarah Ann had suggested iced tea.

Chapter 10

Arliss Hemming shed his western style tux jacket, loosened his trademark bolo tie with its distinctive Mojave turquoise clasp and leaned back in a leather chair, glad to escape to the sanctuary of his studio. The annual Country Music Association Awards parties would go on all night. They could celebrate without him. Those kinds of gatherings were never his cup of tea.

His wife would make the rounds from one bash to another. She could celebrate for him. They'd had words in the limo on their way to the event. Harsh words. Cutting words. Even without the prompting of alcohol, Winnifred could throw daggers from her mouth. What he hated even more than the words; they still hurt, even after all these years. When they first met, and in the early years of their marriage, he had called her Winnie. At some point during those early years the affection instilled in saying Winnie had disappeared. So had the name. He had been calling her Winnifred for so long, he could no longer remember when it had become *Winnifred* and not *Winnie*.

Hemming put his custom-made cowboy boots up on the flat edge of the console and crossed his ankles. He looked around at the darkened interior of the studio, dimly lit by the red and blue lights of the equipment that lined the wall behind the console. They were like tiny unblinking beacons from a hundred different lighthouses. During any storm in his life this was where he came. His sanctuary.

He clasped his arms behind his head, a comfortable position he always assumed to let his thinking focus and his perspective evolve. The walls of the studio were dotted with a small galaxy of the gold and platinum records he had produced. On the console, more than a dozen CMA and Grammy statuettes stood at silent attention around his boots. At the end of the console, standing in regal separation from the others, the award he had casually deposited there after flipping on the dimmed overhead lights of his office—the Country Music Association's Lifetime Achievement Award. It was the ultimate homage by his peers. He had seldom left an awards ceremony in the last twenty years without a piece of metal or glass in his hands. Tonight was the culmination of all the nights and long days he sat at the console in a studio, electronically weaving together each song into a musical Michelangelo. Many ended up on the wall behind his desk, a framed gold or platinum disc.

He should be out celebrating with Winnifred. He preferred being here.

It had been a heady evening for someone else who *was* out celebrating. Jared Parson won four awards: Male vocalist of the Year; Single of the Year; Album of the Year; and Entertainer of the Year. *A big load of tributes for someone who had been on the country music scene for only a couple of years*, Hemming mused.

Jared's debut album had hit the country music world like a bolt of lightning. Doors opened and success streaked right in. He had taken home his first CMA award, Best New Artist of the Year, last year. Jared's second album had been greeted with even more thunderous acclaim. It affirmed him as a top country music artist and reaffirmed Hemming as the town's top producer. So why wasn't he out celebrating? It was a reason he had no logic for—quickly sweeping away the answer from his thoughts.

~

By midnight sleek black stretch limos formed a long line on both sides of Sixteenth Street, outside the NCA Records Building. From the wide glass windows on the second floor poured enough light to make pretend daylight below where the bored limo drivers stood around in small groups, pulling on cigarettes and deciding which of their clients for the night had had the most to drink, who was getting a quick screw before being dropped off, or who had overheard the juiciest gossip from the rear seats.

Sarah Ann had never attended the CMA Awards before. Jill got an annual invitation, but Sarah Ann had politely declined to accompany her last year, not wanting to intrude on her time in the limelight. Tonight had been different. Edgerton Group had Jared sweeping the big awards and another performer taking home a lesser prize. She looked across at their big dog. Jared stood in the middle of the room surrounded by well-wishers. The smile that lighted his handsome features the first time his name was called remained there, like a grin on auto pilot. Beside Jared stood LouAnn, looking happy but fatigued. That was to be expected for someone expecting a baby and dealing with morning sickness.

Each time Jared had galloped up on stage to accept an award he had clutched it to his chest, ducked his head for a moment, then looked out at the audience beaming before launching into his "thank yous." Sarah Ann and Jill were mentioned each time. So were Hemming and Shiring and NCA Records. And LouAnn. With eyes that appeared to radiate love, Jared had pointed the award at his wife. "This is for you, baby." And he silently mouthed the words, *I love you.*

Sarah Ann had applauded loudly, as much for Jared's tribute to his wife as the award he was accepting. It helped dispel, at least for tonight, her unspoken concerns about the nature of their relationship.

Sarah Ann looked across the room in another direction. Her eyes could not miss him. At six-foot-two, he was easy to spot in a classic black tuxedo with white shirt and bow tie. Elegant was the word that came to mind. But then John always was, even when she had been standing beside him.

Now it was Angeline on his arm, with her plump breasts on display in the low cut black sequined sheath gown which accented her slim waist as it flowed over and around her other curves to the floor. Sarah Ann cattily wondered how much those curves and flat tummy were owed to a skilled plastic surgeon and not nature. *Oh well,* she sighed, *nature was having its way with her and she would be damned if she would go under the knife to alter its course.*

"Caught you looking!" Jill gently squeezed Sarah Ann's arm.

"Guilty," Sarah Ann smiled over at her partner. "I'm not sure I looked that good when I was eighteen."

"It has always amazed me why men feel they have to trade in the old model—no pun intended, Sarah Ann—for a new model. It's so middle-aged." Jill looked back in John Bennett Boswell's direction. "But I have to admit, I would trade my old model—if I had one—for one like him."

"Traitor."

"Truth." Jill looked thoughtful for a moment. "You know what the difference is between you and the bimbo. She will always be known as John's trophy wife. You will be remembered as his wife and the mother of his children. That's a bit bigger status in my eyes." Jill turned and wrapped Sarah Ann in a hug. "If it weren't for you, girl, we wouldn't be here tonight. I'm glad you came." Jill stood back and looked at her partner. "I don't know where I would be right now if I hadn't had the good fortune to lose my gallbladder and end up with you for a hospital roommate. I mean that," she added, as tears formed in her eyes.

Sarah Ann was stunned and moved at the same time. Jill seldom showed any emotion. Certainly not like this. She was seeing a rare glimpse of the woman with whom she had worked with these past three years but had never felt really close to; not 'best friend' close at least. Theirs was a convivial business relationship, like two friends working together. Yet it was a relationship both left behind when the workday ended. Jill lived in Nashville above the office—Sarah Ann in Franklin. The closeness they shared in the office and an occasional lunch or after-hours dinner never followed either one home.

A kaleidoscope of emotions played out on Sarah Ann's face before she spoke. "You founded Edgerton Group. It is you who built it from the ground up. It is you who is the reason for its success." Sarah Ann smiled as she took her thumb and gently wiped away a tear hanging on the edge of Jill's eye. "You rescued me with a heaping dose of common sense and then brought me along for this wonderful ride."

The two women embraced again. "Now, go and enjoy a party that, for a change, Edgerton Group isn't paying for," insisted Sarah Ann.

Jill used her knuckle to stem another tear and insure her mascara did not stray onto her cheek. "Love you, girl. See ya later." She sauntered away flicking a wave over her shoulder as she joined the fringe of a crowd ganged around one of the other CMA winners.

Sarah Ann just stood staring at Jill's back, still somewhat baffled, but deeply moved by the affection Jill had just shown her. When a waiter came by a moment later Sarah Ann lifted another plastic flute of champagne from the tray. She tipped the flute in Jill's direction. *Here's to you, partner. May we enjoy many more such nights as this,* she toasted silently. This was her second glass of champagne and she knew she would need food soon to counter the effects of the bubbly. *No Dom Perignon should be disparaged as bubbly* she admonished herself. Len Shiring was sparing no expense. That was reason enough to have a second glass and eat a plate full of finger food.

Her experience with Shiring was that he had a patent on the word frugal. She looked around for the record company executive and found him talking with the managers of two of his label's other top talents.

Sarah Ann heard a woman's ripple of laughter from another group standing near one of the round tables circled with a selection of hors d'oeuvre that would please the most finicky chef, French or otherwise. The woman had her back to Sarah Ann, but she knew from the sleek cut of the pageboy salt-and-pepper hair it was Winnifred Hemming. Tall, almost regal in appearance, in a black dress reminiscent of one of the classic Givenchy's worn by Audrey Hepburn, Winnifred Hemming looked as if she would be at home in the most exclusive country club setting, Sarah Ann thought.

Her eyes drifted around the large reception room as she sipped champagne. Winnifred's husband was nowhere to be seen. She suspected Hemming had dropped his wife off and headed home; maybe even back to his studio. She had come to think of the studio as his lair, a place from which he seemed only to emerge for an occasional trip home to ride one of his prized Quarter horses over the lush meadows and hilly woods of his rural estate south of Nashville.

"Sarah Ann."

Startled, Sarah Ann tipped the flute, spilling a few drops on the carpet below. A crimson flush of embarrassment spread over her face as she looked around at John. He was alone. A smile eased across a mouth that Sarah Ann always believed had been painted on his face by a Renaissance artist because it was so perfectly formed, the lips full and surprisingly soft when they were once pressed against hers.

"I'm sorry. I didn't mean to startle you," John said, looking bemused.

"No problem." She flashed a sheepish grin. "I was just telling myself that a second glass of champagne was dangerous. And I was right."

"Wrong. Entirely my fault. And never argue with an attorney when they're admitting fault."

"Yes, sir." She touched a cocktail napkin to each side of her mouth and wiped the sides of the plastic flute.

"Here, let me take that." He placed the flute on a nearby end table. "I just wanted to say good night, and congratulations on all that happened tonight. You and Jill are quite a success. I think this night proves that." His penetrating blue eyes were mesmerizing. Sarah Ann's voice appeared to be temporarily out of order.

"There you are." The new voice held the same quality as the beautiful face—young and sultry. Angeline linked her hand possessively into John's. He patted her hand in response. "I was just telling Sarah Ann thanks. Great party."

"It is, Sarah Ann. Thank you. We've really enjoyed ourselves," Angeline gushed, parting her lips in a warm smile.

Rediscovering her voice Sarah Ann said smoothly, "I'm so glad you both could come."

John looked around the crowd for a moment and then back at Sarah Ann. "I didn't find Jill. But please pass on my congratulations to her, as well. Good night."

"Good night." Sarah Ann stood in the same spot, not moving, for many moments until she felt a traitorous tear fill one eye. Why, after all this time, did John Bennett Boswell have the same effect on her? Would it never pass? A melancholy descended over her, so deep, it evoked a fear she had not felt since the suicide attempt. *Please, God, give me distance from what was and just let me enjoy what is* she pleaded in silence.

"Terrific party, if I do say so myself. You need to join in." Len Shiring's face was flushed and she knew the reason; the bourbon she smelled on his breath as he clasped her in a tight embrace. Her breasts were crushed against his chest. Sarah Ann smugly wondered what kind of a sexual charge Shiring got from hugging every woman he could in that same manner. Most of the time she was quick enough to avoid such encounters. But not tonight.

"It's a great party, Len," she said as she deftly disengaged herself from his arms. "We have much to celebrate and much of the thanks must go to you."

"Nah! I just print CDs. You and Jill do the heavy lifting," he countered graciously, as he took her hand and headed toward a group of people standing in the center of the room. "There are some people I want you to meet," he said, his words slightly slurred.

Sarah Ann felt herself being encircled by well-wishers; some she already knew, some she was meeting for the first time. The mayor of Nashville gallantly told her she was as beautiful as she was successful. She forced a smile and nodded her thanks.

There was a top executive from a Nashville-based banking conglomerate. "Now that you're so successful Ms. Boswell, we need to lure some of your wealth into our portfolio." She maintained the same smile and nodded to the possibility.

A legendary local television host invited her to be on his program soon and suggested she could bring along a certain singer with the last name Parson. She thanked him for the invitation and offered, "We'll see if that can be arranged." She moved away quickly before being cornered into a firm commitment.

Sarah Ann circled from one group to another. An hour passed before she felt exhaustion descending and excused herself from a small ensemble of fellow talent managers to go to the restroom. It was actually the front entrance that was her intended destination and an escape to deal with the melancholy which had replaced the high spirits with which she had arrived at the party. But first she had to find Jill and say good night. Sarah Ann spotted LouAnn sitting by herself in one of the high-backed chairs ringing the reception area. "Hi, LouAnn. Are you enjoying yourself?"

"I've had a great time, Mrs. Boswell, mm…Sarah Ann. I'm just waiting here for Jared." LouAnn still seemed uncomfortable calling Sarah Ann by her first name.

"And I'm looking for Jill. Have you seen her?"

"Yes, ma'am. She and Jared took off a while back. Said they had something to discuss about a press conference tomorrow. They went down that way," she said, pointing to a wide hallway across from where she sat.

"Thanks. And get some rest, LouAnn. This has been a great night, but you look bushed."

"Yes, ma'am. I am a little. I guess it's the pregnancy and all."

"I'm sure. See you later." Sarah Ann thought how lovely LouAnn looked. She had worn a well-tailored royal blue dress with a boat neck that minimized her slightly protruding stomach and swelling breasts and flattered her blond hair and blue eyes.

Sarah Ann headed across the room, smiling and waving to several who called out salutations as she passed. There was no light reflecting under the doors on either side of the hallway. She knew that at the end of the hallway was Shiring's office. That was probably where Jill was, maybe taking a breather from the thick press of people in the reception area. Sarah Ann opened the door to the office slowly and whispered, "Jill…you in there?"

There was no response, but she heard a rustling noise. With her hand still on the knob, she peered in. Jill was there. She was lying on a deep leather couch against the wall of Len's office with her satin gown pulled up over her hips. Jared Parson was on top of her grunting softly.

Chapter 11

Sarah Ann gripped the steering wheel of her car for several minutes until tears finally came, flushing away the initial anger and embarrassment that swelled from her chest to her throat as she silently closed the door of Len's office. She had hurried past the throng in the reception area, smiling and waving robotically as she made her escape.

It was the sight of LouAnn, sitting in a chair by the front window, looking alone and abandoned, her hands folded in front of her belly, as if trying to hide her pregnancy, which now imprinted itself in her mind. *Did LouAnn know? Did she even suspect why her husband had left her to sit alone, waiting for him to emerge from his 'meeting'? Please God, spare her that*, Sarah Ann pleaded silently as she started the ignition and backed slowly out of the parking space and headed out of the parking lot of NCA Records.

She made no effort to stem the tears as she sped toward the interstate. The initial shock of what she had seen, or mostly heard, was giving way to a sense of betrayal so overwhelming she felt a bolt of queasiness. She braked hard, pulling off to the side of the highway and barely made it around to the other side of the car before her stomach heaved its contents onto the asphalt. Sarah Ann stood gagging helplessly, leaning her arm against the car for support. She watched headlights flash by for some time before finding the strength to get back in the car.

As she pulled back onto the interstate, Sarah Ann let anger overtake tears. How could Jill be so oblivious to the harm she was doing to LouAnn—to Sarah Ann—and worse, to herself? Jill had spent all those years building a business that could be jeopardized by one reckless act. Or was it just one act? How long had this been going on? Jill had been on the road with Jared and his band for weeks at a time, coordinating the events and overseeing the collection of revenues from those events. LouAnn had always remained behind, furnishing the home she and Jared moved into shortly after his second album went platinum. The twelve-room antebellum style brick home, with a sweeping front porch and balcony above, sat in the center of a hundred rolling acres in Leiper's Fork. A picturesque property was how Willie Dell described it after Sarah Ann spotted it among his listings. It was Sarah Ann who had suggested the rural estate to Jared.

Utilizing his long-honed skills as a negotiator, Willie Dell had succeeded in coaxing the sellers down to a favorable price that Jared finally approved. Financial success and the new domestic stability appeared to draw the couple closer in Sarah Ann's eyes. And now they would be welcoming another child into their new home.

Magazines clamored for stories on the young singer-songwriter who had taken the country music business by storm. Picture layouts had shown LouAnn picking out fabric for new drapes and supervising the placement of furniture. Outside, the couple's young daughter, Willow, was photographed happily hugging a teddy bear or grinning atop her father's shoulders as Jared raced around the front lawn neighing like one of the three horses housed in the towering barn behind the house.

One magazine had featured a tearful farewell as Jared boarded his tour bus, affectionately hugging his wife and daughter to him. He and LouAnn reflected a happy domesticity to the readers of the nationally circulated magazines.

If they only knew Sarah Ann reflected bitterly as she turned off the interstate at one of the Franklin exits. Sleep was out of the question. Even with a long, cleansing shower, the foulness of what she had so briefly seen and heard lingered. An overpowering sadness descended back over her, prompting another round of tears.

~

During the hectic three years of their partnership Sarah Ann could not recall any major disagreements. Over lunch, or the occasional after work dinner, they shared plans for the future growth of Edgerton Group. Both felt enough an ease in each other's company to allow an occasional peak into the window of their personal lives. Jill had revealed she left her home in Boston following the death of both of her parents. She had no siblings. The only family member she ever mentioned was her father's aunt. Using the money she inherited from her parents' estate she had followed her own dream to Nashville. There had been a number of boyfriends. Some had been lovers for a time. But permanency with a man was never part of Jill's plan. And through all their sharing conversations, Jill had revealed no clue to what Sarah Ann had discovered in Len's office.

Sarah Ann glanced at the clock. Five-thirty. Willie Dell was probably still asleep, but she dialed his number anyway. The sleepy voice that answered said to give him ten minutes to shower and shave. By the time Willie Dell was seated at the large kitchen island, Sarah Ann had coffee waiting and a platter of bacon and eggs ready to place before him, with the smell from the oven promising homemade biscuits.

Over the rim of his coffee cup Willie Dell could see the fatigue ringing his friend's eyes and the lingering redness of recent tears. He placed the cup back on the saucer, picked up his knife and fork and looked across at Sarah Ann. "Spill it out, baby sister. Whatever it is, it's burning a hole in your heart."

Willie Dell listened, never interrupting, watching the play of emotions flicker across Sarah Ann's face like a silent movie—hurt, anger, sadness, at times outrage at the potential scandal—not to mention how public knowledge of the affair could wreak havoc on their business.

When Sarah Ann's words seemed spent, Willie Dell lifted the tepid remains of his coffee slowly to his lips and studied his friend closely. Sarah Ann was not just hurt and angry, she seemed almost bitter. *So unlike her,* he thought.

In all their past conversations about her business partner, Sarah Ann had never revealed the depth of her admiration for Jill. Willie

Dell assumed their relationship was business only. He felt a small stab of jealousy that someone outside the Prayer Group could lay claim to Sarah Ann's affection. She belonged to them—to him—and had since their friendship was sealed in childhood. Who was this person who had covertly intruded into the tight ring of Prayer Group closeness and seduced Sarah Ann's friendship and affection? *Well, no more*, he reasoned somewhat superciliously.

Willie Dell reached his hand across the wide granite island to grasp Sarah Ann's hand and squeezed it gently. "You know what you have to do, baby sister. You have to confront Jill with a dose of harsh reality. She has to be told how her reckless behavior is putting her client…this lover boy…and her business in great jeopardy." He gripped Sarah Ann's hand more firmly. "It's your business too, Sarah Ann. I've watched you pour your heart and soul into it these past months…years now. Jill has no right to risk all that you've helped turn into a huge success." Then added with a vehemence tinged with indignation, "You don't deserve another Bobby Ray Kendal experience," recalling the man whom he still blamed for nearly ending Sarah Ann's life.

She leaned over Willie Dell's hand and kissed it. He felt tears dampen the hand that held tightly to hers. "I love you, Willie Dell. You'll never know how much, dear friend," she whispered and felt his other hand smoothing her hair.

They remained silent for long moments before Sarah Ann finally raised her head and looked directly at her friend with reddened eyes. "You're right, of course, Willie Dell. I'll have a talk with Jill at the first opportunity." She turned toward the large window over the sink and blinked at the morning glow filtering through the soft yellow silk Roman shade. With the new day came a new wave of dread constrict her heart at what she must do. Jill was her partner; her friend. And LouAnn's betrayer.

Willie Dell put the last bite of a biscuit laden with golden honey in his mouth. Sarah Ann could put together a great meal anytime, and no time better than at breakfast. He dabbed a dribble of honey from the side of his mouth with a paper napkin and sat back in the cushioned stool feeling full and content. Cooking was one of the many things Sarah Ann did well. Better than his mother and that was a Mount Denali high compliment. His expanding waistline was testament to his mother's prowess is the kitchen. The face of a blue-eyed, blond-from-a-bottle, flashed in his mind. Beverly! She couldn't boil an egg, let alone make biscuits from scratch. He shook his head to rid it of the woman who nearly wrecked his life. "Great breakfast, baby sister. Thanks! Even if I did have to haul my ass out of bed before the birds started chirping to enjoy it."

Willie Dell stood up and walked over to raise the shade further and allow the fullness of the rising sun to radiate into the kitchen. "They should all be up by now. If not, we'll make as sweet a bugle sound as any they've ever heard." He turned to Sarah Ann. "Whip up some more biscuits, darlin'. It's time to call in the cavalry."

Chapter 12

Bugles were sounding only in Della Sue Simpson's head as she pushed open the front door without knocking and slipped inside. Shedding her coat and hanging it in the hall closet required movement. Any movement sent the several gin and tonics she had imbibed last night back to war with the several slugs of wine she had swilled straight from the bottle. The two Motrin were so far failing to sound retreat for the worst hangover she had suffered in many a moon.

"Bastard," she muttered under her breath, invoking the nearest thing to a term of endearment for Beaufort Oliver Simpson. It had taken five gin and tonics to fuel the courage to suggest sex, which her husband had declined with a yawn and a saccharin rebuke that began with "Sugar, don't you think we should do it when your head is clearer."

No! her mind screamed as his back disappeared into the upstairs bedroom he had turned into his sanctuary. He had moved out of their bedroom one weekend while she was away four years ago. No, he did not want a divorce. He just wanted to be left alone. "What if I want a divorce?" she had screeched at him. "No," he had replied sharply. There had never been a divorce in his wealthy, deep-rooted Southern family. And he would not be the first to break that tradition.

Sleeping in separate bedrooms should be the woman's choice if Southern tradition were to be upheld. For weeks anger simmered on her surface. Beau ignored it, as he did most things concerning her. Just as she, in turn, learned to ignore him. She lived in one of the largest gated estates in Franklin, had a credit card with reasonable limits and a lot of time on her hands to wonder where the romance that filled and eroticized their early years together had gone.

If clear headedness was the touchstone for spousal sex, then she was doomed to continue living like a nun. *Shit!* She would worry about her need for the bottle later, a need she hid far better than Angela. And there were bigger problems to solve from what Willie Dell hinted when he called an hour ago.

One look at Della Sue sent Willie Dell like a rifle shot to the coffee maker. She was the last to arrive and looked around apologetically. Moments later she was wrapping her slightly shaking hands around a steaming cup and flashing Willie Dell a grateful smile. "Mornin' all," she said between sips after sitting down at the island. "When I make an appraisal of God's greatest achievements, coffee has to be right up there with sex and Clairol heavenly blond."

Laughter erupted.

"I would challenge your choice of color," argued Angela. "Heavenly blond pales in comparison to Gypsy Black."

"But not to sex," retorted Della Sue.

"I'll cede you that one."

Willie Dell filled his coffee cup and then took the carafe around the bar and topped off other cups. "Jeanne Marie, give us a blessing and let's eat our fill of Sarah Ann's wonderful morning cholesterol feast that she's been preparing the past hour. Then we'll get down to business."

Plates were heaped with eggs, bacon, sausage, a cheesy hash brown casserole, several varieties of fresh fruit marinated in a mix of sour crème, confectioner sugar and lemon juice and topped off with a platter of fresh baked biscuits. Silence descended on the Prayer Group as they ate.

Biscuits and thick gravy was a Southern tradition that deserved the reverence of only chewing sounds being emitted by those partaking. When it was Sarah Ann's biscuits and gravy, even more reason to prioritize eating.

By the time she was wiping the corners of her mouth following the final bite of hash browns dipped in gravy, Della Sue decided that what Motrin had failed to accomplish, coffee and breakfast had. Her headache was subsiding and with it her hangover.

"Can I get anyone anything else?" Eyes rolled and heads nodded side-to-side, declining Sarah Ann's offer. The four women cleared away the dishes while Willie Dell measured coffee for a fresh pot.

"All right—what is going on, Sarah Ann Boswell?" Angela could no longer restrain her curiosity. "By-the-way, you look like someone in the first part of a Unisom commercial," she added.

Sarah Ann started to reply, but Willie Dell waved her to silence. "Let me lay out what's happened."

When he finished Angela was the first to comment. "Prick!"

"That part of his anatomy needs to be surgically removed," Della Sue suggested with a glint in her eyes. "Where is Lorena Bobbitt when we need her?"

Jeanne Marie was next to Della Sue and playfully jabbed her in the ribs. "She's sitting by her phone waiting for your call since Beau, *unlike Jared*, seems unable to put his to good use."

"What's her number?" Della Sue asked, her rapidly blinking eyes feigning innocence.

Angela's hands flew upward. "Beau's penis on a platter! Now that's a trophy for over your mantle."

Jeanne Marie shook her head in patronizing disgust. "That may be some gross solution for your problem, Della Sue, but it isn't helping Sarah Ann."

"True," agreed Sarah Ann, "but I want the ticket concession for viewing that artwork." A wide smile momentarily erased her weariness and frown lines. Even Della Sue joined in the laughter.

"Ever the entrepreneur, baby sister." The smile faded from Willie Dell's face. "So, how is your business affected if Jill's little indiscretion gets out?"

Sarah Ann looked thoughtful for several moments before responding, "I don't know, really. Randy Travis had an affair with his manager and they ended up husband and wife. But he didn't leave a first wife pregnant with their second child. A big difference." She looked around at the four faces.

"For one, I suspect, it will not sit well with fans. And they buy his music and fill his concerts," she added. "We've built his image around being the all-American boy who brought his high moral values to Nashville along with his wife, baby and guitar."

"So did Garth Brooks," injected Angela. "And the public fell for it. His career skyrocketed even with all those rumors circulated about an affair with Trisha Yearwood."

"If it *was* going on, nobody knew at the time," Sarah Ann observed.

"Let's face it, men are ruled by their penis, with one exception that shall remain anonymous." Della Sue's mocking eyes trained squarely on Willie Dell.

"I believe the Lorena Bobbitt approach might be justified in the Jared situation. Don't you?" asked Jeanne Marie, also looking at Willie Dell.

"Maybe on Beau," Willie Dell answered cautiously, as his smile faded to a frown. He thought he had heard just about everything over the years from his fellow Prayer Group members. But castration! This was a topper. If other men had as much purview to the machinations of the female mind as he did, they would never marry, always drive in a bullet proof car and hire round-the-clock body guards. Maybe then men would be ruled by common sense and not the most important part of their middle anatomy.

Jeanne Marie felt the familiar pull in her chest for a cigarette. The nicotine patch she was wearing for the umpteenth time was not doing its job as promised in all those commercials. Now was not the time, nicotine fit or not, she told herself and then took a nanosecond to silently compliment her own self-restraint. *Only for Sarah Ann.* "Darlin'," she said, reaching over to grasp Sarah Ann's hands, "I think you need to confront Jill quickly. It will be tough, I know. Lay out the consequences of her fling for both you and her, not to mention that little prick and his pregnant unsuspecting wife."

Willie Dell nodded agreement. "Jill's little peccadillo is putting your future in jeopardy, as well as hers and Jared's. He's making both of you millionaires. Another year with him at the top of the charts and you can retire. Then Jill and Jared can screw to their heart's content. On the other hand, you could be the biggest loser if this affair continues." He reached over and gently lifted Sarah Ann's chin. "Think of it this way, baby sister. Everything you've worked so hard for these past three years could get flushed down the crapper like one of Jeanne Marie's secreted cigarettes."

Sarah Ann's lips trembled at the same time tears shone in her eyes. "She's my friend, Willie Dell. I can't just confront her." Weariness and worry dragged at her and she dropped her head. In a voice so soft that Willie Dell and the others had to strain to hear, she said, "Maybe Jill didn't hear me open the door to Len's office. She may not know I saw what was going on." Her eyes now swimming with tears, Sarah Ann looked around at her friends. "I don't want to hurt Jill." She looked pleadingly at the four faces watching her and asked with words tinged by panic, "What would I say to her?"

Chapter 13

Jill pulled the silk sheet under her chin and sunk lower into the soft mattress as if to hide from the voice that kept repeating itself over and over in her mind, *Jill, you in there?* She had recognized Sarah Ann's voice calling her name. It was like shaking a kaleidoscope again and again, but always seeing the same design.

The whispering voice she heard gnawed at her gut as she lay sleepless since returning from Shiring's reception. She had stared for long minutes at the telephone on the nightstand wanting to call Sarah Ann. Maybe explain. Maybe confront her. Tell her partner it was none of her business. Or even try to persuade Sarah Ann that what she thought she saw was not really what she had seen. It was just a big mistake.

Jill had reached several times for the receiver only to feel the courage to make the call dissipate as the churning caldron of her emotions shifted from contriteness, to defensiveness, to abject guilt—guilt spinning into seething anger—anger that her partner might have been intentionally spying on her.

Is that what Sarah Ann was doing—spying? Had she suspected the relationship with Jared even before opening the door to Len's office? But from the misty depths of her mind the answer surfaced. No! Sarah Ann was not the spying type. She had probably just come looking for Jill to ask about something or maybe just to say goodbye.

Jill thought back to the reception. After making the rounds of other post-CMA parties, she had come in a stretch limo to NCA Records with Winnifred Hemming, Len, LouAnn and Jared. They were accompanied by a security guard who had been hired to keep an eye out for anyone trying to get too close to Jared on his big night. Sarah Ann had driven to the reception by herself.

The guests—some invited—some hangers-on, had broken into whoops and applause as Jared and his entourage entered. He and LouAnn were quickly surrounded by well-wishers. Jill had watched the melee of handshakes, toasts and back slaps from just inside the entry way. Sarah Ann had squeezed her hand and asked her what it was like to finally see her dreams become reality. Jill recalled how touched she was by this tribute from the woman who, she conceded to herself, had been the business force behind Jared's meteoric rise.

Arliss Hemming had come up after the awards ceremony and embraced her and Sarah Ann. "Told you it would happen one day, Jill. All you needed was this good luck charm standing next to you." He had left without saying a word to Jared. Or even to Winnifred.

The party was over. It ended badly. It was time for the *what nows*. How to confront Sarah Ann? How to respond if Sarah Ann confronted her? *It was none of her damn business* Jill raged silently as she slammed the telephone received back on its cradle yet again. But the pesky reality that always trumped her emotions told her the relationship with Jared would have to be explained. It was a confrontation she had been dreading since arriving back at her apartment.

Jared was clueless to her dilemma. He had been too damn busy ejaculating to hear Sarah Ann call out for Jill or even be aware that the door of the office had been partially opened and quickly closed. For the first time since they'd begun having sex, Jill was left unfulfilled. He had always been considerate of her during their lovemaking, insuring her pleasure as well as his own. But never did it seem was there time to relax in each other's arms, as she had with other lovers, and just enjoyed the afterglow of sex. It had ended in Len's office much the same way as it always did. In his usual slam-bam-thank-you-ma'am style he had pulled up his tux pants, kissed her roughly on the lips and slipped out of the dark room to rejoin his wife. She was left to brood over the emptiness she felt in the wake of his abrupt exit and to deal with the rising fear that their affair had been discovered.

Filled with sudden panic that someone else might find her in the dark office had forced her off the leather couch quickly. In Len's private bath she had dabbed her flushed face with cold water, touched up her make-up and smoothed her hair and dress. When she reappeared at the reception with a forced smile clouding the anxiety twisting inside her, Jill had looked around the crowded room but saw neither Sarah Ann nor the guest of honor and his wife.

She shook two Tums from a bottle on her nightstand and tossed them on her tongue, then recalled it had been Tums Shiring suggested when he came over to stand beside her after she reappeared at the party. "You look like you've got heartburn, sweetie," he said as he pulled a small roll of something from his pant pocket. She declined with a smile. "My ulcer's happily asleep. But thanks."

She had given Shiring a kiss on the cheek shortly after that and said good night before grabbing her mink coat from a chair behind the reception desk and throwing it blithely over her shoulder. She had swept out waving to a few who shouted congratulations and blowing air kisses to others. The room was still nearly full even though the reason for the party had departed. *This was Shiring's crowd* Jill conceded silently as she walked the short distance to her apartment above Edgerton Group's office. They drank. They partied. And on a night when one of Shiring's protégés had won four Country Music Association Awards, the party and the drinking would have lasted until daybreak. With Jared gone, Shiring himself would have become the center of attention. *And that's the way he liked it* she thought sullenly.

~

Sarah Ann frowned at her reflection. Sitting in front of the dressing table mirror she could see that even the make-up she was applying did not conceal the weariness in her eyes. A honk sounded leaving her no time to do anything more about what she knew was hopeless anyway. She switched off the bathroom light, bounded down the stairs, grabbed a brown leather jacket from the tall rack near the side door leading out to the portico and raced down the several steps.

Inside the back seat of the Ford Explorer two little arms reached out excitedly from the constraints of the car seat. "Gramma, hug!"

"Hello, little one." Sarah Ann planted a big kiss on the round cheek of her youngest grandchild. His chubby hands held her face in a tight grip. "Tookie, Gramma," he demanded with an ingratiating smile.

"I'm fresh out, John Bennett Boswell the Third," she said with just the slightest trace of guilt, knowing cookies from "Gramma" were banned before church and most other times by her son and his wife, Dominque. They opposed feeding their son too much sugar, a mandate she had ignored while continuing to bake all sorts of sugary treats for her grandson until he himself betrayed her. Her duplicity was revealed when Little John, as almost everyone had called the child since his birth eighteen months ago, blurted out his third word after mama and papa. It was "tookie."

"But I have a big surprise for you when we get home from church—if you're a good boy." That promise was enough to wreath the child's face in a big smile.

Sarah Ann planted another kiss on his plump cheeks, marveling, as she often did, at how much this child was a clone of his handsome father, ignoring any embedding of maternal genes from his beautiful mother with her high cheekbones, amber brown eyes and flowing dark hair. *Typical of the Boswell genes to be so prevailing* she mused again as she leaned back in the seat to buckle her seat belt.

"Mornin', Dominque. Mornin', son," she said, forcing cheerfulness into her voice.

"Saw you and Jill and the Parsons on television last night. Pretty impressive, Mom. Congratulations!"

"Thank you, Johnny. It *was* quite a night, I must say," she added, without betraying any of the bitter emotions left by what should have been one of the highlights of her life.

Dominque turned in her seat. "You looked absolutely beautiful in that green chiffon gown." Sarah Ann also loved the gown that Dominque had helped her select. It flattered her auburn hair and green eyes. Not to mention her newly slimmed figure. Sarah Ann had thought when she tried it on that it made her attractive—at least in a post-menopausal sort of way.

"And I have you to thank for that, Domi," replied Sarah Ann

graciously. "You were the one who found it at Tracy's," referring to one of Franklin's small boutiques owned by the former wife of a country music star. The boutique owner told anyone who would listen that setting her up in a business she loved was the best alimony she could have hoped for when she was cast aside for a younger woman. *Something to keep in mind for LouAnn if she ends up in the same situation*, Sarah Ann ruminated sarcastically.

Dominque's exquisite taste in clothes was just one of many qualities that won Sarah Ann's admiration and affection for her daughter-in-law. Johnny had talked endlessly about her on his vacations at home from college. But it wasn't until his graduation day from Yale Law School that she finally met the mysterious young law student from France who had captivated her son's heart. They were married a year before Sarah Ann joined Edgerton Group and Dominque immediately joined her husband as a partner in his father's law firm.

Surprisingly, Dominque chose to be married in Johnny's hometown. Her parents and two siblings with their spouses and children flew over for the wedding. Sarah Ann insisted on hosting Dominque's family at her large home. If it hadn't been chaotic enough entertaining and feeding six adults and three children, the chaos was complicated by none of Dominque's family members speaking English. Luckily, Sarah Ann had minored in French at Vanderbilt and had remained passably fluent in the language by occasionally reading a novel in French.

Dominque had expressed her gratitude many times for easing the language barrier and Sarah Ann had yet another opportunity to help bridge that barrier when the parents flew over following the birth of their new grandson.

Looking at the heads of the two young people in the front seat, Sarah Ann silently counted her good fortune at having such a handsome son and gracious and loving daughter-in-law. At least for the moment the problem of confronting Jill and dealing with Jared's infidelity was pushed to the back of her mind.

The eleven o'clock Mass was always crowded. Sarah Ann spotted Willie Dell and his mother seated on the other side of the aisle two pews down. He had managed a change of clothes before church and looked no worse for the pre-dawn phone call and the unscheduled breakfast meeting of the Prayer Group. She glanced around but didn't see the other women. She concluded they must have decided they had already done enough praying for one Sunday.

Chapter 14

He took a long gulp from the tall glass and let it float down his throat. Even a draught of the cold beer could not cool the anger aflame inside him. *The sonofabitch was not only likely as rich as ole Croesus. Now he had had to watch Jared prance up on that Opry stage all decked out like one of them ole time movie cowboys and be king for a night. And who the hell was Croesus anyway?* he thought belligerently, slamming the glass down hard enough to draw a look of rebuke from the thin figure wiping the bar at the far end with a rag that looked like it needed more cleaning that the bar.

He emptied the remaining beer down his throat and fished in his back pocket for his billfold. As he drew out three ones, he felt the letter folded on the other side of the bills. It had arrived at the post office box not long after he sent it. *No money* the response had told him with abrupt words. *And worse*, he seethed silently, *the big-headed bastard threatened to sic the law on him.*

He pressed the bills back in the billfold and jammed it back in his pocket, then tapped on the bar with the empty glass. Moments later another beer came sliding his way. *Jared'd regret that threat. Sure as hell. Sure as hell*, he repeated silently as he drew the beer to his lips.

~

The second chiming of the alarm clock was infuriatingly redundant. Jill looked over at the gold face of the clock menacingly before reaching over to pound down the stop button. *Enough! I'm awake already.* Actually, she had slept very little all night. Fear of facing

Sarah Ann today kept her adrenalin pumping at full speed. No food. No sleep. *Maybe a nervous breakdown was in order.*

Warm water from the multiple shower heads rained down on her body. For a few minutes the tension that had gripped her since early Sunday morning was flushed away. Jill never thought herself a coward until now. *It was her company, after all* she thought defensively. *Well, not really.* The partnership agreement she had signed nearly three years ago gave Sarah Ann a fifty-fifty share of Edgerton Group. Jill felt a rebellious twinge of regret at having signed the document, a feeling she quickly shelved. It was Sarah Ann who had become the brains behind the company; Sarah Ann who found Jared Parson; and if she had to be painfully candid, it was mostly Sarah Ann who melded Jared into the polished performer he had become without losing any of his down-home Texas charm.

It was Jill's responsibility to oversee his music and performances; find the best back-up band in the business; sit through long all-night stints—she at the piano—he with his guitar—recrafting a song until they declared it perfect. There had been many such nights. And it was during one of those nights they first had sex on a rug next to the piano.

Sex became as much a part of their song editing as the music itself. And anywhere else they might find themselves together. Jared had become reckless and insatiable. And she had become powerless to stop or even slow the abyss into which they were hurtling.

A shiver of need fluttered through her as the warm water continued to flow over her from several directions. Jill found her own sexual need for Jared matched his for her. It was what made her unable to deny him. She could not give him up. Not now. No matter the consequences. That she loved him deeply was an admission she had made to herself some time ago. She was far less certain about his feelings for her. *Were those feelings only sexual* as she often feared in her infrequent moments of candor? A light kiss when their ardor was spent was generally his only acknowledgement of their lovemaking. He had never said he loved her or even hinted at love.

Jill turned the shower off and wished her tumult of thoughts would turn off as well.

Sitting before the lighted make-up mirror in her spacious bathroom she busied herself applying foundation, then light powder, blush, eye make-up and finally lip gloss. The face that was reflected back looked younger than her years. An attractive face. Pretty. Maybe beautiful. Her eyes had always been her most striking feature. Azure blue. The blue of the Pacific Ocean under a cloudless sky her dad used to tell her when she was a child. The nose—slightly large for her face. The mouth—a little small. But the Creator had infused her with a smile that could fill her face and a lyrical laugh that was instantly infectious to those around her. Arliss Hemming had once described her laugh as part of her charm.

Jill leaned back against the vanity bench covered in a pale peach floral fabric. Dear Arliss. What would he say if he knew of her affair with Jared? Tryst might be a more appropriate word. Arliss would never condemn. It was not his way. He would look at her thoughtfully and then ask if she felt it was the best thing for her. Arliss always seemed to want the best for her—for everyone.

Jill quickly dressed in her usual slacks, heels and silk blouse, adding a string of cultured pearls that complimented the matching earrings and a new ring with three karats of diamonds surrounding a large centered pearl. It suited her now to be simple, a style she had copied from Sarah Ann, who always seemed to look like she had just walked off a page of Vogue. Jill felt the first pull in her stomach. Not panic. Not yet. Rising apprehension maybe? *Dammit—fear!* She was dreading going downstairs. She stood and walked into the small circular kitchen to pour a cup of coffee and held the steaming brew between both hands as she sipped gingerly. She knew she would need all her senses peaking before she reached her office.

The coffee failed to dispel the panic stirring in her gut. Jill closed the apartment door behind her with unusual firmness and started down the carpeted staircase that led directly to her office. She waited several minutes to gather herself before punching the intercom for Viola at the receptionist desk. "Is Sarah Ann in yet?" she inquired in a voice barely above a whisper, knowing full well that at ten o'clock in the morning Sarah Ann would have been in her office for at least an hour.

"Yes, ma'am. Are you officially checked in?" Viola was straight forward with everyone, including her two bosses. And she took no prisoners when it came to screening calls for both Jill and Sarah Ann. Viola Whittaker was by far the best receptionist Edgerton Group had ever employed. That was thanks to Sarah Ann who saw something in the plump, energetic woman, with the glistening ebony skin, who said she needed a job, and enough of a paycheck to support three kids whose father had deserted them.

After telling Viola she was hired, Sarah Ann had pulled a hundred dollars from her purse and handed it to the startled woman. "Consider it a hiring bonus," Sarah Ann had said.

Viola had wiped away tears and then announced she was heading to the Goodwill Store to buy proper clothing to sit at a front desk and welcome folks. And welcome them she did, with a wide smile that displayed Viola's perfect white teeth and deep set brown eyes that remained cheerful even when the smile might retreat from her face.

"Did she ask to see me?" Jill asked hesitantly.

"No, ma'am. You want me to put you through? She said to let her know when you came in, so I already let her know after I heard you come down the stairs."

Dammit! Jill was instantly miffed by Viola notifying Sarah Ann but took pains to hide her irritation. "No thanks, Viola. I'll head her way in just a bit." *Even with doors closed, Viola seems to hear everything. Does nothing escape her?*

Viola added, "And that stack of messages on your desk. They're all from this morning. This telephone hasn't stopped ringing," she said as the ringer sounded again.

Jill glared at the stack of pink message slips and just waved her arm as if to brush away anything that appeared to intrude on her panicked thoughts on how she would handle facing Sarah Ann. Her office was nearest the reception area and just down the hall from Sarah Ann's. At least Sarah Ann could not see the battle playing out on Jill's face. *Time to go on the offensive,* she told herself to bolster her courage.

Sarah Ann had her back to the open door when Jill walked in. "Am I interrupting?" she asked. Sarah Ann turned around in her chair and flashed a smile. "No. Sit down. What's up?"

Jill was taken aback by Sarah Ann's cheery welcome. She had expected—what? *Confrontation? Accusations?* But then, that was not Sarah Ann. She was the least confrontational person Jill had ever known. However difficult the problem she was confronting Sarah Ann approached it reflectively. Never with rancor. And seldom with a complaint. A feeling of such strong guilt swept over Jill, she felt momentarily unsteady on her feet, as if trying to brace against a forceful wind. In that unsettling moment she knew what had to be done.

"We…I need to discuss what you saw Saturday night."

"Then you did know it was me who opened the door?"

"Yes." Jill looked at the large photograph of Jared on the credenza behind Sarah Ann's desk hoping to find courage. But she found no bolstering from the grinning face in the gold frame. Focusing back on Sarah Ann she said haltingly, "I fell in love with him…sometime back…you know…when we spent so much time selecting and rewriting songs for his second album. I guess things started even while we were still on the first tour." She felt tears stinging her eyes. Jill looked pleadingly at Sarah Ann's passive face, "I didn't mean it to happen. It just did."

"Is Jared in love with you?" Sarah Ann's voice was as passive as her expression.

Jill stared at her folded hands feeling like a school girl called before the principal. The first seeds of resentment were sowing inside her. Explaining her actions to anyone, even a close associate and friend like Sarah Ann, was not in her nature. She had built her career in the music management business from scratch, competing against the big boys to gain a toehold on Music Row. And Saturday night she had reached the pinnacle of success in that narrow area of Nashville real estate—a talent she managed won four CMA awards, including Entertainer of the Year. *A talent she and Sarah Ann managed* she corrected silently, sending the budding resentment into retreat.

"He's never said he loved me," she admitted. "But I know he must." Jill glanced again at the photograph seeking support and just as before finding none. "It's complicated, Sarah Ann. I know there's LouAnn and the pregnancy. I think he feels hemmed in by his marriage…that LouAnn is backward…that maybe she's not an asset to his career…not like I could be."

Jill's voice trailed off and an awkward silence hung in the air between the two women, a silence finally broken by Sarah Ann who knew now what had to be said.

"Has he told you any of this, Jill?" There was warmth and empathy in Sarah Ann's voice. "I believe you when you say you love him. I can see it in your face. Hear it in your voice. If he had said he loved you, wanted to be with you, to marry you, then I could understand why you're putting everything you've worked for in jeopardy. Because that *is* what you're doing, Jill: Edgerton Group; Jared; most of all yourself."

Sarah Ann leaned forward resting her elbows on the desk and steepling her hands. "You are the sister I never had. You rescued me when I most needed a lifeline. I owe everything I enjoy today to you. To your generosity. To your great heart. To seeing in me what no one else ever tried to see. If Edgerton Group folds tomorrow I would have no regrets because of the opportunity you extended me without even really knowing me."

Sarah Ann was now looking at Jill's lowered head. "My fear is for you, Jill. There is hurt, and a lot of it ahead, if you continue this affair. Jared has nothing to lose," she reasoned. "His contract is ironclad to a point. If he decides to leave us—you know he can—he'll have his choice of managers. And with his celebrity, he'll always have his choice of lovers. That's the way it is in this business."

Sarah Ann looked appealingly at Jill, whose eyes remained averted. "The only commitment appears to be on your part. Not his," she said gently. "You could lose everything, Jill. Everything," she emphasized. "And the only thing you'll be left with is a ton of heartache."

Jill raised her head and saw the compassion in her partner's eyes. Sarah Ann was right. She had known all this before she stepped into this office. A slight smile creased Jill's lips. "A ton of heartache—great name for a song." The thin smile changed to sadness. "You're right, of course," she conceded as she stood up to leave. "It's wrong in every way. I'll make sure I keep Jared on a strictly professional basis in the future. Sorry you had to see what you did Saturday night."

"Jill. Please don't apologize. This happens." Sarah Ann smiled and tossed her hands in the air. "At least one of us had some good sex. It's been so long for me, I may have to reread—what's that book—*Everything You Ever Wanted To Know About Sex: But Were Afraid To Ask.*"

Jill laughed and then turned in the doorway as she was leaving. "Don't worry. It really is like riding a bicycle. By the way, ton of heartache—that really is a great name for a country ballad. I'll run it by Jared next time I see him." Jill poked her head back around the doorway. "And as soon as I do, I promise you, I'll keep on running."

It was Sarah Ann's turn to laugh. "How about lunch," she proposed.

"Sounds great. My treat. With the damn telephone ringing off the hook," she threw her right arm in the air and shrugged her shoulders as two phone lines rang at once at Viola's desk, "how about driving out to Leiper's Fork and biting into one of Puckett's big thick cheeseburgers? My vessels have been hankering for a heavy dose of cholesterol. How 'bout yours?"

"With onion rings on the side," chimed in Sarah Ann. "That should block an artery or two for the day."

"Let me return a few calls and then we'll head out. We've earned a break from this place."

Chapter 15

Jared Parsons reined in his big horse after the long gallop. "Good boy," he said, patting the animal's neck now slathered with white foamy sweat. He wiped his hand on his jeans and jerked the rein hard to the left, to turn the horse back toward the stable. "How about a run for the hay, boy? Let's see if you can earn your keep."

He dug his spurs into the horse's side and it vaulted forward with a toss of its regal head and a neigh of pain. By the time horse and rider reached the large white stable with its green metal roof, the horse's sides heaved with distress. Parson threw his leg over the left side and leaped to the ground, seemingly unconcerned about the animal.

"Hey, Hershel," he shouted for the farm manager. "Where the hell are you?"

"Right here, Mr. Parson." Hershel Simmons stepped out of a back stall and sauntered toward Parson. "Get a good hard ride in, Boss?" Simmons asked the question facetiously, having heard the horse thundering toward the barn from a quarter mile away.

It was quiet in the country and only the cars of neighbors from nearby estates interrupted that quiet along the two-lane paved road bordering Jared's hundred-acre farm. Watching the horse's heaving side and hard panting incited instant anger but Simmons kept his concern for the animal and his dislike of his boss masked behind a tight smile and expressionless eyes.

By the time Simmons reached the horse Jared had turned on his expensive custom-made cowboy boots and was headed toward the back entrance to the large house on the rise above the barn, flicking his thick riding crop against his right boot with each long stride. As usual he had not responded to Simmons question.

Simmons wrapped his right arm around the horse's neck and stroked him affectionately. "Let's get this saddle off o' ya big fella, and get ya a good rubdown. You'll be good as new," he promised.

Simmons slipped the halter on the horse and then unbuckled the bridle with its double ring bit, a bit he knew was designed to irritate the animal's mouth and add a measure of dominance for the rider. Simmons had been raising and training horses a good part of his life. There was nothing he detested more than this type of bit. Cruel was his assessment. He loosened the cinch and slid the silver studded saddle off the horse, along with the blanket, and heaved them onto a stall gate.

His anger rose with each heavy contraction of the animal's sides. "Come on ole boy. Let's get ya' cooled down."

For nearly a half hour Simmons stroked the brush over the horse's back, neck, legs and even under his stomach as the animal stood patiently tethered to both sides of the barn by long leather leads. After Simmons had brushed away most of the sweat and foam from the sleek hide he took a hose and moved the soft flow of cool water up and down the horse's back, as the animal tossed its head in delight at the feel of the water. "You love a bath, don't ya, boy. Better'n gettin' spiked in the side."

He took a small towel and rubbed gently over each side of the horse where he knew the spurs had left tenderness. *How could a guy who has everything treat a spirited animal like this big fella no better'n a plow horse? Don't make sense lessin' you're stupid or cruel,* Simmons fumed as he led the horse into the largest stall at the front of the barn. *And Jared Parson ain't stupid, that's for sure, for damn sure!*

Simmons closed the stall gate with the name Waylon emblazoned on a well-shined brass plate. The farm manager never called the horse by that name. He thought it defamatory to the namesake for whom he had worked as a back-up musician off and on during Waylon Jennings early days in the country music business. He'd even done a little back-up for Johnny Cash. One thing Simmons knew, *Jennings loved music, his wives, his kids and his animals, just about in that order*, he remembered fondly. Simmons started humming bars from one of Jennings' early hits. That was before Waylon Jennings' slumping career went through a renaissance as one of the fabled Highwaymen with the likes of Chris Kristofferson, Willie Nelson and Johnny Cash.

Now there was a foursome to beat all. Especially Johnny.

Simmons wasn't sure when the two legends had become friends, Jennings and Cash. He had been just another hanger-on in those days, hoisting too much liquor to his lips because one or the other of the two men might be paying the tab on any given night, in any given city where their tour bus was parked. It made it easy to drink. He liked booze so much that it kept him from dabbling in the drugs that bedeviled both Jennings and Cash during their early days.

But there came a time when Simmons' drink tab was pulled only from his own pocket. By that time his music and his family were playing second fiddle to whatever bottle he could afford to buy or bum from a friend or acquaintance.

After years of drifting away from his wife and daughter, from music, and from those he had known in the business, he woke up in a Salvation Army rescue center in Austin, Texas. With help from the A-team there, the nickname for the alcoholics' treatment group, he slowly found God, won his battle with the bottle, joined Alcoholics Anonymous, made his way back to Nashville and turned his love of horses and farming into a job.

Owning a big farm was a status symbol in country music circles. Finding a job was not hard, especially if you were a musician down on your luck that happened to know a lot about horses and farm management. He had come to Jared Parson with a reputation as a top manager and with a sterling recommendation from a couple selling their several-hundred-acre spread in the rolling hills of Williamson County to resettle in the hills above Los Angeles.

It was a bad move on his part he thought bitterly as he finished filling buckets with sweet feed and pitch-forked an alfalfa and hay mix into the large bins hanging in the stalls of three horses and the pony Jared had purchased for his daughter to ride. *Cute little thing, that one. Mostly because she looked the mirror image of her mama. Shy as a deer in hunting season, though. Took after her mama in that respect too.*

Simmons had his suspicions about the introverted mother and daughter. He had seen LouAnn Parson sport too many bruises and black eyes in the months since he'd been hired as manager. She always offered an excuse of falling or bumping into something when the telltale bruising could not be fully covered up by make-up. He knew enough to keep his suspicions to himself. He needed the job. Bankruptcy had bailed him out of most of what he owed, but there was still the monthly payment on the sorry pick-up parked behind the back steps leading up to his two-room apartment above the barn. The living quarters came as part of his salary.

Thrusting the pitch fork into a bale of hay, Simmons strode to the rear of the barn and hurried up the wood stairs to the apartment and jerked open the door. From the refrigerator he reached for a can of Pepsi and pulled the tab as the familiar whoosh of its carbonation exploded from the opened can. He slumped down in a sweat-stained brown leather recliner.

Simmons had met a lot of sonsofbitches in his day, never one to top Jared Parson. *If he takes a whip and spurs to a horse just to show he's boss, who else is the arrogant s-o-b kicking in the balls? For sure he was mistreating his wife.* He was damn sure of that. About the little girl he wasn't sure. Willow was always excited on the three days a week she came to the barn for riding lessons. She displayed a rare enthusiasm for such a shy child. *No signs of abuse there, at least that he could see. Parson seemed to dote on the child anytime she was in the barn with him. Still—it's time to start looking for another job,* he concluded.

Simmons pulled the side lever that sent the chair backwards, crossed his long legs at the ankles and took a long draw on the Pepsi, wishing it was beer—even better—bourbon.

He'd start putting out feelers in the morning.

Chapter 16

Jared Parson did not like Hershel Simmons. *Smug son-of-a-bitch was about as friendly as a pit of rattlesnakes lately. Time to send him packing. He'd ask Jill to help find a new farm manager tomorrow. He'd enough to do without worrying about tending this spread and the animals.*

Jared snapped the cap off a bottle of Corona, pulled the studio chair around with his boot toe and wheeled up to the console. *It was getting there*, he thought with pride, glancing around at the blinking lights on the mixing console. The large soundproof cubicle behind the wide-glassed studio window held a newly installed state-of-the-art microphone and digital teleprompter for the music. The room was dimly lit but clearly visible from the studio. Soon he might have a studio to match Arliss Hemming's. *Maybe do ole' Hemming one better.* Jared grinned at the thought of outdoing Hemming. Even before the end of the studio sessions to cut the first album, Jared sensed aloofness in Hemming; maybe even dislike. Hemming wasn't one to say much. He kept things close to the vest. Jill had warned him Hemming never voiced criticism. He made suggestions. Most of them constructive, Jared had to admit. It was only when Hemming finally said, "it sounds like a wrap to me" that you knew he liked what he was hearing.

Jared was no fool. He let Hemming call the shots in their recording sessions. But that was only because he knew Hemming was getting the best out of him. He and Hemming seemed to be on the same wave link with the final product. "Here's to you, Arliss," he said aloud, tipping his bottle before taking another swig of the Corona. Jared sneered at a picture of him and Hemming hanging on the wall above the mixing console taken when his first album was released. *I get albums that win everything in sight and I'm screwin' the woman you want right under your nose, buddy.*

It had become apparent to Jared within a short time of working with Hemming and Jill, during those long afternoons and some nights the three spent working so closely on the first album, that the record producer had strong feelings for Jill. Jared prided himself on being a keen reader of his fellow man. It was not anything Hemming did overtly that betrayed his feelings for Jill. Just subtle things. The deference he showed her. Always keeping her coffee cup filled from a carafe his assistant kept filled. Rubbing her shoulders when the sessions went longer to ease tension that could build in her voice and temper. Patience was not one of Jill's virtues. Even less so when the recording and mixing sessions dragged on well past midnight as they often did, especially during the cutting of that first album.

Jared had his own way of relieving Jill's tension. *It had started sometime after those long nights at Hemming's studio* he recalled with a crooked smirk as he kicked the chair around in a circle of his studio and extended his arms behind his head. He tried to remember what triggered that first time. Whatever it was, Jill seemed to like sex as much as he did and was always willing when he felt the need, which was just about any time she was around, no matter where they were.

Now it was most often here. He recalled screwing her three times the first night she had come here, and they still managed to finish writing the song that headlined the third album. Sex had become a ritual anytime she came to help with the songwriting.

Jared lifted his booted feet onto the console, crossed them at the ankles and leaned back contentedly. *I've got it all,* he mused silently. The fame—that was the most satisfying—bigger than he had dared dream during those early teen years in Texas when he first set his sights on a country music career. There had been a period when he thought it would all elude him—his dream—the same dream for his future that he had shared only with his mother.

His mother began teaching him to play a guitar before he started school, on the same guitar she had purchased in a pawn shop as a teenager. Her young eyes had also been looking east to Nashville from the squalid doublewide where she was raised just outside Jacksonville, Texas. Her own dream would remain unfulfilled. He was the reason.

She was impregnated at seventeen by a handsome drifter. He had spent two weeks helping her father and brothers during the day pick tomatoes to sell to the broker from the canning factory on the other side of town; and at night sneaking into her bedroom. Before Jared's interest in girls peaked his mother had started warning him "don't let your dick dictate your future. You're don't wanna end up like me," she nagged with harsh vehemence.

He pictured his mother as she was when he was a boy, her long dark hair pulled back in a single braid that fell halfway down her back, shouting at him that he would risk it all; all they talked of; all they dreamed of. And for what—a few minutes of fun. "Not worth it," she always concluded angrily, her voice slurred by booze. "Never worth it."

It had been more than just a few minutes of fun. It began on his second date with LouAnn. She was shy but never said *no*. And he was not one to quibble. *Jesus, that first sex was good*, a slight smile lifting his lips as he remembered LouAnn at sixteen, her long blond hair tangled by sweat from the heat of the cramped back seat of his mother's ancient Buick. He wasn't sure even now which he loved more—LouAnn—or sex. But he knew he needed both.

Remembering that time—a time which now seemed so long ago, he felt the same familiar tug of fear in his gut he had felt then, knowing his mother's reaction if she found out what was going on in the back seat of her car. He knew what he and LouAnn were doing was a betrayal of the promise he had made to his mother long before hormones kicked in and spurred such a betrayal. Everything he had accomplished in his early years had been to make his mother proud of him; all A's on his report cards, becoming an eagle scout, quarterbacking the football team, and being captain of the basketball team. Or was it? Maybe his need to overachieve in everything simply masked the deep-felt shame and resentment he felt toward his alcoholic mother.

Jared shook his head as if to sweep away his lingering sense of guilt. He worked hard to prove he was just another kid, a regular kid, just like the other guys he hung out with. Not a kid born out of wedlock with no father's name on his birth certificate. He knew others knew the shame of his birth—his mother's shame. In a small community such secrets were never kept. He vowed at an early age never to allow anyone to glimpse the sense of inferiority he harbored inside. No one did. And the few who had dared voice an occasional taunt about his mother were soon silenced by his fists.

LouAnn was the first person to whom he had ever revealed his resentment about the circumstances of his birth. She was the one person who seemed to understand the torment inside him. She would hold his hand and remind him over and over it was not his fault. Maybe she understood because they came from similar backgrounds. Like him, she was the offspring of poor working parents. Her father was a janitor at the local elementary school, her mother a waitress at the same café/bar where his mother had worked for years, although the two women seemed to have little else in common besides a work place acquaintance.

It was early April. He and LouAnn were set to graduate the following month. He had taken her to a movie that Saturday night and then finished the date the same way they did each time they were together, having sex in the back seat of the Buick. When he walked her to the door of her doublewide, LouAnn stood with her back against a wooden porch post, her hands clasped behind the post. Jared pressed against her small breasts and caressed her arms as he kissed her goodnight several times. She made no move to go inside or head to the car to finish what he was sure she felt like starting again. When she spoke finally, her words quickly quelled his rising ardor. Tears spilled out with every word. When he made no response, she dried her eyes with a tissue and slipped around him and went quietly inside. He stood alone for several minutes, leaning against the same post LouAnn had, still feeling the warmth from her body. He stood hoping what she had just told him could not be—unwilling to accept the consequence of the word, *pregnant.*

She assured him the birth control pills would protect them after he had complained using condoms was a hassle and took some of the fun out of sex. LouAnn's tears accelerated when she revealed her mother had found the container of pills under the mattress of her bed and threatened to tell her father. LouAnn had lied, explaining to her mother she had secreted the pills away for a friend at school who feared her parents would discover she had been taking them. Her mother accepted her explanation but shook the remaining pills out of the container into the toilet and flushed away the only protection from the dilemma they now faced. Not only that; now she had to admit her own duplicity and face her father's wrath. Her parents were devout Methodists. If she had hoped for empathy from her mother, she knew she had forfeited such sympathy because of her lie about the pills.

High school football had been Jared's stepping stone to college, and he was ready to head to Austin in August for freshmen 'two a days' on a full athletic scholarship to the University of Texas. But as he stepped off the rickety wood porch tethered to the mobile home that April night, his hands jammed in the pockets of his Levi's, he felt the path he had worked so hard to follow folding up under his feet.

He had not offered to stand with LouAnn when she faced her parents. Why should he? This was her fault. She should have told him she wasn't taking birth control pills any longer. Like most of the guys at school he carried a condom in his billfold. And he could buy more at any drug store. By the time he reached the Buick and slammed the door shut, he was seething with rage at LouAnn. How could she have been so stupid? He stomped on the clutch and hit the accelerator as he jerked the shaft into reverse.

His mother was still awake when he arrived home. She saw the anger playing on his face. When she wouldn't stop nagging for a reason he had flung words at her like darts flying toward a target. At first his mother only cried softly. But as the tears continued spilling down the deep fissures in her thin cheeks her own rage built into a storm on her flushed face. It was an anger fueled by the booze she tried to pass off as sweet tea. It finally crowded out the tears in her faded blue eyes and her words then roared like thunder in his ears, calling him names he hadn't heard even in a football locker room. Then came more tears in between gulps of the cheap bourbon. As he sat listening without responding, his mother did what she had always done in any crisis—got stomping mean drunk. The rage and the harsh words subsided into slurs until she finally passed out. Jared then did what he had done so often before, hitched his muscular arms under hers, pulled his mother into the rear bedroom of their cluttered mobile home and laid her across the bed to sleep off her rampage.

In the sanctuary of his small bedroom he cleared his mind of the emotional clutter of anger, resentment, blame and self-pity. He decided in the still darkness what he would do.

Monday at school, Jared pulled LouAnn aside in the hall and whispered his proposal, adding no child of his would be born without a father's name on the birth certificate.

The day after graduation he and LouAnn were married by her parent's minister in a small white clad country church with a steeple that leaned precariously, the victim of too many storms and too little repair. There was no ring. He had no money to spare on even the thinnest band. The ceremony was short, delivered in terse language by the disapproving minister as LouAnn's parents sat alone in the small church, looking somber and reproving. They neither hugged their daughter and new son-in-law, nor wished them congratulations.

Jared's mother refused to attend. He had not seen her since the morning of his wedding and wondered now, as he often did in rare moments of self-reflection, why he didn't care. And the answer he gave himself was always the same. *He just couldn't care less.*

His mother had called NCA Records shortly after the release of his first album and the meteoric fame that followed, leaving her name and address and a message to contact her. He instructed both the record company and Edgerton Group never to accept another message from Willa Parson, without acknowledging to anyone at either organization that she was who she said she was—his mother. In a scribbled note, Jared told Sarah Ann to send her a check for $10,000 with instructions never to contact him again. The check was cashed at a small state bank in Jacksonville, and he had not heard from, or about her, since.

Another demand for money had come several months later in the form of a letter postmarked from a town along the Texas-Oklahoma border. No signature. Only a threat to reveal things in his past that would not fit the image of a small-town boy that Jill and Sarah Ann had so carefully crafted. Jared had shrugged it off as a prank. The next letter a month later was slipped into the mail slot on the front door of Edgerton Group. It was unsigned, and this time threatened bodily harm if the demand was not met. Alarmed, Jill and Sarah Ann wanted to turn the blackmail demand over to police. Jared refused. He suspected the source. His terse response, written that night, carried a more lethal threat. Jared received no further letters.

On the morning of his wedding, Jared had moved out of his mother's trailer, taking with him only his clothes, sports trophies, and the nearly $500 he'd earned from summer jobs and had squirreled away inside one of the sports trophies hidden under his bed. He moved in with LouAnn at her parents' larger, three-bedroom doublewide. He left behind a photo album of pictures taken by his mother when he was a baby and the only photo of mother and son together, taken when he was twelve at a studio in the local Walmart.

Jared found a part-time summer job bagging groceries, and he paid LouAnn's parents most of what he earned for their room and board until the day they left for Austin. They drove away in the seven-year-old banged up Ford Taurus purchased with a down payment from the $500 he kept hidden even from LouAnn.

The day after their arrival in Austin Jared sat in the office of an assistant coach who listened empathetically. Within a week, he and LouAnn were moved into an off-campus, fully furnished first floor apartment. It came complete with baby bed and a small dresser crammed with baby clothes sized from birth to toddler, all in colors of pink, yellow and blue. A sonogram had confirmed the baby girl the young couple should expect to welcome around Thanksgiving.

They named her Willow. Seeing her tiny face peeking out from the papoose-like blanket wrap, Jared felt a surge of protective love he had never before felt for anyone. That night he composed a song to his new daughter. It was one of the songs that made the cut for his first album.

Jared was assigned a token job on campus in the huge library that sat in the center of the Austin campus, a job at which he did little work and received a more than ample paycheck, so they could live comfortably and allow LouAnn to stay home with the new baby. Jared never questioned the beneficence or how it was arranged. In return, he earned his keep on the football field as a tight end with sure hands and a pair of legs that could outrun most defenders. He also delivered grades that gained him status as a top scholar athlete.

In the off season he devoted any time he could to perfecting his guitar playing and writing the songs that would initiate him into the top tier of country music success. Each note he drew on the page, each strum of his mother's old Gibson guitar, edged him one step closer to his dream, a dream he never doubted would be his eventual reality.

He graduated near the top of his class.

The same week he received his bachelor's degree in business, Jared Parson traded in the tired old Taurus for a newer Ford model and rented a small U-Haul trailer. With his wife and child, he set out for Nashville with just enough money to rent a cramped three-room apartment in a seedy part of the city. They had enough money left to buy groceries to last them for maybe a month.

Jared stood up and stretched his long legs. Success had come swiftly and easily. But then he always believed it would, he admitted, as he looked around the private studio with the same sense of satisfaction he always felt in this room. It was his space, built with his money. LouAnn knew better than to intrude—ever.

His wife's face emerged in his mind's eye. It was a pretty face in a sweet, country girl sort of way. Not beautiful. But passable. He had few fears of another man trying to take her from him. She was his—only his.

He had worked hard to provide a luxurious life for her and Willow. Which was why he had no patience with LouAnn's carping. Just weeks before the CMA Awards she had been whining about not seeing him except at dinner. She wanted him to walk with her down to the woods at the back of the property and swim in the stream that flowed through the trees on either side. When he dismissed her coldly, saying he was too busy in the studio, she had started on him about not paying enough attention to Willow. He had yelled he was too busy making a living. It was her job to take care of Willow. *Christ, she could get on his nerves.* He had turned his back on her and headed toward the door to the bedroom when she accused him of not loving her or Willow.

Enough of the goddamned nagging. Rage tore through him at her whining outburst. He rushed back toward LouAnn and slapped her hard across the right side of her face. The force of the blow sent her spiraling backward onto the carpet. Screaming curses, he had pulled her up by her long hair and thrown her roughly onto the bed. "You want attention. I'll give you some attention." He pulled down her tan slacks and ripped away her nylon underwear then pulled down his own jeans and briefs before penetrating her with hard thrusts. When he was spent, he rolled aside and lay silent for several minutes while she sobbed beside him. A short time later he left without a word. LouAnn was still sobbing on the bed.

He sought the sanctuary of his studio and locked the door behind him. Once inside, familiar feelings of guilt and remorse swamped his anger. He had worked so damn hard for her and Willow. *Why couldn't LouAnn just be satisfied with the way things were?* He didn't even pressure her for sex like he used to. No need to anyway. Jill made sex a lot more exciting. She was inventive and pleased him in ways LouAnn had never been willing to try. He felt resentment and anger churning again inside him. *After all, wasn't he giving her everything she had ever wanted that money could buy.*

The money. It had come quickly and in bucketful's. More money than even he dared dream. If he never worked another day in his life, he could live well. The proof he knew was in his burgeoning bottom line, which Jared had wisely put in the hands of Sarah Ann and her ex-husband to manage.

Jared walked over, sat back down in his leather studio chair and leaned back, lifting his feet onto the edge of the console. There were two benefits to having his money managed by Sarah Ann and John. It cost him far less than the usual percentage paid to a business manager. And most importantly, those two seemed to know more about investing than most of the investment brokers and money managers who had contacted him after he banked his first big paychecks from the sales of the debut album.

Real estate. That's what Sarah Ann had suggested. She had searched out some valuable, but overlooked properties around Music Row, a boutique office complex in Cool Springs and this farm. All were purchased for prices well below market estimates. He had to tip his hat to Sarah Ann as a negotiator. Boswell drew up the contracts and within two months the properties had been closed on and the monthly income started rolling in. Smart pair those two. His thoughts focused on his growing wealth, wiping out any lingering feelings of guilt or shame over his abuse of LouAnn.

Chapter 17

"Fire Hershel Simmons! Why? Is he back on the bottle?"

Sarah Ann's voice sounded incredulous. Jared had seemed pleased with Simmons' management of the farm almost since the day she had hired him nearly a year ago, despite knowing Hershel's demons with the bottle. "Is he drinking again?" she repeated. Her question was met with silence at the other end of the line. "Jared…is Hershel drinking on the job?" Still no response.

"Jared…"

"Look, Jill said to call you." More silence. Sarah Ann waited. "No, he's not drinking. Not that I know of anyway. Look…I just don't like the sonofabitch. Anyway, Jill said for you to find me a new farm manager."

Sarah Ann softly cleared her throat. "If you feel strongly about this Jared, of course I'll start immediately looking for a replacement for Hershel." She hesitated, waiting for a response. None came. "But let me mention a couple of obstacles. One, you need a valid reason to fire someone these days or he could get testy and get an attorney. I don't think you want that kind of publicity."

Sarah Ann could hear a heavy sigh at the other end of the line. "Well, shit. It's like I've got no say in any fucking thing…sorry, I didn't mean to toss that word at you." Another heavy sigh, this time filled with unspoken frustration. "I just don't like the guy, Sarah Ann. I should be able to get rid of him without you making a legal case out of it." She sensed rising anger in his voice.

"Jared, I understand your frustration. I don't know that he would or even could sue." She struggled for an instant solution. "Would it help if I had a talk with him and see if I can iron out your differences?" No response. "I know Hershel's doesn't have a lot to say. He probably comes off perhaps a little unfriendly."

"Yeah, he does. The guy's just kinda creepy." Jared knew his response to Sarah Ann's reasoned questions sounded weak and petulant. *He should have made Jill fire Simmons instead of letting her insist Sarah Ann take care of it.*

"One other thing," added Sarah Ann. "He's been efficient enough that the leased portion of the farm has, so far, brought in enough revenue to pay for upkeep of the animals and to cover his salary." She added, "It'll be difficult to find someone willing to work for what he makes. And remember, he also does a lot of the maintenance on the rental properties in town." Sarah Ann let that information sink in, knowing how keenly Jared watched his bottom line, a bottom line made more stellar by the astute investments she and John had made with Jared's growing income. She wanted to scream at him that just because you suddenly don't like someone is no reason to fire a person who is doing a far better than expected job, for a salary well below what a new farm manager would probably demand.

"So, I'm the bad guy here, is that it?"

"No, Jared, you're not the bad guy and you know that's not what I mean. It's *your* farm. Hershel is *your* employee. If you really want him fired, I'll do it." She felt her own sigh echoing between the two phones. "But I worry we won't find anyone as reliable as Hershel has been, despite his past problems with alcohol. And one more thing," she continued. "Hershel seems very fond of LouAnn and Willow. With you on the road so much, it's good to have someone around who will look after them when you're away, especially now, with a new baby coming."

Jared felt some of his initial anger and frustration melting away in the face of Sarah Ann's logic. She was right about Simmons' efficiency. He knew Simmons worked long hours and he had to grudgingly admit, kept the place in top shape. And he hadn't been aware until Sarah Ann mentioned it that Simmons was doing maintenance on some of the Nashville properties. That sure as hell was saving money.

"Okay! Let's drop it for now," he finally relented. Jared forced cheerfulness into his voice. "You're usually right about these things, Sarah Ann." She heard his faint laugh in the receiver. "Guess that's why Jill turns the office over to you and prefers being on the road with me. Works for both of us, don't you think?"

Sarah Ann felt her stomach churn and could not muster words to respond. He did not appear to know she was aware of what had happened the night of the CMA awards.

"I'll let you go. Thanks for smoothing out my thinking." The line went silent and Sarah Ann hung up the receiver and sat back in her chair, jarred by Jared's seeming ignorance of her discovery of his affair with Jill. Or, she thought with rising concern, Jill had not confronted him as she had promised to do and broken off the affair. She rubbed her temples with her fingertips as she felt tension riveting up from her stomach to her head and the beginning of a headache. She had enough headaches without having to deal with the real thing. Anger burst inside her like lightning out of a thunder cloud. Jill's irresponsibility could jeopardize everything they had both worked for—Jill even longer. Why? It was a question she had asked herself a thousand times since the night of the party without ever coming up with a viable answer. Jill was beautiful, smart, and witty. She could have any number of similarly attractive men. She could certainly have Arliss Hemming anytime she finally decided to acknowledge his obvious attraction to her.

Why, why, why? Sarah Ann rubbed her temples again and leaned her desk. She had a pile of calls to return. And her assistant, Nicole, had suggested she call Carl Stone to work out some last minute legal hitches in state fair and concert engagements for a number of Edgerton Group clients that might eventually have to bring John into the conversation.

This was just her morning schedule. Glancing at her calendar she could see the afternoon was equally crowded with appointments. Sarah Ann pushed down the intercom button linking her to her assistant. Natalie Holt answered immediately. "Am I in demand again?" the amiable voice in the office next to hers quipped.

"Yes, you are. Can you pop over for a minute? And I'll tell you just how many demands await you."

"Yo, Boss. Headed your way."

Sarah Ann could not remember a time when her assistant was not amiable and willing, whatever she was asked to do. *A gift from God!* That was how Sarah Ann most frequently thought of her assistant since hiring Natalie Holt the same day she applied for a job two years ago. It happened to be the Monday following Natalie's graduation from Belmont University and she later told Sarah Ann it was the only place she planned to apply. Her eyes were trained on Edgerton Group long before she took her finals. Natalie Holt came armed with a specialized degree in business specific to the music business and something even more valuable; a constant cheerfulness that had so far withstood all attempts to dampen her demeanor by prickly clients and even more prickly vendors: from musicians, to stage managers, to booking agents; even to ex-spouses of the forenamed prickly clients.

The word 'problem' was not in Natalie's vocabulary. What Sarah Ann viewed as a problem was simply viewed as a 'challenge' by her affable assistant and attacked with whiz kid audaciousness and unabashed enthusiasm.

An ever-present smile was radiating on Natalie's round face when her pudgy frame burst through the doorway to Sarah Ann's office moments later. "Mornin'," she said, plopping herself down in one of the chairs in front of the desk. "What's up? You look a little glum and that's not good," she observed. Among Natalie's many attributes was a keen ability to instantly take the temperament temperature of anyone she came face-to-face with.

Just being so cheerfully confronted by her ingratiating smile had the immediate effect of melting away the heaviness Sarah Ann felt. She rallied a pretense of pleasantness and even a faint smile for her assistant. "Good morning, yourself," she said, mustering cheeriness she did not feel as she reached for a stack of paper and notes in front of her and handed it across to Natalie. "You will brighten my day even more than your mere presence does, if you can wade through these. Set up studio time for the listed talents with the erstwhile Mr. Hemming while I busy myself settling problems involving these state fair dates with the booking agency for some of the same bunch."

"Arliss cannot resist me. Consider it done." Natalie noted the hint of a frown still creasing Sarah Ann's forehead. "Why don't I call Arliss and raise you one by calling Stone about those state fair dates and times. If Carl and I can't resolve it, I'll give John a holler. How's that?"

Stone Management had a long-standing contract with Edgerton Group to book its roster of talent into various concert and state fair venues, except of course for Jared. Jill had taken over booking all his concerts in recent months.

"You're a jewel, Natalie. That would be great," replied Sarah Ann gratefully.

"I'd rather be a star in a crown. God likes that, you know. At least that's what the song says," referring to an old gospel tune. She disappeared out the doorway and just as quickly reappeared. "Don't you think Stella is ready to bypass the fair circuit this year?"

"Yes, I do. And I'm going to need to talk with you about some options for her. Jill thinks she's ready to launch on the big venue concert circuit. Can you talk to Carl about our options?"

"Suits me, Boss." And as quickly as she had reappeared she was gone; trailing cheerful energy like the sky streams of a jet, leaving her presence felt even when she was no longer there.

Thank you, God, for small favors and Natalie, was Sarah Ann's unspoken prayer as she watched her assistant disappear out the door. For someone on the plump side, she always marveled at how fast Natalie could move. There was a beguiling innocence about her round face, an unremarkable face except for perceptive brown eyes that missed nothing. Their keen insightfulness operated from just above a pug nose dotted with freckles and a small cherub mouth. Her clothes tended toward the frumpy, indicating Natalie's lack of inclination toward a 'fashionista' bent. With her morning agenda partially cleared Sarah Ann pushed the receptionist's intercom button.

"Yeesss," Viola Whittaker's husky voice drawled.

"Hey, yourself! Is Jill in?"

"Yes'm. But she's got her door shut. You want to open a line of communication?"

"If you would be so kind?"

"Yes'm."

Sarah Ann laughed despite herself. The "slave banter" as she had come to call her give and take conversing with Viola over the intercom never failed to draw a chuckle, from one or the other of them. She heard Viola tell Jill to expect Sarah Ann in a heartbeat. She knew Viola had not waited for a response from Jill. She thought Sarah Ann's habit of asking to see Jill was ridiculous and furthermore, she found no such etiquette requirement in her reading of Miss Emily Post.

Viola also reminded Sarah Ann frequently that Jill never gave notice when she was heading to Sarah Ann's office.

"Thank you, Viola."

"You's welcome, Missus Boswell. I's aimin' to please since it's gettin' close to raise time."

"You're already breaking our bank account."

"On my slave wages?" her cheerful voice aghast.

"Join a union," Sarah Ann suggested laughing as she pushed away from her desk and walked toward Jill's office.

Jill had a cell phone pressed to her ear and waved Sarah Ann to a chair as her lips formed a silent hello.

"I'm working on London as the first stop," she heard Jill say to the person at the other end of the conversation. "London should be first." There was an insistence in her voice. "The venue is bigger. You want to make a big splash at the first stop even though I think all the concerts will sell out early…Of course I'm sure of that. You're bigger than most at this stage of your career. Garth's London concert was huge…Yours might be even bigger."

Sarah Ann knew then it was Jared at the other end. This was the first she had heard about an upcoming overseas tour. At that moment she was glad she had cleared some of her morning calendar and was overhearing this conversation.

"I know what I'm doing. The new album is out in two weeks. That's the perfect time to strike while singles are hitting the high spots on the charts." Jill shifted the phone to her other ear. "Of course, you'll be back before the baby comes." A look of consternation shadowed Jill's face. Her patience threshold was slim at best, even with Jared. "Leave it to me, Jared. Have I steered you wrong yet?" There was a touch of testiness in her tone. "See ya." The phone was clicked off and placed on the desk.

"On the road again, are we?" remarked Sarah Ann in an effort to mask her surprise. "And London bound no less. How come you get Buckingham Palace and Big Ben and I get stuck with state fairs," she said, trying to infuse a little levity into her words.

Jill laughed lightly. "But I thought you loved the fair circuit. Who could pass up elephant ears for London?" Her expression turned serious again. "Anyway, nothing certain yet. Still in the thinking stage. But don't you think he's ready to wow 'em in Europe. It's the inevitable next step." Jill's voice held a hint of a plea for Sarah Ann's approval.

"You would know better than me, Jill," Sarah Ann conceded. "Have you run this past Arliss?" she asked. "He's a pretty good weathervane for these kinds of tours." Jill looked away to avoid answering. "What if the album doesn't do as well as we hope?" Sarah Ann asked.

Jill's face visibly tightened at the question. She scrutinized the phone on the desk as if she was seeing it for the first time. "The album is a killer. You've heard the songs," she added almost reproachfully. "It launches in two weeks. European concerts will be the ideal follow-up. Huge for Jared." She looked at Sarah Ann, a faint smile spreading her lips. "And big bucks for us as well," she added.

Sarah Ann sat back in her chair and considered what she had just heard and what had not yet been said. There was a tone of unreasonableness in Jill's defense of her plan. Her fingers tapped nervously on her unopened daily calendar. She was not acting like the woman Sarah Ann had come to know since joining Edgerton Group. That Jill had a pragmatic business mind which insightfully digested every morsel of an idea or problem, and carefully considered its viability or solution. The woman sitting across from her now seemed steered by emotions, not feasibility or common sense.

"Jill," she began softly, as if her words might awaken a demon she did not want to disturb, "have you really considered the timing for this." Jill looked up as Sarah Ann gathered the courage to suggest. "Or, is this a chance to be with Jared with an ocean separating him from LouAnn and Willow?"

Jill flung her head back, the "No" hissed from her throat sounding like a far-off wolf howl. Her face reddened as she sprang out of her chair, her hands gripping the side of the desk. "How dare you!" she responded in a strangled whisper, her lips quivering in anger.

Sarah Ann was startled by the vehemence in Jill's response and brutal anger in the eyes that looked across at her. "I told you I would end it with Jared. And I did." She spewed the words at Sarah Ann like sparks from a fire fanned by air. "What happened—happened. It's over," she repeated, and then slumped back into her chair, the stark anger of a moment ago replaced by a petulance that prefaced her next words. "Are you going to make me spend the rest of my life serving penance for what happened between Jared and me?"

Sarah Ann leaned in toward the desk. She wanted to walk around the desk and take Jill in her arms and calm the storm between them. But she knew from Jill's reaction her words had wounded deeply. "I'm sorry for upsetting you. You owe me no explanation, Jill."

There was no response. Sarah Ann rose slowly and crossed toward the doorway. Remorse pulled at her every fiber. She had never seen Jill so instantly angry. In all the time they had worked together, there had been few cross word between them. She turned and looked back into the anger still clouding Jill's face. "I was out of line to question your motivation. If you think the Europe concerts are the next step for Jared, I will support and help you in any way I can."

As Sarah Ann sat back down behind her own desk, she knew instinctively the words that had fired such anger in Jill had also touched on the truth of her motivation. A burst dam of regret and dismay flooded through her. She had always dreaded confrontation, with her mother, with John, with Bobby Ray Kendal, even her children when they were young; with anyone about anything. Yet, when she had been forced into confrontations that ruthlessly upended her life, she was the one left wronged by the truth; John Boswell's infidelity which he finally admitted before demanding a divorce; Bobby Ray Kendal's incompetence and duplicity which he blamed on her; even her children's anger directed at her over the divorce until they were seasoned enough by life to admit they had been in denial of their father's actions. From deep within her rose a sense of foreboding that permeated through her whole being. It was a palpable fear—fear that the truth with which she confronted Jill was going to end the same way.

Sarah Ann knew Jill's decision to launch an overseas tour for Jared portended problems far beyond anything they had dealt with at Edgerton Group. And clearly Jill expected to travel with Jared. *That had disaster written all over it,* she concluded mentally. Somehow, she must dissuade Jill from going. But how? Jill had shepherded Jared on his first county fair circuit when he was easy to work with and eager to do whatever was suggested. His meteoric success had changed all that. She must accept that and be prepared to deal with whatever happens. *A pragmatic approach was needed,* she reasoned silently. It also left Sarah Ann feeling as if she had just been kicked in the stomach.

Chapter 18

He drew his fingers along the knife's newly sharpened edge, satisfied. The time was nearing. With a deepening frown, he pulled the crumpled handwritten response from his billfold and read it again. He hadn't really expected to hear from the rotten bastard personally. But there it was, dismissing his threats to reveal his alcoholic mother to the National Enquirer. And worse, threatening to turn his letters over to the cops. *Sonofabitch!* He was just mean enough and selfish enough to do it.

That threat—to involve the cops had put an end to his writing any more letters. He slipped the letter into a narrow box, along with the knife, and pushed it under the seat of his pick-up. He hadn't asked for *that* much money. Enough maybe to buy a new pick-up. And maybe fix up his trailer. He spit tobacco juice so violently it landed several feet away as he stepped out of the battered truck and walked into the convenience store.

He waved to the man behind the counter as he headed for the magazine rack. His eyes lighted on one with a big home on the cover, *a two-story job with a big, wide front porch like that house with them two porches and lots of pillars in Gone with the Wind—that Tara place,* he recalled as he flipped to the story inside.

It showed pictures of a farm with rolling pastures and several horses standing at the white board fence that seemed to stretch for miles. A hundred acres the article said. And there was a picture of Jared looking like he was king of the world from atop a horse. *Living big, the bastard, sure as hell! Well, there was more than one way to skin a cat,* he thought viciously.

~

Jared stood by the side of the bed and pulled the zipper of his jeans up with an angry jerk and yanked the black T-shirt over his head before sitting down on the bed to pull on his socks and boots. Jill was being a bitch about the European concerts. She had argued it might be best to postpone the tour six months. She had even suggested Sarah Ann could accompany him. No way was Sarah Ann going to be over there with him and not Jill. On that he had been abusively adamant. He ended the argument that went back and forth for nearly an hour by throwing Jill on the bed and telling her to shut up while he thrust himself inside her. Only when he collapsed onto her did he feel the wetness of tears on her cheek. His remorse had been instant and genuine. He began softly kissing her cheeks and eyes and then her mouth.

"Don't cry, baby. I didn't mean to hurt you." And he heard himself say the words for the first time, "You know how much I love you, baby."

The rigidness of her body seemed to slowly melt away as he moved his lips down her neck to her breasts and gently suckled each one until the nipples were taut in his mouth as his hand slowly moved downward. He felt her hips arch as she reached a peak of climax soon after he began his soft manipulation. Through the next hour of love making she had been silent until she turned in his arms and whispered in a voice that sounded more like a plea than a question—had he really meant what he said earlier? His response had been to cover her mouth in a long kiss and bring her to another shuttering climax.

Had he meant it? It was not a question he could answer, even to himself. Jill was the first woman who had assuaged his strong sexual drive, and she did it in ways he found endlessly erotic. In a rare moment of contemplation, he passively wondered if sexual attraction equaled love. If sex was an ultimate act of love then, he concluded, there was at least a part of him that loved Jill.

He stood up as he heard the shower come on in the adjacent bathroom. On any other day he would be in there with her, his hands moving over her wet nakedness. Sex in the shower had become almost a ritual ending to a night of lovemaking. He felt a sudden visceral resentment that Jill was now washing off all scent of him. He knew he still smelled of her, something he admitted was pleasurable. And, what the hell! LouAnn wouldn't notice anyway. He could shower when he got back to the farm.

A new burst of anger flamed as he grabbed his leather jacket from the chair near the door remembering what had triggered the long argument last night. Sarah Ann, he thought fiercely, was meddling where she didn't belong. It was Sarah Ann, Jill had said, who cautioned against leaving on a several-week tour with his wife expecting their second child. How would it look to his fans?

"Who gives a shit what his fans said," he had flung back, *"as long as they bought his CDs and downloaded his music."* And the London promoter had assured them the concert tour would be a sellout. The concert tour would go as planned. It didn't matter how pig-headed Sarah Ann might be. LouAnn would stay home, leaving nothing to impede his soaring career or his affair with Jill. He felt a flush of satisfaction as he flung the door open and slammed it shut.

Jill heard the door close as the pulsating shower rinsed the soap from her thin back. The long curve of her vertebrae was clearly outlined, a visible confirmation of the weight she had shed since the onset of the affair with Jared. It wasn't that she had purposely cut down on her food intake, but rather she had to admit she was driving herself at a more frenetic pace. She had always been self-driven. It was what was demanded to reach the summit of the Music City Everest and the rarified air of success she now breathed. Her dreams could just as easily have fallen into the crevasse of failure, where so many Nashville ambitions ended.

But there was an overdrive that propelled her pace in recent months—Jared. Love had proved to be a potent accelerant. He had said he loved her for the first time. The thrill of that stirred inside her only to vanish as she remembered him atop her thrusting again and again, evoking a hurt that even the word love could not vanquish. She winced at the pain of his act and his anger. What was it she did to provoke such a violent reaction in him? It had happened before.

He was always sorry. His apologetic tenderness later proved that.

She threw the towel aside and looked at herself in the wide mirror above the double vanity. It was like viewing herself for the first time. With the lightness of a feather, her fingers traced over her gaunt cheeks and down the top of her arms that now appeared almost spindly. Her hands moved to her breasts. They looked not much larger now than when she was a teenager.

She lifted her chin and shook off the self-repudiation rising like bile within her. Thin was good. Her long legs were more flattering on a slimmer torso. What the hell—better thin than the opposite. And she could always have a breast implant. *Something to consider* she thought as she ran her hands over her flat stomach and the hip bones that now stood like sharp peaks above her long legs. "You don't look like a survivor from a concentration camp, at least not yet," she announced to her reflection with relief as she turned away.

Jill slipped into a sheer dressing gown and headed toward the bedroom. A long day of coordinating plans for the European concert schedule lay ahead and the thought of that sent a spear of new excitement slicing through her psyche. She had conquered Nashville's Everest. She could overcome whatever Sarah Ann or Arliss or LouAnn or anyone else might put in the way of her being with Jared on the European tour.

Jill was at her desk talking with the London promoter about venue arrangements when she looked up as Sarah Ann passed by her door and waved cheerily, mouthing "Good Morning" as she headed to her own office. Jill felt a small measure of stress dissolve within her. At least Sarah Ann seemed to be in good spirits. That would help. The question of the European tour had to be settled today. The tour was going ahead with or without her partner's approval.

Sarah Ann was nearly finished emailing suggested changes to a contract for another budding young talent Edgerton Group had just signed when Jill slipped into her office and took a seat across from her.

"Catch you in the middle of something?" There was a forced lightness etched in Jill's words.

"Nope!" Sarah Ann replied over her shoulder as she waited for a paper still wending its way through the fax on her printer. "Just sending the additions to Stella Wayne's contract to John."

"Think she's as good as I do?"

"She may never be a Jared Parson." Sarah Ann shrugged her shoulders as she placed the final paper on top of the stack and quickly stapled them. "Who knows? She could come close." Stella Wayne was so far exceeding their expectations. Sarah Ann swung around from the credenza behind her desk and smiled across at Jill. "What's up? You look like a cat that just swallowed a mouse."

Jill laughed, but her gelled finger nails continued tapping nervously on the chair arms. Sarah Ann had a gift for relieving awkward moments. "I talked to Jared last night."

"Good. What did he say?" asked Sarah Ann expectantly.

Jill hesitated for a long moment before the words rushed out. "He won't budge, Sarah Ann," and added, "He won't postpone the concerts. And he's insisting I come along. He said as much as he likes you, he feels more comfortable with me handling things over there. He's really adamant about it."

Sarah Ann searched her partner's face introspectively. "I think I already knew that, Jill." She sighed and leaned back in her chair looking beyond Jill to the open doorway and the deserted hallway. "But thank you for making an effort to dissuade him." Her face brightened into another smile. "Now I guess we just have to close ranks and make it a concert tour to rival Paul McCartney."

Jill had expected a confrontation with Sarah Ann. Relief washed over her like a waterfall with her partner's response. "I'm already working on it."

Jill stood up quickly to leave. At the doorway she turned and looked back at Sarah Ann who sat with her head resting on hands folded above her steepled arms.

"You've made losing a gall bladder so worth it," Jill remarked, then turned and hurried back to her office. Sarah Ann knew when Jill lobbed a compliment. She felt a sudden rush of affection for her hard-nosed and sometimes aloof partner. The phone rang, startling her out of the moment of reverie. It was Hemming.

"Got a call from our boy. He wants me to work up arrangements for songs he's planning for his European concerts. Is it a go?" The question was asked blandly, without reproach.

"Yes," Sarah Ann replied. There was a long hesitation from the other end.

"Okay, girl. I'll get cracking on it." Another long hesitation. "Are you going along?"

"No."

"Then I guess that leaves you holding down the fort. Suit you?"

"With you at my side, Sir Arliss, we shall conquer all that rises before us!"

"Going Elizabethan on me, are you?" he laughed. Playing off something Boswell once wrote, he said, "*We will just be a nest of singing birds.*"

Sarah Ann was always pleasantly surprised by his wide knowledge of literature. She prefaced her rejoinder with a laugh. "Or as that sauerkraut-munching Reinhold Niebuhr so aptly wrote, *God give us grace to accept with serenity the things that cannot be changed.*"

"Or, as Shakespeare once wrote…"

"Oh, give it a rest, Hemming. You'll wear out Bartlett's Famous Quotations, not to mention your own mind. Bye!"

The receiver went dead at the other end and she hung up the phone still smiling. Arliss Hemming always seemed to have that effect on her. *How could Winnifred not know what she was missing?* Sarah Ann mused silently.

She was scrolling through her calendar for the week ahead when the phone rang again. It was Viola announcing "da massa" was on the line. John Boswell's deep voice said, "Good Morning."

"Good morning. To what do I owe this pleasure?" Sarah Ann regretted the words as soon as they were past her lips. She still felt immensely awkward at times in her interactions with John, even when it was only business. He seemed to know it and often showed little mercy for her reticence.

"Pleasure! Now that's a word to build a conversation on."

"As long as it's just conversation, build away."

"Touché!"

Sarah Ann felt a deep blush break out on her cheeks. It was the first time she could recall such banter with her former husband since the divorce. She was glad they were telephone lines apart so he could not witness her reaction. She could hear a pleasant chuckle at the other end. "So, our boy is headed to merry ole England with Jill, not you?"

"Yes. It was just confirmed for me this morning."

"Not good is how I'm reading your voice."

"I fear you are right, but only time will tell."

"Anyway, Jill is sending me all the particulars by messenger. I've cleared my calendar so I can review the information and draw up the contracts. But I would like to go over them with you, sans Jill. You available tomorrow evening?"

"Yes."

"My office—or yours? But I would like Jill not to know we are meeting until you and I discuss everything."

"I suppose." She let the silence linger between them. He sensed her reluctance and his voice came across to fill the vacuum. "I know you discuss everything with Jill—and should. She's your partner. But let's be frank. I think as the attorney for your firm, we should take a first look before I go over everything with her. She does have some emotional pull at work here."

He seemed to be telling her he knew of Jill's affair with Jared even though she could not imagine how he had come by that knowledge. "This way we may be able to anticipate any changes she or Jared want…" His voice trailed off and she knew he was reluctant to say they could demand changes that would not be in the best interest of the firm or her.

Sarah Ann knew instinctively John was right. Yet, if she agreed, it would not be without feeling she was being disloyal to her business partner. There had always been an unspoken agreement between them—to share everything involving their business and take no major action without the other's input. She would be breaking that unspoken bond by agreeing to John's terms, something she had never done until now. But she knew she must.

"I should have everything drawn up by late tomorrow afternoon. How about around six? My office would probably be better,"

"Sounds good," she replied, knowing immediately it was not a decision she felt comfortable with on more than one level.

"Later." That abrupt word had always substituted in John's vernacular for goodbye.

Chapter 19

Shortly before six the next evening it was with no small amount of trepidation Sarah Ann approached the front door of the downtown bank building. The butterflies roiling in her stomach would be worse if not for Sam. It was the same Sam, ever smiling, who greeted her at the front desk when she came through the large glass revolving door.

"Mr. Boswell mentioned you'd be coming Miz Boswell. It sure is good to see you after all this time." His dark face beamed with pleasure as he came out from behind the circular counter of the welcome desk. "I think I need a hug, Miz Boswell."

"It's so good to see you again, Sam," she said as he wrapped his beefy arms around her and she planted a quick kiss on his thick cheek. Aside from a wider girth, he had not changed in the five or so years since she had last seen him, which had been often before her divorce.

Sam Henry was born with the frame of a Sumo wrestler, but even on the football field as a center at the University of Tennessee, he was ever the happy warrior. When he failed to make the National Football League draft, Sam Henry simply chucked his dream of football glory and riches and with the same good humor with which he approached life in general, he chose to become a Nashville police officer.

After a quarter century of doing his part to keep the drivers and the criminals under control who came within the benevolent borders of his patrol territory, he had traded his blue uniforms for the brown and tan ones provided him by the bank. With the new uniforms came more regular hours and a weekly paycheck that came reasonably close to his police pay. He left the police department with his pension and a 9mm Glock and holster, now anchored on a leather belt around his waist.

Sarah Ann first encountered Sam shortly after he joined the bank and immediately fell under the spell of his genial nature and often in those early encounters, envied his seemingly endless good spirits. She wondered then, as now, if he ever felt down. She doubted it.

"I didn't expect you to be working the evening shift. What a nice surprise," said Sarah Ann as she signed the obligatory check-in sheet.

"Just fillin' in for another guy on vacation this week, Miz Boswell. Back on days next week."

"How are Loretta and Sam, Jr.?"

"Couldn't be better. Loretta's still teaching third graders and Sam, Jr. will be a senior at Vanderbilt this fall. He plans to go to medical school after graduation." The pride was evident in his voice.

"Med school. That's great, Sam." She laughed and added. "Get ready for a big drain on your savings account."

"You got that right, Miz Boswell." His laugh seemed to rise from deep down, split his wide lips in a broad smile and radiate up to his eyes. "You may see me on double shifts here come this fall." He was still chortling when the elevator arrived with a chiming ding to take her to John's office on the eighteenth floor.

Sarah Ann took a deep breath and entered the office through the unlocked front door and glanced around. The elegant reception area that she had decorated shortly after John relocated here was largely unchanged. A sixteen-by-twelve silk rug they purchased on their first trip to China remained in place between two high-backed Henredon wing chairs flanking an ornate table. A lamp on a teak base with an intricate oriental design around its glass middle sat on the table. She remembered spotting it in a little antique store in Franklin. Across from the chairs was the antique Queen Anne couch she discovered in the back of the same store, dusty and forlorn, stacked with other items waiting for display space on shelves and cases. She had the couch refinished and then recovered in a muted sapphire fabric—a fabric that complemented the stripped design in the chairs. A wide, tall mahogany breakfront dominated the back wall. It's shelves were filled with leather bound books and intricately carved jade figurines and colorful porcelain vases.

Sarah Ann's mind flashed back to that first trip to the Far East nearly two decades ago. She and John had boarded the first-class cabin for the trip home bent over by backpacks and pulling bulging carry-on luggage filled with many of their purchases now being displayed. The only clothing in the bags was used to wrap around the more fragile pieces. She loved the reception area after its completion and still found it just as much to her liking now. Whatever else may have been lacking in her marriage to John, it certainly was not her good taste and skill as an interior decorator.

"Hasn't changed much in here."

Sarah Ann started at the sound of John's voice behind her and turned quickly. He was standing in the entryway next to the receptionist's desk which led to a wide corridor with offices of attorneys and paralegals scattered down both sides. As the founding partner of Boswell, Jardine & Boswell, she knew his office was the large one at the end of the shortest corridor.

"Sorry to startle you. I've been keeping an eye out for you and thought I heard the front door open."

"Tis me," she said, smiling awkwardly and feeling the flutter of butterflies again.

"Come on back." He waited for her to catch up before walking beside her toward the double stained-glass doors that welcomed clients into his office. The doors were striking in their brilliant hues of sapphire, teal green and a variety of blending colors detailing a silk tree and several birds sitting on its gently curving branches on each side. Sarah Ann could not restrain herself from reaching out and momentarily tracing the raised glass etching of a Yellow Finch sitting on a branch. She had worked weeks with a stained-glass artist to finalize the design.

"This must have been our Chinese period," she teased as he ushered her to a chair in front of the ebony desk with thick ornately carved legs they had spotted in a shop in Xian. John had bartered for several minutes, at one point walking away, only to be followed by the frantically waving merchant who finally agreed to John's price.

After arrangements were made to ship the desk, a chair and several other items, they had left feeling jubilant and then joined hundreds of other eager tourists to view the magnificent Terra Cotta Warriors.

"It seemed to be a good period that has stuck with us," he replied mildly as he walked around the wide desk. "Everybody here likes the motif. Isn't that how you women describe such handiwork? Or is a better word, ambience?"

"That's as good a word as any, I suppose." Sarah Ann felt a small pull of first wife glee, wondering if Angeline had wanted to make changes in the office and John had refused. She felt a flush of guilty triumph at the thought.

John picked up a stack of folders on his desk and came around to sit in the chair across from her, pulling it so close she could smell his subtle after shave lotion, the same richly masculine scent he had used for years. "I've included the changes you suggested in some of the contracts," he said, referring to a conversation they had had earlier in the afternoon. He handed her the folders. "The changes are on the pages marked with the yellow tabs. Everything else is pretty standard."

Sarah Ann opened the top folder and leafed through the multi-paged contracts one-by-one reading the changes denoted by the tabs. When she looked up, John appeared to be studying her closely and again her butterflies fluttered wildly.

"This all looks fine, at least at first glance," she said, training her eyes back on the open folder in her lap and forcing her voice to sound business-like. She felt like a deer in front of headlights and wanted to bolt for the door. But she remained planted. "I think the changes you've made are needed and will certainly close some glaring loop holes."

"Good." He took the folders from her lap and placed them back on the edge of his desk.

"Sorry," John said, as he turned back toward her. "I seem to have forgotten the manners my mother drilled into me at a very early age. Can I get you a cup of coffee? Or better yet, a glass of wine? After all, you were holding on your lap a *lot* to celebrate."

"A glass of wine would be lovely..." Sarah Ann regretted the words as soon as they were spoken. She glanced hastily at her watch not really seeing the time displayed on the gold Rolex, the one John had given her their last Christmas together; the same month he met Angeline.

A stab of hurt shot through her like a spear. "Oh wait, Johnny." She hesitated; momentarily embarrassed at using the name she called him in their more familiar days. "I didn't realize how late it's getting." She suddenly had no idea what time it was or how long she'd been there. "Anyway, I'm driving."

"Sarah Ann," his voice sounded so smooth and persuasive, "you've only been here an hour. Take a moment to share some wine. Let's toast your success. Please."

"Of course." She felt herself sinking back in the chair. "Thank you… that's very kind." The butterflies were rampaging. Sarah Ann felt a flush drape over her face as John walked over to the large credenza behind his desk. He had his back to her as he pulled a bottle of wine from a hidden cooler, and two wine glasses from a neat row hanging in the section next to the cooler.

"Anyway, if one glass of wine impairs you enough to be arrested and sent to the hoosegow overnight," he chuckled, as he walked back toward her with the goblets, "you know where to call for a good attorney to spring you." She remembered his laugh, husky and merry, a laugh that she could never resist joining in with.

He handed her the wine. "I'll drink to that," she said, raising her glass to cover the tension she felt at his closeness.

"Sarah Ann, let's drink to more than that." He reached out his hand and he guided her to her feet. "Let's toast your success." Even standing, he still stood several inches above her and his eyes locked on hers. "You are a great success. I don't think you realize how much you are respected in Nashville business circles. If it weren't for you, Jill would still be signing opening acts for state fairs." He raised his glass. "To you and your continued success."

Their goblets touched lightly, and each lifted the pale wine to their lips. Then John bent down and kissed her lightly on the right cheek. "You deserve all that you've worked for."

Sarah Ann felt a flush returning to her cheeks as she sat back down.

"It's nice to see a woman who can still blush at a compliment." His smile was warm, tempering the hint of genial taunting in his words.

"It's the Beth March side of me," she said, referring to one of her favorite characters in *Little Women*. "But thank you." She looked down at the glass she held to hide her embarrassment, studying the tiny bubbles floating to the top of the white wine like miniature balloons trying to escape into the air. She swished the wine gently out of an old habit and lifted it to her lips. "The wine is delicious, John. It reminds me of that wine in Australia…" Her words tapered off remembering the wine they both loved from a small vineyard in the Barossa Valley region near Adelaide.

"You remember well," he replied, bringing the goblet to his lips, his eyes never leaving her face. "It is Australian. The same brand we brought back from our trip there. I keep it stocked here at the office. It can now be ordered on Amazon," he added.

The wine warmed all the way down, and she felt some of the tension melting away as she recalled driving through the sweeping countryside of the Barossa Valley, its hills undulating with neat rows of grape vines. They had stopped for lunch at a small vineyard and the couple that owned it had given them a tour through the winery operation, past the processing area into a shallow rock cave where giant barrels were stacked five deep aging in a constant temperature that only Mother Nature could provide. The constraints of the cave size were what kept the vineyard from expanding the owners had explained. "Only so much room for aging the stuff, you know," she remembered the husband saying.

"But we like our smallness," the wife said. "It suits us."

They spent most of the afternoon visiting with the friendly couple and purchased two cases of a white and a case of robust red wine before reluctantly parting and heading back to Adelaide, both slightly tipsy from the several glasses of wine imbibed during their stay at the winery. It was well past nightfall when they arrived at their quaint hotel. They had made love on a bed that had an innerspring mattress and laughed at what sounds the guests in the room below them must be hearing.

How could they have been so happy? What had gone wrong in

such a short span of time after they returned home? She knew the answer—Angeline. Sadness descended on Sarah Ann, a sadness so palpable she feared it showed on her face.

"A penny?" John asked, interrupting her reverie.

"Sorry, the price has gone up. Inflation you know."

He smiled at her response. "You were far away, Sarah Ann Boswell."

"I'm back. Just enjoying the good wine," and tipped her glass to him.

They sat quietly, sipping the remaining wine. When her glass was empty he reached over and took it from her hands. "Can I get you another?"

"No thank you, John." She reached for the stack of duplicate contracts neatly divided into folders that he had prepared for her. "I really must be going."

"I'll see you out." He reached for her coral Coach bag on the floor beside her chair and slipped the strap up her arm onto her shoulder. It blended with the bright floral ankle-length skirt and coral silk blouse she was wearing. As he punched the call button for the elevator, she turned to face him and said, "Thank you, Johnny…for the wine and working up these contracts so expeditiously."

"You're welcome."

The chrome elevator doors opened slowly. As she moved to enter the elevator, he grasped her arms gently and kissed her on the cheek before letting her slip into the elevator.

"Did I tell you how lovely you look tonight?"

"No…but thank you." She could feel her cheeks turning red as the elevator doors were closing.

"You're blushing again." The last thing she heard was his soft laughter as the elevator began its descent.

Chapter 20

"Oh my God!" It was all Willie Dell could think to say.

"He could not have been nicer," Sarah Ann said, summing up her meeting with John as she tossed the dish towel to Willie Dell.

"He actually kissed you on the cheek twice?"

"By actual count!"

"I wish I could have been there to see both." A wicked smile crept across Willie Dell's lips. "Better still, I wish the ever-lovely Angeline could have been there to see that."

Sarah Ann turned away toward the sink, suddenly pensive. "No, Willie Dell. I may get some compliments from him, but she has his heart."

"Maybe; maybe not?"

"No maybes. Anyway, thanks for helping with the clean-up."

"It was my turn. But then, I used to get a pass before women's lib."

Sarah Ann turned back toward him and stuck out her tongue. "Nice try. But I remember when you were helping your mom with the dishes. That may've been before the Mayflower landed." She squealed and jumped sideways as he flipped her with the towel he had been twisting.

"What's going on in there you two?" It was Angela's voice coming from the front parlor.

"Hurry up. I need booze," Della Sue shouted.

Willie Dell held the door leading from the kitchen for Sarah Ann to pass and then walked down the hallway beside her. Sarah Ann caught his arm as they approached the wide foyer. "Now remember, not a word to the others, please."

"You know me better than that, baby sister," he smiled, patting her hand. "I'll take the right turn to the study and get the port." Sarah Ann turned left into the spacious parlor where their friends were gathered. "The booze is on the way," she announced.

Willie Dell came in shortly balancing the tray with a Waterford decanter filled with a favorite brand of port and five small matching goblets. "I passed Home Economics with an A. And I've been promised extra credit for serving this after dinner delight." He placed the tray on a side table with a marble top and poured an even amount into each small goblet before handing one to each of his fellow Prayer Group members.

"And mind you, there is brutal torture followed by certain death if any of that port splashes on my new couches," warned Sarah Ann, referring to the off-white couches she had recently purchased as part of her redecoration of the downstairs rooms. The elbowed couches artfully defused the more colorfully covered side chairs and window treatments.

"Now there's a *not-so-veiled* threat if ever I heard one," drawled Jeanne Marie, feigning a fearful expression as she started to lift the port to her lips, albeit carefully.

"Before we drink—a toast to our hostess—superlative as always." Willie Dell tilted his glass in salute to Sarah Ann before taking his seat in one of two wing back chairs on either side of the table with the port tray.

"I'll drink to that and to the fabulous new look of this room," praised Della Sue. "You've gone from post-Civil War chic to absolutely beautiful. What an elegant update." Angela and Jeanne Marie added their compliments.

"Well, I owe a lot of these choices to Willie Dell who went with me for the final selections."

"That's only because you women can never make up your minds." His words were met with hoots and boos.

"The last thing I would take you for, Willie Dell Winstead, is a chauvinist pig." Angela's face wrinkled into a faux frown of rebuke.

"Since I have been associating primarily with four women since shortly after the change from diapers to training pants, I'll put that accusation right up there with being a eunuch or being gay. I had to marry the one woman who gave banshees a good name to disprove the latter. Since I fortunately failed to impregnate Beverly, I have yet to dispel the former." He took a slow sip of the rich port before adding, "Whether or not I'm a eunuch is still up for debate."

"All right!" exclaimed Della Sue, "I know just the way to dispel that ugly rumor. Drop your drawers." Over the eruption of laughter, Willie Dell jumped to his feet and started to unbuckle his belt.

"Stop—wait! No drawer dropping 'til we get a measuring tape," gasped Jeanne Marie, holding her sides as she laughed even harder at the sight of Willie Dell who was now swinging his hips provocatively and humming a strip tease tune. "Sarah Ann, GPS me to your tool box."

"Never mind, Sarah Ann, I carry just such an item in my purse." Angela jumped up to get her purse. It sat beside two other purses on an ornate round mahogany table Sarah Ann had recently acquired for the wide foyer.

Enough, y'all. Everyone back in your seats," Sarah Ann loudly ordered over the clapping and Jean Marie's shrill whistles. "How can I avoid indigestion when you have me laughing so hard?"

"I carry a roll of Maalox," replied a straight-faced Angela. "They're right beside the measuring tape." Another eruption of laughter.

"Stop it now! I mean it y'all. Keep encouraging him and next thing you know he'll be trying out for *Dancing with the Stars*."

Jeanne Marie's whistles hushed, and Willie Dell bowed with a flourish of his right arm before buckling his belt and plopping back in his chair. "Anyway," he said to Angela with a droll upturn of his lips, "your tape measure would probably prove inadequate for the job."

"Who needs a cabin boy when we have you, Willie Dell," Della Sue piped in.

Sarah Ann tapped gingerly on the table to get attention. "Which brings us back to the subject of tonight's gathering—our upcoming cruise. Our travel planner extraordinaire, Jeanne Marie, has the floor.

Jeanne Marie whipped a blue cloth carryall bag from beside the couch where she sat. It was emblazoned with Franklin Luxury Travel in bright red lettering. "A gift from our friends to moi. Don't be jealous. There's one for each of you." She started handing a bag to each of the others. "Della Sue, peep inside yours," she said, exaggerating her words. "They threw in a little something extra just for you, darlin'. They're massaging condoms to keep you happy and safe, all at the same time."

Another burst of laughter as Della Sue waved the little red carton around. "Thank you, sweetie. A more thoughtful gift I can't remember," she drawled. "The happy part I'm looking forward to. Nature has pretty well taken care of any worry over safety concerns."

"Please, ladies. No menopause recounting tonight," pleaded Willie Dell.

"Oh, Willie Dell." Jeanne Marie raised her eyebrows and shook her head before a sly smile broadened her lips. "You haven't looked inside your little goody bag yet."

He looked inside. "If what I think I see in here is what it is, it's staying put right here in good ole Franklin."

"Over my dead body," threatened Della Sue. "Out with it!"

"Careful what you wish for. Beau would be in my eternal debt."

"Out with it." This time it was Sarah Ann making the demand. Willie Dell held up the bikini style Speedo and a pair of boxer shorts made from cotton plastered with small hearts complete with chubby cupids. "Thank you, Jeanne Marie, my travel wardrobe is complete."

"Okay, enough of this," ordered Jeanne Marie. "Here's the suggested revised plan for our week together. We leave from beautiful Vancouver, British Columbia one month from today and will spend a blissful week sailing the inland passage of America's last frontier aboard the merry ship M/S Amsterdam with a side trip to Anchorage and Denali National Park." She looked around at the startled faces staring back at her, except for the two who already knew the destination.

"Amsterdam," said Della Sue with rising wariness in her voice. "I don't recall that being one of the Carnival fun ships."

"Not even close, but the Amsterdam does come complete with cabin boys. Only on the Amsterdam they're called cabin stewards."

"You say Vancouver…and last frontier," injected a skeptical Angela. "As best I recall there were no cruise ships leaving for the Caribbean from British Columbia last time I checked. Or is my geography directionally impaired?"

"Give that girl an A-plus for geography. We are going to Alaska," declared Jeanne Marie.

"Alaska! No way, Jeanne Marie Osborn. I want my bikini clad butt on some warm sand, not the frozen tundra." Vehemence coupled with disappointment in Della Sue's voice.

"I know guys." It was Willie Dell. "It is hotter than Hades in the Caribbean in early August, not to mention its hurricane season, and Jeanne Marie had to work the trip around Sarah Ann's schedule. Flights were more convenient to the west coast."

There was silence for a moment. Then Angela blurted out, "What in the hell do you do in Alaska, build igloos with the Eskimos, swim with the whales?"

"No, silly." said Della Sue, who was sitting next to Angela and jabbed her in the ribs, "We go bear sighting and then eat salmon right out of the stream, just like the bears, before the poor fish can commit suicide after doing their duty as prodigious procreators. I saw that on the National Geographic Channel."

"It's called spawnin', darlin'," informed Angela in a professorial tone. "I saw the same show." And she added, "If I had to be a pro-digious procreator, I most certainly *would* commit suicide." She looked quizzically at Jeanne Marie, but the initial disappointment had faded from her voice.

Sarah Ann looked around at her friends. "Look. I don't have to go. Y'all can plan a later vacation. It doesn't have to be next month." Her suggestion was met with a chorus of "No Way."

"We all go or not at all," declared Angela. "Alaska it is. Anyway, Della Sue," she said, returning the jab, "I will buy some furry ear-muffs big enough to keep your butt warm while you sun bathe on the tundra."

"I didn't know earmuffs come in butt sizes, dearie." Della Sue blinked her eyes at Angela. "I'm truly dazzled by the extent of your knowledge of such fashion accessories."

Jeanne Marie ignored her and said, "So if everyone's on board with our dream trip…?" Jeanne Marie left the question hanging as she glanced around at the faces around her. "Oookay! Then I'll make the final arrangements Monday."

"Do you need us to write you a check tonight?" asked Angela.

"No, actually…" Jeanne Marie hesitated, glancing over at Sarah Ann sitting beside her. "I forgot to mention. No checks needed. Sarah Ann is paying the entire tab for the trip, including airfare to and from, and our deluxe penthouse suites."

"Not gonna happen, baby sister. Very generous of you, but way too much," protested Willie Dell.

"I agree with you, Willie Dell," echoed Angela, "even though Charlie's parsimonious accountant's heart would go into cardiac arrest if he heard me saying this."

"Par-sa what!" exclaimed Della Sue.

"It was one of Bill O'Reilley's words of the day, darlin'. Or think of it this way. Parsimonious is to Charlie what livin' like a monk is to Beau."

"Well! No need for Mr. Webster when you put it that way."

Willie Dell picked up his glass of remaining port. "If this is how you want to spend some of the millions you'll be making from Jared Parson's upcoming tour, then we promise to be the most grateful business write-offs you'll ever have." He raised his crystal goblet to Sarah Ann. "To the beautiful and generous founding member of the Prayer Group."

"Here, here," chorused the voices around him as they raised their glasses to Sarah Ann.

Willie Dell set his empty goblet on the tray. "Now let's say a word of thanks and then get on with the business of entreating whatever else we want the Almighty to do for us this month.

Chapter 21

It was money Jared Parson had on his mind as he lay on the long soft leather couch in Jill's apartment. There was a private entrance he used out of view of anyone in the office below. With Sarah Ann gone their privacy was insured. She was the only one ever allowed to come up to Jill's apartment using the outside stairs.

Jill was tucked in beside him, her warm bare back against his chest, his knees bent into hers. By her measured breathing, he could tell she was asleep as he aimlessly stroked one breast. Even asleep she responded to his touch. The nipple his fingers gently circled firmed under his persistent stroking.

She had topped off their coupling by telling him advance ticket sales indicated a record gross per concert since tickets went on sale two days ago. The London concert was nearing a sellout. The other five concerts were not far behind. "A September to remember" Jill had defined it. The thought of such success stoked his senses even more than the afterglow of sex.

Net sales of tickets, she assured him, could set a new record for a country music star. It would crown his status among his peers. Money was the truest measure of success, he reasoned. As he savored his success, he had to acknowledge the burn within him to achieve even more—the status of legend. He breathed deeply as if to underscore his inexorable future. The money would keep flowing in with each new song and each new album. But it was no longer only money that drove him. That he would admit. It was fame that now fired his ambition even more.

Jill finally stirred in response to his stroking fingers. The burn of his thoughts transferred to his genitals. He turned Jill in his arms and kissed her drooping eyelids. Her eyes opened slowly, and he kissed the tip of her nose, then traced his lips down to hers.

~

Sarah Ann sat in a chair on the veranda outside her room watching the round of the sun's head begin to lift above the high slopes of mountains to the East. It looked like the top of an orange, gaily festooned with pink ribbons the color of cotton candy rising above the grayish green of the distant timber lines. She was the only one awake to view the start of the day from their hotel overlooking Vancouver Harbor. They had spent the whole of yesterday touring quaint Victoria Island and Butchart Gardens. *If ever she had a soul garden, it would be Butchart,* she thought whimsically. They had spent more than four hours meandering through the lush botanical beauty of the extensive gardens and still regretted there was not enough time there.

For dinner they chose a small French restaurant in Victoria recommended by Sarah Ann's daughter, Anna Leigh and her husband, who had vacationed in British Columbia. The Prayer Group was not disappointed, lingering over a second bottle of a delightful California merlot. It was the surprising suggestion of the sommelier from an extensive wine list proffering many higher priced selections.

Despite the late hour they had arrived back at the hotel, Sarah Ann found herself awake at the usual five-thirty, in ample time for the glorious Canadian sunrise to which she was being treated at this moment. As much as she loved the three women and one man which whom she was traveling, Sarah Ann cherished this brief period of solitude.

In the nearly four years since she had joined Edgerton Group she could probably count on both hands the number of days she had been away from the office. Travel always involved business. In the hectic week before leaving for this vacation she had versed her assistant on everything to expect or to cover during her absence. Natalie seemed always to be one step ahead of her as they reviewed the work she would be taking over. Even then Natalie had called Sarah Ann three times before the Nashville take-off and had left two call-back requests by the time they had landed in Vancouver. Sarah Ann's cell had been suspiciously silent the rest of the day. That was probably Viola Whittaker's doing. She laughed softly thinking of the devious ways Viola would find to obstruct calls to her without having to reveal the reasons to Natalie. Somehow she knew the uber-efficient Natalie would find a way to solve whatever problem Sarah Ann's absence might present. "Thank you, Viola," she whispered softly to herself.

"Who in the world are you talking to at this ungodly early hour?" Jeanne Marie's voice sounded husky with lingering sleepiness.

Sarah Ann turned toward her friend and patted the chair beside her. "Myself! Who else?"

"That's dangerous, you know, talking to yourself." Jeanne Marie wagged a warning finger at Sarah Ann as she dropped into a chair beside her. "First step toward the ole dementia ward at your friendly neighborhood nursing home."

"Well, if that's the case I'd better check in quickly. Thanks for the cheery salutation. Good morning, yourself."

"I did forget Good Morning. Sorry. Miss Manners will probably order a proper flogging now that we're in one of jolly ole England's commonwealth countries."

"Then we have no choice but to escape to Alaska."

"I believe that's on the schedule for today.

The cell phone in Sarah Ann's lap sounded the first bars of Nessun Dorma. Before she could pick it up Jeanne Ann jumped up. "I'll make coffee." She blew a kiss as she slipped back into Sarah Ann's suite.

"Hello."

"It's Jill. Did I wake you, vacation girl?"

"No. Just sitting here watching a Canadian sunrise on the balcony of our hotel which overlooks beautiful Vancouver Harbor."

"Is that in Alaska?" inquired Jill.

"Not yet. We're still in Canada. What's up?" There was a long hesitation at Jill's end before she answered. "Everything is just about set for the overseas tour." The line went quiet for a time.

"That's great," inserted Sarah Ann. "Kudos to your planning skills. Where are the final venues?"

"London to start. Then Edinburgh, Amsterdam, Stockholm, Copenhagen. We finish in Berlin.

"What about Paris?"

"Jared didn't approve the arrangements, so I dropped it."

Sarah Ann felt her anger rise instantly. Jill had not discussed this with her and she knew it would be too late now to try and schedule another concert. Jared had initially approved the Paris venue and they might face penalties for any cancellations, but she suppressed her anger and stated in a measured voice, "Our contract with Jared requires a minimum of seven concerts. If he couldn't agree on Paris, he could have selected from among at least five other choices of concert venues."

Again there was a long pause before Jill answered. "He didn't want to be gone from home so long…you know, with the new baby coming and all. He thought seven concerts was too much time away."

"Did you remind him the contract he signed calls for that number?" Sarah Ann regretted the words before she finished the sentence. And Jill's response was immediately defensive.

"We can't push him too far, Sarah Ann. He could jump ship and then where would we be?" This had become Jill's standard rejoinder of late when Sarah Ann questioned Jared's growing recalcitrance to abide by some requirements of his contract. It was ironclad. She believed John after inquiring about enforcing its provisions if Jared did indeed sign with another manager. He would lose financially, big time, John had assured her and pointed to the contract's clauses which underwrote that assurance. John had also observed it would make Jared a pariah in the tradition steeped world of country music. Loyalty carried an inestimable value along Music Row.

Sarah Ann could see no advantage in pressing her point. "I can understand his reluctance to prolong the tour, so he can get back home to LouAnn and Willow and be there when the new baby arrives," she conceded. "But that isn't the reason you called. Sorry for sidetracking you."

"Well…" Jill seemed to be searching for words and finally blurted out, "Jared wants a bigger share of the take."

Sarah Ann was thunderstruck. She and Jill had met with Jared before drawing up the contracts for the tour. He had agreed to the standard flat amount plus a share of ticket sales. Sarah Ann wanted to raise the issue of his contract terms but hesitated, fearing another counterattack from Jill. "How much more does he want?" she asked impassively.

"He says ten-percent more of gross ticket sales."

Jared had stunned Jill with that figure when they were in bed, her nakedness covered by a silk sheet, watching him pull on the personalized cowboy boots she had had made for him in Amarillo. He had quickly justified his demand by pointing out two of the concerts were sell outs already. "I'm the one busting my ass to make people want to buy tickets." He had then leaned over and kissed her, letting his lips linger while his tongue teased provocatively, and his thumb fondled a nipple through the silk sheet. "Anyway, baby, the more I make, the more we'll have in the future when it's just me and you."

She heard the door to the back stairs closing before what he said cleared the jumble of her thoughts like sunshine penetrating fog. She had never allowed herself to divine a future with Jared; only a present. Yes, he had said he loved her. But only in passing. And only once. Never until now had he intimated a future together beyond their current relationship. She had never dared reveal the depth of her own feelings for him for fear she might drive him away.

Jill had dreaded phoning Sarah Ann. What Jared was asking was excessive. The business side of her acknowledged that. But she also accepted she could not tell him no, especially now that he had attached the caveat of a future together to his demand.

"Are you serious?" Sarah Ann exclaimed. Jill could discern the thinly-veiled anger beneath the surface of her partner's retort. She had tried to brace herself for just such a reaction, but now words failed her.

Sarah Ann sensed the discomfort at the other end of the connection. It was enough to calm her furor over Jared's demand. "Jill, he isn't being reasonable. Surely you know that?"

Her question hung in the miles of space that separated them. "Let me talk with John and get him involved," Sarah Ann finally suggested, sensing that Jill was a woman made vulnerable to Jared's demands for fear of losing him. "He can deal with Jared and insulate you from what will probably be a contentious exchange, knowing Jared. Trust me. John has a way of making rejection sound not so bad after all." Before Jill could respond Sarah Ann added, "It's what we pay him to do, and it will keep you from being caught in the middle. You have enough to do coordinating all the arrangements for the tour."

Sarah Ann was making sense Jill admitted to herself. But her fear of the anger certain to erupt in Jared trumped common sense. Even more, she feared that denying him additional money would jeopardize any future with him. Such an outcome was now unthinkable. She could hear the desperation in her own voice when she suggested, "What if I waive my share of the proceeds? It might be enough to cover what Jared is asking." Jill's mind was in such chaos she could not estimate what the firm's share of the tour profits would be or if her half of those profits would even equal the ten-percent additional Jared was demanding.

Jill's proposal stunned Sarah Ann. Clearly, Jill was not thinking straight. And the only answer to Jill's irrational proposal struck Sarah Ann like an anvil to the chest. The certainty of what confronted her sent the air pouring out of her lungs. *Oh, God* she thought. *Jill had not ended the affair with Jared.* The realization of being blind to Jill's duplicity shocked her even more, leaving her chest heaving. She turned the cell phone away from her mouth so Jill could not hear her strangled breathing. Why had she been so blind to what was happening? Someone else needed to bring Jill to her senses. It was now clear to her that she could not.

Maybe Arliss could intercede. He would be reluctant, she knew, and probably decline to get involved anyway. Her thoughts rushed back to John. If she could just persuade Jill to discuss it with him, John might be able to sway her from this ruinous path. She took a deep breath and lowered the phone back to her mouth. "Why don't we let John evaluate what Jared is asking?" Sarah Ann suggested in a soft, appeasing voice. "He may have a better solution than you taking a hit financially."

Jill's voice was laced with anger when she answered. "He's a lawyer. He'll just say Jared is in the wrong and that we should hold him to the contract. "Right?"

Sarah Ann could not argue with that reasoning and instinctively knew any further argument right now would only kindle Jill's anger further. "Look Jill, if you think your proposal is the best solution then I'll accept that. If it works for you, it works for me," she offered, trying to defuse the charged conversation. "Anyway, it might save on attorney fees," she added trying to insert levity into the strained conversation.

Jill felt an immediate rush of relief. She had dreaded telling Sarah Ann of Jared's demand. Now she was being given a free hand to accept it. Suddenly, she realized Sarah Ann's income would also be affected. A nagging guilt clawed at her. Giving Jared a bigger share would reduce the share for Edgerton Group. Both Jill and Sarah Ann took an annual salary. In addition, they each took a bonus at the end of the year based upon the profits of the firm. Last year's bonus had been in the high six figures, thanks primarily to Jared's music and concert sales. He was the firm's cash cow.

Why shouldn't he have a bigger share? she silently rationalized. But then had asked herself, *Am I trying to vindicate what clearly would have risen to the level of avarice if Jared were any other talent Edgerton Group managed? But he isn't. He is our biggest client.*

Jill knew Sarah Ann was no fool and would know, or at least suspect, the reason she had been bullied into acquiescing. At that moment Jill was grateful her partner was two-thousand miles away and she was not face-to-face with Sarah Ann. And wouldn't be for at least another week. Maybe it would be enough time to find a way to close this latest fissure in their business relationship. Shame at what she had just done and what she had revealed churned in the pit of her stomach. Panic gripped her throat stifling further words. With a shaking hand her thumb pressed the disconnect button.

Chapter 22

Sarah Ann saw the disconnect notice appear on her phone and put it down on the table. The same sickening feeling engulfed her that she had felt once before—when John had announced he wanted a divorce. *Please God, this can't be happening* she moaned inwardly. She had capitulated then just as now. Why could she not stand firm? Challenge the wrong being done to her.

The faces of people who had wronged her, skewered her with hurt and humiliation, played across her memory like a never-ending reel of video tape; her father leaving one day when she was five and never returning; no goodbye hug; never a phone call; never a letter to explain why he left or even to say he still loved her, or if he had ever loved her.

John announcing late one night he was packing some clothes and would send for the rest of his things; no goodbye hug; not a word of explanation; only a certified letter several days later, signature required, and inside a several-page document stating in impersonal and pitiless legalize that masked the reasons for his departure and why he would not return. And Bobby Ray Kendall, unfurling a verbal red flag starred with all her shortcomings as executive director of his family foundation, and waving it in her face.

"Coffee?"

Sarah Ann was startled out of her gloomy reverie by Jeanne Marie's return. "Good God, girl, you look like you just lost your best friend," she said, her brow furrowing in sympathy as she handed the cup of black coffee to Sarah Ann.

Sarah Ann made a feeble attempt to smile. "Not if you still want to hold that title," she replied while lifting the steaming cup to her lips in an effort to momentarily banish the sadness she knew Jeanne Marie had so quickly perceived.

"And to hold that honor in the face of such snippy stiff competitors like my fellow travelers of the Prayer Group brings me close to a real Southern Belle swoon." Jeanne Marie took a long gulp of coffee before setting the mug down on the table and fixing her piercing scrutiny on Sarah Ann. "Don't try to hide whatever Miss "roll in the hay" was imparting was good news. I saw you on the phone. Fair warning. Your face is, and always has been your worst enemy when you attempt to fib. So spill it!"

"Has anyone told you lately how bleeping nosy you are?"

"Often, but to no avail. Spill it."

"Coffee, tea or me?"

"The latter."

The banter had given Sarah Ann time to push back the despondency that had swamped her only moments before. "I fear Jill has not finished her "hay rolling" as you called it."

"And you know this *how*?"

"By supposition, by extra-sensory perception, by osmosis. I don't know." Sarah Ann turned her face toward the sunrise, set the cup down on the small round veranda table and stared across at the skyline of Vancouver with its backdrop of forested mountains in the distance while she repeated what Jill had just told her.

When she finished Angela exclaimed, "Good God, but he's a greedy bastard."

"You forgot talented and a major money maker."

"Okay! Talented, clanging cash register bastard."

"Better."

"Sweetie, I'm sorry." Jeanne Marie drained her cup in one last gulp and stood up. "You stay here. I'll bring the pot. We both need a refill."

As Jeanne Marie stood up Sarah Ann reached out and touched her arm. "No mention of this phone call or any of its gist to the others. Okay, girlfriend?"

"Sure enough." She patted Sarah Ann's arm reassuringly. "Just remember though, secrets are toxic; sharing is cathartic. I swear I can't remember who said that," she said, as she turned toward the sliding door.

"No one. You just made it up."

As Jeanne Marie turned toward the door she nearly bumped into Della Sue coming through the sliding panel with Angela at her heel. "Made what up?" Della Sue asked in a voice still thick with sleep.

Jeanne Marie shrugged a 'don't know' as she stood back for her two friends to pass. "Mornin' you two," she said cheerfully. Della Sue simply nodded and pointed to the cup in Jeanne Marie's hand as did Angela as they stepped out onto the veranda. "Mornin' yourselves," Jeanne Marie answered sarcastically, responding to the non-verbal orders for coffee. "Grab a seat. Coffee will be ready in a jiff. I'll be right back."

"Thank God," said Angela in a voice somewhat akin to a zombie. "A pox on the devil who devised time zone changes. No respect for sleeping habits." Both women thumped down into deck chairs.

"Mornin' glories. Are we suffering from a case of the pre-coffee grumps?" Both women nodded agreement which forced a smile from Sarah Ann who stretched her arms upward as she looked at the sun now fully ascended, still splashing the horizon with streamers in an assortment of dazzling hues. "Looking at this sunrise, I may just break out in song like…what's his name? Oh yeah, I remember… Gordon McRae…like he did in that movie *Oklahoma*."

"Spare us," pleaded Angela. "Anyway, Gordon McRae was an alcoholic, so I imagine he was hung over and not believin' a word of *Oh, What a Beautiful Morning*."

"Wasn't he on a horse when he sang that?" threw in Della Sue.

"Yes, I think I recall that, though they probably had to tie him on. And I bet it was filmed in the afternoon anyway." Angela sighed heavily. "Nobody in their right mind sings this early in the morning."

Jeanne Marie returned shortly with the coffee container in one hand and the second finger on her other hand looped through the handles of two mugs. "Folgers to the rescue," she smiled sweetly as she began pouring.

"So back to my question," said Della Sue, "made what up?"

"Nothing," replied Jeanne Marie. "Anyway, I can't remember."

Della Sue's head rose from hanging over the steam coming from her coffee cup and her face lit up. "Okay now, what *is* up you two?" The sleepiness that shrouded her eyes a moment before lifted from her face like a rocket. Her eyes were suddenly bright with inquisitiveness. "*Nothing* is an unacceptable response in this group."

Angela shook her head in assent as she took her first gulp of coffee.

"God, but you're nosy, insistent B-I-T-C-H-E-S," Jeanne Marie retorted, raising the cup to her lips.

"Are we slinging insults before even boarding the ship to 'snow queen' paradise?" Willie Dell followed his remark with a "tsk, tsk, tsk" as he pulled the sliding door closed behind him.

Four pairs of female eyes trained on him as he made his way to the remaining deck chair. He looked around at the four faces devoid of any humor. "Was it something I said or has the coffee not kicked in yet?"

"Both!" the four female voices responded in unison.

"In that case I must find sanctuary in caffeine."

"Grab a cup from the cupboard and I'll fill 'er up," said Jeanne Marie, holding up the half empty glass carafe of coffee.

As he pulled the sliding door shut he saw three heads bent over coffee mugs, the fourth head lifted toward him with mischief in her eyes. "Sarah Ann's keeping secrets," declared Della Sue in a sing-songie voice.

Willie Dell eased into a chair and trained his eyes on Sarah Ann. "No secrets allowed in this confessional of friends. Spill it out, baby sister. I'm all ears," he prompted Sarah Ann, as he reached out his cup for Jeanne Marie to fill.

When Sarah Ann had finished, she realized with what tawdry colors she had painted Jill and felt an immediate pang of remorse. From a well of empathy buried deep within her, she knew that her business partner was more a victim, but of what she wasn't quite sure. Being an older woman with a hard outer shell who had allowed a younger man to pierce the fiercely independent, tough minded, tougher talking, wise cracking veneer that presented itself to the Music Row community, belied her understanding of Jill Edgerton. She was the founder of Edgerton Group, which now managed two of the hottest talent in country music. Maybe it was simply what it appeared to be, just a lonely older woman who had fallen for a randy younger man. Whatever the reason, Sarah Ann knew that the affair could not end well for them or for her.

"I say 'eunuchize' him and that will solve the problem," suggested Della Sue with a wicked grin. Laughter erupted. Eunuch seemed to have become a favorite word in her vernacular.

"Oh, God! That hurts just hearing you say it." Willie Dell shook his head as if warding off a sudden chill. "With thoughts like that floating around in that vacuous head of yours, if I were Beau, I would be long gone and quick about it."

More laughter.

"Vacuous? How did such a fine little word like that float up through the empty space between those jumbo ears of yours," Della Sue snipped back.

Jeanne Marie stifled her giggling and lifted two fingers to her lips and let loose with a muted whistle. "Enough, y'all. This is not helping." She looked around at her fellow Prayer Group members and said impishly, "Or we could pray for terminal cancer to befall Jill, something that takes you quick. You know, like the kind Michael Landon had; he only lasted a few weeks."

"That's a horrible thought, Jeanne Marie," exclaimed Angela, feigning shock. "I wouldn't wish such a thing *even* on my two ex-husbands." When the laughter quieted, Jeanne Marie slipped out to brew another pot of coffee while her four friends seemed content to stare at the gentle disturbance of the quiet waters of the Inland Passage by a passing ship's wake.

The reverie was broken by Della Sue. "I was just thinking. You know if I had cancer and knew I was not long for this world, I would blow all my money and take a trip just like this—maybe longer—and go until God decided it was time for me to disembark."

"Nice thought," said Jeanne Marie, returning with the steaming coffee, "except when you 'disembark' on a ship as you have described your passing, they store you with the steaks in a big freezer. It subs as a morgue until the hearse arrives at the next port to off load you."

"Party pooper!" Della Sue exclaimed with feigned vehemence.

"You could wipe the smile off Beau's face after our annual sex on his birthday." Della Sue held out her cup for a refill. "What?" she said in response to the astonished look on Jeanne Marie's face. "Sex is cheap. And anyway, Beau already has too many neckties."

Chapter 23

Sarah Ann stood at the railing watching with fascination as the big ship was maneuvered slowly parallel with the dock. Moments later she walked to the starboard side and trained her binoculars to where sunlight danced on the snow-bleached cap of Mt. Rainier. Mother Nature gave promise of yet another spectacular day.

She and her four companions had also seen the spectacle of Mt. Denali in all its sun-bathed splendor just days before when they had taken a train from Denali National Park to Anchorage. Locals called it "her coming out" since the tallest mountain in North America preferred her cloak of clouds most of the year. From Anchorage they had flown to Fairbanks and boarded another Holland America ship for the return voyage.

"I wondered where you were hiding, sneaking off after breakfast like that."

Sarah Ann smiled over at Angela as she grasped the brass railing beside her. "I didn't sneak off. I'm right here in plain sight for all to see who seek me out."

"Don't we sound poetic this morning?"

"It's the latent Wordsworth bubbling up in me. Happens at the strangest times. It must be the sight of Mt. Rainier." Sarah Ann handed the binoculars to Angela. "Have a looksee. It may bring out a little Shakespeare in you."

"Great view," Angela said with the binoculars pressed against her eyes. "But, oh damn, alas, I feel no words pouring forth from my somewhat less than ample bosoms to indelibly imprint this moment in time for all posterity. All I see are two fat buttocks rising from the steam."

"What!" Sarah Ann looked where Angela was pointing the binoculars toward the upper deck of another cruise ship docked in front of theirs. A tubby man was wrapping a towel around his exposed rear end. "That is definitely not Mt. Rainier."

"Could have fooled me," quipped Angela, handing the binoculars back to Sarah Ann.

"I better head back in and throw the rest of my stuff into the carry-on." She started toward the door and then turned back and wrapped her arms around Sarah Ann's shoulders and pulled her close. "Thank you for these wonderful last few days, even if Della Sue didn't get to screw one of the cabin boys. It has been as close to perfect as you can get. Love you," she said, kissing Sarah Ann on the side of the cheek.

"Stay put you two, time for a group hug." Della Sue stepped through the door followed closely by Willie Dell and Jeanne Marie. They wrapped arms tightly around the two women at the railing and around each other, standing like a multi-colored human ball swaying slightly in the softly filtered light of early morning.

When the hug released, Della Sue addressed Angela with faux petulance, "By the way, missy, just how do you know I *didn't* have my way with a cabin steward."

"Remember, darlin'," replied Angela in an exaggerated tone, "you were assigned to my suite and never did my hound dog nose detect the scent of eau de semen."

"I agree. You do have a nose that would make any self-respecting hound dog proud."

"Enough, you two," Sarah Ann interceded. "We have to be off this boat in an hour or so and time it is a wastin'."

She had pleaded the need to catch up with her computer and opted for a seat near a window after boarding the late morning flight to Nashville. She sat across the aisle from the other four in the spacious business class section of the plane. But her laptop lay unopened as she stared out at the thick white clouds through which the plane was making its rapid ascent.

The discussion with the Prayer Group played over and over in her mind as she wrestled with the advice that had finally come out of the confab that had stretched well into the early hours. Her friends had been unanimous. *Compromise.* Allow Jared to drop the additional venue from the contract but rebuke his demand for a greater share of the proceeds, even if Jill were willing for it to come from her share.

It was the ever-pragmatic Jeanne Marie who suggested having one less venue for Jared to play. Eliminating all the physical hassle of staging the venue was a better alternative than yielding to his demand for a bigger share of the proceeds. Giving in to such a demand, she reasoned, would insure his take would be higher for all future concerts.

Willie Dell had questioned why Jared was suddenly making such demands while his career was still on an upward trajectory.

Della Sue surmised he had to have coerced Jill into agreeing to his demands before she even discussed them with Sarah Ann. The others agreed.

Angela rationalized, "You can't really stop her from carrying on the affair. She's on a self-destructive course. You can only try and keep it from taking you and the business down with her."

How? That was a question the Prayer Group had debated long into the night, a debate which finally ended when Della Sue suggested encasing Jill's groin area in a medieval chastity belt with a sturdy lock, the key to which would remain safely stuffed in Sarah Ann's bra. That was enough to send everyone chuckling back to their suites.

Chastity belt aside, Sarah Ann knew Angela was right. Jill would go to Europe with Jared. The affair would continue. *That she could not control*, she agreed silently, as she continued staring at the white clouds below and the bright azure of the sky above as the plane leveled out. The ethereal beauty of what she was seeing did little to lift her spirits. At the same time, she felt her spine straighten slightly. She would once again have to confront Jill; confront the reality of her relationship with Jared but insist on a compromise solution to his demands. If she was to save their business from the consequences of her partner's libido, she must at least restructure Edgerton Group to succeed with or without Jill and Jared.

Sarah Ann opened her computer and when the page she wanted

appeared, her fingers flew across the keys as the strategy to achieve the goal she was settling on began to fill up the screen.

~

John Bennett Boswell thoroughly disliked the man slumped in the maroon leather chair across from him. But he was a good enough attorney to let not a scintilla of his feelings penetrate the pleasant professional veneer he displayed to the glum face peering back at him. He had taken it upon himself to meet with Jared after reading "trouble" between the lines of the carefully worded email.

"Sarah Ann emailed me and said you have some concerns about your contract for the upcoming tour. She won't be back until this evening. I thought we could meet, just the two of us, and perhaps ameliorate those concerns before she gets back." There was no response from Jared and his expression remained stony. "By the way, congratulations on the new album. Sales are terrific. Bumped into Arliss Hemming recently and he predicted just that. There's no better judge of such things than Arliss. Don't you agree?"

Jared stirred in his seat. "I guess. He's a good producer. I'll give him that." He took another gulp from the chilled bottle of Michelob John's secretary had handed Jared after he arrived and had rudely waved off an accompanying glass with a flip of his hand.

Arrogant bastard. You bet your life Arliss is a good producer or you wouldn't be where you are now, John fulminated silently, struggling to keep his thoughts from betraying the mild pleasantness on his face. "Sarah Ann touched on some of the changes you would like." John waited for a response. Jared remained silent, but a wary expression closed over his handsome face.

"I thought Jill and me had that all worked out. Why is Sarah Ann even involved?" The tone was flat, veiling the anger gathering inside him.

"She's Jill's partner, Jared. Any changes to your contracts affect both of them."

Jared leaned forward in his chair. "Not if it doesn't affect Sarah Ann's bottom line." There was a hint of belligerence in the words.

"And that may be," John countered evenly. "Let's discuss the changes you want to make and see what we can work out."

Jared succinctly outlined his demands. "I know better than half the revenue coming into Edgerton Group is coming from my music sales and concert tours. I deserve a bigger cut of the take," he added, slumping back in his chair and taking the last swallow of the beer.

"Would you like another one?" asked John, nodding at the empty Michelob.

"Yeah, sure. Why not? I guess I can call my manager to chauffeur me home. I'm sure neither you nor Jill wants this cash cow to have a car crash." There was an obvious smirk in the words and on his face.

John let a trace of a smile be his answer as he pushed a button on his telephone. "Miss Jane, could you bring another Michelob for Mr. Parson?"

John's secretary arrived with the frosty bottle of beer moments later. "Is there anything else I can get you, Mr. Parson," her voice a dead giveaway to her Nashville linage.

"No, ma'am. Thanks."

She turned to her boss and bathed him with a bright smile that dimpled her plump cheeks. "May I bring you some coffee, Mr. John?"

"Not now, thanks. "

Jared had turned to watch her leave. When the secretary closed the door quietly behind her he turned and remarked. "Not the secretary I would expect a successful guy like you to have." He tossed back a long gulp of beer.

"She's been a fixture here since I hung out my shingle. She knows my business better than I do." John steepled his arms and tapped his clinched hands against his chin. "Now, Jared, let's look at what we can do to make your life happier with Edgerton Group. I believe we can work out canceling the one concert. It will take some negotiating with the management agent in London. But I'm optimistic we can achieve that with a minimal cost. As for your request for a larger share of the ticket proceeds—that is a little more complicated."

"Complicated how?" Jared lifted the bottle to his lips without taking his eyes off John.

"You have a contract with Edgerton Group that binds you to it for nearly two more years. Both partners would have to agree to any changes. Unfortunately, Sarah Ann is not willing to do so at this time."

"Then I will sue to nullify my contract."

"On what grounds, Jared?"

"Inadequate representation."

"Yes, you could try to sue on those grounds. I suggest you first find another attorney familiar with the music business to review your contract. I think they will reach the same conclusion I have. It is ironclad." *And I wrote it, you horse's ass,* John sneered silently as he looked reflectively at the younger man across from him. "And I believe the success you've achieved would certainly contradict your claim of inadequate representation."

Jared took another pull of beer. "But, then there is the issue of you," he said accusingly. "You've got an obvious conflict of interest, Sarah Ann being your ex-wife."

"And you, Jared, have a conflict of interest," John countered smoothly. "You're screwing Jill." John continued to tap his clasped hands against his chin as his eyes bored into the man across from him

"It's none of your business who I'm screwing," Jared snapped, his face reddening as anger welled up.

"It is when the woman you're screwing is a partner in a firm I represent."

Jared fought to control the blinding rage that pressed him to lash out at the bland face across the desk. In an effort to contain his anger, he gripped one arm of the chair so tightly his knuckles turned white. When he finally spoke, his voice was harsh. "I'm busting my butt to succeed, and Sarah Ann has done damn little to promote my career. It's been all Jill's effort." Jared waited for a reaction. There was none. "Maybe what needs to be done is Jill and I both see about cutting loose from Edgerton Group—or better yet, finding a way to fire your ex-wife."

"May I also remind you Jill and Sarah Ann have an ironclad partnership contract?"

Jared took the last gulp of beer and banged the bottle down on John's gleaming desk. "This doesn't end here, you bastard. Sarah Ann will regret this."

"I hope that isn't a threat." John stood up, his face no longer a mask of pleasantness. The anger in his eyes belied the control in his voice.

"Because if it is, and if you harm Sarah Ann, or Jill, in anyway, you will answer to me." John punched the button on his telephone. "Miss Jane, could you please come and show Mr. Parson to the waiting room while I call for a car to take him wherever he wants to go."

Jared bounded out of his chair pushing it roughly aside. "Save it, you sonofabitch. I'll drive myself."

Jared had crossed to the door just as Miss Jane opened it. She shot a worried glance over his shoulder to John as she partially blocked the doorway.

"Wait up, Jared," said John, pushing hurriedly away from his desk. "I was planning to head home early, and I'll drop you wherever you'd like."

Jared spun around, his face still streaked with rage. "I told you I'd drive myself." He turned on Miss Jane and snarled, "Get out of my way, lady."

"Her name is Miss Jane." The hand that restrained Jared's shoulder was surprisingly strong and it detained him from forcing the office door fully open. "Two beers will get you a DUI." John's voice was as steady as his grip on Jared's shoulder. "Music City isn't as tolerant of such infractions of the law as they were in former days. I'll drive."

Despite Jared's antagonism John's words penetrated. The warning registered. The two beers here had come after two he drank for spine-bolstering before tearing into the city to confront John. "I guess I pay you sure-as-hell enough to get a free ride out of the deal." He jammed the tan Stetson down on his head without any acknowledgement to the woman who had politely handed it to him.

John nodded reassuringly to evaporate the cloud of frustration gathering on his secretary's usually calm face. "I'll check in with you later, Miss Jane. Forward any important calls to my cell," he requested in a placating tone as he slipped into his suit jacket."

"Have a good afternoon, Mr. Boswell." She turned and disappeared back into the office.

Chapter 24

Viola Whittaker was whistling softly as she unlocked the brightly painted front door of the large 1950s bungalow that housed Edgerton Group along Music Row. The blue front door, with its oval cut-glass window, had a refreshing Caribbean look that appealed to Viola's love of colorful anything, except the language she occasionally overheard her oldest son using when he thought she was out of earshot. "Ghetto speak" he called it. Trash was what she called it. *When would that boy learn she had ears like a lynx?* She shook her head as she eased her bulk into the chair behind the large ornate desk from which she guarded the entrance with a wide smile, a cheerful hello and a "no nonsense" look that dampened any hope of getting past her without a firm appointment.

Viola noticed the telephone light on for Jill's office. She peeped around the corner and saw the door closed. *In early are we, Miz Jill. Wonder what's up?* Before she was seated back behind her desk the main line rang.

"Good morning, Edgerton Group."

"It's me, Viola. I'm stuck on the interstate." The voice was weighted with exasperation. "There's an accident. I should be around it shortly, but don't look for me for another half hour."

"Mornin', Miz Sarah. Welcome back. Glad one of those big ole brown bears didn't make a dinner of you."

"Mornin', yourself. As for bears, we saw zilch of the creatures. They apparently headed into early hibernation when they heard the Prayer Group was coming."

"Maybe thought you were missionaries from the Nashville Zoo."

Sarah Ann laughed. "No doubt. We are a bit intimidating." There was a brief silence and Viola heard a long sigh followed by a nearly inaudible "Shit!"

"Miz Sarah! What language!" Viola chastised with feigned astonishment. Actually, it *was* the first time she had ever heard Sarah Ann curse.

"Did I just say what I think you heard? Sorry," came the contrite apology. "Have I told you how much I hate commuting? When I get rich, I'm buying a helicopter and turning the back parking lot into a heliport. See you shortly."

Before Viola could hang up the receiver the intercom buzzed. "Was that Sarah Ann?" Jill inquired.

"Good mornin', Miz Jill. Yes, it was."

"Let me know when she gets in."

"Will do."

Twenty-some minutes later Sarah Ann swept into her office and tossed her briefcase on the desk. "God, I hate commuting," she muttered again under her breath as she sat down and looked with annoyance at the several neatly stacked piles of paper awaiting her perusal. The need for coffee beset her immediately.

"Black and here are two sugars just in case you dropped your Weight Watchers pledge to ban sugar." Viola placed the steaming cup in front of Sarah Ann.

"Have I told you lately that you are the nearest thing to a St. Bernard on a mercy run? Thank you and good morning." Sarah Ann looked up at Viola's beaming face appreciatively and tore open the two packs of sugar and dumped them unceremoniously into the cup. "God and Nutrisystem or whoever will just have to forgive me." She sipped and closed her eyes.

"I hired a brass band to welcome you back. They couldn't stay." Viola turned in the doorway. "I'll remember the St. Bernard reference come pay hike time. And Miz Jill wanted me to alert her as soon as you came in. Welcome back."

"Thanks."

It's good to have you back, girl Viola thought as she turned to leave.

"Oh wait, Viola." Sarah Ann opened her Coach brief case and

pulled out a small narrow box before rushing out from behind her desk.

Viola stared at the changing colors of the large ammolite pendant dangling on a gold chain she lifted from the box that Sarah Ann had handed her. "It's so beautiful, Miz Sarah," she whispered, staring in fascination at how the colors changed as she lifted it to the light. She looked up at Sarah Ann with liquid brown eyes. "Nobody's ever given me anything like this. I don't know how to thank you."

"I could use a hug."

"You got it." Tears spilled down Viola's plump cheeks as she wrapped Sarah Ann in a tight embrace. "It was one fine day when I came to work at Edgerton Group."

"You're welcome." As Sarah Ann turned to head back to her desk she remarked, "It was my good fortune when you walked through our front door."

"Thank you."

She raised her voice at the disappearing Viola. "Oh, and you can forget I said that come raise time." Sarah Ann heard "Not this elephant" and laughed out loud as she slipped back into her desk chair.

She leaned back in her chair and felt the butterflies of panic gripping her stomach. Sarah Ann could think of nothing she dreaded more than confrontation. And she fully expected that would be the reaction to the plan she had so carefully crafted on the plane. But confront Jill she would in the gentlest, but firmest way she could. She knew that the end result might be not only the loss of her friend, but the dissolution of a lucrative partnership.

Sarah Ann reached for the folder with the written proposal inside. As she crossed the hall to Jill's office she was suddenly awash in doubt and felt her resolve vaporizing like steam from a tea kettle. Clutching the folder as if to draw courage from its flimsy sides, she knocked softly before entering. "Good morning."

Before the words were hardly out, Jill let out a squeal of delight and bounded from behind her desk and wrapped Sarah Ann in a tight hug. "Am I glad to see you, girl. Welcome home."

Taken aback by Jill's friendly embrace Sarah Ann was left momentarily speechless. Was this the same Jill she had been talking to from Vancouver; the angry distant Jill; the sarcastic Jill? It was that incarnation of Jill that Sarah Ann was expecting to greet her. Not this enthusiastic, smiling woman who gripped her in an affectionate vice of a hug.

"Thank you," was all Sarah Ann could manage.

"Take the weight off." Jill pointed to the chair in front of her desk as she walked around her desk and sat back down in an oversized desk chair and learned back. She fixed Sarah Ann with an appraising eye. "You look rested. I think the trip did you good despite having the four horsemen of the apocalypse along for the ride."

"You know I could never leave home without them," Sarah Ann drawled, attempting to match Jill's good humor.

Just then a cloud passed over Jill's face, dimming the smile that had brightened it only a moment ago. "So, back to the grind stone. What's up?"

Sarah Ann knew that signaled what she must do. She lifted the file folder unto the desk.

Jill eyed the manila file warily. "What's this?" she asked bluntly.

"A proposal."

Jill leaned back in her chair again, a guarded expression spreading across her face like a distant thundercloud across the horizon.

Sarah Ann began. "I did a lot of thinking after our last conversation. I knew you were upset with me, Jill."

Jill remained silent, her expression now morphing from wary to obdurate, as if preparing to hear something disagreeable and already deploying resistance. Sarah Ann had seen this reaction before in her partner.

"I put my thoughts on how to resolve our issues on paper," Sarah Ann said in as placating tone as she could muster.

Jill opened the file and read silently, her face inscrutable as her eyes drifted down the page and then the second. When she finished reading she slowly set the pages on the desk beside the open folder before looking up. "So, you would give up your cut of the income from Jared and give me full control of his management."

"Yes."

"And you would settle for making your living off our string of 'maybe somedays'? And the only thing you want is to purchase the office real estate and add your name to the company logo?"

"Yes." Having my name attached to Edgerton Group would give me some—how can I put it delicately—balls in this business.

A flicker of a smile banished the skepticism from Jill's face at hearing her partner use such course vernacular. It was so unlike Sarah Ann. She lifted her panted legs onto the desk, crossed her ankles and leaned back in her leather chair. "Okay. I'll take that as a compliment. But what do you need with this house which we've talked about selling anyway so we could rent classier office space."

"It's not just an office. It's more like a home."

Jill studied her partner thoughtfully. They were of one mind on that. While she had suggested more elegant digs for Edgerton Group more than once, she was content to stay put and glad Sarah Ann agreed. But it still bothered her that Sarah Ann was willing to give up any part of Jared's income flow. "And you're *really* okay with giving up any income from Jared?" she asked, a hint of skepticism in her words.

Sarah Ann weighed her response thoughtfully then sat forward, her chin resting on her crossed hands and looked directly across at Jill's impassive face. "You taught me everything I know about this business and were willing to take a chance on someone who had to learn it all. Then along came Jared. I couldn't have managed him. He has succeeded because of your knowledge and contacts. My contribution has been filling in a few details. You made him Jill. He may not give you credit for that, but he should. He would be back in Texas playing weekend gigs at bars without your experience."

Jill opened her mouth, but Sarah Ann shushed her before any words came out. "Let me finish. I can handle the talent we have now. You've taught me enough that I think I can do a good job of helping them achieve success in this business. And with a little luck one of them may just prove to be another Jared. I'm happy…actually. I'm challenged doing just that, and letting you take the reins of Jared and the income he brings in. I've made more money…"

Before Sarah Ann could finish Jill interrupted, "Do you realize what you're giving up, Sarah Ann?" Jill's question was again laced with incredulity.

"Yes, I do. He may be worth millions more to you, me and this firm. But, as I started to say, I've made more money than I ever dreamed of having. And I'm content to try and pan for gold among the other clients we have now. Stella Wayne is looking very promising at the moment." She took in a deep breath. "Anyway, it's enough for me. As for the office, it would be a good investment. You don't need the hassle of overseeing its maintenance and it is plenty of storefront for the talent I'd be managing. You keep your office here and the apartment upstairs—rent free—that way I still get to see you when you're in town and not on the road with Jared." Sarah Ann sat back reflectively and again silently weighed what she knew she must say next. "I know you love Jared…"

Before she could finish Jill sprang to her feet and leaned forward across the desk, her blue eyes swathed in anger. "What if I do?" she demanded fiercely. "What does that have to do with anything involving you or Edgerton Group? Any feelings I have for Jared are my business and not yours, not anyone else, you hear." Jill's chest heaved, and her cheeks flamed from the abrupt outburst. As suddenly as the anger appeared, it vanished, and she sat down wearily, looking drained, as if the broaching of the subject that had remained such a source of silent contention between the two partners had deflated the balloon of emotion prompted by Sarah Ann's words. A terse silence ensued between the two women.

It was Sarah Ann who spoke first. "You know and I know it has everything to do with our business," she said gently and braced for another angry response. There was none. Sarah Ann continued, "I owe you everything as a business partner. Even more as your friend. Because of your special relationship with Jared, it is imperative that you not have me or anyone else standing in the way of wherever that relationship takes you. I want only your happiness. More than that, I want you not to be mistreated. I can no longer stand by and see that happen as I have been doing and not interfere."

"How dare you!" Jill sprang to her feet again and pounded her knotted fist on the desk. "How goddamn dare you suggest Jared mistreats me?" Jill began pacing back and forth in the space behind her desk. "You know nothing about how he treats me. Jared loves me."

This was the confrontation Sarah Ann had feared, but she was not prepared for what came next. In an accusatory voice Jill lashed out, "You're just doing this because Jared wants a bigger share of the gate. Even if we give it to him you would still be getting a lot of money. So would I. So would this company. Why in the hell can't you be satisfied?"

Sarah Ann kept her voice even. "I am, Jill. That's why that proposal is in front of you. You're right. Your personal relationship with Jared is none of my business. I value our working relationship too much to allow Jared to come between that and our friendship. You—this company—mean everything to me. And I know there's certain conflict ahead if I don't step aside and let you focus all your considerable energy and hutzpah on making him the greatest country entertainer ever." Sarah Ann looked directly at the angry face across from her and added, "And I know you will. I believe Jared knows that to."

Another long silence as Jill nervously fingered the two sheets in the open folder in front of her before finally stuffing them back inside. "It's a lot to think about. Can you give me a day or two?"

"Whatever time you need." Sarah Ann stood up to leave and stopped when she reached the door. "Peace pipe time. You bring the marijuana or whatever and let's have dinner at Puckett's tonight. I've always fantasized sitting on the front porch out there and getting high."

The dark cloud seemed to lift from Jill's face. "You have a date. What time."

"Hey, we're the bosses. Whatever time your rumbling tummy ordains."

"I have to meet with Arliss this afternoon to finalized arrangements for the band and meet with Lowell to go over them. He's Jared's new band director. Should be free by four or so."

"Good. We can beat the worst of the traffic. I would need something stronger than weed to calm me if I have to battle I-65 at five."

Before Sarah Ann could close the door, she heard Jill ask mischievously, "By the way, did that Prayer Group of yours get you into bad habits like smoking dope while you were in the frozen north?"

"I'll only tell in the dark of the confessional," Sarah Ann threw back as she crossed the hall to her office.

Chapter 25

It had started out a typical Friday; the welcoming smile from Viola followed by the steaming cup of coffee placed in front of her along with five pink message notes to return calls. Those should have been the first clues that her day would go astray and quickly. Sarah Ann could not remember a day when she had spent so much time on the telephone. She silently thanked the inventor of the speaker phone or she feared she might be minus a hand to dry rot from holding the receiver so long.

Viola ducked her head in the door. "I'm just headed out. You need anything before I go?"

"No. But thanks. Have a better evening than I've had a day."

Viola belted out her melodious laugh. "Goin' home to my brood? If you only knew what that's like," she chuckled. "It makes the worst day that the devil himself could possibly divvy up at work look like a gift from God. Have a good weekend, Miz Sarah." She waved her hand, still chuckling as she disappeared down the hallway leading to the parking area behind the office.

"You too!" Sarah Ann called out as she glanced at her watch. Five fifteen. John would be here anytime now to go over the new partnership agreement and the contract to purchase the building that housed the soon to be renamed firm of Edgerton & Boswell Management.

The dinner at Puckett's a week ago had proved cordial and productive. In between biting into thick cheeseburgers and dipping homemade onion rings into ketchup, she and Jill had agreed on a framework for the new partnership and a price for the firm's property. To Sarah Ann, Jill seemed not only happy with the proposed arrangement, but even appeared relieved. They had seen little of each other this week. Jill stayed closeted in her office most of the time working on final arrangements for Jared's European tour except when she was dashing out the door to Hemming's studio to finalize music arrangements with Jared's band. Amid all that, not only was one venue not dropped, but two more were added. It would keep her and Jared in Europe until only three weeks before his new baby was due, something he had been so adamantly opposed to until now.

Sarah Ann shook her head. *Hers was not to reason why!* She did wonder how LouAnn was dealing with her husband not being with her during part of the difficult last weeks of pregnancy. But she dared not ask. Jared would be Jill's client exclusively now, in body and bankroll.

Midweek Jill had ducked into Sarah Ann's office long enough to announce she would be vacating the apartment above the first-floor offices shortly to move into a condo she was purchasing in Brentwood. She described it as three stories of luxury and convenience. Sarah Ann was taken aback by Jill's announcement but later admitted to herself a feeling of relief. If the affair with Jared continued, and she had no doubt it would, the tryst would not be on the premises of Edgerton & Boswell Management.

The ringtone of her cell phone broke into her reverie. "I'm at your back door and it's locked."

"Sorry. Be right there." She had meant to tell Viola to leave the door unlocked. She caught a glance of herself in the hall mirror as she flashed by, her lips blanched of lipstick and her hair in need of a little tidying up. Oh, well, John had seen her look worse. Only then she had been younger and 'worse' didn't look as unappealing as it did now that she was older.

She unbolted the lock and swung it open for John. He looked as dapper and fresh as always. Why in hell was life so unfair? His lips didn't require lipstick and if the wind ruffled his thick salt and pepper locks, it only made him look more attractive. Sarah Ann quickly repressed the swell of feelings that bubbled to the surface anytime she saw her former husband.

"Hi."

"Hi, yourself." John slipped out of his suit jacket and draped it on a coat rack just inside the door. "You women have it good you know."

"How's that, Mr. Boswell?"

"Women don't have to wear coats during the hottest time of the year or feel a hangman's noose clutching at their throat for most of the day." She hoped he missed her eyebrows lifting. He loosened his tie and unfastened the top button of his crisp white shirt. "That's better," he said as he picked up the leather briefcase from the floor beside him.

"Good," she said as they headed down the hall to her office. "I thought for a moment I was going to have to fish out a five to put in your pant waist."

John laughed and followed her into her office. "I must come cheap if all I can seduce from my audience is a five-dollar bill."

"John Boswell, Esquire, you are by no means cheap and you command your pricy fees without the inconvenience of having to undress."

"If that's the case, I may need to consider a new business model."

Sarah Ann slid into the chair behind her desk. Having casual banter with this man, who still had the power to make her feel the pain of their parting despite the passing years, was far beyond her comfort zone. To conceal her discomfort, Sarah Ann lowered her head and opened her drawer and snatched a pen. She tapped the ballpoint twice on the desk as if calling the meeting with John to order.

"I'm sorry," she said standing back up. "Where are my manners? May I get you something to drink—some coffee or a soda?"

A faint smile flickered across John's face as he recognized her unease. "No thanks. I'm good."

Sarah Ann reclaimed her seat as he pulled two thick packets from his briefcase and slid one across the desk. "I've tabbed the changes to the partnership agreement and there is space on the margin to initial your approval. Same for Jill. The contract for the sale of the property is fairly standard and Jill emailed me you won't need the addendum allowing her to remain in the upstairs apartment. Did you know about that?"

"Yes. She's bought a condo in Brentwood and plans on moving

out in the next week or so. She's anxious to move before heading overseas for the tour."

John looked at Sarah Ann thoughtfully. "You know you're passing up a lot of revenue from that tour. And a lot of revenue from Jared's future earnings," he added. "There's no question he's the biggest name in this town. He'll peak at some point, but you're giving up a lot before he reaches that summit."

"I know, John." She knew it was his job as the firm's attorney to advise her of the financial downside of her decision and she suspected he thought her a fool for making this change. But she had made her peace with the decision the morning she left Seattle. "The Alaska trip allowed me time to think. I believe this is the best way forward for me. *And* for Jill," she said, adding with a self-deprecating smile, "I'm sure Jared is also applauding my decision."

"No doubt," John replied.

He was all business as they went over the changes to the partnership agreement and the real estate contract. When she finally closed the thick packet, she felt the warmth of the descending sun on her back as it filtered through the partially open shafts of the wooden blinds on the window behind her desk. They had been at this for more than an hour.

John placed his copies of the contracts back in the briefcase and then stood and stretched his tall frame with the languorous movement of a big cat rising from an afternoon nap.

"Long day?" asked Sarah Ann.

"Actually, a short night. Comes with age I guess."

"Can't be, Mr. Boswell. Only women suffer the pangs of aging and insomnia."

"You must be reading too many women's magazines, Mrs. Boswell. You need to brush up on the latest edition of Men's Health."

Sarah Ann felt a lurch in her chest and a flush spreading from her neck upward at hearing John call her Mrs. Boswell. It seemed so long since she had filled the role that came with that title. "Well, I think we can call it a day here, or what's left of it," she said lightly, glancing over her shoulder at the gathering dusk outside the window. "I'm ready to call it a week and enjoy the weekend."

"Actually, if you *are* calling it a day how about joining me for dinner? I skipped lunch and I'm famished."

"Oh gosh, I don't know…," the rest of the sentence was left unsaid.

"Angeline is out of town, if that's the reason for your hesitation." An uncomfortable silence followed his statement. "I would welcome some company. Anyway, when was your last meal?"

"This morning," she admitted. "I grabbed a coffee and muffin at Starbucks on the way in."

"No wonder you're looking so svelte."

She smiled at his selection of such a complimentary adjective to describe her weight loss in recent months. Willie Dell had not been as kind, calling her 'positively bulimic' and nagged her incessantly to eat more during the cruise.

"How about Jimmy Kelly's? They still have the best steaks in Nashville."

"Sounds great. I haven't been there in ages." In fact, Sarah Ann could not remember the last time she had been to the famed steakhouse. It had once been a luxury date, one she and John could only afford a couple times a year when they were married, and the children were young. She felt a stir of nostalgia. There had been good times with John, prompting the inevitable question. *What had happened to change those happier times* she asked herself silently, wistfully?

"A thick filet should find plenty of room to wrap around those skinny ribs of yours."

As she stood up she felt like having a good stretch herself. "Give me just a moment to freshen up and make sure the alarm is set." Sarah Ann lifted her purse from a desk drawer and slipped out of the office.

The face that peered back at her from the mirror looked pale and a little worn from the long day. *Looking a tad old, are we?* she admonished the reflection. She touched up her blush and lipstick and went up front to double check that the alarm system was engaged. It was. Viola was always reliable where security was concerned, especially when she knew Sarah Ann was working late.

John was back in his suit jacket and his tie back in place when she returned. "Ready?"

"Yes," she replied as he ushered her out the office and toward the back of the building. She noticed the alarm for the rear door had not been set. She was sure she had reset the alarm after ushering John in. Frowning, she typed in the code before they exited into the parking lot now shadowed by the fading daylight. Sarah Ann moved toward her car and felt John's gentle restraint on her arm. "Why don't we take my car? I'll drop you back by after dinner."

"Are you sure? I don't mind driving."

"My invitation. Let me be the chauffeur." He took her elbow and guided her toward his car parked in a visitor's space. As she slipped into the buttery soft leather seat of the Jaguar convertible, Sarah Ann noticed Jill's car in the secluded spot nearest the outside stairs that led up to her private quarters. She wondered why Jill had not stopped by to say hello. Sarah Ann had told her John was dropping by after office hours and to poke her head in if she came home in time. That question evaporated as John pulled onto the street and Sarah Ann felt the butterflies of tension stirring.

How long had it been since she had sat in the front seat of a car with John? *Years*, she thought as she stared silently at the passing lights of buildings as they sped by, her hands gripping the purse in her lap like the handles of a life raft. Would she never again feel comfortable with this man with whom she had shared a bed for twenty some years?

The silence between them now reminded her painfully of the muteness that deepened long before the papers were signed that silenced their marriage.

"A penny?"

She glanced across at John, grateful he had interrupted her despondent thoughts. "Sorry," she smiled, realizing her silence bordered on rudeness. "Just enjoying Nashville at twilight. I never seem to take notice when I'm behind the wheel."

"Are you coming to Little John's birthday bash next week?"

"Wouldn't miss it," she replied, thankful he had veered the conversation into comfortable territory; their grandson. "Rumor has it the little cowboy is getting his first pony."

"Yeah," he chuckled. "Rumor has it the pony is way too tall for the little boy, but then who is measuring a birthday gift by how many hands tall it is compared to its rider."

She laughed and found her tension releasing its hold on her stomach. "Any bets on how long we'll wait for a table since we're showing up unannounced?"

"Oh, ye of little faith. Leave it to my ever-charming devices and see if they can't squeeze us into a discreet table for two in the back."

And that was where Sarah Ann found herself sitting within minutes after their arrival. The tenderloins John ordered were excellent and she marveled that he remembered just how she liked her steak—medium rare—topped with Jimmy Kelly's tasty variation of Hollandaise sauce that added an extra dimension of flavor to the meat. John reached over and poured more of the excellent California merlot in her glass before she could protest. "If I didn't know better, Mr. Boswell, I would think you were trying to get me inebriated."

"That's a tough accusation to make. Inebriated? No way. Maybe just a little drunk."

"Then maybe just a little sip or two more," she said, raising her glass and tipping it toward his. "Here's to a new standard in attorney-client relations."

He held her eyes as he sipped his wine, his expression impassive. This made her even less prepared for what he said next. "Come home with me. Spend the night."

Sarah Ann dropped her eyes and stared at the wine where a variegated light danced on the ruby surface of the merlot as she nervously swirled the wine. It took her a few moments to recover her words and look back over at him. "Despite living like a nun for as long as I can remember, I'm sure that would not be a good idea," she said, trying to cover her shock at his proposition with a lighthearted answer.

He laughed softly. "I could always count on your sense of humor to cover your uncomfortable moments." He held the wine to his lips and slowly emptied his glass. "I didn't mean to make you feel uncomfortable, Sarah Ann." He seemed to be gauging the impact of what he said next. "I miss you, Sarah Ann. I miss the good times we had. I regret letting them get away—letting you get away."

Before the words of rebuke forming in her head could pass her lips, she felt a presence standing by their table. "Please excuse this intrusion, Mrs. Boswell. I saw you when you came in and wanted to introduce myself before I left." Sarah Ann looked up at the tall, slender man extending his hand, his handsome face crowned by dark blond hair streaked with silver. But it was the piercing dark eyes that held her gaze for longer than politeness dictated before she finally reached out and took his hand. His firm grip hinted at the strength of the man hidden beneath a well-cut dark blue pin-striped suit. "I'm Ross Lambert of NCA Records.

"Please, it's Sarah Ann," she told him graciously. "Nice to meet you." The name was not familiar, and she thought she knew most of the executives with NCA. Lambert held her hand an inordinately long time before releasing it and turned to John who was pushing back his chair. "John Boswell. I'm the attorney for Sarah Ann's firm," he said as he stood up. The two men shook hands cordially while each took mental measure of the other.

"Your reputation precedes you, counselor," said Lambert. "And I mean that in the most complimentary way."

"Thank you. I appreciate that. Will you join us for a glass of wine?"

"No thanks. Perhaps another time." He turned to Sarah Ann. "May I call you next week? I'd like to take you and your partner to lunch when it's convenient. I just arrived earlier today from Los Angeles and haven't had time to contact one of NCA's biggest clients or his managers." It seemed an obvious referral to Jared Parsons. He was NCA's top selling artist.

"I'm sure I speak for Jill Edgerton in saying we would be delighted to join you for lunch," Sarah Ann smiled, still mesmerized by Lambert's compelling eyes.

"I'll give you a ring. Enjoy the rest of your evening. And again, I apologize for intruding." He nodded to John. "A pleasure to meet you, counselor," he said before turning and walking back to a table near the front of the restaurant where two men stood up as he approached, and the trio headed out the front door.

"Interesting," observed John after sitting back down. "I heard a couple of weeks ago Len Shiring might be getting the boot. I wonder if Lambert is replacing him or just here to wield the axe?" he speculated.

"I don't know," Sarah Ann replied, somewhat puzzled and astonished at hearing Shiring might be replaced. "I had no idea Len was under the gun. But then I'm just back from vacation."

"That'll teach you to take a few days off." He leaned back and studied her thoughtfully. "Shiring's a little bit old school, Sarah Ann. Technology has pushed the country music business into brave new worlds and guys like Shiring may not be keeping up with the changes. I get the impression he's still hawking CDs at a time when more and more music is being downloaded onto smart phones or streamed onto I-pads."

A frown eclipsed Sarah Ann's smile. She didn't question John's assessment. The rapid digitalization of the music business was something both she and Jill were struggling to keep up with themselves. "I've only known Len for a couple of years. He certainly has been great to work with." She lifted her napkin and dabbed the edges of her mouth. "I hope for his sake you're wrong."

"Yeah, me too. I actually like Shiring a lot. He's a straight shooter in a business that unfortunately does not always take that into account." John picked up the wine bottle and topped off Sarah Ann's glass. "Enough talk of business."

"Now, I *know* you're trying to get me tipsy, Mr. Boswell," lifting the glass to her lips.

He tipped his glass toward her. "Without fear of sounding too prosaic—yes."

Sarah Ann detected playfulness in his voice that belied the seriousness in his eyes. "Come home with me tonight," he urged again. "I want to have more than dinner with you."

Her eyes wavered under his unrelenting gaze. As if the turmoil of her thoughts were not enough, she suddenly became aware of the noise around her. A waiter at a nearby table was reviewing an order and the sommelier was extracting the cork from a bottle of wine at the table behind them. *This could not be happening. How long…how often had she ached to hear the very words John had just uttered?* For months after his exit from their marriage she had fantasized about his return to their home—to her bed. And just as tonight, she and John sharing a glass of wine while he murmured sensual words which had once evoked so much response from her. That was before carpools and teenagers; before so many missed dinners that became so many missed nights, before middle age thickened her waist and tiny lines slithered out from the sides of her eyes. It was a fantasy that had finally exploded into the nightmarish reality of a near death experience. The pain of that experience scorched her heart.

Sarah Ann set down the glass of wine and looked over at John. "We can't John. I…I can't." She refused to let her gaze falter from his stoic face. "I loved you so deeply." She reached across and laid her hand on his, a rueful smile creasing her lips. "Maybe I still do," she shrugged. "But we can't recapture what time has taken away. And I can't do to Angeline what was done to me."

John set his glass down and lifted her hand to his lips. He turned her hand and she felt his warm lips on her wrist. "Have I told you lately what beautiful hands you have? They go with the face, of course." His words came in a whisper as tender as the kiss. "As for Angeline—she and I have separated. But I'm sure she would appreciate the concern you expressed." There was remorsefulness in his words that reflected the pain in his eyes.

She was stunned by the disclosure. "I'm so sorry, John…for you and for Angeline."

"Thank you. It's…," he hesitated, searching for the right words. "It's for the best for both of us. Angeline agrees." He kissed her hand again before releasing it. "You are my loss, Sarah Ann. My greatest regret." His voice was again thick with remorse as he continued, "I'm sorry I hurt you so deeply. Attorneys are supposed to be callous by nature. I'm afraid I did not disappoint." A thin, self-effacing smile etched across his lips.

Now it seemed her turn to ease the awkward silence that followed. "You will never know how much your words mean to me. I'm grateful," she said as she reached a hand across to cover his. "Thank you."

He smiled sardonically. "Thanking me for what. Screwing up our marriage?"

"We've survived. Me literally," she smiled, and then winced, remembering the suicide attempt which nearly succeeded. "And there is this," she reflected as her smile widened to a grin, "it's been so long since I've had sex I'd have to take a 101-refresher course before hopping into the sack."

He laughed and patted her hand. "Not to worry. Haven't you heard, it's like riding a bicycle."

"Something else I haven't done recently."

He chuckled softly. "I love you, Sarah Ann Boswell. And I promise you this won't be the last time I hit on you. In the meantime, I'll find you a book on sex 101."

Placing her elbows on the table she rested her chin on folded hands before countering good-naturedly, "Sounds like really raunchy reading. Will it measure up to Danielle Steele?"

"Only if she's a best seller in adult book stores." He shook his head as if to answer his own question. "Let me get the check," and raised his hand to signal their waiter.

Chapter 26

The ringing telephone on the round table by Sarah Ann's bed seemed far away. The fog of interrupted sleep gave way to the same recurring nightmare that haunted her dreams when her children were young, a savage dream that was always her sleep companion when her children were away from home. It most often occurred when she opted to stay home when John took the children for a long weekend with his parents to their North Carolina mountain retreat. She avoided going whenever she could muster a convincing reason because of her in-laws' overt coldness toward her; their aloofness sprang from their conviction John had married *beneath* him. It was a conviction she was never able to dispel. In the dream, John and the children were lying on the side of a highway embankment crying out for her help. She was running to them but could never quite reach them before she would wake up shaking and perspiring. Now, Sarah Ann rocketed up in bed at the insistent ringing and glanced at the clock near the telephone—4:32. A phone call at this hour could mean a wrong number or something urgent. Fear constricted her throat and panic gripped her stomach as she threw back the satin duvet.

She grabbed for the phone. "Hello."

"I'm calling for Sarah Ann Boswell." A male voice, brusque and deep. She felt her throat tighten. "Yes, this is she," her voice barely above a raspy whisper.

"This is Metro Detective Marlin Hotchkin. Sorry to disturb you, ma'am, but I was wondering if you would mind coming to your office. We have a situation here."

"Situation?" she repeated in a baffled voice.

"Yes, ma'am. It's something we need to talk with you about in person."

"Has there been a break-in, Detective?"

"It's a little more serious than that, ma'am. If you can't drive, I can send a car to pick you up."

"No, Detective, that won't be necessary. I can drive. I live in Franklin. It will take me a half-hour, forty-five minutes or so to get there." She was fully awake now and the tentacles of fear began to wrap around her. "Please, can you tell what this is about?"

"When you get here, ma'am. Better that way."

"All right. I'll be as quick as I can."

"Thank you, ma'am." The dial tone announced he was gone.

As she threw on the jeans and pull-over blouse she'd worn last evening her mind was racing. *What in God's name could this be?* She had double checked the security system when she left the office with John Friday evening. Jill had mentioned on Friday morning she planned to be at her condo Saturday awaiting delivery of new furnishings, adding she would probably sleep there that night. Anyway, why would anyone break into the office? No money or anything of particular value was kept on the premises. A sign hung on the front door alerting would-be thieves to those facts. As for Jill's apartment, the trappings of her wealth were not displayed in expensive art or jewelry or furniture or anything else that Sarah Ann could think of. And she knew Jill kept very little money in her purse, let alone in her apartment.

Turning onto the street that ran in front of her office, even from two blocks away, Sarah Ann could see numerous police cars, some double parked, the lights on the cruisers rotating like a myriad of blue saucers being hurled into the pre-dawn darkness around the vehicles. The fear that had gripped her insides when she had answered the phone now felt like a cinch that threatened to squeeze the last breath from her lungs.

A Nashville police car was parked behind wooden barricades blocking the street just ahead. An officer emerged from the cruiser and walked toward her as she lowered her window. Thick humidity rushed in making her face feel as if it had been immersed in a sauna as the early morning air collided with the air conditioned cool of the car's interior.

"I'm sorry, ma'am. You'll have to go around another way."

"I was called by a detective and told to come here. My name is Sarah Ann Boswell. I'm with Edgerton Group. Our office is in the middle of this block." Charged by rising panic, her words rushed out as if she were a truant child showing up late for school.

"Oh, yeah. Sorry, ma'am. Detective Hotchkin said to let him know when you arrived." He pressed the button on a small radio receiver in his hand. It squawked like an angry crow before she heard, "*Hotchkin.*"

"Miz Boswell's here," the young uniformed officer said, turning away from her. When he turned back he motioned her to follow him as he pulled aside two of the barricades nearest the left curb. "He's waitin' for you just down there, ma'am." He was pointing toward the largest group of police vehicles.

As she eased slowly forward between police vehicles, she saw a sturdy built man of medium height in a rumpled dark blue suit walking toward her, a hand-held radio pressed to his mouth. She stopped as he came abreast of her car. "Just park in that driveway there, Miz Boswell," he said indicating the open driveway of a house across the street and three doors down from Edgerton Group. "I need to keep a path open on the street." Before she could ask any of the questions that sprang to her lips he raised the radio and barked something at someone on the other end.

She pulled into the driveway and stepped out of the car, trepidation now mixed with the panic already churning inside her. "Please tell me what's happening, sir?"

"Detective Marlin Hotchkin, ma'am. I think it's better if we talk inside." He led the way across the street and past several police cruisers to the walk leading to the Edgerton Group building. Yellow crime scene tape was stretched across the front porch where another uniformed officer stood guard outside the front door that reflected the rotating blue police lights on its own cheery blue veneer like unwelcome new paint. Several unmarked cars, some sedans, some SUVs, were parked behind each other along the length of the narrow driveway that led to the parking lot in the rear of the building.

The detective led her toward the rear of the building. In the back parking lot was a large van marked Metro Police Crime Scene Unit and behind that unit was another smaller van marked Metro Coroner. Only as she followed the detective up onto the small covered porch leading to the back door did she notice Jill's car parked in the shadow of the aluminum topped carport. Suddenly Sarah Ann felt fear, and it tasted like bile in the back of her throat.

Hotchkin had seen her hesitate on the step and followed her eyes to the car. "Come on inside, ma'am." He reached back and nudged her elbow. "Let's go inside where we can talk."

She suggested her office and he followed her down the hall. Above, she heard the sound of footsteps. Jill's apartment. Sarah Ann sat down behind her desk, laid her purse on the floor beside her and clinched her hands together in her lap to constrain the shaking. The fear that had assailed her outside now turned to terror.

Hotchkin pulled a chair up closer to her desk and seemed to read on her face the fear she was feeling. He had seen it all too often in his nearly twenty years as a homicide detective, most often in witnesses and family members, sometimes even in suspects. It was always his job to figure just who he was dealing with. In a voice that was as inscrutable as his facial expression he said, "I called you, Miz Boswell, because your number was listed to notify..." he hesitated, before continuing. "Sorry to tell you this, Miz Boswell, but a woman we believe to be Jill Edgerton is dead." He studied her face closely as he continued, "It's still early yet, but it appears she was stabbed to death."

The words did not have the ring of reality. *Jill dead? Stabbed to death?* Sarah Ann moved her clenched hands from her lap to the desktop and stared at them, willing them not to shake; willing the words the man across from her had spoken so unemotionally not to be real. Hotchkin watched Sarah Ann's struggle to control herself. When finally she lifted her face and looked at him, tears were moistening her eyes, but he could see she was winning the battle for control. "You're sure it's Jill?" she asked, in a quiet voice.

"We'll need a family member to confirm the identity for sure, ma'am. But it appears the victim is Miz Edgerton." Hotchkin pulled a small note pad and ballpoint pen from the breast pocket of his rumpled suit jacket. "We've not been able to find any phone numbers for her husband or family. Can you help us with that?"

A lone tear slid down Sarah Ann's cheek. *Husband?* As much as they had discussed Sarah Ann's former husband, Jill had never mentioned if she had ever been married. Her parents were dead. Jill had told her when they first met that her parents died even before she moved to Nashville from…Sarah Ann's mind went blank. *Where had Jill moved from? She couldn't remember. Was it California? No, Boston. That was it. God, please let me remember. Please let me wake up and find this has been just a bad dream.* She clenched her hands even tighter, fighting again for control as more tears trailed down her cheek. "I'm so sorry. I know her parents are both gone. I know she was an only child. I can't recall if she has any close relatives." She looked at the Monet print on the wall to the side of her straining to remember. "There was someone…I believe an aunt…her father's sister, if I recall correctly." She turned her hands upward in a sign of helplessness. "Jill never really disclosed much about her personal life."

Sarah Ann realized suddenly how little she knew about Jill. They had been business partners for more than three years. She felt the penetrating scrutiny of the man across from her. "I can't imagine what you must think of me, not even knowing if my friend has an aunt or grandparents…"

Sarah Ann looked distractedly at her clenched hands. "We never took time to talk much on a personal plain. When we'd get away for lunch or dinner occasionally, our conversations always seemed to revolve around business."

Sarah Ann tried to remember what they had discussed at their dinner in Leiper's Fork. *Was it only a week ago?* She looked around the top of her desk and labored to recall what they had talked about. *Oh yes, the new partnership agreement. And how excited Jill was about going to Europe with Jared and his band. Jared. She hadn't even thought about him. He would have to be told about Jill. What would happen with the upcoming tour? Everything was in the works. Could they cancel the venues? Oh God, what did it matter now? Jill was dead. Someone had stabbed her. Who would stab Jill? Why?*

Hotchkin watched the drama tracing across Sarah Ann's face. He knew she was losing her battle for control. He needed to snap her back to reality.

"Can you tell me where you were yesterday and last night, Miz Boswell?"

The bluntness of the question had the needed result. There was a long silence before she spoke. "Let's see. Yesterday was Saturday. I went shopping with my daughter-in-law. We had a birthday party… for my grandson…and then I helped her fix dinner last night. After my grandson went to sleep…let's see…I guess I left sometime later… just went home."

"And Friday evening, Miz Boswell. Can you tell me where you were?" Hotchkin knew the coroner was still upstairs and had not yet told him the approximate time of death.

Sarah Ann looked at the detective blankly for a moment and then said in a hushed voice. "I was here meeting with our attorney. We were going over a new partnership agreement and then we went out to dinner. He drove me back here to get my car. Then I drove home."

"About what time was that?"

"I got home about eleven, so I probably left here about ten-thirty… maybe a little later."

Hotchkin nodded and scribbled the time on a small pad and added new partnership agreement. "Who is the attorney you met with, Miz Boswell?"

"John Boswell." Hotchkin recognized the name. *Big shot attorney in the music business.*

"Any relation?"

"Yes, he's my former husband."

Hotchkin kept his expression impassive. *Interesting*, he thought. "Was he the firm's attorney or your personal attorney?"

"He represented both of us—me and Jill—our firm," she added hastily.

"So, were you and Miz Edgerton ending your partnership?"

"No, no, of course not." She looked over at him sharply. "We were splitting the responsibilities because of Jared. Jared Parson."

Hotchkin nodded his head as if the name was familiar. Actually, it was very familiar. *So, this management company has a big-bucks talent on its roles.*

"He's been so successful…," Sarah Ann stopped and once again seemed to be trying to find words. "Mostly because of Jill…and she was going to manage his career full time. I was going to manage the other talent here."

There was a rap on the door and the partially bald head of a man with a pudgy face and a paunchy midriff looked in toward Hotchkin. "Sorry to interrupt, Marlin. Can I see you a moment?"

Irritation at the intrusion brushed across the detective's face but vanished just as quickly. He pushed the chair back and rose. "Excuse me, Miz Boswell."

Sarah Ann could hear mutterings outside the office but none of it registered in her mind as she tried desperately to absorb the tragedy that had befallen Jill. Jill was the reason Sarah Ann was sitting in this very office, in this very building; the reason she had restructured the insipidness of her life almost four years ago into a meaningful synergy of work and accomplishment; the reason she had found to get past her divorce and the hole it had left in her heart.

"Sorry, Miz Boswell," Hotchkin said politely, interrupting her reverie. He sat down brusquely. "Now, where were we?" he said flipping through two pages of scribblings in the worn notepad before looking at her. "You said you and the deceased…," he stopped after seeing the pain leap into Sarah Ann's eyes at the word deceased. "Sorry, Miz Boswell," he apologized again. "You said you and Miz Edgerton were kinda' restructuring your partnership agreement. Do I understand that correctly?"

"Yes."

"And under this new agreement you were splitting your responsibilities, you said?"

"Yes."

"Did that change of responsibilities affect the income either of you receive?"

Sarah Ann wasn't certain how to respond. She looked pensively at Hotchkin whose face remained expressionless. "Since Jill would be managing Jared's career fulltime, she would retain all management revenues from his performances and royalties…except for what she would pay as her share of the office expenses."

Hotchkin jumped in when she hesitated. "So, since Mr. Parson is so successful, I presume she would be making more money than you? Would that be the bottom line, so to speak, of this new contract between you and the…Miz Edgerton?"

"Yes, that would probably be the bottom line, as you say, Detective." Sarah Ann felt the first stirrings of alarm at where the questioning was going. She pulled open her desk drawer and handed Hotchkin the copy of the new agreement, the one John had left for her to give Jill Monday—tomorrow. "That was the copy I was to give Jill for her to look over. We had not yet signed it."

Hotchkin noted the numerous colored tabs as he flicked through the several-page document before laying it aside and returning to his notepad. "Mind if I keep this for the moment?"

"No, of course not."

"I'm curious about one thing, Miz Boswell. Why would you give up income from such a big earner like Mr. Parson?"

A hint of a smile flickered across Sarah Ann's face. "Our attorney asked me that same question Friday evening. I'll tell you what I told him. I've made more money than I ever dreamed of earning. What I will make from the other talent we manage is enough. And Jill was doing the lion's share of the work to manage Jared's career." She could tell from the skeptical look on the detective's face that her answer strained credulity in his view. But she could not tell him the real reason that prompted the new partnership agreement. As far as she knew, only she and John were aware of the affair between Jill and Jared. And she would not allow the woman who had been her friend and partner to be smeared by an unnecessary scandal that would hurt not only Jill's reputation, but deeply wound LouAnn. Jared's young wife did not deserve that any more than Jill.

Hotchkin instinctively knew the woman across from him was holding something back, but he chose not to press her, at least for now. She seemed genuinely shocked by her partner's murder.

"I would like to call my…," Sarah Ann started to say husband and caught herself, "our attorney. He would want to know about Jill."

"Sure. Absolutely. Give him a ring," he said, pointing to the phone on her desk, "but I would appreciate your staying here." He pushed away from the desk again and stood up. "I need to check with some other folks here." He turned in the doorway. "I appreciate your cooperation, Miz Boswell."

John sounded chipper when he heard her voice. That instantly changed when she told him the reason for her call. "I'm so sorry for your loss, Sarah Ann. Where are you now?"

"I'm here, at the office. A Nashville detective called me earlier this morning. He didn't tell me she had been…," her voice caught. "I didn't know she was dead until I got here. I'm so sorry to call you like this, but he's asking me questions about the new contract…I don't think he believes me. Oh, John, I don't know what to do…what to say." For the first time since learning Jill had been killed, Sarah Ann wept, sobs tearing at her throat as tears spilled down her cheeks.

"Stay right there, Sarah Ann. And don't say anything more to that detective or anyone else. Do you understand me?" When she didn't respond he said again. "Sarah Ann, do you understand what I'm saying?"

"All right…yes, John, I won't say anything more."

"I'll be there as quickly as I can." The dial tone told her the connection was ended and she set the receiver in the charger with a mechanical move of her arm. She bit down hard on her lower lip and willed her emotions under control. She needed coffee. Slipping out the door she started toward the back kitchen break area, but a uniformed officer held up his hand to stop her.

"Sorry, ma'am. No one past here—Detective Hotchkin's orders.

"I was just going to make some coffee…there in the kitchen," she said pointing to a room off to the side toward the back of the building.

"It's okay, Harris," she heard Hotchkin's deep voice thunder out from the front reception area. "If you could make a big pot, ma'am, I'm sure we'd all appreciate it."

The young officer stepped aside, and she headed toward the break room. Several minutes later the 12-cup carafe was steaming, its contents wafting aromatically through the room. She poured herself a large mug and one for Hotchkin. "The coffee's ready officer," she said as she passed the policeman. Hotchkin was sitting at Viola's desk and took the coffee mug from her with a grateful nod as he pressed a cell phone to his ear. "Sugar and powered cream are in the second drawer," she whispered before heading back to her office.

Above her there was the thumping of several sets of feet. She wondered sadly about Jill up there somewhere, alone, no one to mourn her as the tramping feet moved around her. The tears came again. *How sad to die so savagely and so alone* she thought, sitting back down in her comfortable chair. The memory of her own near-death experience washed over her. *I was alone then too. But alone by my own choosing and attempting to take my life by my own choosing,* recoiling as she always did from the memory of that bleak chapter of her life. The nightmarish vision of a knife slashing down into Jill as she slept filled her mind's eye. The even more nightmarish scene of Jill awake as her attacker's weapon ripped into her flesh assaulted her mental vision. "Oh, God, please let her have been asleep and not felt pain," she whispered.

"Unfortunately, that wasn't the case, ma'am." Sarah Ann looked up startled. Hotchkin stood framed in the doorway. "She was a brave woman. She put up quite a struggle from what we can determine from the preliminary investigation." He sat back down in the chair across from her. "Have you thought of anyone we should notify yet?" he asked.

"No. But someone who has known her for many years is Arliss Hemming. He's a music producer with a studio just off Music Row." She lifted the steaming coffee mug to her lips to help repress tears misting her eyes. "He might know more about Jill's family," she said with a hint of apology in her voice. "I could call him," she offered.

"Better if I do it, ma'am. What's the number?"

Sarah Ann fished in her purse for her cell phone and turned to contacts. She handed the phone to the detective. He punched the call sign and walked back into the hall. Again, she could hear only muffled words. Then silence. Then more muffled words.

When he stepped back inside he explained, "I reached his wife. He apparently spent the night at his studio working. It's close by. I'm heading over there right now," and added, "I'd like you to stay here, if you don't mind. I shouldn't be too long.

"Detective." Sarah Ann lowered the cup to her desk. Hotchkin turned back toward her. "When were police alerted that Jill was…," she couldn't bring herself to say the word murdered, "that something was wrong?"

"Sometime around eleven last night. Actually, by an anonymous caller, Miz Boswell. A male voice. Wouldn't give his name to dispatch. Just said something awful had happened to Miz Edgerton and for us to get right over here. When the first patrol cars arrived, they couldn't find signs of a break-in or anyone around. Just Miz Edgerton upstairs. She was already deceased."

"Do you know how long Jill had been…dead?"

"We're not sure, ma'am. We'll know more when the coroner finishes her work."

He left, and she sat in silence. Only the tramping of feet above her intruded on her silence. *An anonymous call to police. Was it the killer?* She wondered absently. *Who would want to harm Jill? How did they get in? It was unlikely someone attempted to rob her*, she thought, trying to find answers. *There was no money to speak off. Jill used a debit card for personal expenses and a company credit card for anything related to the business.* Sarah Ann let her panicked mind scan through her memory of the rooms upstairs again and again. She had only been up there a handful of times. She could not recall seeing anything of great value. Nor could she remember any photos of Jill or family members or friends. *A robber would have left mostly empty-handed* she surmised.

Hadn't Hotchkin said there was no sign of a break-in? Why would Jill let someone in at that hour? Only Jared had a key to the apartment. A dark thought intruded into her thoughts—*Jared's volcanic temper and the abuse she suspected he inflicted on his wife. Did he do the same to Jill?* She immediately banished such suspicions and forced her thinking back to how an intruder might have gotten in. There was one other key. It was in Viola's desk in case Jill needed her to go upstairs and do something for her when she was away from the office.

Sarah Ann stood up and walked toward the front. Early morning sunshine slanted through the partially open wood blinds on the picture window that flanked the front door. She opened the bottom drawer where the key was kept on a ring attached to the side of the drawer. It was there. She would have to remember to tell Hotchkin about the key when he returned.

She walked back to her office, mystified by what the detective had told her. If there had been no break-in, then Jill may have known her attacker.

A great sadness washed over Sarah Ann as she pictured her friend battling for her life. But then, that was Jill, scrappy always, blunt, no nonsense, shrewd; a woman who knew the front doors and the back doors of the music business; a woman who went toe-to-toe with record company executives to win favorable contracts for any talent she represented; the same qualities she had gently tutored and nurtured in Sarah Ann. She owed so much to Jill. Had she told Jill often enough how much their partnership had meant, how it had changed her life.

Now, Jill was gone. And she would never again be able to voice her gratitude to this woman for giving her a life she never visualized leading; a success she never anticipated achieving. Jill had reached out and lifted her from the depths of a personal hell and led her onto the plateau on which she now stood. Sarah Ann buried her face in her hands and wept, deep sobs racking her body with a torment of agony over her remorse and loss.

When the sobs finally quieted, Sarah Ann sat staring vacantly at the print of a field of bright wildflowers by Monet. She loved the painting that contrasted so colorfully with the bland beige wall paint.

"Miz Boswell." The same bald pudgy-faced detective who had interrupted Hotchkin stepped into her office. She looked up at him with red-rimmed eyes and wondered distractedly how he could ever give chase to a fleeing criminal when his paunchy stomach hung over so far it hid his belt. "There's a man in the back. Says he knows you and you're expecting him."

"Thank you." She rose unsteadily, aimlessly smoothed the front of the long-sleeved silk shirt she had thrown on over jeans and walked toward the rear of the building. John stood there, his cheeks shadowed by a day's growth of beard, his expression solemn. He opened his arms and she felt them wrap around her as the sobs returned.

"I'm so sorry, Sarah Ann," his voice as soothing as the hand that stroked her hair. He kept her in a tight embrace until he felt the sobbing finally abate, then pulled a hanky from his pant pocket. She accepted it gratefully as his arms fell away. "Let's go sit in your office."

John made a fresh pot of coffee and set a fresh cup in front of her before taking the chair where the detective had sat. In the minutes that followed Sarah Ann told him everything that had happened from the time she received the call from Hotchkin. He listened intently, without comment.

"From what you've told me the police have no theory about how the intruder got in except there is no indication of a break-in."

"Apparently not."

John leaned back and crossed his long legs. They had been sitting there quietly conversing for more than an hour, attempting to avoid the reason they were there together on a Sunday morning, when they heard footsteps pounding down the hallway past Sarah Ann's office. They could hear raised voices coming from the rear parking lot. "Stay here," John motioned her to remain seated and stepped out. It was several minutes before he returned, his face drained of color.

"What is it, John," her voice filled with alarm.

"The coroner's office just removed the body. Apparently, the media got wind of it and it was a zoo back there while they were loading…," he left the rest of his sentence hanging in the air unspoken. "I went up to Jill's apartment with Detective Hotchkin. Says he's the lead investigator." Again John hesitated. "Sarah Ann, you may need to move your offices somewhere else temporarily," his expression grim as he added, "Whatever you do, don't go up there."

John sat back down and reached his arms across the desk to gently fold her hands in his. "Hotchkin said he'll give a brief statement to the media and be back with you in a few minutes." He searched her face before asking, "How much has he told you?"

Sarah Ann started to answer and suddenly found her mind blank. Tears welled in her eyes again and she turned away under John's unyielding gaze. He felt the tremor in her hands and grasped them tighter, trying to impart reassurance. When she looked back over at him, her hands had steadied. "He told me Jill fought with her attacker. And he said the police were notified by an anonymous caller sometime around eleven last night."

"Have they said when Jill was killed?" he asked.

"The detective said they weren't sure. The coroner would have to make that determination."

John sighed deeply and released his grip on her hands and sat back in his chair, a deep frown furrowing his brow. "I need to be with you whenever you speak to this detective," he said, with an emphasis on "whenever". And we may need to hire an attorney to help you."

Sarah Ann looked bewildered for a moment and then shook her head in disbelief. "Surely they can't think I would have harmed Jill." Her eyes reflected the pain in her words. "Oh, dear God! They *can't* be thinking such a thing," a hint of panic in her voice.

John rubbed his chin thoughtfully as he measured the effect of what he was about to say. "The detective said you gave him a copy of the proposed partnership agreement which neither one of you had yet signed. That leaves the original partnership agreement still in effect." He watched Sarah Ann closely to insure his words were being fully understood. "You may recall that under the original agreement, in the event of one partner's death, the remaining partner would become sole owner of Edgerton Group and all of its assets."

Sarah Ann looked at him sharply as the impact of his words became clear. "Are you saying that I could be a suspect?"

"Yes."

The bluntness of his answer caused a momentary wave of nausea. "For godsakes, John, you of all people must know…"

"Sarah Ann. I *know* you're not capable of such a thing. And if you were, I've no doubt I would be your only intended victim," John said with a hint of irony in his voice. His attempt at levity was lost on the woman staring back at him, panic still registered in her eyes.

"Sorry to keep you folks waiting." The natural ruddiness of Hotchkin's face had deepened to crimson and was shiny with perspiration from standing out in the morning sun on a day that held the promise of typical early September heat and humidity. The statement he gave to the news media had been as short on information as it was terse. The questions that followed were met not with answers, but his back, as he stomped into the building, silently dismissing the reporters as a pack of rabid dogs. And that was his label for the media on a good day. He knew he would hear again about his public relations shortcomings from the captain when he got back to the station. *What the hell*, he thought rebelliously, *he had his thirty years in. Let the captain and the police department spokesman deal with the bastards.*

"Detective Marlin Hotchkin," he said, extending his hand as John stood up. John pulled a chair next to Sarah Ann and signaled the detective to sit in the chair he had vacated.

"Mind if I take off my jacket, folks. It's already a scorcher out there." Hotchkin deliberately took his time retrieving his rumpled notepad and pen from the inside jacket pocket before draping the jacket over the back of the chair. What he had learned from the coroner was going to make this interview a little more challenging.

Chapter 27

He woke with a start and rubbed his eyes. He wasn't sure how long he had slept with his back against the wall. He rubbed his left cheek where blood had crusted on jagged scrapes. He pulled a grubby hanky from his pant pocket and spit on a corner and rubbed off some of the dried blood. As he attempted to crawl toward the far window he felt stiffness in his knees and back from being too long in one position. As he glanced at his large Timex it reminded him how long he had been there. And for the first time since breaking into the vacant rental house he felt a gnawing thirst. He couldn't remember when he had last had a drink of water, a drink of any kind for that matter, or something to eat. One thing for certain, he could sure use a beer.

Streaks of sunlight splayed across the room from the partially opened Venetian blind covering the back window, a window that allowed him a narrow bird's eye view of the happenings across the alley. Lots of commotion there. He could not have found a better spot from which to watch it all.

He had just managed to break into this house before the first police unit arrived. It was he who had summoned the police with his call from the pay phone outside the convenience store last night. It was a good thing he brought plenty of change with him. Even a 9-1-1 call cost these days. A far cry from when a call was a dime to anyone or anywhere in town.

He had watched the two officers who arrived first as they swished their large flashlights around the edges of the building across from him before searching around the rear doorframe and testing the door knob. It was locked. He knew that already. And the alarm was on.

The police officers had then trained their lights inside the car parked under the aluminum canopy, peering in the front seat and then the back seat before finally going up the outside steps to the apartment. They knocked several times and announced Nashville Police. No response. He knew there wouldn't be. Because he had left the door unlocked, they had no problem getting in. He wanted to make it easy for them to find her. What seemed like only seconds later one of the officers rushed down the stairs and vomited in the shrubbery shielding the parking area from the house next door. *This must've' been his first murder* he speculated.

The first sirens sounded shortly after that. Shielded in darkness, he surreptitiously watched the small rear parking lot fill up with police vehicles over the next hour.

Sometime after three a.m. he had slipped out of the house and walked two blocks to where his battered pickup was parked and drove back to the convenience store, parking a block away and walked back to the pay phone, carefully avoiding the view of the two outside surveillance cameras. The number he dialed rang several times before it was answered. He hung up seconds later, reassured. Driving back toward the house across the alley, he kept telling himself it would be all right. Somehow, it had to be all right.

Again, he parked two blocks away and made his way in the concealment of pre-dawn darkness to the vacant house and slipped back in easily, having left the side door unlocked.

He rubbed his eyes. He must have drifted off to sleep before all the commotion across the way woke him up. Good thing. He watched as two men carried a black body bag down the stairs to a waiting gurney. A small woman in a dark pant suit, with a clip board in hand, watched as the body was loaded into the back of a van. She talked briefly with the pair before they climbed into the front of the van and drove off. Then she turned to the outstretched microphones of the several radio and television crews surrounding her. He reckoned she must be some big shot and pondered what she might be telling them reporters about the woman in the body bag.

Then a man in a rumpled suit talked briefly with the same group.

He didn't seem to say much and looked pissed before turning to go back inside the building.

He would have to slip out of the house soon if he was going to be back in his motel room in time to catch the early newscast and hear what all they had to say.

~

Hotchkin now knew the woman sitting across from him could not have committed the murder of her partner. In a bewildered voice the daughter, Leigh Ann, confirmed her mother had had dinner with her family at their Franklin home and had left sometime after ten o'clock, at least an hour after the time the coroner estimated Jill Edgerton was stabbed to death. Shocked and tearful at learning why the detective had called, Leigh Ann insisted on driving to Nashville to be with her mother. He dissuaded her from coming only after a stern "No" and a firm promise he would ask Sarah Ann to call her as soon as possible. Leigh Ann finally yielded.

The alibi eliminated opportunity. But not motive. That was abundantly clear after the attorney described to Hotchkin in detail the terms of the partnership agreement which left Sarah Ann the sole owner of a business he suspected raked in a lot of money from Jared Parson's earnings alone.

The detective had listened intently, nodding from time to time. Sarah Ann Boswell was no longer talking. That was clear. And that only caused the nagging in his gut to feel like a burning ulcer. *What was it she was holding back?* Hotchkin was an experienced and savvy hand at interrogating. He could wait her out.

The detective fiddled with his notepad and pecked the desktop with his pen. Silence seemed to have a chokehold on the interview until Hotchkin finally broke the impasse by asking Sarah Ann, "Since Miz Edgerton appears to have no immediate kin here, could you go down to the coroner's office and identify her remains." He noted she appeared visibly relieved the interview was over.

Sarah Ann glanced at John and then nodded her head. "What time should I be there?"

Hotchkin pulled his cell phone from his pant pocket and dialed a number he knew by heart. He was told, "as soon as possible," by the person at the other end.

"Can you tell me where I should go?" asked Sarah Ann, after agreeing to go immediately, visibly relieved the interview appeared to be over.

"I know where the coroner's office is, Sarah Ann. I'll drive you there." John looked over at Hotchkin. "Will that be all, Detective?"

"Yes sir, for right now," Hotchkin replied in a dour tone. "I may have more questions later. I appreciate your cooperation, Miz Boswell. And you counselor," he added, nodding at John as he pushed back his chair and stood up. "I'll be in touch, Miz Boswell.

The coroner's office was in a building adjacent to Metro Police Headquarters which stood in the center of a complex of government buildings. They were met in the lobby by the same woman who had been at the crime scene. She had shed her pant suit for blue scrubs and a white coat. The name badge pinned on her coat identified her as Chief Coroner Dr. Jean Chambers.

After shaking hands with both of them, and saying in a kind, but businesslike voice that she was sorry for their loss, she directed Sarah Ann and John to follow her through a double door and down a corridor to another double door with a cautionary notice 'Authorized Personnel Only'. It opened into a large windowless room with muted lighting. In the center of the room were three large steel tables. Sarah Ann felt her chest contract. On the nearest table, bathed by a large operating room style light, was a body covered in a white sheet. Standing like a silent sentinel on the far side of the table was a younger man in identical blue scrubs, his head covered with a white cap, and his hands gloved in vinyl.

Dr. Chambers looked at Sarah Ann. "I know this is not easy, Mrs. Boswell. Are you ready?" she inquired in a kindly tone. Sarah Ann nodded, and she felt John's hand touch her shoulder as the man pulled the sheet back just enough to reveal Jill's face. Sarah Ann gasped as her hands flew to her mouth. "Oh, dear God," she whispered and felt John's reassuring arm tighten around her shoulder. She leaned into him for support.

Dr. Chambers asked softly, "This *is* Jill Edgerton?" Sarah Ann nodded her assent. "Would you mind stepping over to my office to sign some paperwork?"

The coroner led them back through the double doors to an office just off to the left. Inside its small confines were warmly painted walls, a sharp contrast to the sterile white and stainless steel of the autopsy room. Lining the wall to one side of the desk were framed diplomas and other recognitions that spoke to Dr. Chambers' qualifications and status in the world of medical examiners. On her desk were framed photos of two children at various ages.

"I know how difficult this must be for you, Mrs. Boswell," the doctor said sympathetically. "There are a few things we need. I understand you and the deceased were business partners," her voice assuming a more businesslike tone. "Do you have power of attorney for Miss Edgerton?"

Sarah Ann stared at the coroner, her mind a blank. It was John who answered. "She does. It's included in their partnership agreement. I'll have a copy of the power of attorney sent over to you tomorrow first thing, if that's satisfactory?"

"It would be. Once we have it, we'll be able to discuss further arrangements." Dr. Chambers pushed a form across to Sarah Ann. "This is a statement attesting that you have identified the deceased as Jill Edgerton."

Sarah Ann scribbled her signature and slid it back to the coroner.

"Again, I'm sorry for your loss, Mrs. Boswell. I appreciate your coming on such short notice," she added, placing the form in a basket on the side of her desk. "If there are no further questions, I'll take you back to the lobby."

It was late that afternoon when Sarah Ann pulled under the portico of her driveway. She felt exhausted, mentally and physically. John had offered to drive her home and stay with her. She had declined, feeling a desperate need to be alone. The blinking light on the answering machine greeted her as she entered the kitchen. The first call was from Willie Dell. "I just heard. Let me know what I can do to help you deal with this horror. Love you, baby sister."

She would call him back later. There was one call she must make first.

As usual Jared didn't answer until the final ring before voice mail. "Hey, Sarah Ann. What's up?" There was a hint of irritation in his voice.

"Jared…" She felt sobs tugging at her throat again. "Jill is dead." She hadn't intended to be so blunt. There was a long silence until finally she said, "Jared, are you still there?" She could hear his breathing become raspy as he fought for control.

"Yeah, I'm here. Wha… what happened?"

How to answer that question had been weighing heavily on her during the drive home. She knew how deeply Jill had loved him but was doubtful that her love was reciprocated. Sarah Ann remained deeply suspicious of Jared's motives. She had even gone to a darker place, wondering if he and Jill had quarreled and it had turned violent. It was only when she heard his strangled cry, and the obvious tears, that she felt a sudden rush of guilt. "Jared, someone murdered her. She was stabbed to death."

"Stabbed," he repeated, seeming not to comprehend. There was a prolonged silence before he asked in a choked voice, "When."

"Police say it was sometime last evening in her apartment above the office." Jared's chocking sobs went on for some time as Sarah Ann waited patiently, trying to think of comforting words. When the sobs finally abated, Jared said, "I know you never believed it, but I loved her." The connection went dead.

She hung the phone up slowly, dumbfounded. Jared had loved Jill? Her mind rejected his declaration. Sarah Ann had suspected for some time that Jill had suffered abuse at Jared's hands after seeing bruises on her arms more than once and even a bruise on her cheek which Jill explained away as a fall in the bathroom. *How can you love someone you probably physically abused? How can you love someone and use them the way you so blatantly used Jill?* her mind screamed. *To demand a greater share of income at her expense. That was greed, not love; certainly not the love Jill deserved from the man she worked so hard to groom for success.*

A torrent of emotions flooded through her, a deep sadness at the realization she would never see Jill again; a deeper anger that someone had so brutally taken Jill's life. Jill did not deserve such a violent end to her long years of hard work climbing the pinnacle of success in an industry that had demanded so much of her for so long before finally giving back.

Sarah Ann looked around the kitchen at the beautiful new white cabinets, the elegant new granite countertops, the muted stainless steel of the upscale appliances, the kitchen she had so longed for. A kitchen made possible by the income she derived from a career she owed entirely to Jill. She clutched her throat and felt tears stinging her eyes.

Suddenly she did not want to be alone; could not be alone. John and both children had offered to stay with her or for her to stay with them. But it was not her family she wanted at this moment. She reached for the telephone on the wall. Willie Dell answered on the first ring as if he had been standing by the phone. He heard the grief tearing through her. "Hold on, baby sister. I'll be right over."

Chapter 28

Willie Dell held his friend tightly, rocking her gently in his arms, trying to ease the sobs that seemed to levitate from deep within. When the tsunami of sobs fell quiet he pulled a handkerchief from his pocket and lifted her chin, dabbing away the rivulet of tears that left red streaks down her cheeks and around her eyes. "Blow," he commanded with the same gentleness with which he held the hanky over her nose.

"Have you told the others?" He knew she meant his fellow Prayer Group members.

"Yes. They'll be here shortly, baby sister. And I suspect they'll bring a pack mule train of food."

A thin smile creased her lips. "Why is it, Willie Dell, we Southerners find such comfort in food. In any crisis of our lives, we eat."

"Didn't you know food is the great assuager? It's what I tell my Weight Watchers coach and she falls for it every time."

She patted his plump cheek and slipped from his arms. "You could always brighten my spirits, even when I was forced to invade your sacred tree sanctuary."

The doorbell chimed. "I believe the food train is pulling into the station," he announced. "I'll get it."

Jeanne Marie hefted two large bags bulging with take-out from Panera Bread onto the large island in the center of the kitchen, and then drew Sarah Ann into her arms. "I'm so sorry, darlin'…so very sorry. I can't imagine what you're going through." She pushed Sarah Ann slightly away and saw new tears streaming down her cheeks. "You cry, honey. That's what tears are for, to wash away pain," then she pulled Sarah Ann back into her embrace and held her tightly until the doorbell sounded again moments later.

"I've got it," said Willie Dell as he hurried toward the front of the house.

Della Sue eyed her two friends as she placed bags from Publix and Cheesecake Factory beside the bags from Panera. "Beau heard about Jill on the news," she said as she grasped Sarah Ann's hands. "We love you, darlin', and we're goin' to help you get through this."

"You take Sarah Ann into the living room while I take care of this food," instructed Jeanne Marie, waving her hand at Della Sue. "You too, Willie Dell. I'll man the kitchen. It *is* a woman's domain, you recall," shooing them out of the room with an insistent wave.

"Funny, I must have missed that gender lesson," was Willie Dell's good-natured riposte, tossing her a kiss over his shoulder as he departed for the parlor. Before he could take a seat near the two women huddled together, the doorbell chimed again. He opened the door and stepped aside as Angela swept in, her bleached blond hair askew, several plastic bags clutched in her hands. "I picked up a few things at Publix," she explained, slightly winded by the walk from the car.

Willie Dell relieved her of the plastic bags straining her arms and motioned her toward the kitchen. "I'll help you unload and then we'll head to the parlor," said Willie Dell in a hushed voice. "Jeanne Marie's volunteered for kitchen duty."

"How's she holding up?" whispered Angela, nodding toward the front room as they walked down the hallway and into the kitchen.

"Not too good."

Twenty minutes later they were all gathered back around the kitchen island. It was food and the familiar chatter of her friends that provided Sarah Ann an ephemeral respite from the horror of seeing Jill dead on the cold steel table in the autopsy room that was playing like a video in her mind, over and over. It was a picture which threatened to release another stream of tears. By sheer force of will she held them in check behind the dam of fear that she would reveal too much of the shock of this day to the friends now gathered around the kitchen island.

"Cheesecake—red velvet, my personal favorite, or the Yankee version—New York." Jeanne Marie pointed a silver cake server at Sarah Ann.

"No thanks. I couldn't."

"Never say you can't when confronted with this nirvana of heaven-blessed comfort food." Jeanne Marie waved the cake server with the authority of a teacher wielding a pointer at a blackboard. "I repeat—red velvet or the Yankee version."

"The Yankee version. Small."

"You make my Confederate gray blood run blue, but Yankee version it is. How about the rest of y'all?" she demanded, swinging the cake server in a loop around the granite covered island.

Angela topped off their glasses with the smooth Mimosas she had stirred up. "Drink up, baby sister," urged Willie Dell. "It might help you sleep later."

Sleep, and the nightmares she feared would invade that sleep, was the very thing that Sarah Ann was most apprehensive about right now. Staying awake seemed a better alternative. She sipped the tangy Mimosa obediently. Welcomed warmth from the fruity drink permeated through her. During the meal she had recounted most of what had happened, even about not sharing with Detective Hotchkin Jill's affair with Jared.

"Is it really any business of the police?" Della Sue reasoned. "Anyway, it would only besmirch Jill, and surely cause a scandal for Jared and his wife." She left unsaid what it might do to the reputation of Edgerton Group and indirectly to Sarah Ann. *Lord knows, she already had enough to be upset about*, Della Sue thought as she watched her friend with growing concern.

"But oh, how Music Row loves a scandal," Jeanne Marie chimed in. Della Sue tried to shake her head nonchalantly to dissuade Jeanne Marie's line of thought. Oblivious, Jean Marie plunged ahead, "The Tennessean would certainly love it," her voice dripping with sarcasm. "It might even spike their sagging…ouch," she exclaimed feeling a sharp jab from the toe of Della Sue's high heels.

The Nashville newspaper was a frequent target of Jeanne Marie's barbed criticism since it had purchased the local newspaper last year and promptly fired her as society editor. A superfluous position the newly installed young executive editor had explained. "Superfluous, my ass," she had hurled at him as she headed out the door after clearing out her desk. In a show of solidarity, all the members of the Prayer Group had dropped their subscriptions except for Willie Dell, who surreptitiously re-subscribed under a fictitious name, with delivery diverted to his post office box. A realtor could not be without a local newspaper.

Angela began clearing away plates. "I'll take clean-up duty since Jeanne Marie served up this elaborate feast from the kitchens of Panera and Publix. Why don't y'all take your mimosas and retire to the front parlor."

Della Sue spoke up. "I'll give you a hand."

Angela shook her head emphatically. "No need, darlin'. You just hurry your little 'knickers' down the hall." She smirked wickedly at her friend. "Anyway, cleaning up a kitchen makes me feel like I'm channeling Beau."

"May the good Lord smite you with a severe case of dishwater hands," Della Sue flung back, as her heels clicked toward the doorway.

"Is that what's wrong with Beau?" Angela inquired mischievously.

"Dishpan hands isn't one of Beau's problems," Della Sue tossed back. "His afflictions affect a different part of his anatomy. Anyway, he's now immunized against dishpan hands. Didn't I tell you? He just had a new dishwasher installed."

Angela laughed and started filling up Sarah Ann's new dishwasher.

In the parlor, Sarah Ann sat on the couch leaning against Willie Dell, his arm protectively around her shoulders. Jeanne Marie stood up and walked over to one of the floor-to-ceiling bookcases flanking the marble fireplace, opened the leaded mullioned glass doors and pulled out a CD. "I believe we could all use a little Pavarotti."

Just as the music began the telephone rang. Jeanne Marie picked it up and listened silently. "I'll get her." She padded across the deep, soft carpet in her bare feet, having shed her shoes in the kitchen, and held out the phone to Sarah Ann who looked at her quizzically. "It's John."

"Hello."

"How are you doing?"

"I'm all right. Some friends are here with me."

"The Prayer Group?" Absent from his voice was any hint of the hostility he had so often directed at her childhood friends in the past. It had been an ongoing source of contention during their marriage.

"Yes."

"I'm glad they're with you." There was a prolonged silence. "Tomorrow, after you've rested, we need to talk, Sarah Ann. Hotchkin called me tonight. He wants to meet with you again." More silence. "I'm afraid he suspects you're holding something back." Again silence. "Sarah Ann."

"Yes, I'm listening."

"I know how difficult this must be. The police have located an elderly great aunt who appears to be Jill's only living relative. She lives in the Boston area. Hotchkin said she hadn't seen or heard from Jill in years. But we can discuss all that tomorrow." Another prolonged silence. "Try to get some rest. Call me if you need anything." And he was gone. Jeanne Marie lifted the phone from Sarah Ann's trembling hands.

"I'm glad he's at your side on this one, baby sister." Willie Dell pulled her back against his chest and tucked his arm around her shoulder. "John can be a prick, but a prick that'll have your best interests at heart. And he'll protect you."

A short time later Jeanne Marie joined her friends as the emoting voice of the fabled tenor swelled in the background. They talked, skirting the tragedy that had befallen Sarah Ann, and kept to lighter things that had touched their lives. And so the evening passed in much the same way all Prayer Group meetings had—with stories and gossip, recounting past memories, belly laughs when Della Sue declared Beau the reincarnation of an Egyptian court eunuch, but with certain physical characteristics intact. And as always there were the prayer requests. They varied little, but tonight a prayer was added, for the repose of the soul of Jill Edgerton.

Unspoken were the prayers for Sarah Ann to find the strength to deal with what had befallen her.

Chapter 29

Ross Lambert announced himself to Viola. Her large brown eyes remained rimmed with tears as they had since arriving this morning. He reached his hand and she hesitantly took his. For just a moment he held hers in both of his. "I'm so sorry for your loss. I can only imagine what you and the rest of the staff are dealing with this morning."

You have no idea, mister, and how would you know anyway? It wasn't your boss who was murdered flashed through Viola's mind.

Viola was a quick study of those who walked through the front door of Edgerton Group's modest office. But she felt herself being drawn to this man whose dark brown eyes, shaded by thick brows, shown with kindness. His thatch of wavy silver streaked blond hair added a mature handsomeness to his chiseled features, supported by a strong chin with a deep cleft. "I called Mrs. Boswell earlier."

Viola retrieved her hands from Lambert. Her normal skepticism of anyone she did not know walking through the door returned. *Kind or not we'll see if Miz Sarah Ann has time to deal with the likes of you.*

"Sorry to intrude, Miz Sarah. A Mr. Lambert says you knew he was coming." She listened and then nodded. "You can go back, Mr. Lambert," her voice assuming its usual courteous, businesslike tenor. "Second door on the right."

The first door past the conference room across from her was a coat closet, and Viola couldn't begin to count the number of times people had opened it thinking Sarah Ann would be sitting there, something that never failed to amuse her. But not today. This was a day for tears and ample tissues. She would need another box of them before this day was over—snatching yet another wad from the box and pressing them to her swollen eyes and blowing her nose stoutly.

"Good morning." Lambert opened the door so gently Sarah Ann didn't notice. He stood framed in the doorway, his head nearly touching the top. "Is this a good time? Or would you rather I come back."

"No please, do come in and sit down," she invited, appearing touched by his concern about intruding. She punched the intercom. "Could you please hold any calls for a few minutes, Viola?"

She stood up and they shook hands. "What can I do for you, Mr. Lambert?"

She was getting right to the point, which meant he probably was intruding, but she was a polite enough business woman to allow it, since he represented Edgerton Group's most successful artist's record label. He pulled a single page from his narrow briefcase and pushed it across the desk to her. Sarah Ann read the first few lines and then reread them before looking back at Lambert, her features cloaked in confusion. He noticed the dark circles beneath her eyes, two dark emeralds, softly misted by tears. She had the haunted look of someone who had shed too many tears and had too little sleep.

"What is this, Mr. Lambert?"

"My resume, Mrs. Boswell."

Her expression changed from confused to stunned. "Your resume! I don't understand." Her voice had dropped to almost a whisper.

"You're going to need someone to handle Jared Parson for the European tour that launches in less than a month." He saw a dark cloud of wariness descend over her face. "I was the manager of a couple of top groups in my earlier days. That's before donning a suit and tie and joining NCA five years ago. You're going to need a road manager for Parson. I'm applying for the job."

"Mr. Lambert, I haven't had time yet to even consider the tour. There are a number of things I need to deal with first, but I…"

He cut her off gently. "I know. What's ahead of you the next few days will be overwhelming. That's why you'll need someone to finalize arrangements for the tour. I can do that," he concluded simply.

Watching Lambert, Sarah Ann was stymied momentarily by the

warmth of his brown eyes and the empathy clearly emanating from them. "We may have to cancel the tour, at least temporarily," she said. "I'm meeting this afternoon with Jared and our attorney to discuss the ramifications and to consider possible alternatives."

Lambert leaned back in his chair and observed Sarah Ann introspectively. "Include me in that meeting," he suggested. "Depending on how the contracts are written—I suspect they're fairly standard and ironclad—Edgerton Group could face severe financial penalties if you cancel now, even if you try to reschedule in light of this tragedy."

"I understand that, Mr. Lambert. But I also have to weigh what Jared wants to do. As much as I appreciate your concern and willingness to help, I have to consider Jared first."

"You have a lot on your plate, Mrs. Boswell. I may be able to clear away a part of that. And if I prove myself satisfactory in handling the tour for Edgerton Group and Jared, I would like to buy in as a partner, even as a minority partner."

"Now you *are* getting way ahead of yourself, Mr. Lambert." Sarah Ann was shocked by his broaching a possible partnership at this time. She felt a hint of irritation evolving toward anger at his audacity. "You're right, Mr. Lambert…"

"Please," he interrupted, "call me Ross."

"All right, Ross," she replied in a flat voice. "You were right when you said I have a lot on my plate. I don't mean to appear rude, but I must bring this visit to an end." She stood up and extended her hand across the desk. "I hope you understand. Thank you for coming."

"I do understand, Mrs. Boswell." His lips lifted in an apologetic smile. "I've cleared my afternoon calendar if you change your mind." At the door he looked back at her still standing behind her desk. "I'm deeply sorry for your loss. Jill Edgerton was highly respected in country music circles. Her death is a great tragedy." She looked for any hint of insincerity in his eyes and saw none. They were a remarkable map of his emotions. "Again, I'm available if you think I can help."

"I very much appreciate that, Mr. Lam… Ross. Thank you." She smiled wanly. "And please, call me Sarah Ann." Before Lambert could clear the doorway, Sarah Ann said, "On second thought, Mr.

Lam…Ross. Why don't you come to the meeting with Jared and John? Your presence could prove helpful."

Lambert nodded. "See you then."

She sat back down slowly. Had what just happened, really happened—that the new head of NCA records wanted to take over as Jared's tour manager and then join Edgerton Group?

She shook her head in disbelief. It was the last thing she would have expected on what was already turning into an extraordinary day.

The intercom buzzed. It was Viola. "I have a Detective Hotchkin—I think that's his name anyway—on line one."

"Thanks, Viola. Oh, and Viola, could you do me a favor? Call Jared and ask him to call me when he has a moment. Thanks."

Sarah Ann punched line one. "Yes, Detective?"

"Just wondering if you and I could meet for a short time yet today? Got a few things I'd kinda like to go over with you, if that's all right."

"Of course. I'm meeting at one with Jared Parson and our attorney. Could it wait until after that?"

"As a matter-of-fact that works fine for me. I need to talk with Mr. Parson as well, so maybe I'll catch both of you right after your meeting."

"May I ask why Jared needs to be involved? It's a really busy time for him since Jill had been in charge of coordinating arrangements for his upcoming European tour."

"I'm sure it *is* a busy time for him, ma'am. So I'll keep my time with both of you short."

It was clear she would not be able to put him off. "Would about three be convenient," she offered.

"Just fine, ma'am. See you and Mr. Parson then."

"Hotchkin punched off his cell phone. He hated having to wait on the interview. Chances were that attorney would stick around. He could screw things up and advise them both not to talk. Hotchkin slammed the door of his unmarked car and walked toward the Employee's entrance to the police department. At least knowing what he did now would put him in the cat bird's seat when he got into a room with that pair. He wondered if what he now knew was what Miz Boswell was holding back. *Whatever it is, she sure as hell was holding something back.*

Sarah Ann heard Nessun Dorma sound on her cell phone and pulled it from the purse at her feet. It was John. "Are we still set with Jared for one?"

"Yes. He called me right after talking with you."

"I've already gone through the contracts Jill signed on his behalf. The penalties could be steep for pulling out. The two outdoor stadium venues are narrowly written on ways to default without penalty. Almost the same with the indoor venues. Of course, if Jared becomes seriously ill, is injured or dies, the concerts can be postponed or obviously cancelled without penalty. Unfortunately, having a manager murdered is one eventuality not covered."

"What is the liability for Edgerton Group if he refuses to go?"

There was a heavy sigh at the other end of the line. "I had to be a little more persuasive with both Jill and Jared on that score. Edgerton Group has no liability. But Jared does. It was the compromise I hammered out with him after he demanded a bigger share of the box office take. I included an insurance policy to cover his liability. It's with Lloyd's of London. Jill insisted Edgerton Group pay half to write the policy. But otherwise, there is no financial consequence for you and the insurance should minimize Jared's out-of-pocket loss. It's something I'm exploring further. Hopefully, I'll have an answer when I see you at one."

There was a brief silence broken by John. "How are *you* holding up?"

"I've been on the phone all morning, even with Viola screening calls, and Natalie helping her. Keeping busy is helping. Thanks for asking."

"Do you need some extra help? I could spare Jane for the rest of the day. We have a temp in this week who could take over here for a few hours."

"Thanks for the offer. But I think we're okay for now."

"I hope it's all right with you, Sarah Ann. I've asked Johnny to come with me. I think a second pair of legal eyes and ears could prove helpful. No extra charge," he added smoothly.

Hearing their son was accompanying his father jogged Sarah Ann's memory. "I had a visit a short time ago from Ross Lambert at NCA. He's offering to fill in for Jill as road manager for the tour and asked if he could sit in on our meeting." She didn't mention his offer to buy in as a new partner in Edgerton Group. "What do you think?"

"Fine with me. Maybe Jared should hear what he has to say." She could hear his pen tapping on his glass topped desk, a habit John had for as long as she had worked with him from early on in their marriage. "Is it just NCA trying to protect their investment in Jared?"

"There's more to it than that, but I'll tell you later." Sarah Ann's name sounded on the intercom. "I'd better go, John. I'm glad you're bringing Johnny. See you at one."

Lambert arrived early bearing a subway sandwich and potato chips. "It looked like you might have missed breakfast," he explained. Sarah Ann accepted it gratefully and as she took a small bite of the sandwich he said, "I thought I should explain something before the others arrive. Leaving the distribution end of the music business has been my goal for some time. I wish the circumstances were not what they are, but Jill's death provided an opportunity to jump ship from NCA and start working in a part of the industry that holds keener interest for me." He looked at her with piercing eyes, gauging her reaction. "Timing is dictated by the situation, in this case an unfortunate situation."

Before she could respond the intercom buzzed. "Mr. Boswell and your son are here," Viola announced with the formality of a palace butler.

"Tell them to come on back."

After being introduced to Lambert, Johnny walked around the desk and wrapped his mother in a hug. "I'm so sorry for all you're going through, mom. We'll help you get through it." He kissed her on the head and cheek. "Love you." She patted his cheek and for the first time since arriving at the office early this morning, tears threatened. She willed them away and took her seat. The three men sat down in chairs ringing her desk.

John placed his briefcase on the edge of the desk and looked over at Lambert, "I don't mean to be impolite," he remarked, "but I'm not completely sure why you're here, Mr. Lambert. Or even if you should be."

Lambert seemed to take no offense at John's bluntness. "I under-stand, Boswell. I told Sarah Ann earlier I'd like to fill in as Jared's manager during the upcoming tour, assuming that arrangement is agreeable with Jared."

"It's fine with me." Jared strode into the office, closing the door sharply behind him. "Sarah Ann called me and said it was up to me to do the tour or not. She'd back me either way. I talked to LouAnn and she wants me to go. So, I'll need a manager." Jared shook hands with John and John Jr. "You must be Lambert," he said cordially, holding out his hand.

"Good to meet you, Jared. Sorry it's under these circumstances. Sorry for your loss."

"Yes, sir, I appreciate that." Jared turned and surprised Sarah Ann by walking around her desk and wrapping his arms tightly around her. "Who could have done this to Jill?" he whispered in her ear. She felt the dampness of his tears against her cheek. "I just don't understand who…who could have done this to Jill?"

Sarah Ann was staggered by Jared's depth of emotion and she drew her arms protectively around him. "I don't know, Jared, but the police will get to the bottom of it."

"Yes, ma'am, they will," he said as he released her and brushed tears away with his shirt sleeve. John Jr. had pulled another chair around the desk and Jared sat down. Sarah Ann noticed the dark circles under his eyes and evidence of worry in his furrowed brow. "Are you sure you want to make the tour, Jared," she asked, voicing her concern.

"Yes, ma'am. As I said, I talked it over with LouAnn. She thinks I should go. And if you're good with it, we are too."

John spoke next. "Have you ever managed an overseas tour, Lambert?"

"No, but I speak French and German, and in my early days in the business was a road manager for a couple of top rock groups on the West Coast. I worked up most of the musical arrangements for those groups, as well as booking gigs in some major venues." He added, "It's all listed in the resume I gave Sarah Ann earlier today."

Sarah Ann handed the two attorneys and Jared copies of Lambert's resume. After long moments of silence John looked up. "Obviously you have the qualifications," he agreed. "If you're the man Jared and

Sarah Ann want, I'll let them work out your financial compensation, and we'll draw up a contract and have it ready for signing at your earliest convenience."

Jared reached across John and shook hands with Lambert. "Thanks for coming on board. I appreciate it, man."

"Now that that's settled," said Sarah Ann, "let's discuss the particulars of the tour and make sure everything is in place." The discussion of the tour details lasted for the better part of the next two hours, with Lambert inserting suggestions from time-to-time that brought nods of approval from Jared and Sarah Ann. John seemed relieved that none of the changes required addenda to the tour contracts.

After settling on a salary and percentage Lambert stood up to leave. He smiled and noted with ironic humor that the biggest beneficiary of the change could be Len Shiring, who might just keep his old job after all.

John Jr. left with Lambert, discussing some details to include in his contract as they walked toward the reception area. Sarah Ann closed the door of her office and slipped back behind her desk and glanced at her watch. "Jared, a Metro detective is coming shortly. He wants to talk with both of us. I think John should stay with us for the interview."

"Sure…I guess." He looked suddenly devoid of his usual swagger and for the first time Sarah Ann saw something in his eyes she had never before seen—fear.

"I should absolutely be with you both anytime you're interviewed by the police," insisted John.

"Yes, thank you, John. I agree. Don't you, Jared?"

"Yes, ma'am," he said emphatically. He stood up and walked behind Sarah Ann's desk and opened several slats of the vertical blind to stare out at the grassy median separating the driveway from the house next door. "Did he say what he wanted?"

"He didn't say," answered Sarah Ann. Turning in her chair, she added in a low voice, "I've told him nothing about your relationship with Jill."

She heard a heavy sigh. "I told LouAnn about us…'bout me and Jill. I thought she should hear it from me, and not someone else."

Sarah Ann was startled by this revelation. She glanced over at John. A look of concern suffused his handsome features. "How did she take it?" John asked.

Jared walked back and slumped back in his chair. "She cried a lot. Didn't say much." He seemed to be studying his hands which were gripped tightly together in his lap. "She asked me if I loved Jill. I told her no. I didn't want to hurt her anymore." Looking over at John, tears swam in Jared's eyes; the same eyes John remembered reflecting only distain akin to hatred when he had last seen the singer in his office. Now those eyes reflected only pain. "Is it possible to love two women at one time?"

John was taken aback by the question. "I suppose," he answered speculatively.

"I do, you know…love them both."

"If that's the case, Jared," said John, "you have a chance to make amends with your wife. And refocus your love on her. Not every husband who strays has a chance to do that."

Sarah Ann felt her own heart lurch at John's words. She knew they were meant as much for her as for Jared.

The intercom buzzed. "Two detectives here, Miz Sarah." Viola's usually crisp voice was low, almost a whisper. "You want me to send them back or let them cool their heels for a little while. I told 'em you were in a meeting."

Hearing two detectives were here took Sarah Ann by surprise. Hotchkin had not indicated he was bringing anyone else along. "No, it's all right, Viola, you can send them back."

John stood up and opened the door just as Hotchkin and a second man appeared from the front. "Good to see you again, Detective Hotchkin. And this is…?"

"My partner, Detective Jim Morgan. Jim, this is the attorney I mentioned, John Boswell." Actually, he had done more than mention Boswell. The two men had looked him up on line, read the resume on the webpage for Boswell, Jardine & Boswell, checked cases Boswell had been involved with, and even scanned his divorce petition. Hotchkin had learned early on in his career that when a man files for divorce, it usually means he has a piece of ass on the side pressuring him to make the relationship respectable. That was underscored when he read Boswell had married his second wife two weeks after legally ditching his first. Peering at the long-haired beauty on Boswell's arm, smiling back at him from a story about a charity event carried in the Tennessean, Hotchkin could understand the attorney's second rush to the altar.

Hotchkin nodded a terse greeting to Sarah Ann. "You must be Mr. Parson. My partner, Detective Morgan." Both men shook hands with Jared. "And, Jim, this is, ah, Miz Edgerton's business partner, Sarah Ann Boswell," he said as she emerged from around her desk.

"I just returned from vacation today," Morgan explained, extending his hand to Sarah Ann. "Pleased to meet you, ma'am."

"Won't you gentlemen have a seat?" John said and pointed to the chairs vacated by Lambert and his son.

When everyone was seated, Hotchkin said brusquely, "Let's get down to business."

"You two are looking into Jill's death?" Jared asked pointedly.

"Yes, sir, we are." Hotchkin answered. "And first things first, Mr. Parson. Where were you Saturday night when your manager was killed?"

"I was at my farm in Williamson County, mostly working in my recording studio."

"About how long were you in there, in the studio, would you say?" It was Hotchkin asking again, while his silent partner jotted notes in a small spiral notebook.

"We had supper about six. Me and my wife and little girl. Then I went into the studio right after that. Worked until about midnight, best I can remember."

"And can anyone verify that's where you were."

"Well, about eight or so my wife called me in the studio. We went and tucked our little girl in bed. I promised to read her a story, but I needed to work in the studio so LouAnn—that's my wife—read her the story so I could get back to work." Jared looked at John as if seeking reassurance he had said the right things.

"Do you know of anyone who had threatened Miz Edgerton, or who would wish her harm, Mr. Parson?"

"No, sir. Everybody liked Jill. She was the best. You know, the best manager you could have in this business. I owe everything to her and Sarah Ann."

"How close was your relationship with Miss Edgerton, would you say, Mr. Parson?" It was Morgan speaking for the first time.

Sarah Ann saw a flash of alarm flicker across Jared's face, but his tone was even when he responded. "Miz Jill and I worked pretty close. It's the way it is between a singer and manager. She even helped with a lot of the music arrangements." He hesitated and seemed to grip the sides of his chair a little tighter. "She had a music degree and played the piano well enough to be a performer on her own. It wasn't something she shared with many folks." He glanced at Sarah Ann and knew from her expression this was the first she knew of Jill's musical talent. "She was savvy in all aspects of our business," Jared continued. "Told me one time she considered trying the performing end of the business. Then figured she could make more money managing people like me." He looked unblinkingly at Morgan. "I'm sure glad she made that choice." There was a catch in his voice when he continued. "I'm really going to miss her."

"I'm sure you will, Mr. Parson," Morgan returned evenly in an urbane voice, very different from his more colloquial partner. "Would you describe your relationship with Miss Edgerton as strictly business, strictly platonic?"

John interjected. "I believe Jared has already answered that question, Detective."

"That may be the case, counselor, but a Mrs. Winnifred Hemming told us…" He made a point of leafing through the notebook before looking directly at Jared, "that she believed you and Miss Edgerton were having a sexual affair." He let the statement sink in a moment before asking, "Is that true, Mr. Parson?"

Jared looked stricken. "You sonofabitch," he choked, leaping up from his chair.

John moved with a natural quickness and placed his hands on Jared's shoulders. He pushed Jared gently back into his seat. "I would advise you to say no more, Jared." He turned to the two detectives. "That's clearly hearsay. And you know it, Detectives. I believe this interview is at an end. If you have anything further to discuss with

Mr. Parson or Mrs. Boswell, please contact me and we'll cooperate, I'm sure." He pulled a slim silver case from the inside pocket of his suit jacket and handed each man a business card.

"Glad to hear it, counselor," Hotchkin responded in a pedantic tone. "We'll need to go over a few things with Mrs. Parson. Could you arrange a time convenient for her?"

John glanced at Jared who shook his head vehemently but remained silent.

"Mrs. Parson is in the advanced months of a pregnancy, Detective. I'm sure you realize how upsetting such an interview would be for her. Is it really necessary?"

Judging by Parson's reaction, Hotchkin knew it definitely was, but chose to let the matter go unanswered for now. He stood up. "You'll be hearing from us again, Mr. Boswell. Ready, Morgan?" The second detective stood up with a clear show of reluctance and followed Hotchkin out the door held open by John. Now *we know what Miz Boswell was holding back* Hotchkin thought as they approached the front door.

"You buying that shit, Marlin?" Morgan spit out, as they walked down the front steps toward their unmarked car parked at the curb. "It sure as hell is obvious they don't want us talking to that guy's wife."

Hotchkin nodded agreement. "Boswell's right about one thing. What Miz Hemming told us is hearsay unless we can prove it. To me it sounded like she was into the sauce heavy when she called, so I don't think we can put much store in what she's told us. Not at this point, anyway." He opened the passenger side door as Morgan walked around to the driver's side.

"I still think we need to have a little talk with Parson's better half and find out if she suspected her husband was screwing his manager. And if he was and she knew it—just how pissed she was.

"Pissed enough to kill like that when you're way along in a pregnancy?" questioned Hotchkin as he pulled the door shut.

"Who knows?" Morgan pulled away from the curb and headed toward Belmont Boulevard. "If she *was* pissed enough to kill, it's the husband I'd have stabbed."

Chapter 30

He saw the unmarked car driven by the younger of the two detectives only for a moment from his vantage point across the alley from Edgerton Group before it left his line of vision. How much had they learned so far? He wished he could have been a fly on the wall.

Jared had looked scared—real scared—when he plopped himself down in his fancy new Mercedes convertible and tore out from the parking area behind the house he was looking at across the alley. He'd be more than scared when the cops found what he'd hidden in Jared's studio 'cause the bastard would be in jail facing murder charges. Them two detectives might just have to get a little nudge in the right direction to make sure that happened. He eased out of the vacant house and made his way in the shadow of the alley, back to his battered pickup.

The setting sun slanted through the partially opened blind leaving parallel streaks of bright light cascading over Sarah Ann's desk where she sat when the phone rang. It was Ross Lambert reporting he had resigned from NCA Records effective immediately. Len Shiring would be keeping his job, at least temporarily.

Sarah Ann wanted to feel a big weight being lifting. Soon, perhaps. Just not yet. She welcomed him aboard and gave him Jared's unlisted home phone and cell phone numbers. Jared was now in Lambert's hands. She hoped *good hands*. Leaning back in her chair, Sarah Ann rubbed the back of her neck with both hands to ease the strain from sitting too long. She looked up at the wall clock above the door. An hour yet before her appointment at the funeral home in Brentwood. Just enough time to freshen up in the bathroom and maybe grab a hamburger from a fast food restaurant.

Hotchkin had allowed John to search Jill's office after the meeting and rummage through a safe in her apartment to look for a will or other important papers that might shed more light on her past. He found none. Only a passport, a gold pocket watch with an inscription—'To George from Lucille, December, 1945'—and a framed black and white photograph of two people; the man in a military uniform he knew was Army Air Corps from World War II and a pretty girl with a mass of long curly hair and a smile that looked strikingly like Jill. When he had returned from the apartment his face was pale, his expression grim. Jill's blood had soaked into several areas of the light blue carpet fibers and dried to an eerie dark red, like a splatter of dark clouds on a pale moon. John had handed Sarah Ann the items he found and warned her again, not to go up there. With no will, and only an elderly great aunt in a nursing home, it had fallen to Sarah Ann to make arrangements to bury her friend and business partner.

This she did in a cemetery in Brentwood where grave stones read like an early 'who's who' of country music legends. The memorial service in the funeral home's spacious chapel the following Friday was filled to capacity. Sarah Ann sat flanked by John and her children and their spouses on one side and Willie Dell on her right, who held her hand throughout the service. Seated just behind Sarah Ann were the rest of the Prayer Group, along with a somber Jared and a tearful LouAnn.

Arliss Hemming followed the minister to the podium. He had mentored Jill during her early years in Nashville, had known her the longest. He delivered the eulogy. In his soft-spoken way, his simple words paid a touching tribute to his friend. Sarah Ann knew that hidden in his simple words was a much deeper loss.

Hemming's wife, Winnifred, did not hear the eulogy. She was falling-down drunk by the time her husband left for the funeral.

Jared then stepped to the front with his guitar, and accompanied by his piano player, sang a mournful *Amazing Grace*. When his voice cracked with emotion, many in the audience took up the song and the solo became a choir. Tears were still being wiped away with tissues as the line of mourners filed out of the chapel.

The wake followed at Sarah Ann's home. Natalie and Viola helped Monet serve a delectable array of hors d'oeuvres, sandwiches and desserts the maid/chef had spent the better part of yesterday and the morning of the memorial service preparing.

Sarah Ann moved among the guests with her social skills on autopilot, accepting condolences, and listening to the recounting of endless stories about Jill. She had proved to be a tough and colorful part of that tight little community called Music Row. "We'll miss her," was said to Sarah Ann over and over. And she knew many of them meant it.

Members of the Prayer Group were sitting together at the far end of the large parlor, following their fellow member as she shook hands, listened to words of sympathy and awkward inquiries about the progress of the investigation into Jill's brutal murder. It was Angela who determined Sarah Ann needed a break. With the silent approval of her friends she walked over and gently guided Sarah Ann out of the room and out to the screened-in back porch.

On the way, Angela plucked a chilled glass of sweet tea from a tray being passed around by Natalie and handed it to Sarah Ann. "Drink," she ordered after they were settled on the cushioned porch swing. Sarah Ann obediently lifted the cool drink to her lips. "I can't be away long," she insisted.

"You just needed a little break."

"Thank you."

"You're welcome," replied Angela, squeezing Sarah Ann's hand.

As Angela propelled the swing back and forth with her feet, Sarah Ann stared out beyond the wide flower beds and the neatly trimmed boxwoods to where an ancient magnolia tree towered. A gentle breeze rustled its fat leaves. The magnolia dominated the center of the large backyard, its wide trunk wrapped with a wrought iron bench in need of paint. Some of the wood steps John had nailed into its truck when their children were young, now hung precariously at different angles, minus a nail or two. *Such happy times* Sarah Ann silently recalled, hearing again the squeals of delight as her two children scampered up the tree. Sometimes their adventuresome antics had brought her heart to her throat just watching. Somehow both had made it into their teens without busted heads or broken bones.

Sarah Ann forced herself back to the present. "They keep asking me why this happened to Jill, Angela. All I can do is shake my head." Tears that had been restrained all day threatened. "I better go back in," she said, taking another gulp of iced tea. "Thank you for spiriting me away for a little while."

As she stood up, Sarah Ann noticed Arliss Hemming standing just beyond the big magnolia. She handed the glass to Angela and walked out toward him.

"Hey, Arliss."

"Hey, yourself."

"It was a beautiful eulogy. Thank you again for doing that for Jill."

"No problem," he said tilting his head toward her. Stray tears were curving languidly through the crevices of his cheeks. She stood beside him for a moment, silently staring in the same direction as he. "I think of all of us who knew Jill," Sarah Ann said softly, "you will miss her the most."

He patted her arm. "You know I'm here for you too, Sarah Ann. I hope you carry on for Jill." He turned and looked down at her. "It's what she would have wanted. You were the best thing that could've happened for her."

"Thank you, Arliss. I will. I promise." She reached up and kissed him lightly on a cheek still wet with his tears.

Back inside the kitchen Angela was waiting and they walked back into the parlor together. Fewer people remained. Within an hour, even those who had lingered were gone. Leigh Ann and Dominque ordered Sarah Ann to remain with her friends while they helped clean up.

It was only after she sat down in the circle of the Prayer Group that she realized Jared and LouAnn had not come to the wake. She'd been surprised to see LouAnn at the funeral. *Maybe Jared has the good sense to work things out with LouAnn and keep his family together,* she thought silently, as her eyes lingered on a picture of her and

John with their children when they were still in elementary school.

She must remember to call LouAnn tomorrow and let her know she could call on her for anything she needed while Jared was in Europe on tour. She must also remember to check with Lambert first thing in the morning to see if he nailed everything down for the upcoming tour. They would be leaving in two weeks. It was a tight deadline to meet in light of the tragedy of Jill's death. She suddenly felt the crush of all that had happened closing in on her and reached over for Willie Dell's hand.

"I'm right here, baby sister."

John sat with his son and son-in-law in the loveseats on either side of the large fireplace in the center of the room. Each man sat with his arms on his knees, a bottle of beer hanging from one hand, their heads bent close, as if carrying on a confidential conversation. John had seemed somewhat aloof today, remaining close to his children since arriving for the wake, almost as if he were avoiding her. Maybe it was just his way of giving her space on a day he knew she was grieving and knowing he could not offer her the same solace she drew from the Prayer Group. Yet, she had to admit to herself, he had been stalwart these past few days. He and Lambert might prove to be the rocks on which she could continue to build the company that was now her sole responsibility. She mused at the heretical use of sacred testament to illustrate her situation. She whispered a quick prayer of forgiveness.

"Sarah Ann, what are you mumbling about?" demanded Della Sue good-naturedly.

"A prayer, Della Sue. Isn't that the purpose of our little group? Something we set in stone when we were seven or eight."

"I thought it was wreaking havoc on hapless nuns. But darlin', I could simply be misinterpreting the preamble to our Prayer Group constitution."

The faces around her erupted in laughter and for the first time since the horrible Sunday that seemed an eternity ago, Sarah Ann joined in. *If laughter was good for the soul, my soul is getting a rejuvenating massage.*

When her laughter quieted to a smile Sarah Ann explained, "If you must know I was thanking God for having John Boswell, Esquire, and Ross Lambert, in my camp as I go forward. I would describe their support as stalwart."

"Stalwart," repeated Angela. "Sounds like something you would heap on a Knight of the Round Table."

"Shush! John will hear us." Sarah Ann glanced across the room and saw John and the two younger men looking toward them. He nodded to her with a thin smile. "He has been a Godsend and Lambert may prove to be manna from heaven," she whispered.

"Sarah Ann's right on both counts," agreed Willie Dell. "Maybe we need to join her in a prayer of thanksgiving for having them to work with at this dire time."

"Later," suggested Sarah Ann. "There are some who might compare us to Haitian Voodooers if we break out in prayer while others are in the room. I remember when Jill told me about y'all praying over me when I was hospitalized for trying to beat God to the final punch. She described you, Willie Dell, as a Roman God with his Vestal Virgins, or something like that." A dark cloud moved over her features. The memory of that time still evoked pain and guilt at her weakness and narcissism. She shrugged away the memory. "Anyway, I need to attend to my remaining guests."

Standing at the door, Sarah Ann held Viola and Nicole in a long embrace. The tears that sprang to her eyes seemed to mute the words she wanted to say for how grateful she was to have both of them at Edgerton Group. "You get a good night's rest and we'll see you in the morning," said Viola, brushing away her own tears. This was a weekend when all hands would be on board at Edgerton Group. "Or better yet, we'll see you when we see you. No need for you to come in while we're there to hold down the fort." Sarah Ann was still holding a plump hand in hers until Viola took a step beyond her reach.

John held Sarah Ann for an uncomfortably long time in front of their children. In her ear he whispered. "Whatever you need, just call me. Especially anytime the police contact you."

"I will," she whispered back, before withdrawing from his comforting arms. "Thank you for everything."

She stood in the doorway until the cars carrying John and her children and their spouses pulled down the boulevard before stepping back inside. *Why did it take such a tragic event to bring them all together again under one roof?* she wondered as she closed the door.

Sometime later it was Jeanne Marie who insisted she go to bed and found a pair of pajamas in a drawer while Sarah Ann sat before the bathroom dressing table removing her make-up with a moistened towelette. The make-up came off exposing dark circles of fatigue under her eyes. At that moment she felt like she could sleep for a week, but dutifully pulled up the wake-up alarm before slipping into the pajamas. Jeanne Marie drew a light cover over her and tucked it under her chin. "You sleep well, darlin'. Willie Dell will lock up and set the alarm as we head out. Sweet dreams," she murmured as she bent and kissed Sarah Ann on the forehead.

"I'd settle for no dreams at all at this point."

"Then no dreams it is." Jeanne Marie turned and blew a kiss from the doorway and said, "Love ya," before closing the door behind her.

Sarah Ann fell asleep almost immediately, but the dreams did not rest. She saw Jill's pallid face exposed when the sheet was rolled back, lying in a pool of blood on the cold steel table. She awoke with a start, her heart banging against her chest wall in the dark room. Around her she felt a presence. For a few moments her body was gripped by a palpable fear that left her shaking. With an unsteady hand she turned on the lamp by the bed and began to question her sanity as she lay back on the pillow. *Get a grip, girl, it was only a nightmare.* She glanced at the bedside clock. Four a.m. Sleep was behind her. She rose slowly and headed to the shower.

The eastern sky was still being painted with thin streaks of pink and orange to welcome the new sunrise when Sarah Ann arrived at the office. If additional sleep proved impossible, so was the work load ahead for this day, she realized, even if it was the weekend. She settled behind the desk and booted up her laptop to peruse her calendar. Sitting back in the chair with a heavy sigh, she suddenly felt a dark sense of foreboding pervading her again, the same menacing emotion that had awakened her with such terror. She shook her head in an effort to exorcize the demon and bent over her computer to respond to several emails that she had marked priority, including some brief thank you notes to be written to a number of the country music elite who honored Jill with their presence at the memorial service.

One would be to Len Shiring, who seemed truly grieved at Jill's loss. He had not mentioned Lambert when they'd conversed briefly at the wake. She said nothing about his usurper's new affiliation with Edgerton Group. If he knew about it, Shiring chose not to mention it, averting what could have been an awkward moment. While still engrossed in making the list of notes to be written, the cell phone ringing startled her.

"Sorry to call so early. Hope I didn't catch you at a bad time."

"No. I'm at the office," she assured Lambert, noting it was just after seven and felt the pulling need for coffee. "What's up?"

"I'm at the back door with a spare Starbucks, but no key to get in."

"You are an answer to prayer. I'll be right there."

The coffee was still steaming, and she felt revived with the first few sips. "What brings you to the office so early? I hope you are the bearer of good news."

He took a long pull from his own coffee before answering. "It's not." She felt her spirits sink precipitously. "Jared called me last night and says the two detectives investigating Jill's murder want to talk with LouAnn. They didn't tell him why. They did say they were coming this afternoon and would be armed with a search warrant." He looked at her searchingly. "Do you know why?"

"Maybe. Although, I'm not sure why a search warrant." She turned away from his trenchant gaze that held a silent rebuke for not sharing with him something that he must have figured out on his own.

"Jared was having an affair with Jill. It's been going on for some time. Am I right?"

There was just a trace of irritation in his commanding voice. She looked up at him, her expression a silent plea for understanding. "I gave my word to Jared that I wouldn't tell anyone; not you; not the police. I wanted to allow him time to work things out with LouAnn. They were together yesterday at Jill's memorial. I think they're trying to do just that."

"Do you think the detectives suspect anything?"

"Yes, I fear they do. I'm even more fearful of what this could do to Jill's reputation and Jared's career," she added with concern, "not to mention the hurt it will further inflict on LouAnn if it becomes public." She looked away and focused on the familiar colors of the Monet print. "I've been in LouAnn's shoes."

"I know." He did not elaborate or say how or what he knew about John's abrupt departure from their marriage. She was a little offended he seemed to know so much about her, and she so little about him. "I'm headed out to the farm for a meeting with Jared and the band. Once I've broached it with Jared, you and I will have to figure out how to deal with everything." Lambert tipped the paper cup up and drained the remainder of his coffee. "The police will find out, if they don't already know." He pitched the crumpled cup into the small trash can at the side of her desk.

"Good shot."

"Thanks. I was a point guard on my high school team." He grinned sheepishly, as if she might think he was bragging. "A demanding coach meant you better hit or else." The humor was supplanted by a troubled frown. "If they put the question square to Jared and LouAnn, they'll have to answer truthfully. We should arrange for an attorney to be with them when she's interviewed."

Sarah Ann nodded agreement. "I'll call John."

Chapter 31

The two detectives arrived with two uniform officers and presented the search warrant as they stepped into the wide foyer of the graceful home. It was a home made more stunning to the two detectives because it had been built on a rise overlooking the rolling pastures on either side of the long, tree-lined lane leading to the horseshoe drive in front.

Jared and LouAnn sat holding hands in silence in the large living room, with John sitting across from them sipping coffee the housekeeper, Jeannette, had provided before she excused herself to take Willow outside to play. They could hear the footfalls of the searchers upstairs, of drawers being opened and closed; doors being opened and shut; then periods of silence.

It was Detective Morgan who came down and asked Jared to take them to the studio he had built over the four-car garage attached to the rear of the sprawling house. John squeezed LouAnn's hand reassuringly before telling the detective he would accompany Jared.

He and Jared stood silent as the two detectives, and the accompanying officers, rummaged through a large closet where several guitars stood tilted back on large wood racks. They lifted stacks of sheet music neatly stored on shelves and displaced a number of items as they reached under and around everything. After foraging through the recording studio, they returned for a final look behind and under the large console with its myriad of small blinking lights.

"Better come here, Marlin." It was one of the uniformed officers. Hotchkin bent down and with his vinyl gloved hand picked up a large hunting knife, its blade streaked with what appeared to be dried blood. Hotchkin was almost certain of that as he walked slowly over to where Jared stood beside John. "This belong to you, son?"

Jared stared at the knife, his eyes reflecting recognition and shock. "Did you use this to kill Miz Edgerton, son."

Jared's head jerked up. "No sir, I didn't…I didn't kill her."

John interposed immediately, "I would advise you to say no more, Jared."

Hotchkin ignored the attorney. "But you've seen this knife before, haven't you, son?"

Jared just stared at the bloody knife Hotchkin held in his right hand. "Is this your knife?"

"No, sir," Jared answered emphatically.

"But you know whose knife this is, don't you, son?" Hotchkin was certain he had seen recognition flash across Jared's face when he was shown the knife.

Jared looked at John apprehensively. Then he lowered his head under Hotchkin's unyielding gaze but remained silent.

"Detective, I can't allow this interview to continue." John turned and looked squarely at Jared. "Don't say anything else. You could be putting yourself in jeopardy."

Jared seemed not to hear the admonishment and looked up at Hotchkin with pleading eyes. "I swear I didn't kill Jill. I loved her. Someone's trying to put the blame on me." There was a fevered vehemence in his voice as he clinched and unclenched his fists. "I just want to find Jill's killer."

"We want the same thing, Mr. Parson," Hotchkin replied taciturnly, as he placed the bloodied knife in a clear plastic evidence bag. He turned back to Jared and John. "How 'bout we go back downstairs and let's see if we can get to the bottom of this."

Hotchkin followed Jared and John down the stairs. He became more certain with each step down that Parson was telling the truth. The knife had been planted. That was now obvious. It was meant to be found. The voice on the tape had told the dispatcher the knife was in the studio near *all them computer machines.* Hotchkin had played the tape back several times.

It was a male voice with a distinctly southern accent. Someone was making a poor attempt at framing Parson, maybe even trying to frame his wife.

On the drive there, through the verdant rolling countryside of Williamson County, he and Morgan had determined LouAnn Parson could well be the key to solving the murder of her husband's manager. What she might tell them could be pivotal to the case. On that he and Morgan concurred. But getting her to do so might not be in the cards with John Boswell running interference.

LouAnn sat next to the attorney, looking very pregnant and very scared. John seemed acutely aware of her discomfort. He wrapped an arm around her shoulders and patted her arm gently in a gesture of support. The detectives had specifically requested that Jared wait outside in another room with the two uniform officers. He had reluctantly consented after receiving assurances from John that it would be all right.

When the two detectives seated themselves across from LouAnn the attorney asked politely if they would like something to drink, a coffee or soft drink. They both declined.

LouAnn kept her hands tightly folded in her lap as John told the two detectives he was convinced she had nothing to do with Jill Edgerton's murder after talking with her at length. The detectives sitting on the couch across the large marble-topped table from the attorney and his client were unconvinced. In Hotchkin's long experience, Boswell was doing what attorneys were paid to do— thinking their client as unblemished of the sin of crime as a newly resurrected soul. It had been his experience that he and God knew better. And he was as sure as the sun rising that LouAnn Parson knew something that could be vital to solving this case.

She had been home with Jared and their daughter the night of Jill's murder. When asked if anyone besides Jared could verify that, LouAnn summoned a man named Hershel Simmons, whom she introduced as the farm manager when he appeared from the back of the house. He had joined her and Jared and Willow for dinner the night of the murder and stayed for a while after Jared retreated to his studio. Simmons seemed visibly ill at ease with the two detectives. Still he answered their questions succinctly and without hesitation.

After dinner he said he helped LouAnn stack dirty dishes in the dishwasher. It was the housekeeper's day off and she was away from the farm visiting her sister in Murfreesboro. LouAnn had asked him to see if her husband could come tuck Willow into bed. He remembered the light outside the studio being on. That light meant nobody could go in. He picked up the phone outside the studio and told Jared he was wanted in his daughter's bedroom and Jared had said "okay." He then headed back to his quarters behind the big horse barn and did not see Jared or LouAnn after that.

"About what time was that, Mr. Simmons?"

A little after eight, Simmons recalled. Neither detective questioned Simmons' version of that night further. But there was something about the guy that bothered Hotchkin. He would check on Hershel Simmons, farm manager, sometime country musician and song writer and gauging by his sunken, ruddy cheeks, still a heavy drinker unless he had disavowed the bottle more recently.

Hotchkin frowned as he recalled Parson's version of the dinner that night. He never mentioned Simmons and said it was his wife who had asked him to tuck their daughter in. *Could be an outright lie*, he reflected silently. *Could just be a memory lapse by Parson.*

Impatient with Hotchkin's slower, more measured approach, Morgan blurted out, "When did you first discover your husband was having an affair with his manager?" If looks could kill, the malevolent stare Hotchkin turned on his partner could have done the job as effectively as a 9mm bullet through the heart. But Hotchkin said nothing as he looked back at LouAnn for her response and watched her eyes fill with tears.

John squeezed LouAnn's hand again gently. "Tell them what you know, LouAnn."

Tears slide silently down LouAnn's cheeks as she looked over at the two detectives. "He told me about it after he learned Jill was killed. I didn't know 'til then."

"Did he tell you how long the affair had been going on?"

"He didn't say. Jared said it just happened because they were spending so much time together." She looked stricken as tears continued spilling down her cheeks.

John pulled a handkerchief from his inside coat pocket and handed it to the distraught young woman. He felt a wave of guilt washing over him as he watched LouAnn dabbing the hanky over her cheeks and eyes in an effort to stem the flow. His mind strayed back in time. *Was this how Sarah Ann had reacted when he told her he wanted a divorce and admitted there was someone new in his life? If she had shed tears, he couldn't remember. And if she did, he could not recall even offering her a handkerchief, only turning his back and walking out of the room without a backward glance. It had taken more than five years to finally realize how much he had lost the night he had exited their home and their life.*

"Did your husband ask you not to talk with us about what he had told you, Mrs. Parson?"

"No, sir."

"You're sure about that?" It was Morgan.

"Yes, sir. He and Mr. Boswell both told me just to tell you what I knew if you ask and to tell it truthfully."

"We thank you for that, Miz Parson. You're doing the right thing," Hotchkin said soothingly. "I need to show you something we found up in your husband's studio and see if you recognize it." He pulled the evidence bag from beside him, walked around the table and placed it in front of LouAnn. She recoiled visibly at the sight of the bloodied knife. "Do you recognize this knife, Miz Parson?"

She remained silent, staring at the knife, and began shaking. John drew her closer to him.

"You do recognize this knife, Miz Parson?" Hotchkin gently repeated.

"It looks like one my daddy has," her answer barely audible.

"Sorry, Miz Parson. Who'd you say this knife belongs to?"

LouAnn looked up at the stern detective, her eyes brimming with tears. "It looks like one my daddy uses to skin deer with when he hunts back home in Texas."

Hotchkin picked up the evidence bag and sat back down next to Morgan. "Have you seen your daddy lately?"

"No, sir. Not for a while. Not since we moved up here. Jared and my daddy didn't get along so well."

"Do your parents ever call you?"

"Last time was a few weeks ago. I had called my mama when Jared was gone. He told me not to talk with them. When my daddy came on the line, he just wanted to talk with Jared. Jared told me later, daddy probably wanted some money again."

"Did your husband ever give him any money?"

"No, sir."

"Was your daddy angry?"

"Jared said he was. Real angry."

"Where do your folks live, Miz Parson?"

"In Jacksonville, Texas." She gave them the address of the trailer park.

Hotchkin jotted down the address and nodded his head gravely, while seeming to be studying his rumpled notepad. John sensed the interview was winding down. Moments later Hotchkin stood up. "I guess that'll be all for now, Miz Parson, unless Morgan here has anything more."

Morgan signaled he didn't with a quick shake of his head, but his face remained wreathed in a skeptical frown.

Not seeing Jared, John accompanied the two detectives to the front door. "Counselor," said Hotchkin affably, extending his hand.

"You'll let me know the results of the fingerprint tests?" John asked, handing Hotchkin another business card.

"Sure thing, Mr. Boswell."

John extended his hand to Morgan who answered with only a cursory shake and left without another word. The other two officers came out of the kitchen where they had been waiting with Jared, who hung back by the kitchen entryway.

After closing the door John felt an almost visceral relief at seeing the four lawmen descending the steps toward their cars.

"Well, she sure as hell has motive, Marlin," Morgan observed, after starting the engine and cracking his window as he lit a cigarette with the sterling silver lighter his wife had given him for his last birthday. He turned the unambiguous engraved message away from him. It was as much a habit as the Marlboro's he'd pulled from the pack in his shirt pocket. *Cigarettes are going to kill you,* it read. *So what? This job already had a head start on his demise.* "You think that Simmons guy was telling the truth?"

Hotchkin studied the road ahead before he answered. "Yeah. You can usually tell when someone is lying. He said both of 'em were at the farm about the time the woman was getting stabbed. Anyway, it would be hard for someone Miz Parson's size to jab a knife in that deep and push upward. That's something they teach you in the military."

He partially opened his passenger side window to let the smoke escape. He was trying to quit again and resented the hell out of Morgan for lighting up. Hotchkin swallowed his resentment in silence. No sense causing a rift. Good partners were hard to come by. And Morgan was a step up from some who had been assigned to him over the years. "I think we might definitely be lookin' for a perp who's had that kind of training. We could even be looking for Miz Parson's daddy."

When Morgan just took another pull on his cigarette and didn't respond, Hotchkin reflected to himself, *Maybe we might just get lucky and find some fingerprints on the knife.*

~

He watched them leave. He had a vantage point which allowed him to remain invisible to the detectives, and anyone else inside the house. He hoped this visit by the cops didn't involve LouAnn. She wouldn't deserve that. This was all Jared's fault. And he'd heard on the television news that Jared was supposed to be flying across the ocean. That would leave LouAnn to deal with this mess by herself. She didn't seem to have no friends, at least none he'd seen come visitin'. Not a time for Jared to be gone, what with her pregnant and just the plump girl to help with little Willow.

He wondered just how much help she really was. He also wondered if Jared was screwing her, too. He wouldn't doubt it. Jared couldn't seem to keep his pants zipped any more now than when he was in high school.

Then there was that other lady at the office where Jill had worked. Was he messin' with her? She seemed a little old for him when he had watched her from the cab of his pick-up as she walked in front of LouAnn and Jared at the funeral—on the arm of that same attorney in the house now. Maybe she was spoken for? But then, she was the only one in the bed when he'd slipped into her big house the other night after disabling the alarm system.

Piece of cake that alarm system, he chortled mirthlessly. What a rip-off. When he'd been installing them, those security companies charged a hefty price to put 'em in. And a sizable amount every month to keep 'em beeping when a code was dialed in. He didn't need no code. He could disable just about any of 'em blindfolded.

He felt a rumbling in his stomach and couldn't remember when he last ate. Time to grab a bite. He felt the shuttering of the battered truck as he turned over the ignition. It was pretty near a death rattle, truth be told. But it had got him this far. He couldn't complain. He pulled from the secluded spot where he had observed the arrival and departure of the police and headed down the same road in the opposite direction.

Chapter 32

Stella Wayne sat across from Sarah Ann beaming. And with good reason. She had just learned the title song from her second album had soared to number one on the country music charts.

Viola popped her head in the office. "Coffee, tea, coke?" Sarah Ann pushed her empty cup across to Viola and mouthed a grateful thank you.

"I'll take a diet coke if it's not out of your way, ma'am."

"Coming your way, Miss Stella."

Stella brushed back a miscreant lock of thick, curly raven hair that kept escaping the clasp holding it back from her face; a face blessed with a creamy complexion, with only a light sprinkling of freckles dotting the slim nose and blue eyes that seemed to radiate a never-ending smile. It was a face imbued with the same mix of beauty, sweetness and strength that found its way into the words of each song Stella wrote and sang, with a voice that spoke to her Oklahoma roots.

For only a moment the smile dimmed in her luminous eyes. "I'm sure sorry about Miss Jill. I just can't get over it. Murdered right here. I sure hope they find out who did that to her real soon. Have the police said anything yet?"

"Thank you, Stella. I do too. So far the police haven't indicated they know much."

Viola swept back into the office, a steaming mug of coffee in one hand, which she handed across the desk to Sarah Ann, before pulling the tab on the canned soft drink and pouring it over a small glass of ice. "Thank you, ma'am," said Stella.

"Anything else I can get you ladies?"

"We're good. Thanks Viola. You can send Jerry back."

Jerry Goshen was an old hand who had been around the block in the country music publishing world with the entertainment sections of both Nashville newspapers, a couple of local publicity agencies and now with an industry weekly. He considered himself more 'country' than the publications he represented.

"Howdy do, Miz Sarah Ann," he said, announcing his presence with his signature greeting as he ducked his tall, tubercular-thin frame through the doorway. "Sure sorry about Miss Jill. Awful thing that. Just awful. How you holdin' up?" he asked with genuine sympathy, clasping Sarah Ann's hand.

"It's still a little rough right now, Jerry. But thank you." Sarah Ann pointed to the empty chair next to Stella. "Jerry, I'd like you to meet Stella Wayne."

"Pleased to meet you, young lady." Stella's petite hand disappeared into a hand that was sized for a Paul Bunyan. "I guess congratulations are in order," he said, flashing a wide grin that seemed to split his face in two, as he eased down in the chair and stretched his long, jean-clad legs out in front of him.

"Thank you, Mr. Goshen."

"Jerry, young lady. Miz Sarah Ann can tell you I never stand on formalities." Stella warmed to the gregarious reporter immediately. "So, tell me all about yourself and how you managed a chart topper from your second big album."

Sarah Ann watched silently as the savvy reporter gushed and plied, all in the same breath, it seemed. He had a way of mining for a good story that left most of his competition following in his wake. And he did it with the veneer of a good ole' country boy; a veneer Jerry Goshen had carefully nurtured during his thirty years in Nashville. Sarah Ann knew she was probably one of the few people who knew Jerry Goshen's good ole' country boy veneer was just that—a veneer. He actually hailed from a small town in northern Indiana. It was over too many beers at a Second Street honky-tonk that he had admitted his non-Southern roots to Jill. Except for telling Arliss and Sarah Ann, Jill had kept Jerry's secret safe.

When the interview was over, Jerry arranged for a photography session to go with the story. Sarah Ann frowned at her crowded calendar and mentally moved things around to accommodate tomorrow afternoon. That would fit Jerry's deadline for the story to run in the next edition.

After Jerry bid a jovial goodbye with another ear-to-ear grin, the two women walked back to the break room where Sarah Ann refilled her coffee mug. "You did great, Stella.

"Thanks, Mrs. Boswell."

Sarah Ann placed her hand maternally on Stella's shoulder. "When will I convince you that it's Sarah Ann? Calling me Mrs. Boswell makes me feel ancient."

"You are anything but, Sarah Ann," declared Stella sincerely.

"Your mama raised you right."

Stella laughed. "I hope you'll remind her of that. She and dad are coming to see me perform at the Grand Ole Opry. Mama's convinced Nashville and country music have totally corrupted my Baptist upbringing and eviscerated the good manners she spent years implanting in me."

Now it was Sarah Ann's turn to laugh. "And she'd be wrong on both counts. But if you throw around a word like eviscerated in this town, people will be convinced you've done something that should land you on the sex offender's list."

Stella laughed. "I promise to mind my vocabulary in the future."

"Good girl."

After Sarah Ann said she would arrange for a hairdresser and make-up before the photo shoot, the two women parted; Stella skipping happily out the back door to the parking lot, and Sarah Ann heading back to a workload that would keep her in her office until well after dark. So little time, so much to do with Jared and his band heading to England in a few days.

She had asked Nicole to assist Lambert with whatever he needed done. With Nicole's help they had quickly hired an experienced talent manager whom Nicole said wanted to make a change. After giving notice one day she was on board with Edgerton Group the next day, assuming Nicole's duties in a fluid transition. To Sarah

Ann's appreciative eyes, Carol Bennington had simply morphed, like Harry Potter wizardry, into Nicole.

Sarah Ann then snapped up a grateful Abe Winters. He was not only eager to earn a steady paycheck but also proving to be a gifted organizer who coordinated bookings and travel arrangements through Carl Stone's agency.

While the brutal death of Jill had placed a pall on the office, the work had to go forward. That much Sarah Ann knew. She owed it not only to the talent they represented, but the woman who had founded Edgerton Group. And now Stella's career was firmly off the launch pad—a career that could eventually rival Jared's.

At Sarah Ann's insistence, Ross Lambert had taken over Jill's office. At first he balked, saying it should be her office. He relented only after Sarah Ann pointed out the practicality of having all of Jared's history with the agency, stored in Jill's files and on her computer, at his fingertips.

Lambert was in his office each morning before she arrived. They would then meet to discuss the upcoming European tour. He was juggling a lot, but the bulk of his long days were spent with Jared and the band at Arliss Hemming's studio, where practice sessions started before noon, and often went well into the night.

Lambert had not broached the subject of a partnership again. But then there hadn't really been any time. He never failed to praise Nicole, whose work days now mirrored his own. Sarah Ann would make sure Nicole's annual bonus reflected their appreciation.

It was nearing six when Sarah Ann glanced at the wall clock just as the desk phone rang. The voice at the other end was chocked with sobs. "What's wrong LouAnn," her voice rising with alarm.

"It's my daddy, Miss Sarah. My mama called me." Through the strangled sobs Sarah Ann heard only "You've gotta come out here now. Please."

Chapter 33

Sarah Ann held LouAnn's trembling hands in hers. When she arrived at the farm, LouAnn's sobs had quieted, but it was clear from her red eyes and blotchy cheeks her crying had been prolonged. Willow was clinging to her mother and appeared frightened by her mother's emotional state. So Sarah Ann summoned Hershel Simmons on his cell phone.

He arrived shortly, doffed his sweat stained Stetson and mumbled a greeting to Sarah Ann before scooping Willow into his arms. He brought an end to the child's tears with a promise she could help him finish feeding the horses before hoisting her onto his sturdy shoulders. Her tears were replaced by delighted giggles as they went out through the mud room to the back door.

After making a pot of coffee, Sarah Ann sat LouAnn down beside her at the kitchen table in an alcove surrounded on three sides by tall windows. They looked out on the rolling pastures, now in shadow as dusk was quickly retreating into night.

Her coffee untouched, LouAnn explained her father was overdue from a hunting trip he had left to go on more than three weeks ago. "Mama said it's too early for hunting in Texas. And he didn't exactly tell her where he was going."

"Has he not contacted your mother at all?"

"No, ma'am." LouAnn gulped back more threatening tears. "She did get a call a few days ago, but nobody said anything on the other end. She thinks it might've been daddy but doesn't know for sure."

Sarah Ann sipped her coffee and LouAnn continued. "He goes off from time-to-time to hunt this time of year. He doesn't always tell Mama where. But he usually calls her to let her know he's okay."

"Is he not answering his cell phone?"

"No, ma'am. They…my folks…they don't have cell phones, just the landline." Sarah Ann had trouble wrapping herself around the concept of not having a cell phone in this day and time. As if reading Sarah Ann's thoughts, LouAnn explained her father thought cell phones were a waste of hard earned money.

"Has your mother notified police that your father may be missing?"

"I don't think so, ma'am. She told me she's afraid it would really rile him when he got home to find out the law was looking for him."

"Have you told Jared?" The sudden fear that flickered in LouAnn's eyes was Sarah Ann's answer.

"Jared and my daddy…they never got along too well." Not wanting to let go of Sarah Ann's hands, LouAnn rubbed away a stray tear against her shoulder. "My daddy is a God-fearing man, Miss Sarah. He was truly disappointed in me when I became pregnant. Jared and me had to marry in a hurry. I'm an only child. Mama said he's never gotten over it."

Sarah Ann tightened her grip on LouAnn's hands to calm her trembling. "Mama told me a ways back that my daddy even quit going to church after I left home. And then he wouldn't even drive my mama there anymore. We never missed services when I was growing up—every Sunday morning and every Wednesday evening, faithful as could be 'til I went and got in a family way." LouAnn looked at Sarah Ann with her swollen eyes. "I just know something bad is going on with my daddy, Miss Sarah. I just know it."

Deep sobs shook LouAnn's body and Sarah Ann pulled her into her arms to comfort her. "Why don't we call you mother right now," she suggested, "and just *see* if maybe your daddy has checked in with her."

Sarah Ann released LouAnn's hands and walked over to the counter to fetch her cell phone from her purse. "What's the number for your folks, LouAnn?" she asked, sitting back down beside the distraught younger woman. "What's your mother's name," she whispered as the distant phone started to ring.

"Betty Murray. My daddy's Lester Murray."

A thin voice at the other end said hello. "Mrs. Murray."

"Yes?"

"My name is Sarah Ann Boswell. I'm a friend of your daughter, LouAnn." There was no response from the other end of the connection. "I'm sitting here with your daughter and she's worried about her daddy and wanted me to call and see if you've heard from him."

"Who is this calling?" There was a plaintive tone in the voice asking the question.

"Sarah Ann Boswell, ma'am. I'm a friend of your daughter's," she repeated.

There was a prolonged silence then, "No, ma'am. You can tell her I haven't heard a word from her daddy." The instant anger in the thin voice lingered even after the line went dead.

Sarah Ann held the phone pressed to her ear for a long moment before punching it off. "I'm sorry, LouAnn. She says she hasn't heard from him." LouAnn was watching her searchingly, pain evident in her eyes. "She hung up before I could ask anything further."

LouAnn turned and looked out the window at the gathering darkness. "I appreciate your calling her." When she turned back her eyes were red, but dry. "If you'll excuse me, Miss Sarah, I'd better go get Willow. It's getting close to her bed time."

"May I come with you? I'd like to visit with Hershel. I haven't seen him for a while."

Sarah placed her phone back in her purse and followed LouAnn out the back door. Their motion prompted flood lights on the house to light their path. From inside the barn they could hear Willow's enchanting little girl laughter. It seemed to flow around Sarah Ann's sadness like sprinkles of fairy dust, bringing a smile to her lips as she followed LouAnn inside the open door of the barn. Children were such vessels of unadulterated joy. She made a vow to herself to spend more time with her own grandchildren when this nightmare, that blighted her every waking hour, finally passed. But she knew that would not be until Jill's murder was finally solved. *Please God, make it soon* she prayed silently.

They found Willow still atop Hershel's broad shoulders, handing hay to a handsome bay horse in one of the back stalls. The barn interior and stall doors had been painted a mellow tan and brown since the last time Sarah Ann had been here. New lighting brightened the interior. Across from the large tack room at the rear of the barn she noticed wooden steps leading to the small enclosed quarters Hershel occupied.

Hershel nodded to both women as he lifted Willow over his head to the ground. Despite the growing bulk of her pregnancy, LouAnn bent down to Willow's level. "It's time for your bath and a bedtime story." LouAnn's pronouncement was met with a pout on the pretty little oval face, which made Sarah Ann think that must have been how LouAnn looked at seven years old. "Tell Mr. Hershel thanks and wish him good night." But unlike most children her age, Willow made no effort to resist her mother. She reached her arms out to Hershel, who bent down to welcome her hug. She kissed his gaunt cheek, roughened like hide and deeply fissured by sun and life.

"Goodnight, little one. Sleep tight."

"Can I help you feed the 'horsies' when I wake up?"

"You can help me anytime your mama says okay."

"Bye, Miss Sarah." Sarah Ann bent down and gave the little girl a hug. "Goodnight, dumplin'. Sweet dreams."

After LouAnn and Willow set out for the house, Sarah Ann turned to Hershel, who was holding his ancient Stetson against his thigh and leaning against an empty stall. "Something on your mind, Miz Sarah?"

"I was just wondering how you were doing, Hershel? We haven't talked in a while."

"Can't complain." He ducked his head and studied the hard ground beneath his boot as if it were a puzzle he was trying to solve. "I'm real sorry about Miss Jill." His eyes remained fixed on the ground. "I didn't hold with her carrying on with Jared, but she didn't deserve to have that happen to her."

"So, you knew about the affair?" Sarah Ann was stunned by Hershel's admission.

"Yes, ma'am, I did." Hershel made no attempt to hide the condemnation in his response.

Sarah Ann realized that could account for the antagonism Jared had toward Hershel. Maybe even the real reason Jared had wanted him fired.

"How long have you known…about Jared and Jill?" she asked mildly.

"A while now." He batted his hat against his thigh to sluff off imaginary dust. "Those two detectives ask me about Jared and Jill, but I didn't feel right telling them anything, so I didn't."

"It's all right, Hershel. You did the right thing. LouAnn told them. It was best coming from her."

"You don't think…" he fell silent and looked beyond her into the darkness outside the barn. "Jared is many things I don't like, Miz Sarah, but he ain't no killer."

And she knew in her heart at that moment that neither was he. She felt a flush of relief and realized she had come to the barn with a nagging suspicion that it might have been at Hershel's hands, Jill was murdered. She silently rebuked herself for even harboring such a thought about this shy, gentle-spirited man, who had pulled himself up from the abyss into which his life had fallen. She knew his descent into alcoholism had banished all that had once been important: his family, his career, famous friends who came with that career. Those friends now as lost to him as his years spent drinking. Yet, he laid blame only at his own feet and no others'. Hershel Simmons was certainly no killer.

"Would you walk me to my car, Hershel."

"Sure thing, Miz Sarah."

He pulled his hat on and they walked out of the barn and into the night air, heavy with fall humidity that bode of an approaching storm.

He opened the car door and she sank into the comfortable leather seat. "Thank you, Hershel." He backed away as she started to pull the door shut, then paused and said, "And thank you, Hershel, for caring so much for LouAnn and Willow. They'll need you even more when Jared leaves for Europe."

"Yes, ma'am," was all he said in reply. And she knew inherently in those short words was a promise he would keep. As she drove around the horseshoe shaped drive and headed down the lane leading to the road, she glanced in the rearview mirror and saw Hershel still standing there, a distant shadow as she swung left onto the two-lane road. She tapped the phone knob on the side of the steering wheel. A Siri-like voice asked what name. John picked up after the first ring.

"Just the voice I was hoping to hear," he remarked casually.

"Actually, I'm on my way from Jared's. LouAnn called me earlier this evening and what she told me is troubling." She proceeded to tell him about LouAnn's missing father and the long-standing rift between Jared and his father-in-law.

"What you've told me *is* troubling," John agreed, after allowing her to speak without interrupting. "Hotchkin needs to know about this development. The father-in-law being overdue may just be coincidence. But I tend not to put much store in coincidences," he observed. "Do you want me to call Hotchkin in the morning and set up a meeting?" And added, "I think I should be there with you."

While John was talking, she noticed the lights of another vehicle behind her in her side view mirror. They bounced up and down as if the vehicle was driving over rough terrain instead of a smoothly paved road. "I would appreciate you're contacting Hotchkin for me," she said absently, her eyes darting from the bobbing lights in her rearview mirror back to the road ahead. She was approaching the cutoff to highway 96.

"What time would be convenient for you?"

"Oh…gosh, I'm not sure. I don't have my laptop with me." She could tell the vehicle behind her was gaining. "Can I call you when I get home?"

"Sure." There was a new inflection in her voice.

"Is everything alright, Sarah Ann?" he asked with rising concern.

"I'm fine. Just tired."

"Where are you right now?" he asked.

"Turning onto 96. I should be home in fifteen minutes. I'll check my calendar as soon as I get there and call you back." She punched the call cancel button. She had gone half a mile on 96 and saw no lights behind her; no lights in either direction. There seemed to be little traffic on this stretch of the highway, which linked the western part of the county with Franklin. She sat back in the seat and for the first time noticed her heart thumping like a Jamaican steel drum in her chest. Until now she hadn't realized the toll the events of the last weeks were taking on her nerves. The Lexus topped a small hill and sped down to the level plain ahead. The dashboard clock neared nine o'clock. She ordered up her favorite Nashville country music station from the Siri-like voice that answered her command. Maybe she would hear Stella's big hit. It seemed indelibly imprinted in the music rolodex of her brain; but still, she hadn't heard it played on the radio yet, with a live DJ praising it.

Another hit was playing and a second had started when she glanced into the rearview mirror. The bobbing lights were back. A streak of adrenaline flashed through her—a streak of panic. Only one other car had passed, and it was going west. The bobbing lights were coming her way, east, and once again, gaining. A deep sense of foreboding draped over her. Sarah Ann's voice commanded John's number from the accommodating computer voice. This time he didn't answer until the third ring.

"Sorry. I went out to clear out the mailbox, which I haven't done for a week, and heard the cell ringing as I came in the door," he explained a little breathlessly. "It was upstairs."

She knew that meant he had to climb two stories to get to his bedroom in his upscale high-rise condo. "I know this may sound crazy John, but I think someone may be following me."

"Where are you now?"

"Still on 96, just west of Franklin."

"Go directly to the police station on Columbia Avenue. I'll meet you there." The fear that gripped her strangled any reply. "Sarah Ann, you okay?"

"I'm sorry." She felt the first sting of tears. "It's been so bloody awful…everything… these last few days. I think I'm losing my mind."

"Just go to the police station. I'm going to call and ask someone to meet you outside and stay with you 'til I get there." She heard him snatching his car keys from somewhere, and then rushing down the stairs. "Leave your cell phone on. Don't hang up so I know when you reach the police station. I'll call them from my landline."

John—the commander-in-chief. John in charge. John knowing what to do in any situation. She had relied on that John for all the years of their marriage. Then that John had left. And she had had to learn to cope…learn to be in charge…seek her own destiny… be her own commander-in-chief. She floored the gas pedal and the Lexus leaped to her foot's command. The bobbing lights behind her began to grow smaller.

~

He stomped the old pick-up's gas pedal to the floor and held it there. The motor sputtered in protest, but grudgingly sped up. Still, the backlights he'd been following with ease since the bitch pulled out from the farm were now fading. Did she suspect he was following her? *No way she could*, he decided. He'd been too careful, keeping to a place across the road from the farm's lane where nobody could spot him unless they came directly looking for his truck. How would she know it was his truck following her anyway? Well, no matter. If he couldn't do his mischief tonight, he knew where she lived, and he would just bide his time. It *would* end here. If not tonight, then tomorrow. But he also knew his patience and time were already stretched. He'd make them all pay, and he'd do it quickly. He knew time was running out.

Chapter 34

After crossing into the city limits, Sarah Ann slowed, but only when she hadn't spotted the bobbing lights in her rearview mirror for the last couple of minutes. She turned off onto Columbia Avenue, the historic street and hallowed ground along which much of the bloody Battle of Franklin was fought in the Civil War. The parking area next to the stately columned building that housed the Franklin Police department was just blocks from the Carter House, ground zero in the battle that claimed the lives of five Confederate Generals, and the highest per capita casualty rate of any battle in the four-year war that brought the old South to its knees.

John was actually waiting for her just inside the parking lot flanked by two uniformed officers. He must have driven even faster than she. Then Sarah Ann recalled his new condo was just blocks away.

After turning off the ignition Sarah Ann leaped out of the car. She felt John's arms wrap immediately around her, as the fright bottled up inside spilled out with her tears. "Let's go inside," he suggested, his arms firm around her shaking shoulders.

One of the officers took her keys and moved the Lexus to a visitor space, while the second officer guided them through a side door of the department. They were ushered to an office where a man in a suit was waiting. The officer who had parked the car soon caught up and handed Sarah Ann her large purse and the car keys, before disappearing down the hallway.

"Sorry for your troubles, Mrs. Boswell," offered the young officer. "This is Lt. Michaels. He's gonna take things from here. Evening, ma'am, Mr. Boswell," and tipped his hat slightly before walking out of the office.

Michaels, who had stood up when they came in, reached out his hand to John and then Sarah Ann. "Steve Michaels. Glad to meet you both. Have a seat, won't you please," he said, pointing to two cushioned chairs in front of his desk. A mild voice matched his manner. His dark wavy hair was threaded with silver which contrasted with a handsome, unlined face. The effect was to make the veteran police lieutenant look younger than his biological calendar. But it was his hazel eyes that were his most striking feature. They complemented his handsome features and added warmth to his calm face.

"Tell me about the vehicle that was following you?" he began. As Sarah Ann's answers streamed out, she became painfully aware of how vague she was sounding. She was grateful for Michael's patience as she continued, revealing the reason she had gone to Jared Parson's farm in the first place, and about the failure of Mrs. Parson's father to contact his wife after leaving his Jacksonville, Texas home for an extended hunting trip.

"You must think me a ditz. I can't give you a description of anything but bouncing lights from what appeared to be a pick-up truck." She gripped John's hand more tightly.

"Not at all, ma'am. The movement of the headlights indicates this is probably an older vehicle, maybe in need of new tires or new shocks." His next words were spoken with a wry smile. "We don't see a lot of those in Williamson County." She silently agreed. It was a county she knew was regularly listed as one of the top twenty most affluent in the entire country.

"I'm sorry I can't be more helpful, Lieutenant. I'm afraid having my business partner murdered such a short time ago has left me a little jittery. Actually, very afraid."

"Understandable, ma'am." Michaels leaned back in his desk chair. "What you've told us about Mrs. Parson's father could be of interest to the Metro investigators. Do you have the father's name?" Michaels jotted down the name on the legal pad on which he had been taking notes, as Sarah Ann talked. "If you'll excuse me, let me see if we can run a check on any vehicles owned by this individual."

When she no longer heard the lieutenant's footsteps in the hallway she turned to John with a rueful expression. "I'm wasting this man's time." She felt dreadful at that moment and could feel the stirring of queasiness in the pit of her stomach. That's all she needed now was to get sick to her stomach after laying out such a lame reason for involving the Franklin police.

"Before you beat yourself up anymore, let's see what Michaels finds out. He looks like a pretty savvy guy to me. I don't get the impression he thinks what you've related to him is so lame, to borrow your description." John reached across and drew her hands into his. "It's been more than two weeks since Jill's murder. And I get the impression from Hotchkin they don't have much to go on and each day that passes the trail gets colder. Let's see what Michaels comes up with."

Time crawled as they waited. When Michaels finally returned he had a paper in his hand still warm from a computer printer. "We may have caught a break," he opened cautiously. "There is a 1992 Ford pick-up registered to a Charles Lester Murray at the same address you gave us in Jacksonville. A truck matching that description was reported to the Williamson County Sheriff's Office two days ago by a neighbor of the Parsons, who thought someone had abandoned it off the road near Parson's place. He said it looked like there was a man sleeping inside the truck, but it was pulled off in some heavy brush, so he couldn't be sure. By the time the deputies got out there, the truck was gone. Tire tracks indicated the truck had been there. Since there is no stolen truck report from elsewhere, they had no reason to follow-up further."

Michaels sat down behind his desk and trained his eyes on Sarah Ann. "Have you noticed an older truck parked near your house or your downtown office anytime lately?"

Sarah Ann scoured her memory for any such sighting and came up blank. "I sorry, but I haven't noticed one."

John interposed, his mellifluous voice filling the small office. "Is it possible to provide some extra surveillance around Sarah Ann's home until we find out for sure what Mr. Murray may be up to? Or, if it is his truck that was spotted here?"

"I was thinking along those same lines. We could post a patrol car outside your house, ma'am. What's that address?" Michaels jotted it down in his scribbled cursive. "I'll alert the Metro detectives and fill them in on Murray and his truck. And I'll call the sheriff's department to let them know about the situation. See if they can keep their eyes on the Parson farm."

Michaels looked solicitously at Sarah Ann. "Are you going to be all right, ma'am? You can rest assured, now that we know Mr. Murray may be in Williamson County, we'll be keeping a close eye on you. Try to go home and get some rest," he urged gently.

She'll be safe, Lieutenant," John assured him. "I'll stay with Mrs. Boswell tonight," adding, "I have a carry permit."

"Are you carrying now, Mr. Boswell?" John unzipped a blue windbreaker to reveal a shoulder holster with a 9mm Glock secured within its leather confines.

"I think you can feel safe tonight, Mrs. Boswell," Michaels smiled reassuringly. "And I'll make sure we touch base with Metro right away."

Sarah Ann's weary face reflected the relief she felt. They appeared fairly certain about who had followed her—LouAnn's father. *But why* she had to ask herself.

Michaels watched this play out on her face. "You weren't seeing a ghost. It seems likely Murray's truck was the one following you, and rest assured, if it *was* him, we'll find out why, Mrs. Boswell." Again, the calm voice and soothing manner.

"Thank you, Lieutenant. Franklin is fortunate to have officers like you."

"Your tax dollars at work, ma'am," he said with facetious humor. "It was the mayor's main pledge during the last election, to keep the community safe in light of the rising crime rate in Nashville." His lips inched apart in a puckish grin. "We try to ensure our politicians' promises are kept."

Michaels escorted her and John out to the parking area through the high ceilinged front lobby, and after a quick handshake, he slipped back inside. As John tucked her into the front seat of the Lexus he said, "I'll be right behind you," and closed the car door.

He quickly reopened the door part-way, "And I won't be behind you with 'bobbing for apples' lights." The door closed again.

She nestled back in the seat, strapped herself in, and fired the ignition. It was approaching midnight when she turned onto Shiloh Lane. She was surprised to see several cars parked in front of her house, cars she readily recognized. As she pulled under the portico, the Prayer Group came swarming out the side door. They waited until John pulled up behind her before rushing between cars to embrace Sarah Ann.

"What are you doing here?" she exclaimed, and quickly lowered her voice for fear of disturbing her neighbors. John came up and stood behind her.

"It was Angela," answered Willie Dell. "She was listening to the police scanner when your name came across. Monitoring the police is to Angela what *Dancing with the Stars* is to the rest of us. She triggered the Prayer Group hot line. Reporting for protection duty," he said, saluting smartly.

"Shhh," Sarah Ann cautioned. "We'll wake the neighbors, and then they'll notify our neighborhood Crime Watch Captain."

"Who's that?" whispered Della Sue.

"Mary Ellen Carter."

"Oh, sweet Jesus," lamented Jeanne Marie. "This could just be the excuse she needs to have us all arrested and put in the Williamson County Sing Sing."

"Bitch," muttered Della Sue under her breath.

"Snitch is a better adjective," suggested Willie Dell.

"Snitch, bitch. Take your pick, Willie Dell," said Jeanne Marie. "They apply in bushels to Mary Ellen Carter," she added with a sneer. "Let's get inside."

All five Prayer Group members had disparaging memories of their high school nemesis who had delighted in reporting their numerous infractions of the rules to the principal.

John motioned with his arm and pulled Willie Dell aside after they stepped inside the door. "Are you carrying?"

"Right here, bro." Willie Dell patted the holster under his shirt. "Glock nine, hollow point. Should stop the Incredible Hulk if I aim right."

"I know you're a good shot, Willie Dell. Still a reserve deputy?"

"Badge and cuffs to go with the Glock right here in my pocket." Willie Dell looked at John kindly. "You look beat, Johnny. Go home. Get some sleep. We'll take this watch with Sarah Ann. I promise I won't leave her alone until everything is sorted out, whatever this horror from hell that is going on."

John felt the bone weariness Willie Dell could see. He nodded gratefully. "Any of the women have weapons for back-up."

"It scares the hell out of me if you must know, Johnny, but Della Sue and Jeanne Marie are both packin'." He chuckled and added, "If I were Beau Simpson, I'd be running for the North Carolina line right this minute. It wasn't so long ago she was talking about castration."

John winced, "Ouch!"

"I know. As much as Della Sue drinks, with a gun to boot, if I were Beau, I'd be wearing a titanium protector over my balls.

John laughed. "Me, too!" His weary features quickly turned serious. Clapping Willie Dell on the back he said, "Many thanks, Willie Dell. Call if there's anything you need." He hesitated as he pulled a business card from his wallet, "Or if Sarah Ann needs anything."

"Sure thing." Willie Dell stood watching John back out the driveway before going into the house. He set the alarm and made sure the motion sensor was on for the outside flood lights. They had been installed only yesterday after he had insisted Sarah Ann light the full perimeter of the large home.

The scent of fresh roasted coffee wafted in to the wide foyer and seduced Willie Dell back to the kitchen like Odysseus to the song of a Siren. Sarah Ann handed him a steaming cup with a dollop of cream and two sugars. He smiled his gratitude and let the aromatic steam drift into his nostrils. As he observed the four women gabbing animatedly across the kitchen island, he settled on a workable protection plan.

Sarah Ann was exhausted. She was going straight to bed. No arguments.

Della Sue looked like Beau had bested her over whatever turf they were currently tussling. She could take the room next to Sarah Ann. He already knew Della Sue slept at home with her gun beside her pillow. He'd make sure she did it here as well. *Not a bad thing her having a gun so handy, unless of course, Beau ever made the mistake of trying to sneak into her bedroom. Fat chance that!* He shook his head at the conflicts the 'sacrament of marriage' exacted on his friends and issued a quick prayer of thanks that he had had the good sense to excise Beverly before she put him in the poor house, or worse, on death row for murder—hers.

Angela would be needed for kitchen duty early. She could take the guest room adjacent to the stairway. No closed bedroom doors, he decided.

Jeanne Marie he would post in the rear of the house. She was a crack shot. He would keep watch in front near the staircase. Tomorrow they would hire some off-duty police and deputies to help with protecting Sarah Ann until this craziness was resolved. He knew several who would welcome the extra income.

Willie Dell took a long draw of his coffee and felt the sweet liquid warm as it rolled past his tongue. "Okay, ladies. Here's the plan for tonight." Surprisingly, when he finished there was no grumbling. *This had to be a first,* he thankfully observed.

After the three women were in bed, Willie Dell doubled checked every window downstairs to make sure they were locked. He trusted the alarm sensors on those windows. But he trusted his own eyes more. After a final check with Jeanne Marie, he went to the front of the house, double checked that his cell phone was on, and sat down in a shadowy corner of the foyer to watch and listen.

Passing by at frequent intervals was a Franklin Police cruiser. Inside two pairs of eyes scanned the large porch and the wide veranda above it for any signs of break-in. The police car also drove down the alley to which the homes on Shiloh and Manassas backed up. Their flash lights flickered over the backyards and their eyes scanned for any signs of movement or any fresh tell-tale disruption of the graveled alleyway by wheels of another vehicle. None were seen.

~

He had watched all the commotion across the street, his thin frame concealed behind the deep shadows cast by a large tree separating two side yards. At first, a small dog had been yapping, sending his heart into this throat. But when the commotion across the way died down, the dog quit barking.

It was clear to his way of thinking that the cops were onto something. Seeing the police cruiser pass by the first time was all he needed to convince him of that. Anyway, he was bone tired from snatching sleep whenever he could in the pick-up. Danged uncomfortable! His back hurt like the devil. His stomach rumbled its emptiness. And worse, he was about out of money. Could be it was time to end all this.

It was clear, getting to that Boswell woman was right near impossible now. So maybe he might just have to let her live. B*ut not her 'bread and butter.'*

Chapter 35

Aloud clap of thunder trumpeted the start of the downpour. Flashes of lightning lit up the western sky giving him only brief light to see by as he walked nearly a mile back to where he had parked the pick-up behind a church on Natchez Street in a less affluent part of Franklin. He figured no one would take heed of a beaten up old pick-up in this area of town. His empty belly rocked with a mirthless chortle just thinking about how short the distance was from where he parked the pick-up to that fancy police department.

He waited for a crack of thunder before starting the pick-up, and kept his headlights doused as he pulled out on to Natchez Street. Keeping to side streets that pretty much paralleled Columbia Avenue, he drove south. He wondered how many of the folks who lived along here worked in some of those big fancy houses like Miz Boswells. Probably a lot of black folks here, he surmised. Poor whites like him mostly lived in trailer parks.

At least folks could live today in an area and it didn't much matter about skin color. Not so back in the day. Then everybody was poor where he growed up on a forty-acre cotton patch, in the delta of Arkansas, where the border ran close with Louisiana. White folks and Colored folks didn't mix much back then. Times were better now. He nodded his head in silent agreement. *Things changed when ole Lyndon B. took the reins. He was a right fair man. He made things better for most poor folks. Yes sir, he did. Now things was all screwed up again.*

He had scouted a number of back roads that would lead him deeper into the county. He had a knack for keeping directions straight in his head. Never much need of a map once he got the lay of an area. But the blasted rain was making it hard to see as he strained forward against the steering wheel and squinted. It was all the worn windshield wipers could do to keep enough rain off, long enough for him to see in the pitch black ahead. As if the rain and black night weren't enough to deal with, he had to crack the windows a piece on both sides to keep the windshield from fogging up, or it was near impossible to see at all.

Normally he could pull off the road and wait out a rain like this, maybe under an overpass, or even in a parking lot. Too dangerous tonight if his suspicions were right, and the cops had somehow gotten onto him. Well, he couldn't dither much longer on anything. Tomorrow or maybe the next day…but soon…he would get it done and over with. And that would be that.

~

It was after nine when Sarah Ann arrived at the office which was abuzz. She had told Viola on the telephone about being followed by the pick-up with bobbing lights and about the Prayer Group spending the night with guns loaded. "Scary!" Viola kept repeating as Sarah Ann described the ordeal. One detail she purposely hadn't mentioned was LouAnn's father gone missing in an older model pick-up.

Lambert, Nicole and Carole Bennington had been waiting for her at the back door. "Are you sure you should be here today?" Nicole asked, as Lambert handed her a mug of fresh coffee. She accepted it gratefully, hoping it would help dispel the bone weariness she felt after not being able to shut down her fear-cluttered brain. She draped a smile on her face and greeted the trio with forced cheerfulness and words of reassurance, despite the terror stirring about inside her like the panicked fluttering of a wild bird trying to escape through a closed window. She was determined the internal fear would not be allowed to consume her, or cast a pall on today, or the celebratory weekend just ahead. One of their young talents was about to reach an early pinnacle on her climb to stardom, and another would crown his climb by leaving in a few days on a tour that would touch tens of thousands of fans on another continent.

She appreciated their concern. Missing work, even being late as she was now, was not an option this week. Saturday night, Stella was making her debut on the Grand Ole Opry. There were final arrangements to coordinate with Carole on the party Edgerton Group and NCA Records were co-hosting afterwards for Stella at the Hermitage Hotel.

Stella's parents, siblings and spouses and several uncles and aunts were being flown in or driving in for the celebration. They would have to be shepherded to the Opry and the later festivities. Even Jared would be there. He was scheduled to perform just ahead of Stella, and then introduce her to a nationwide cable television and radio audience. If only Jill could be there to see her. How pleased Jill would be to watch their top performers on the same stage.

Lambert touched her arm, his deep voice laced with concern. "You okay, Sarah Ann."

"Sorry. Just thinking how proud Jill would be if she could be there Saturday night." She shook her head slightly to banish the sadness threatening to unmask her forced cheerfulness.

"Can I get a moment with you before I head over to the studio?"

She quickly nodded yes to Lambert and turning to Carole said, "I'll get with you in just a little bit if that's okay."

"Sure thing, boss," Carole responded brightly and bounced off down the hall toward her office. Nicole followed in her wake. Sarah Ann watched them with envy. *Such energy. She could use a thimble full or two of that right now.* Lambert was still standing there. "Something else, Ross?" Worry descended like a shroud over her features.

"You have visitors waiting in your office." Before she could ask who, he answered. "It's Marlin Hotchkin, that detective from Metro, and his partner. I forget his name. They got here about a half hour ago."

"Thanks." She walked over and topped off her mug. "I think I may need a lot of what this has to offer today," lifting her coffee mug in a mock salute.

He gave her a droll smile as they started down the hall together. "I'll let Viola know to hold your calls," he said, as she turned into her office and closed the door behind her.

Both detectives stood up. "Good morning, gentleman. Sorry I'm so late getting in. Had a house full of company last night I had to help feed before I could get away." She slipped her purse off her shoulder and into a drawer in her desk, before setting the briefcase at her feet.

"Heard you had a little excitement down your way last night," Hotchkin revealed nonchalantly as he and Morgan sat back down. She spied the empty coffee mugs on the floor beside their chairs.

"Refills, gentlemen, before we get started?"

"No, ma'am." Morgan just nodded his decline.

"I'm presuming the Franklin Police filled you in on what they learned?"

"Yes, ma'am. A lieutenant…" Hotchkin thumbed through his rumpled notepad… "Michaels left me a detailed message. Told me about you being followed and about Miz Parson's daddy being missing, along with his pick-up." The detective looked up to measure her reaction and found her expression mute. "Did a little checking on my own. Found out Mr. Murray is a Vietnam War veteran and was part of some kinda clandestine unit over there, you might say, that trained Vietnamese fighters in guerrilla tactics, liked how to use knives to kill."

"Dear God…," Sarah Ann's face blanched. "You think he may have killed Jill?"

"I'd say we have a prime suspect, ma'am."

"But why…why Jill?" Sarah Ann seemed at a loss for words, trying to digest what Hotchkin had just imparted.

"Won't really know until we have a chance to talk with Mr. Murray. We're hoping Mr. Parson can help us figure it out. We'll be talking with him a little later." Hotchkin studied his notes again before looking back up. "Anything more you can think of, Miz Boswell, which might help us."

Her head was bent down, and a lingering silence ensued before she looked back up. "I'm sure you think I was wrong for not telling you about Jared and Jill." She felt the catch in her throat. "She was my friend. A friend I deeply miss." Her eyes pleaded with the older man across from her. "She truly loved Jared. I didn't want my friend's reputation sullied when she was no longer here to speak for herself."

It was Morgan who responded. "It's all right, Mrs. Boswell. We knew you were holding something back. We understand now." He glanced at his partner, who grudging agreed with a gruff nod of his head.

The empathy in his voice surprised Sarah Ann. In their previous interviews, she felt they were still looking at her as a possible suspect. John had agreed. The incongruity of being viewed in such a way had filled her with a deep chill of fear. "Everyone is a suspect to police initially," John had explained, trying to ameliorate her fears. He had tried to reassure her that police investigations were a process of elimination…to stay calm, and not be afraid of the truth.

"Thank you, Detective."

"Its okay, ma'am."

Hotchkin tapped his pen impatiently on his pad. "Have you ever had any dealings with Mr. Murray?"

"No, not that I recall. I've never met him or his wife."

"Can you think of any reason why he would be following you?"

"No. None. As I said, I've never met the man." She looked at Hotchkin's inscrutable face, his sagging cheeks streaked with the stress of age, his thick, untamed eyebrows shadowing deep set eyes, weighed down by bulging bags. He was a man who looked older than his years. He seemed oblivious to her scrutiny. "So, Miz Parson's parents never came to any of the big events, like the CMA Awards, to see their son-in-law honored?"

"Neither Jared nor LouAnn have ever even mentioned her parents to me."

"So, you don't know the relationship between the Parsons and the in-laws?"

"I only know Jared is estranged from his mother, I don't…"

Morgan interrupted, "Wha'da you mean by estranged, ma'am?"

"He has no contact with her to my knowledge. He had our attorney…"

"You mean Mr. Boswell?"

"Yes. Jared asked John to send her a large check…for ten thousand dollars, if I remember correctly, enclosed in a letter that requested she never contact him again."

"Did he send money to the Murrays?"

"Not that I'm aware of."

Hotchkin thumbed through his notepad again. "But I believe you told us, you and Mr. Boswell advised Parson about investing his income. So you might know if his father-in-law was hitting him up for money."

She hesitated, not sure how to answer. Jared took a generous monthly stipend from his income. She had no idea how he spent it. "I can only tell you we never sent any money to his in-laws from this office. As I told you, all of the bills for the farm are paid from here, from a domestic account we set up for Jared. He receives a flat sum to do with whatever he and LouAnn want."

Hotchkin perused his rumpled notepad for another minute or so before abruptly tucking it in his jacket pocket and standing up. "Thank you, ma'am. I guess that's all for right now, unless you have something Morgan?" The unobtrusive younger detective shook his head.

With the departure of the two detectives, the morning dissolved into a whirl of frantic meetings, more meetings, phone calls and finally a harried Nicole ducking into Sarah Ann's office to announce the expedited passports for two of the band members had finally arrived. Cross off one crisis!

Lunch was ordered in for the staff. It was Viola who came to the office door early in the afternoon with a paper plate piled with warmed up bar-be-que ribs, baked beans, cole slaw and an array of fresh fruits in a Styrofoam bowl. "Eat," she commanded. "Coffee or diet coke?" she asked. Before leaving to fetch the soft drink, she insisted at least half the plate be empty before she returned, as she fluttered her hand for Sarah Ann to start eating. Sarah Ann looked at the plate without enthusiasm, but rather than risk Viola's attentive wrath, she picked up a greasy rib, slathered with sauce, and nibbled away. Viola nodded approval as she sat the diet coke on the desk and hurried out the door as the telephone sounded up front. A moment later Sarah Ann's intercom buzzed.

She had barely said hello when an excited Stella described how well the practice session went for her performance Saturday night. And how great the dress looked that Sarah Ann helped her select. Stella's enthusiasm, basted with joyfulness, helped Sarah Ann shed the cloak of worry which had pervaded her spirits since meeting with the detectives. She said a silent thank you to the young singer as she hung up and was leaning back in her chair when the intercom buzzed again. "Detective Hotchkin," Viola announced acerbically. "You here or you out?"

Sarah Ann sighed heavily. "I'm here." *What now?*

"Just take a minute, Miz Boswell," Hotchkin opened in a raspy voice. "From the sound of things, your receptionist may have me on a timer."

Sarah Ann laughed. "She's just playing palace guard, a role she takes seriously."

Hotchkin just grunted, and then continued, "Had an interesting conversation with Parson. Seems there *is* bad blood between him and his father-in-law. Goes back to when he lived in Texas. He hasn't allowed the Murrays to see their daughter and grandkid since they moved up here." She waited, knowing a question was coming. "How much did Parson tell you or Miz Edgerton about his outs with the in-laws."

"If Jared ever discussed it with Jill, she never mentioned it to me. Some weeks, maybe months ago, I lose tract of time, we were contacted by Mrs. Murray, who wanted to get in touch with her daughter. We passed it along to Jared through Jill. I don't know if, or how he responded."

Hotchkin cleared his throat roughly, the sound of a long time smoker trying to forge an opening to his lungs. "Some sheriff department investigators down in Texas talked to Miz Murray this morning. They went with a search warrant at our request. Seems a serrated hunting knife Mr. Murray kept under the bed is missing, along with him. The knife used to kill Miz Edgerton had a serrated blade, just like the one we found at the Parson place. And it's got one identifiable fingerprint that didn't get wiped off. Also Miz Edgerton's DNA from scrapings the coroner found her fingernails."

He cleared his throat again, this time more gently. "Mr. Murray is now what we like to call a person of interest, Miz Boswell." He fell silent, letting the impact of his words sink in. "An arrest warrant is being issued as we speak."

"I'm not sure I understand, Detective. Why would he target Jill… or me, for godsakes? I've never met the man. And I don't think Jill had either."

"Well, ma'am, that's a question we'll put to Mr. Murray when we find him." She heard him attempt to ignite a lighter several times, probably the same one she saw bulging in front of the cigarettes stuffed in his shirt pocket when he was in her office earlier. It was the first time she had noticed him with cigarettes. She pictured a cloud of smoke ringing his head.

"None of my business, of course, ma'am, but have you taken any precautions, like maybe staying with a friend…maybe hiring some private security…just until we locate Mr. Murray?"

"Some friends are staying with me at my house. I do have a security system on all the downstairs doors and windows."

"That's good, ma'am. Any of these friends staying with you handy with a gun?"

"I'm afraid so, Detective. But I can't vouch for their aim," she added smiling.

A wheezy laugh rasped up from his throat. "Best to hire some off-duty cops, ma'am."

"Our attorney hired a private security firm to protect the office round the clock. I'll talk with him about securing their services for my home."

"Good idea. Well, you take care, Miz Boswell. I'll be in touch." He was gone before she could say goodbye.

As soon as she hung up, Nicole and Lambert walked through her doorway. "Got a minute?" Lambert asked, flashing a grin. "I bear tidings of great joy."

"In that case, sure. Pull up a chair you two."

For the next half-hour Lambert went over finalized plans for the tour, with Nicole occasionally interjecting details of travel and accommodations. Sarah Ann marveled at how seamlessly he had taken over the management of Jared and his band and ironed out so many wrinkles that had plagued Jill and Nicole. He was proving a gift from the country music gods. And proving he'd make a more than capable partner in the future. But that was still to be resolved.

He seemed content to postpone finalizing any such plans until after he returned from the tour.

"Shiring is flying to London for the first concert. NCA wants to record the concert live for an album and release it in time for Christmas sales." Lambert grinned. "I told you I was the bearer of glad tidings. What'd you think?"

"Great! Excellent!" She found herself clapping her hands with excitement. "How is Jared with all this?"

"He had the same reaction as you," Lambert replied, his grin easing back to a smile. "Maybe less clapping. Maybe a few qualms about recording live. But he's good."

She sighed heavily and rubbed her eyes. "Let's hope the British like him as much as we reconstructed Southern "Yanks."

"They will."

She hardly noticed the remainder of the day rush by until the familiar tones of Nessun Dorma sounded on her cell phone.

"I'm in the parking lot," John said. "Are you ready to call it a day?" He had insisted on driving her to work this morning, and when she balked initially, the Prayer Group ganged up, putting down any chance of a rebellion. Together, they were circling around her like a wagon train to provide a protective ring. "I'll be right out."

The after-hours security guard John had hired for the office walked her to the back door and out to where John was parked, the top of his Jaguar convertible down to enjoy the evening air, devoid of the clammy humidity of recent days. It was the opening act of a colorful fall with tepid temperatures that made middle Tennessee such a pleasant place to be during this particular season.

John had his cell phone to his ear as she came down the steps. Even in profile, he remained as good looking as the younger version she had fallen in love with so many years ago. What had it been… thirty years…more? His gray hair only accentuated his handsome features, giving them a distinguished maturity.

Why was it women looked old with gray hair—men looked distinguished, she moaned inwardly. *Life is so damned unfair. But there's no promise of fairness when the doctor signs your birth certificate. C'est la vie!*

She opened the door and felt herself sinking into the plush leather seats. She was going to have to treat herself to one of these someday. But then she would have to carry a head scarf, and lather with sunscreen. On reflection, maybe her Lexus wasn't so bad after all.

"Hey," he said, leaning over to kiss her lightly on the lips. She must have looked as surprised as she felt. "Caught you blushing," he teased. "Good day I hope. I'm assuming that, since your attorney did not get a call from you."

"Busy, busy…but I promise tomorrow to bug you silly."

"Deal," he said swinging out of the parking area and down the rear alleyway.

He delivered her to her side door under the portico where she was met by Willie Dell. From the kitchen wafted a flavorful bouquet of Mexican spice. She knew Jeanne Marie was cooking her favorite Taco casserole even before she came bounding out from the kitchen to greet Sarah Ann, wiping her hands on her apron. "I hope you're hungry, darlin'.

Despite her pleas, the Prayer Group had insisted on taking turns spending the night, with Willie Dell to be a constant every night, his granddaddy's sixteen gauge shotgun loaded by his bed in the upstairs guest room across the hall from Sarah Ann, and the 9mm Glock now tucked in the small of his back.

Willie Dell had lived next door to Sarah Ann since before either started school. He moved away only once, for what would become the longest twelve months of his life, when he lost his bachelorhood to the demonic charms of a mortgage banker named Beverly Eddings. She proved the banshee antidote to any lingering desire he held for home and family. His mother's unremitting crankiness, topped only by her ceaseless complaining, had blossomed like bacteria in a petri dish in the year he lived away.

He survived the transition by doubling his work hours and building a two agent real estate firm into the largest in Franklin and his net worth into seven figures. Willie Dell Winston had long ago come to terms with living like a monk.

The only woman he ever really loved lived next door, but she might just as well have lived on a far continent, for the divide he placed between the close friendship he cherished and his latent romantic feelings.

As the years passed, his responsibilities grew for caring for an aging mother, whom he had bundled off earlier today, amid wails and tears and gnashing of false teeth, to stay with her younger sister in Nashville. "Just until all this fuss blows over," he promised without divulging too many details of the 'fuss', as he hustled her into his aunt's house.

Sarah Ann ate a polite, but smallish serving of Jeanne Marie's prized casserole, served by a smiling Monet. *Extraordinary*, thought Sarah Ann. Monet made no secret of her resentment of the Prayer Group and began grumbling under her breath in her distinctive, often indecipherable dialect, several days in advance of the Prayer Group's monthly meetings. Whatever magic spell Jeanne Marie had cast over the cantankerous Monet was welcome.

When Sarah Ann attempted to help with the after dinner clean-up, she was barred from the kitchen and exiled to the front parlor to keep company with Willie Dell. Noting the weariness in her eyes, he soon ushered her upstairs with instructions to bathe, go to sleep, and call him if she needed anything. Jeanne Marie had peeked in a short time after Sarah Ann burrowed under the covers and kissed her on the cheek. "I hope you sleep well, darlin'," before tip toeing out.

Sleep proved elusive, despite a week that was proving exhausting with the weekend still ahead. The tumult of the weekend kept reigniting her wake cycle like a snooze alarm going off repeatedly. Just before midnight she heard her bedroom door open quietly, and for a moment her body froze with terror until she realized it was Willie Dell shadowed in the dim light from the hall. "Come in. I'm awake," she whispered.

She sat up and patted the side of the bed. He sat down and took her hands in his. "Can't sleep, baby sister?"

She shook her head, "Not a wink." She leaned against his shoulder. "I keep thinking all this is just a horror fantasy like we used to spin as kids. Only reality is far more horrid than we could ever imagine."

Willie Dell folded her into his arms. "It'll all be over soon, Sarah Ann. The police will catch the crazy s.o.b., waterboard a confession out of him, or whatever they do these days instead of rubber hosing. Then the great State of Tennessee will fry him. In the meantime, we get to hold Prayer Group meetings every night. So what's not to like about that?"

"Not a thing…not a thing." She reached up and kissed him on the cheek. "Promise you'll always be my best friend."

"Promise, cross my heart."

"John and Angeline are separated."

He looked stunned as he pushed gently away to see her face. "When did this happen?"

"I'm not sure. He just told me a few days ago." Sarah Ann turned away as she felt tears forming. "He wants to get back together." She turned and buried her face in Willie Dell's neck. "He said losing me was the worst mistake he's ever made."

He patted her back trying to ease the sobs tearing through her. "And you know what, Willie Dell?"

"No, what, baby sister?" he whispered soothingly in her ear, as he rocked her gently.

"If he had said that to me even six months ago, I would have rushed back to him without a second thought. But now…"

"But now?"

"But now I'm not so sure." She pulled back again and wiped away the tears with the hem of the sheet. "What's wrong with me? When I couldn't have him, I thought I couldn't live without him. Now I can perhaps have him, and I'm not sure it's what I really want anymore."

Willie Dell's face cracked into a mischievous smile. "Some psychologists might call that being a woman."

She laughed, and more tears fled down her cheeks. "I never took you for a chauvinist pig, Willie Dell Winston," smacking him lightly on the shoulder.

"I've been called that and worse by other members of our little prayer klatch." He took the sheet and tenderly wiped away the remaining tears. "Now lay back and try to get some sleep. Holler if you need anything." He bent down and kissed her on the forehead. "Love you, baby sister."

It was well after 2:00 before her mind finally shut down and she slept.

Chapter 36

Jared Parson was scared—scared shitless. He hadn't seen his father-in-law since the week before he and LouAnn left Texas. Police knew, and Jared knew, it was he that Lester Murray was gunning for. Jared leaned on his arms looking out over the balcony balustrade, distractedly watching the two mares and Willow's plump pony munching grass contentedly near the white fence along the lane leading to the road. On a rise overhung with tall oak trees across the lane, his frisky stallion was rolling in thick grass, still soft and damp from a mid-morning rain.

Below him, the trees lining the long drive were showing pale hints of the radiant oranges and reds that would brighten as the green vanished from the leaves, nature's colorful signal the season was changing. Fall would soon be on full display. His favorite time of year and he would miss most of it because of Europe.

He lingered on the balcony, the gentle fingers of a cool breeze stroking his grim face and teasing the natural waves of his dark hair. His childhood dream was laid out before him; this home and the rolling lush land surrounding it.

It had been a far distant hope, bound in the hazy gauze of childhood daydreams, when he was growing up in a trailer, the stench of his mother's alcohol and cigarettes permeating the air that even open windows could not purge. Only the shouts and applause as he entered a stage, and doffed his signature tan Stetson, and lifted his custom designed Gibson guitar in salute to a packed venue, even came close to rivaling what he felt now, looking out on the fruits of his achievement.

He would experience that same familiar high when he stepped out on the Grand Ole Opry stage tonight.

But it wouldn't be the same tonight, goddammit. He roughly brushed away a stray tear from his cheek with his hand. He would look out and the one seat he most wanted filled would be empty, a seat that should have been filled by one of the two women who had made all he looked out on possible.

Jill was dead because of him. He knew that now. The cops did too. *God, I'm sorry, Jill.* His body convulsed with sobs. *Why in hell didn't I just send him the money?* It was the same question which had haunted his thoughts since learning Lester Murray was suspected of stabbing Jill with that big knife of his, the one he used to skin deer he mostly poached in the off season. The coroner had found traces of animal DNA mixed with Jill's. The older Metro detective said a fingerprint on the knife, found in his studio, was Murrays. Now they just had to find Murray. And right now they had no clue where he was, which scared the hell out of him.

Jared noticed movement behind the barn. Probably ole Hershel. Another man who hated his guts. But thanks to Sarah Ann he was still here. Right now, Jared needed him. He knew Simmons would do him no favors, not if he could avoid it, but might if it involved LouAnn and Willow. And this did.

He walked down the back stairway from the balcony and out to the barn. Simmons was mucking straw and loading manure into a wheel barrel.

"Hey, Hershel." The older man straightened up and leaned on the pitchfork. "Got a favor to ask?" Simmons nodded. "I've got to be in Nashville this evening. Could you stay up at the house with LouAnn and Willow? She's not feeling so good. The baby's been giving her fits at night kicking, and she's still kinda down. This thing with Jill… now her daddy…it's left her pretty unsettled."

"Sure. What time?"

"I need to leave in an hour or so." Jared stuffed his hands in his jean pockets and lowered his head, pawing at the dirt floor of the barn absently with the toe of his boot like a skittish horse. He knew Simmons suspected he had been carrying on with Jill. Maybe

LouAnn had told him. He knew she talked to Hershel a lot. He felt a pang of guilt. Lonely, probably. Who wouldn't be, stuck out here with Willow, him working long hours—*not to mention the nights he spent with Jill*—and no one else to talk to except the housekeeper or Hershel. They seemed to be her only friends. He *was* grateful for one thing. Simmons was protective of LouAnn and Willow. "How handy are you with a gun?" Jared finally asked.

For an instant Simmons looked incredulous, then rubbed his chin bristled with a couple day's growth of whiskers. "I guess handy enough."

"You probably already know the cops think LouAnn's daddy may be who killed Jill. They said he might be after me next." Jared stared off to the side of the barn and felt tears burning his eyes. He swallowed hard to gain control. Hershel Simmons was the last man he would want to perceive him as weak. "I guess I've screwed things up royally, Hershel. Somehow, her daddy must've found out about me and Jill and took it out on Jill." He could see the accusation in Simmons eyes. *What the hell, he deserved it*, he admitted silently. *He had treated Hershel like shit.*

This time the tears would not hold back. "I told LouAnn. She's really hurt." His lips trembled, and he gripped the top of the stall door nearest him. "I've been a real shit. Can't let anything happen to LouAnn and Willow," he said, shaking his head. He looked up and saw the intractable expression had faded from Simmons face. "I'd be grateful if you'd stay with my girls until I get back tonight."

Simmons shifted the small wad of chewing tobacco from under his lower lip to his cheek. "I'd feel more comfortable with a shotgun. Been a few years since I handled any handguns."

"Okay. I've got a sixteen gauge up at the house. Holds three shells."

"Sounds like that'll do. Let me get the horses in here and fed, and I'll be right up." Simmons stood the pitchfork against the stall and walked toward Jared with the bull legged gait of a man who had been around barns and horses a good deal of his life. "No worry about Miz LouAnn and little Willow." He lumbered off toward the fence.

As he walked back to the house, Jared heard Simmons call the horses with a two-finger whistle. The animals answered with loud neighing. Jared found LouAnn in the playroom with Willow and the housekeeper. His daughter was squealing with delight when Jeanette grabbed her from behind as she hid in the large playhouse and swung her around and around after pulling her out. He stood in the doorway watching, trying to recall when he had last played with his child. He was never there to play with her, seldom took time to read her a bedtime story, or take her riding on her pony. No wonder the little horse was getting so rotund.

Things would change when he got back from Europe. He would take some time off. Maybe take his two girls and the new baby to Disney World, or someplace like that, if LouAnn was feeling up to it. *Yeah, things would change when he got back.*

~

Sarah Ann rode in the stretch limousine with Stella and her parents and her two older sisters and their awestruck spouses from the Opryland Hotel, the short distance to the Grand Ole Opry. Stella looked radiant in a royal blue gown she and Sarah Ann had selected for her Opry debut. The radiance in Stella's blue eyes competed with the sparkling sequins covering the bodice of the gown.

She and Lambert had met the family entourage at the airport yesterday morning and whisked them to the hotel where Nicole and one of her assistants had spent the rest of the day guiding them around Nashville's famous sites, before Stella joined her family for dinner at a posh Green Hills restaurant. Sarah Ann had arranged a limo service for the entire weekend stay, much to the delight of both Stella and her family.

It was a gregarious group that piled out of the limo in front of the famous Opry. Stella hugged her mother, from whom she had inherited her beauty, before being wrapped in a bear hug by a doting father who towered over his petite wife and daughters, his once sandy hair nearly turned to grey. It was clear it was he who had imparted to each of his daughters his keen sense of humor and extroverted personality. Sarah Ann gave silent kudos to the two sons-in-law who seemed content to remain on the quieter periphery of the high decibel interaction between members of the Wayne family.

After handing over the family to the ever-genial Nicole, Sarah Ann escorted Stella backstage to her dressing room. As she turned to leave, Lambert approached. His silver streaked hair and good looks stood out in the navy blue blazer and tan slacks, complemented with a blue and beige striped silk tie.

"You look beautiful, Mrs. Boswell," he complimented as his eyes roved appreciatively over the pale blue silk shantung cocktail length dress she was wearing, with a matching bolero cut jacket.

"Thank you, Ross. I dress to impress," she replied with self-deprecation, attempting to conceal her sudden awkwardness at his perusal. "How's our boy?"

"I was just headed to his dressing room. He's a little tired. I think the long practice sessions are wearing on him. And on the band." Lambert led the way down a brightly lit hallway.

"Maybe he'll catch some rest this weekend." They stopped at a door with Jared's name inserted in a wide brass slot and knocked.

"Come on in."

Jared looked up. Lambert was right. She was shocked to see the weariness ringing his eyes. But he smiled a greeting as he pulled on his second boot.

"You all set, Jared?" She was sure he was. Whatever fault she had with his temperament, he was a consummate professional.

"All set," he answered, standing up. The boots he had just put on seemed to emphasize his height. "How's Stella holding up?"

"Excited. But nervous."

"That figures. I was too the first time." He stood before the floor length mirror and tugged his muscular shoulders into a colorfully hand-tooled leather vest, with his first name on each side. "Still am and probably always will be."

"If you are, it never shows," Sarah Ann observed kindly. "I better get back out front. Good luck, tonight." She patted his arm. "And thanks again for opening for Stella."

"Give 'em hell, son," Lambert added, as he opened the door for Sarah Ann.

Out front, Opry goers were flooding through the doors and scurrying to seats that arced around the large stage. There was merry mayhem, front row center, where the Wayne family sat chattering amongst themselves at a volume that would be the envy of Minnie Pearl's fabled entrances. The decibel level dimmed only when Sarah Ann interrupted to introduce Lambert, who got a kiss from Mrs. Wayne, and a bear hug and bracing pat on the back from the ever convivial Mr. Wayne.

Seated in back of the Wayne family were members of the Edgerton Group staff, along with spouses and dates. Viola gave her a hug and introduced her to the three children who were astonishingly polite after being described to Sarah Ann with adjectives like 'hellions' and the 'devil's own', etc. The younger son and daughter, who were eight and eleven, shook her hand. And their older brother, who was the mirror image of Viola and six inches taller than his mother, thanked her for inviting them. It was their first time to see the legendary country music show. After more introductions, Sarah Ann excused herself and whispered to Lambert that she was meeting John and some other friends in the lobby.

He was standing there talking with Willie Dell. The female members of the Prayer Group were scattered behind them.

"No spouses," Sarah Ann inquired, somewhat facetiously, knowing spouses were persona non-grata at most gatherings of the Prayer Group.

"Beau and Charlie are at your house, darlin'," Della Sue smiled wickedly. "They're on guard duty tonight, armed with shotguns and a six pack."

"Then God help any intruders," quipped Willie Dell half seriously.

"But only if the intruders get there before the six pack is finished," warned Angela.

Sarah Ann was laughing as she waved them to follow her, ushering them to their seats. "Next time, darlin', let me know when I have to walk so far for a seat down front, and I'll take a pass on my daily Jane Fonda's," Jeanne Marie cheerfully complained, as she took a seat in the front row next to Willie Dell. John was the last to sit down and smiled his thank you to Sarah Ann for holding a seat for him next to her.

When Jared finished his song, a hit from his latest album, he stayed on the stage to introduce Stella, who made a beaming appearance. Her family greeted her entrée with exuberant applause, and her performance was complimented with prolonged applause. Then a surprise, an encore appearance by Jared. Stella smiled and blushed with appreciation.

"How about a duet with this beautiful young lady," Jared asked the audience. They roared their affirmation with applause and whistles. He whispered something in her ear and she nodded before quickly tuning her guitar, while two members of his band stepped back on stage.

As Stella and Jared faced each other to sing a Dolly Parton classic, *I Will Always Love You*, Sarah Ann felt John take her hand in his. After Jared and Stella exited the stage, Lambert, who was sitting directly behind Sarah Ann whispered in her ear. "Can I take her to Europe with me?"

"First things first," she countered. "She's only fresh off the state fair circuit."

He laughed and whispered, "I think she may get a pass on serving any more of those dues."

By the time Sarah Ann and Lambert made their way backstage to the dressing rooms, a glowing Stella said that Jared had already left and offered his regrets for not attending the after show party. While making their way back to the lobby from back stage, Stella was congratulated by some of the veteran Opry performers and several wished her a great future. To Sarah Ann's thinking, that was a given after her performance tonight.

It took nearly an hour for the four limousines to ferry all the staff and invited guests through the tangle of traffic outside the Grand Ole Opry to the downtown Hermitage Hotel. Sarah Ann had managed to pawn chaperon duty for the happily riotous Wayne family off on John and Lambert and nestled herself in the limo with the Prayer Group.

"Is my house still standing," was Sarah Ann's first question, as she slipped in next to Willie Dell.

"Yes, but Beau and Charlie were about to pop the last of that six pack," reported Della Sue, swinging her cell phone in the air. "So who knows, darlin', what you'll find when you get home." Then added officiously, "May I remind you, Beau's services do not come with liability insurance or guarantees of any sort."

"Ditto that for Charlie," agreed Angela as she popped open a can of beer from the built-in cooler. There followed a quick cacophony of popping beer tabs. Willie Dell raised his can, "To Sarah Ann and her success."

"Here! Here!"

Della Sue looked around the spacious interior of the stretch limo, "You know what," she noted provocatively, "there's ample room in here to do more than drink beer."

"And what would that be Della Sue," inquired Willie Dell, in a voice thick with sarcasm.

"Darlin', if you have to ask, you have too much in common with that Dalai Lama fellow, which I believe in fact you do, since you suffer from a bad case of monkism."

Angela quickly leaned across Jeanne Marie. "Who has what in common with Dolly? Is that her married name? And what in the hell is monkism anyway? I've never heard of it. Is it contagious?" Angela's question sent her friends into hysterics.

"Not *Dolly*, silly. Dalai! You've heard of the Dalai Lama, the guy from India who dresses in that funny red color and sits with his legs tucked under him all the time and took a vow of chastity before he was born," Jeanne Marie instructed condescendingly. Then added in a puzzled tone, "I've never heard of monkism either."

Willie Dell took a pull of beer. "Actually, Jeanne Marie, the Dalai Lama's from Tibet.

"Whatever," Jeanne Marie jabbed back, as she waved his sarcasm away like a pesky fly.

"As for monkism," continued Willie Dell. "I believe Della Sue is referring to my sex life or the lack thereof."

"Only to the lack thereof, darlin'." Della Sue hoisted her can in a mock salute.

"I have managed for the nearly fifty years since the formation of the Prayer Group, to keep that particular private subject *private*. If I ever revealed anything to this group, I'm sure it would show up under a banner headline in the newspaper."

"Then your secrets are safe with me, darlin'. I only subscribe to People Magazine."

"Della Sue, darlin', that gives me more relief than a roll of Tums." Willie Dell popped another can.

As the banter continued, Sarah Ann could feel the stress of the past week gliding away. She wondered silently how different her life would have been without these friends who had been such pillars of support during both good times, and periods of tribulation. Then her mind drifted to another friend, Jill, who had cast a lifeline to her from a hospital bed and made climbing the pyramid of success she now enjoyed possible. She finished her beer and shrugged off the shroud of grief that threatened to descend and darken her mood. She was happy tonight—happy and laughing. It felt too good to let go of.

During the dinner, Willie Dell and John had excused themselves and Sarah Ann turned around and saw them huddled in conversation just outside a sign for restrooms. When they returned to the table it was John who sat down beside her. "I'm on guard duty tonight. Willie Dell is taking a well-deserved night off. Is that all right?"

She looked at him with teasing eyes and whispered. "And is this fair warning, Mr. Boswell, to don my chastity belt."

"Don't bother," his blue eyes dark and inscrutable as he bent and kissed her on the lips.

"That will get you nowhere if Della Sue's downstairs on guard," she whispered.

"Willie Dell is rescheduling her shift."

"My concerns are assuaged, counselor." She tipped her wine glass to his. "Except for one. What about the current Mrs. Boswell?"

She filed for divorce and agreed to the generous financial settlement I lavished on her. Papers are signed. Divorce uncontested. Final in seven weeks.

"Good. Anyway, I misplaced the key to my chastity belt."

His deep laugh was as melodious as his rich voice. Sarah Ann smiled and looked around her at the gabbing, happy faces that were her circle of life. She issued a silent prayer of gratefulness for the wellspring of happiness that had once again emerged from one of her darkest periods. How blessed she was.

Chapter 37

He parked the battered pick-up about a half mile down on a rough path off the main road, in a dense coppice of thistle and vines. The opposite direction from which he knew the slick car with the low growling mufflers would be coming. The old shotgun hung heavy in his right hand, heavy enough that he shifted it from one hand to the other every hundred steps or so. "I knew them snickers bars I swiped from that convenience store a couple o' nights ago wouldn't hold me long," he muttered. *But then they're probably enough,* he added silently. *Won't need no more, not where I'm was headed.*

He burrowed into the culvert under the lane, at the edge of the two lane road. It smelled of damp, and he could feel water seeping into his pants where he sat. *Plenty cover, this.* He stretched his long skinny legs as far as he could, which wasn't far enough to keep his knees from making tents, and settled back against the cool metal to wait.

A wash of guilt splashed over him—guilt he couldn't seem to scrub from his conscious. He hadn't meant to kill that woman. It was the man having carnal relations with her he had come to punish. He tried to get her to shut up, but she kept screaming. He just pulled the knife to scare her silent. It only made her holler louder. She was still screaming when he plunged the knife in the first time. She just looked at him with terror in her eyes, her blood seeping through his hand covering her chest. She started to cry out again. He couldn't stand it. He yelled at her to stop screaming. But she just kept on as she slid to the floor. He had to silence her. Someone downstairs or next door would hear. He knelt over her and plunged the knife in again and again, finally jerking it up to her heart like they trained him in the army. She went silent even before then; just staring at him until her eyes went blank. He shook the memory from his mind. *What was done, was done. No going back now.*

The Bible admonished, *cleave to your wife.* That same Bible also taught the Ten Commandments and sternly admonished against murder. He had learned it all at his daddy's knee, every night after the evening meal when the good book was recited before bedtime. The Commandments also taught, *Thou Shalt Not Commit Adultery.* Tonight he would teach that sinning sonofabitch a final lesson on that score, and patted the shotgun lying across his cavernous belly.

~

Jared swung into the lane and parked in front of the house. It was nearing midnight. Moonlight cloaked the trees along the lane in a silvery hue. The night air touched his face like a feathered hand as he bounded up the front steps. Before he could put his key in the brass lock of the wide oak door, it opened.

"I saw you drive up, Mr. P."

Hershel Simmons stepped aside to let him in and then peered out into the darkness, long enough to let his eyes adjust. Satisfied nothing was moving outside, he closed the door and turned the dead bolt lock.

"Everything quiet here," he reported, before a question could form on Jared's lips. "I just checked on Miz LouAnn and Willow. Both asleep."

"Thanks, Hershel…for taking care of my girls."

"No problem, Mr. P. Guess I'll head back to my place unless there's something else?" He handed the shotgun to Jared. "Keep it," Jared said. "I might still need your help."

"Sure thing." Simmons shifted the gun under his armpit and started toward the back of the house when Jared asked. "Did you see the new girl tonight? She did great don't you think?"

Simmons stood framed in the doorway leading into the kitchen. "Yes, sir. Watched her…with Willow and Miz LouAnn." Over his shoulder he added, "You did great yourself."

"Thanks, Hershel." A moment later Jared heard the back door open and close and a key turn in the lock.

He sat on the stairway and yanked off his custom leather boots, the boots Jill had made for him in Amarillo. The soft leather felt like the firm skin of a woman's breast—her breast. His chest tightened in pain and he felt hot tears sting his eyes. For the first time since Jill's murder he felt the need for sex. He shook his head as if to dispel the urgings of his loins. LouAnn was too far along for them to have sex. Maybe she would never want him again after what he'd done. Forgiveness she had granted him immediately. Burying the hurt he had inflected would take more time. He would give her whatever time she needed. It was the vow he made to her as he buried his head in her lap sobbing his apology.

He picked up the boots and ascended the elegant winding stairs quietly, his steps soundless on the thick carpet in the hallway as he entered the bedroom. He looked down at LouAnn breathing the steady rhythm of sleep. She looked like the same teenager he first met in high school.

He watched her for a few more moments. Her childlike features appeared almost translucent on the ivory silk pillow, paled by the faint light of the moon slanting in through the partially opened drapes of the French Doors which led out to the front balcony. He marveled at how much Willow looked like her mother.

He slipped into the dressing room adjacent to the bedroom and closed the door quietly, before turning on the light. He unsnapped the holster for his Glock from the back of his belt and set it on the side of the white marble vanity. He crossed the spacious room to finish undressing, draping his clothes over a regal Queen Anne chair. He debated sleeping in one of the guest rooms. But this was not a night to be far from LouAnn's side. He turned out the light before opening the door. He stepped noiselessly to the bed and eased his way beneath the covers, trying not to disturb LouAnn.

"That you, Jared?"

"It's me, LouAnn. Go back to sleep. Sorry I woke you."

She turned on her side toward him. "We watched you on the Opry…me and Willow and Hershel. You did great."

"Thanks, baby. What did you think of Stella?"

"Sings like an angel. You think she'll be a star?"

"Probably. Sarah Ann and Ross think so."

"But not as big a star as you, Jared."

He leaned over and kissed her softly on the lips. "You've always been my biggest fan. Couldn't have done it without you."

"Do you mean that, Jared," she asked, her eyes watering as she touched his cheek lightly.

"I mean it, LouAnn. Love you." At that instant, he thought he heard a sound from downstairs, like a door opening. Maybe Hershel forgot something. He reached across to the night stand for his gun and remembered leaving it in the dressing room. "Be right back." He didn't want to alarm her as he padded into the dressing room and fingered in the dark for the holstered gun on the vanity.

Just as he stepped back into the bedroom he saw a slightly bent, sparse shadow framed in the double doorway by the dim ambient light from the wide hallway behind. "Forget something, Hershel?" he asked, as he unsnapped the holster.

"It ain't Hershel." The response was a reedy voice he didn't recognize. "It's me, you sonofabitch."

Then he knew. Before Jared could pull the gun free from the holster, the first blast tore through his chest, sending him crashing against the wall separating the bedroom from the dressing room. The second blast tore into his shoulder. He was dying before his body slumped down to the carpet.

"No daddy, no." LouAnn screamed, frozen in the bed by the horror of what she had just witnessed, paralyzing any movement.

"I did it for you, LouAnn. He was no good for you from the start."

The sound of her father's voice seemed to snap her paralysis and she swung out of bed and rushed over to where Jared lay. His head was slumped at a sharp angle against the wall. She placed her arm under him and pulled him into her lap. "Oh, please God. Don't take him from me," she moaned, as she rocked back and forth.

From another room came the sleepy voice of a child. "Mommy, come get me, come get me. I'm scared." The voice seemed not to penetrate her grief.

He was standing over her now looking down impassively. "I did it for you, LouAnn," Lester Murray repeated. "He wasn't no good for you. Never was. He was a sinner. This is God's will, you know."

He was still staring blankly at his daughter and dead son-in-law when he heard boots pounding up the stairs. The shotgun hung limply in his hand, one shell left in its chamber. He turned and walked back toward the double doors opening into the bedroom, toward the pounding footsteps, holding the shotgun in front of him.

Hershel Simmons burst onto the landing. Simmons saw the slim figure in front of him bring the shotgun to his chest. Before Murray could shoot, the shotgun Simmons held thundered in the still night knocking the spare target back several feet.

Simmons stepped over the thin figure partially blocking the wide entrance into the bedroom, kicking the shotgun out of reach of the dying man. Then his eyes took in the scene. He stumbled over to where LouAnn was holding Jared's bloodied body against her protruding stomach. He knelt down, setting his gun aside, and placed two fingers against Jared's neck. He moaned softly before gently moving Jared from her lap. He firmly clasped LouAnn's trembling shoulders and pulled her up.

"Come with me, Miz LouAnn. There ain't nothing more we can do for him now."

She swayed against him. Fearing she would fall he lifted her into his arms and carried her out of the bedroom, stepping around the body of her dead father. It was when he put her down by the stairway that LouAnn noticed the blood dripping from a wide gash on the side of his head.

"Hershel, you're hurt," she cried in alarm.

He staggered sideways momentarily before righting himself. "I'll be okay, Miz LouAnn," he said. Leaning heavily against a wall he fished in his pocket for his cell phone to dial 9-1-1.

When the first sheriff's deputies arrived, they found Hershel holding Willow on his lap and reading to her from one of her favorite books. LouAnn sat beside him, leaning her head against his shoulder, his arm around her protectively. Blood from his gaping head wound mixed with the blood that had already soaked the front of her cotton nightgown.

"Upstairs," was all Simmons said to the arriving deputies.

The first paramedics arrived only minutes later. Simmons insisted they take LouAnn to the hospital in the first ambulance. When the paramedics lifted her gently to her feet, her eyes stared blankly from a face blanched by shock. Simmons had to ply free her grip from his hand and smoothed back the hair from her forehead. "Willow will be fine, Miz LouAnn," he assured her. "Jeannette's on her way. She's going to keep your baby girl safe while you get well." LouAnn seemed neither to hear nor comprehend, and did not respond to the paramedics questions as the gurney was loaded into the ambulance.

Jeannette arrived just behind the second ambulance and lifted Willow from Simmons' arms to hers. He had tried to stand and collapsed, blood still streaming from the wound inflicted by Lester Murray with the stock of his shotgun which he slammed into Simmons' head as the farm manager had been crossing toward the barn. Simmons told the deputy who rode in the ambulance with him he had not heard the older man who seemed to appear out of nowhere. The blow had dazed him. He remembered the attacker unsnapping the ring of keys from his belt. He wasn't sure how many long moments passed before he was able to stand and stumble back into the house. "Too late. Oh God, I was too late," he lamented, over and over, sobs choking his throat, as the paramedics worked to stem the bleeding.

~

Their lovemaking had been long and satisfying. John brushed her lips with a light kiss before sitting up on the side of the bed. "For a couple of mid-lifers, we do this quite well, don't you think," he said smiling, and bent over to kiss her warm lips again before pulling on his pants and trotting downstairs. John was uncorking a bottle of their favorite Australian chardonnay when the phone rang, the intrusive sound eclipsing his buoyant mood. He glanced at the wall clock above the sink before placing the newly opened wine bottle on the counter. At this hour it was never good news.

It was Sarah Ann who took the call on the bedside phone. A sergeant with the Williamson County Sheriff's office announced himself. She listened with rising horror.

Epilogue

There were two funerals held the same day.

Just outside Jacksonville, Texas, a lone figure, in a dull dress, which hung limply on her gaunt frame, stood vigil above the open grave, while a plain steel casket was lowered by a creaking mechanical winch. She said no prayers. She carried no flower to drop into the grave. She said no goodbyes. When it rested on the earth below she simply walked away.

At that same time a packed Ryman Auditorium was hushed as the young widow, her hand gripping that of the pretty little girl beside her, bent and kissed the floral wreathed casket. Television cameras at the back of the legendary first home of the Grand Ole Opry and a former house of worship, captured the touching moment. It would be replayed on the evening news on the Nashville channels, the three major networks, and repeatedly on the cable news channels.

Sarah Ann and Ross Lambert stood by the casket on either side of LouAnn. As they turned away, Sarah Ann took LouAnn's hand in hers and Lambert lifted Willow into his strong arms. Behind them followed the slow parade of mourners.

After handing Willow off to Sarah Ann's daughter, Anna Leigh, LouAnn had insisted on standing beside Sarah Ann at the front of the auditorium, with Lambert on one side of the widow and John flanking Sarah Ann. For nearly an hour they shook hands, returned embraces and listened to words of condolence from the several hundred attendees.

In the short span of time it took for Jared Parson's meteoric rise to stardom in country music, he had reached an envied pinnacle just below legendary. His untimely death would catapult him into that fabled strata, in much the same way James Dean's untimely death at twenty-four had ensured his status as a Hollywood legend.

There was no public wake following the funeral. The burial was more private; by invitation only. Those invited were seated on both sides of the casket, perched above the grave opening in the same cemetery where Jill Edgerton had been laid to rest.

Today they gathered to support LouAnn and her daughter, Sarah Ann and John on one side of the young widow; Ross Lambert on the other. Seated behind them were Sarah Ann's children and their spouses and the entire staff of Edgerton Group. Behind them sat the members of Sarah Ann's Prayer Group.

Looking across the casket Sarah Ann watched Arliss Hemming struggle to hold back tears. Len Shiring sat near Hemming with members of Jared's band and their spouses, and in the back row, feeling uncomfortable in a new suit, shirt and tie provided to him by John, sat Hershel Simmons. One side of his head was swathed in gauze, his eyes still swollen and blackened by the concussion he had suffered at Lester Murray's hands.

Jeanette reached over and took his hand firmly in hers when his head bent in grief. Simmons had been hailed a hero by the local media. Such praise made him far more uncomfortable than the new suit.

Willow glanced shyly at the faces around her, her small, sad face not fully comprehending what had happened to her daddy, or why he was never coming home again. Johnny's son, Little John, was snuggled on Sarah Ann's lap and talked to Willow from time to time, the way children do, oblivious to the soft-spoken minister standing at the head of the casket reading verses from the Bible. LouAnn counted their childhood banter a blessing and smiled down at her daughter and the beautiful dark haired boy. From time-to-time, she felt the gentle kick of her own son inside her.

When the brief burial service ended, Sarah and Lambert stood at LouAnn's side as the guests shook her hands, hugged her neck once again, whispered more awkward words of condolence and promised to keep in touch. It was the right thing to say to a grieving widow. But life moved on. And so would most of them, the burial of the murdered Jared Parson just an afternoon when they had had to reschedule commitments to a later time on their busy calendars.

After entrusting a visibly weary LouAnn and Willow to Hershel and Jeannette for the limo ride back to the farm, Sarah Ann hugged Lambert and said she would meet him in the office the day after tomorrow. She had given the entire staff an extra day off to help them absorb the tragedy that had befallen Edgerton Group. She also knew they faced long days of dealing with the loss of their top talent and the cancellation of his sold out European tour. Insurance would cover any financial fallout from the cancelled tour, but there were numerous other events, future concerts, that would have to be dealt with.

Abe Winters was moving into the office next to Lambert as his new assistant now that Lambert was about to sign a partnership agreement. He and Abe would take over responsibilities for managing Stella Wayne. The success of her new album, and her stunning appearance on the Grand Ole Opry, had catapulted her to a high demand talent on the concert circuit.

Sarah Ann had quickly expanded Nicole's duties, and told her to bring on a second assistant to help with managing their growing list of talent. Carole Bennington would become Nicole's chief assistant, which left Sarah Ann to find her own new assistant. She had someone already in mind, but it would take some cajoling. Viola would have to be coaxed from behind the comfort of the reception desk to take the cubby-hole office next to Sarah Ann's, a move which boded a livelier tenor for Sarah Ann's work week.

The day-to-day business of Edgerton Group promised to be more hectic than before. But then, she though silently, resting her head in the crook of John's arm as the limousine sped toward Franklin, this is what she and Jill had worked so hard for; had dared to dream would happen during their discussions as they had chased juicy cheeseburgers with hand-breaded fried onion rings at Puckett's.

Her two children and their spouses sat across from her. "You two getting back together?" It was Anna Leigh who broached the subject, prompting a gentle jab in the ribs from her husband. John Jr.

already knew his father's answer to that same question but watched his mother inquisitively.

"Actually, I haven't had a proper proposal," Sarah Ann responded in a teasing tone, looking up at John.

"I'd get down on my knees. The space here, though, is a little cramped."

"Actually, Dad, admit it," John Jr. said in a cheerfully mocking tone, "if you got down, you probably couldn't get back up at your age." Dominique was cradling a sleeping Little John in her lap, but still managed to nudge *her* husband in the ribs. "What?" he exclaimed innocently.

"Watch it, buster," replied his father. "The name on the law firm I helped found can be changed with the flick of a brass plate."

"Sooo?" insisted Anna Leigh, this time with her arm defending against any rib jabs from her spouse.

John lifted Sarah Ann's chin and gave her a long kiss. When he lifted his lips from hers she was blushing. "Not in front of the kids…" her words were cut off by his lips over hers. "Say yes, and you'll get a lot more where that comes from."

"Yes," she replied in a voice barely above a whisper. She wiggled out of his arms. "Wait! Has the ink dried on your divorce?"

"Maybe in four, maybe five more weeks, give or take a day or two."

"I don't know if I can wait that long, Mr. Boswell. After all, we've already consu…" she caught herself just in time before finishing the word 'consummated' in front of her children, and blushed furiously, setting off howls of laughter.

"We'll discuss this later," she said archly, trying to salvage her dignity and leaned back in the crook of his arm.

When all the goodbyes were said, John walked her to the door. "Won't you come in?"

"The Prayer Group is here."

"I'm sure they won't mind. Come on in."

He shook his head. "I made a vow a long time ago that I would never intrude on a gathering of the Prayer Group." He leaned down and kissed her. "Good night, my love."

She stood on the porch watching him walk to his car parked

behind hers under the portico, and waved goodbye before letting herself in.

Succulent smells drew her to the dining room where a veritable feast had been laid out. The din of conversation ceased as she walked in. Willie Dell stood up and pulled her into a hug. "How you holdin' up, baby sister?"

"Better now that I'm here with you," she replied graciously, meaning it. "Where are Beau and Charlie and Stuart?"

"You know our husbands, darlin'. They run for cover when the Prayer Group gathers."

"That's how John reacted a moment ago when I invited him in."

"You trained him early, and well, a long time ago," Jeanne Marie observed with a wicked smile.

"And here I assured him that if he came in we would make him an honorary member."

"Not a chance," Angela insisted. "We closed membership to this less-than-secret society when we were in third grade. And I, for one, *will not* vote to open it up to John, Beau, Stuart, and least of all, Charlie."

"Maybe Tom Selleck, if he asks us real nice," drawled Della Sue.

It was Willie Dell who noted the look of expectation on Sarah Ann's face. "What is it, baby sister? You look like a dam about to bust."

"John and I are getting back together." A pandemonium of shouts rattled the crystal chandelier as three sets of high heels clacked on the rich parquet floor like a din of cicadas. She was pulled from one hug into another, with clamors for details, and finally a skeptical Della Sue demanding to know when and how this came about under the nose of, and without the advice and consent of, the Prayer Group.

"That's not exactly correct," Sarah Ann said. "Willie Dell pretty well knew this was coming. Anyway," she added, "John just asked me to remarry him, in front of the children, as we were being driven home.

Three faces turned on Willie Dell. "And you didn't tell us…not even drop a teensy tiny hint," admonished Angela.

"I believe I recall something to the effect that anything of a private nature shared with you three is likely to make the next edition of the local newspaper."

"You know that's not true," Jeanne Marie chided Willie Dell. "Haven't we always abided by that slogan Las Vegas plagiarized from us—what is said in Prayer Group stays in Prayer Group."

"I think the plagiarizing part may be wrong," corrected Della Sue. "But I'll stand by the rest."

"Hey, I'm hungry, and the food's getting cold," complained Willie Dell. "Let's eat. Y'all have no trouble talking and eating at the same time."

"Chauvinist pig," Jeanne Ann muttered as she took her seat.

"Oink, oink!" Della Sue stuck her tongue out at Willie Dell.

"Let's offer thanks," commanded Willie Dell. They held hands. Sarah Ann's was tucked in Willie Dell's on one side and Angela's on the other side. She could feel the warmth of their long friendship flowing through her like a gentle stream of tonic that lifted her spirits as nothing else could.

"God bless each of us and those we love. Keep them from harm. Help us overcome whatever adversity He may see fit with which to challenge us. May He infuse us with His grace to deal with whatever besets us with patience and faith; to not lay blame; and to find charity in our hearts to support and love those God entrusts to our care, most especially Della Sue where Beau is concerned." He raised one eyelid slightly to check her reaction. She raised one eyelid part way and smirked. "And most especially may God give Sarah Ann the sustenance she needs to see her through the difficult days ahead and ease the pain in her heart from the losses she has suffered. We ask this in Jesus' name. Amen."

The chorus of *Amens* was followed by a polite scramble to fill plates from the several dishes in the center of the oval table, the preparing of which had consumed most of Monet's workday.

"Willie Dell, I think you need to plan a bachelor shower for John and have the invitee's bring either Viagra or Cialis."

"That's a sweet thought, Della Sue," responded Sarah Ann. "But I'm quite certain such gifts are not necessary, if you get my meaning."

"Then maybe a condom shower would be in order," suggested Angela.

"Oh darlins', as much as I appreciate your thoughtfulness for wanting to hold a shower, I assure you it isn't necessary," said Sarah

Ann. "I've reached that magical age. I'm still young enough to live in sin, and *enjoy* it, without having to worry about any consequences that nature might inflict on me." She looked around mischievously. "Something itsy bitsy from Victoria Secret might be a more *thoughtful* wedding gift."

Shock stood out on the faces of the four people around her. "Did she just say what I think she just said," Jeanne Marie inquired of her fellow Prayer Group members.

Angela assured her she did.

"I believe our prudish and puritanical Sarah Ann has finally emerged from her Catholic closet," Willie Dell intoned, in his best imitation of Gregorian Chant.

"Some advice, darlin'," Della Sue lobbed across at Willie Dell. "Stick to your day job."

"Pass those yummy scalloped potatoes, won't you Della Sue," drawled Sarah Ann, "and a shaker of aphrodisiac to sprinkle on them."

"Gladly, but only if there's enough left over to shower on Beau."

Later that night, when the dishes were cleared away and the three women had gone, Willie Dell took Sarah Ann by the arm and led her out to the backyard. They walked arm-in-arm to the big tree that overlapped their properties. Both stared up at the rickety, long neglected tree house. A half-moon peaked above the lopsided roof, its pale light cutting shafts through the sparsely-leafed branches of the thick oak.

"We met here, you know," Willie Dell noted quietly.

"I remember it well," Sarah Ann replied, laying her head on his shoulder. "Has it been so long ago?"

"Sorry to remind you, baby sister, but it has."

For the next several moments they were each lost in their own thoughts before Willie Dell pulled her even closer. "You know what we need to do?

"No, what?" she asked.

"We'll have the tree house rebuilt and make it big enough to accommodate monthly meetings of the Prayer Group. Since it hangs over both our properties, we can alternate hosting duties."

Sarah Ann pulled away and stared at her best friend aghast. "Have you gone stark raving, Willie Dell Winston! There is no way I'm climbing that tree at my age to host a Prayer Group meeting… in a tree…even if it would have a refurbished house," she concluded with genuine fervor.

"I will build it and you will come," he countered smugly. "And so will Della Sue and Jeanne Marie and even the ever tepid Angela."

"Dream on, little brother." But she laughed and clapped her hands in delight. "I dibs the ticket concession. The whole town—the old timers at least—will pay big to see Della Sue Simpson shinny up a tree. Even Beau might buy a ticket."

"None of us will have to shinny. I'll build an elevator. It might cut into your ticket sales, but you won't mind, will you?"

Sarah Ann lifted her face to the sky and let out with a full-throated laugh. "Now I know it's time to call in the men in white coats.

He was staring at her now, his eyes kind. "That's the first time I've heard you laugh like that in such a long time."

She knew it was true and suddenly realized how much lighter she felt, as if the emotional burdens of the past weeks and months, had been lifted, for a short time at least. How good it felt. "Thank you, Willie Dell, for helping me feel alive again…to feel a little joy again." Sarah Ann threw her arms around his neck and kissed him lightly on the cheek.

"You're welcome," he whispered in her ear.

Arm-in-arm they walked back toward her house. "And I *am* going to build another tree house back there. With an elevator, of course. And you *will* come," he insisted.

When they reached the back porch, Willie Dell glanced back to where the old tree house hung precariously from high limbs, its flaws veiled by night shadows and shook his head solemnly. "We'll call it The Prayer Group Tower."

As they entered the back door her laughter trailed behind them like the ghost of a moon fading into a sky coloring with the subtle pigments of an approaching dawn.

About the Author

Alice Jackson is a retired journalist, broadcast professional and world traveler, having visited more than 123 countries since 2002.

She majored in journalism and political science, at the University of Tulsa, married the editor of the university newspaper, and raised four children and a younger brother. She worked in local television as a reporter, anchor and news director for 20 years before purchasing a small radio station in Franklin, Tennessee, which she sold in 1997.

When her dearest friend died of cancer in 2000, she adopted his adult, special-needs son, Robert. It was the first adult adoption in Williamson County, Tennessee. In 2007, she moved with her adopted son to Indianapolis to be near her daughter to insure care for Robert.

Robert passed away in 2011. Since then, Alice has traveled and focused her attention on her writing.

Also Available From

WordCrafts Press

Maggie's Song
  by Marcia Ware

End of Summer
  by Michael Potts

The 5 Manners of Death
  by Darden North

Odd Man Outlaw
  by KM Zahrt

Home
  by Eleni McKnight

Martyr's Moon
  by J.E. Lowder

Ill Gotten Gain
  by Ralph E. Jarrells

www.wordcrafts.net

www.ingramcontent.com/pod-product-compliance
Lightning Source LLC
Chambersburg PA
CBHW060954120726
47910CB00002B/636